AN UNDENIABLE ATTRACTION

Devon took a deep breath. His arm slid down the rough wood, then his fingers tangled in the unruly curls at her nape.

"Don't," Felicity whispered.

"What if this is what I want in exchange for taking you to New York?"

"You don't mean that." His fingers on her neck sent shivers down her spine.

"Don't I?" Bending his head, Devon placed his lips on the curve of her shoulder.

"Please." Felicity turned enough to push him away.

"Please?" He bared his teeth in a mockery of his usual grin. "Please what? Don't act the demure maiden about to be ravished. We both know a kiss is all the force I need."

"No, I don't—" But the rest of her words were lost as his mouth swooped down on hers. His lips were hungry and hard. He demanded, his tongue and teeth forcing her mouth open, filling her completely.

She acknowledged his claim. He needed no more than a kiss . . . a touch to liquify her resolve. Yet she tried to fight her body's reaction to him, forcing her palms against the solid strength of his shoulders. She pushed, her arms quivering from desire as he thoroughly explored her mouth.

Then with a moan, Felicity surrendered, abandoning any claim she had of resisting him.

D0775748

PUT SOME PASSION INTO YOUR
LIFE . . . WITH THIS STEAMY SELECTION OF
ZEBRA *LOVEGRAMS!*

SEA FIRES (3899, $4.50/$5.50)
by Christine Dorsey
Spirited, impetuous Miranda Chadwick arrives in the untamed New World prepared for any peril. But when the notorious pirate Gentleman Jack Blackstone kidnaps her in order to fulfill his secret plans, she can't help but surrender—to the shameless desires and raging hunger that his bronzed, lean body and demanding caresses ignite within her!

TEXAS MAGIC (3898, $4.50/$5.50)
by Wanda Owen
After being ambushed by bandits and saved by a ranchhand, headstrong Texas belle Bianca Moreno hires her gorgeous rescuer as a protective escort. But Rick Larkin does more than guard her body—he kisses away her maidenly inhibitions, and teaches her the secrets of wild, reckless love!

SEDUCTIVE CARESS (3767, $4.50/$5.50)
by Carla Simpson
Determined to find her missing sister, brave beauty Jessamyn Forsythe disguises herself as a simple working girl and follows her only clues to Whitechapel's darkest alleys . . . and the disturbingly handsome Inspector Devlin Burke. Burke, on the trail of a killer, becomes intrigued with the ebon-haired lass and discovers the secrets of her silken lips and the hidden promise of her sweet flesh.

SILVER SURRENDER (3769, $4.50/$5.50)
by Vivian Vaughan
When Mexican beauty Aurelia Mazón saves a handsome stranger from death, she finds herself on the run from the Federales with the most dangerous man she's ever met. And when Texas Ranger Carson Jarrett steals her heart with his intimate kisses and seductive caresses, she yields to an all-consuming passion from which she hopes to never escape!

ENDLESS SEDUCTION (3793, $4.50/$5.50)
by Rosalyn Alsobrook
Caught in the middle of a dangerous shoot-out, lovely Leona Stegall falls unconscious and awakens to the gentle touch of a handsome doctor. When her rescuer's caresses turn passionate, Leona surrenders to his fiery embrace and savors a night of soaring ecstasy!

Available wherever paperbacks are sold, or order direct from the Publisher. Send cover price plus 50¢ per copy for mailing and handling to Zebra Books, Dept. 4322, 475 Park Avenue South, New York, N.Y. 10016. Residents of New York and Tennessee must include sales tax. DO NOT SEND CASH. For a free Zebra/ Pinnacle catalog please write to the above address.

CHRISTINE DORSEY

SEA OF TEMPTATION

ZEBRA BOOKS
KENSINGTON PUBLISHING CORP.

ZEBRA BOOKS are published by

Kensington Publishing Corp.
475 Park Avenue South
New York, NY 10016

First Printing: October, 1993

Printed in the United States of America

To my daughter Elizabeth, who embodies the beauty, intellect and spirit of a true heroine . . . in my totally unbiased opinion.

And, as always, to Chip.

"Chasing a sail is very much like pursuing a coy maiden, the very coyness sharpening the pursuit."

Captain Raphael Semmes,
Confederate States Navy

Prologue

May, 1862
New York City

"I don't believe I understand what you're proposing."

Felicity smiled, her blue eyes shining bright with amusement. It was no wonder Jebediah Webster's thick brows were raised in surprise. He probably never anticipated he'd be the recipient of such good fortune.

"What exactly don't you understand?" To Felicity's way of thinking she'd explained everything quite nicely. Her plan might be a shock to Jebediah, but that didn't mean Felicity hadn't thought long and hard about it. She wasn't frivolous and light-minded as others . . . as her father seemed to think. And this would prove it.

"Miss Wentworth," Jebediah began, then paused, his prominent Adam's apple quivering when a soft feminine hand covered his.

"Don't you think you should call me Felicity?"

"Miss Wentworth," Jebediah continued. He slid his hand from beneath Felicity's and ran the tip of his finger under the starched wing collar of his shirt. "I'm flattered, of course." Pushing palms against knees that appeared bony even through his thick wool pants, the young man stood and walked to the marble-top table in the center of the room.

Then he *had* understood everything she'd said. Felicity folded her hands primly and sat, her back straight, not touching the velvet brocade settee. She'd lured Jebediah to the drawing room because it offered privacy and an intimate setting.

Perfect for a proposal.

"Jebediah." Felicity rose, straightening the wide expanse of her emerald silk skirt. Grimacing momentarily, she tucked a stubborn curl of red-gold into the chignon at the base of her head and moved toward the object of her affection. He stood tall and poker straight, his narrow back to her. "You needn't say anymore."

As she stepped beside him Felicity laid her fingers on his sleeve. Of course he was flattered. Felicity never doubted his emotions. After all she knew exactly what she was offering.

The Wentworths had amassed a fortune through the years. And though her father supported Jebediah and other abolitionist ministers like him, the amount was nothing compared to what Felicity—and her future husband—would have at their disposal.

But though he needed money for his cause, Felicity knew Jebediah didn't have a mercenary bone

8

in his body. He was too fine a man. Stalwart, steady and God-fearing.

The perfect man for her.

And she would be a good wife for him. Besides her money, Felicity was offering herself. Enough young men had courted for Felicity to know in all humility that even without her inheritance, she was desirable. Little wonder the recipient of all this good fortune was temporarily stunned into silence.

Out of all the young men in New York, she had chosen him. Felicity braided her fingers and gave her hands a squeeze of excitement. This would prove to everyone that she was a serious young woman.

". . . serious."

"I beg your pardon." Felicity's cheeks reddened as she looked into the thin face of the man she loved. She needed to stop wool gathering and pay attention. She didn't want to miss anything her beloved said.

"I said," Jebediah began again with a sigh. "You can't be serious about this."

"Oh, but I assure you, I am." Felicity looked up at him through her thick fringe of auburn lashes—a look that had brought more than one young man to his knees.

"Do you ever hear a word I say from the pulpit?"

"Yes, of course." He had a strong beautiful voice, deep and dramatic when he preached. She could listen to him forever. Actually, it was during one of his talks on the horrors of slavery that she first conceived the idea of marrying him.

"Today? What did I speak of today?"

Was this a test? If so, she was likely to fail miserably. As Felicity sat on the hard pew beside her father today, her thoughts were on her upcoming proposal, not on the minister's words. "Well, I . . ." Felicity snapped open her fan to give herself more time to think. Besides, if she glanced at him just so, *he* probably wouldn't remember what he said.

"I thought as much." Jebediah turned away, puffing air out through the space between his front teeth. "You have no inkling what I'm about."

"No inkling?" Felicity's eyes opened wider. Perhaps her mind had wandered this morning, but she'd been to enough of his sermons and heard enough of his discussions with her father to understand. She wasn't a dolt. Felicity opened her mouth to tell him so, but he cut off her words.

"You think a little money spread over the evils of mankind will pave your way to heaven."

"Money?" Felicity stepped back. Her wide skirt tangled on a chair leg but she paid it no heed. His voice could be very loud and overpowering. Especially up close. "I wasn't talking about money, it was . . ."

"No. In your case you're willing to sacrifice your lovely body on the altar of redemption. Did you honestly believe silken clothes and rouged lips would entice me?"

Her lips weren't rouged. They were naturally

pink. But before Felicity could point that or anything else out, Jebediah continued.

"If you had listened this morning, you would have heard me tell of Negress, Esther, and her flight to freedom. Of the children she was forced to leave behind and the horrors those poor innocents are now living at the hands of their devil masters."

"I heard you speak of Esther." The unfortunate woman was at this very moment sitting in the library of Wentworth House. Her presence was the reason Felicity had difficulty persuading Jebediah to join her in the drawing room.

"Then how can you flounce about and flirt when there is evidence of such cruelty under your very nose?" Jebediah paused as he wiped his bony fingers down across his high cheekboned face. "Forgive my abruptness, Miss Wentworth, but the woman I marry will possess deeper qualities than a beautiful face and a coffer of gold. She will be committed to the cause. As committed as I. And we shall work together, side by side, to eradicate the evil of slavery from the world."

"But I could be that woman." Felicity hated the pleading in her voice. A Wentworth did not beg.

Jebediah looked down at her and for a fleeting moment Felicity thought he would agree with her . . . see the error in his ways. But before Felicity's amazed eyes he shook his head, turned, and walked away.

"I don't think so," was all he said before leaving the room.

11

Felicity watched him go, her eyes wide in disbelief. She expected at any moment Jebediah would stop and race back to her, begging her forgiveness for his momentary lapse of sanity. It wasn't till he disappeared up the wide staircase that Felicity began to realize that probably wasn't going to happen.

"Well, I . . ." Felicity fanned her suddenly hot cheeks and backed onto the settee, sinking down in a swish of crinolined silk. She, Felicity Wentworth, had been rebuffed, rejected.

Rejected.

The idea was numbing. Not that she always felt loved. But her father's rejections were subtle. Closing her eyes, Felicity forced her thoughts away from Frederick Wentworth's reaction to his only remaining offspring.

Besides, her marriage to Jebediah Webster was supposed to change that. To make her father see. To make them all see.

Biting her lip, Felicity tried to fight back the tears stinging her eyelids. This was not the way it was supposed to happen. At this very moment her father was to be hugging her; congratulating Jebediah and proclaiming this the most perfect match.

Her mood brightened slightly with the thought that perhaps Jebediah didn't truly understand her proposal. But with a delicate sniff she accepted that that wasn't the case.

He understood.

He simply found her lacking in the same area that her father did. Jebediah Webster was to be her salvation, her proof of worthiness. Instead he only confirmed her father's opinion.

She hadn't had a good cry since they received word of her brother Arthur's death, but Felicity felt the need for one now. As she reached in her reticule for a handkerchief—there was no need not to be prepared—she heard movement in the hallway.

So Jebediah *had* come to his senses. Felicity turned, a watery smile on her lips. But it froze when she saw Esther, the woman Jebediah had brought to the house.

"Mr. Wentworth asked me to fetch you, Miss Felicity." The woman gave a little bow and looked at Felicity with dark almond shaped eyes that held a trace of fear. She wore a fresh dress and apron, thanks to Wentworth money, and her shoes were so new they squeaked with every step. She was obviously ill at ease and Felicity could certainly empathize.

Her mother had taught her better than to show her emotions in front of the servants. And though Esther wasn't actually in the Wentworth employ, she had known nothing but servitude during her lifetime. She probably wasn't used to seeing her mistress on the verge of tears.

"Please . . . Esther . . . please sit." Felicity swept aside her skirts and smiled invitingly at the woman. She only wished to make Esther feel more at ease. Her own reluctance to go upstairs—and face Jebediah—had nothing to do with her actions.

"I ain't sure I should. They's . . . that is Mr. Jebediah's expectin' me back."

"He'll understand." She'd almost said, 'Let him wait,' but decorum won out. "I believe Mr. Webster wishes me to know more about you."

Felicity felt a pang of guilt as Esther reluctantly lowered herself to the far edge of the settee. But she wasn't actually lying. Jebediah *did* want her to know more about Esther and people like her. Wasn't that the message of nearly all his sermons?

"What ye wantin' to know?"

She was used to this, Felicity realized. The poor woman expected to have to tell people of her private grief. She should spare her the retelling, but something in Felicity couldn't do that. Instead, she sat and listened; listened to the tortured story.

"How old are they? How old are your children?" Felicity asked when Esther paused. The escaped slave's dark eyes shone like jet and her chin trembled.

"Ezra, he's the oldest. He's nearly grown. He can do as much work as a man. He'll be gettin' on okay, I imagine," she said with some pride. "But Sissy ain't real well." Esther shook her head. "She's a mite sickly. And Lucy ain't more 'an a babe off the tit."

Esther was going to cry. Felicity realized that as well as she realized the woman didn't really know exactly how old her children were. As Felicity handed over her handkerchief, she searched for something to say, some words of comfort. Jebediah would know what to say. But nothing came to her.

Esther had been sold off the plantation where her

children lived. Sold because the mistress of the house suspected Esther of inviting attentions from the master. "I ain't never wanted him to touch me," Esther said. "Never!" She turned her face away. "When I had the chance to leave, I'z took it. But I had no way to get my childs."

Felicity stared down at her folded hands and wondered why nobody did anything about Esther's children. Of course there was a war on, a bothersome evil war, but traveling south wasn't that difficult. After all, less than three years earlier, Felicity had done it herself to visit a distant cousin who lived in Charleston.

Esther wiped at her nose, then looked up apologetically. "I'll wash this for ye, Mistress."

"What? Oh, you needn't bother. Just keep it." Felicity had more handkerchiefs than she could ever use. But giving the poor woman one of them didn't seem enough to make up for her loss. Felicity opened her mouth to offer more . . . money, perhaps, then she remembered Jebediah's words. Did she seek to buy salvation? And more, did she expect to impress Jebediah and her father by giving money?

As Felicity looked up at Esther an idea sprang into her mind. One that would benefit everyone—Esther, Felicity and even Jebediah. Because he would get the wife he deserved—her.

"Esther!" Felicity could barely suppress the excitement in her voice. "Where are they? Where are your children?"

"In South Carolina." Her black eyes were weary. "Why?"

"Because . . ." Felicity wasn't going to tell her now. But she'd find out soon enough. They all would, including Jebediah and her father. There'd be no denying she was as committed as Arthur had been. Because a Wentworth never gave up. And Felicity Wentworth planned to prove herself worthy of the name.

One

June, 1862
Charleston, South Carolina

He hated black.

Devon Blackstone leaned his hip into the sharp-edged windowsill and smiled at the irony. A Blackstone hating black. But it seemed every time he returned home more bright silks were shed in favor of morbid black by Charleston's daughters.

He absently watched the woman struggling along on the street below. She was swathed in widow's weeds, the heavy material covering her completely. Another casualty of the damn war.

"Such a waste," he mumbled, grimacing when he realized he spoke aloud.

"What did you say, honey?"

"It was nothing." Devon glanced over his shoulder to where Lil sprawled enticingly across the bed. The gossamer veil of mosquito netting was pushed aside and she beckoned with her finger, her red lips forming a provocative pout.

"Come back to bed and you won't have time to talk to yourself."

Devon's chuckle was devilish. "I think perhaps I'm talking to myself *because* of the time spent in your bed."

"Complaints from the infamous blockade runner?" Lil lifted a smooth bare shoulder, letting the sheet fall from her rounded, pink-tipped bosom.

"I think you know better than that." Devon forced himself to look away. "But if I climb back in that bed neither of us will come up for air for the rest of the day, and I do need to pay my respects to my grandmother."

"I saw Mrs. Blackstone last week, did I tell you?"

"No." Lil hadn't done much talking since Devon showed up at her place of business this morning. The *Intrepid* ran the blockade of Federal ships last night. As usual, the danger and excitement stayed with Devon as they docked in Charleston. And as usual, Lil was only too happy for Devon to release some of that excess energy with her. He still felt tense, like a boiler with its safety vent blocked, but he didn't think another round in Lil's bed would help.

He turned, doing his best to ignore her generous breasts and listened to her go on about his grandmother.

"She was riding down Meeting Street in her carriage and she actually had her driver stop to thank me for my donation to the hospital fund. Imagine that."

"She thanked you?" Devon arched a brow. "That doesn't sound like Grandmother."

A slow flush spread up Lil's neck and face. Devon wouldn't have thought her capable of blushing, but he supposed if anyone could illicit one it was his grandmother. "Well, actually she told me it was about time I used some of the profits I . . . em . . . earned to help with the suffering caused by this war."

Devon threw back his head in laughter. "Now *that* sounds like Grams."

"Well, she thanked me none the less," Lil said defensively.

"I'm glad." Devon turned back toward the window, casually searching for the widow he noticed earlier. Lil continued to talk about his grandmother, saying what a fine lady she was, but Devon paid little attention. Not that he didn't agree. He adored his grandmother, though he was the first to admit that her tongue could be rapier sharp. But Devon spotted the widow again, still struggling with her heavy bag, and he couldn't stop watching her.

She was young. That was obvious even without seeing her face. Her body was slender, and though the carpetbag dragged her arm down, her movements were graceful.

The street was crowded, clogged with sailors and soldiers—another effect of the war—and the woman seemed out of place. A regrettable commentary on Charleston and the hard times that plagued the city.

The morning was sultry, humid and hot. The sun

hung hazy over the harbor, with only an occasional breeze off the bay to offer any relief. Perspiration glued Devon's linen shirt to his upper body. He couldn't imagine how warm the widow was beneath the heavy hat and veil.

But she kept plodding on, clutching her carpet bag as if her life depended on it. And Devon kept watching. When a maverick breeze came off the bay, bringing with it the scent of sea air, it caught at the widow's skirts, swirling them around her ankles. And it momentarily lifted the black veil.

Before her black-gloved hand shot up and dragged the drape back down he caught a glimpse of her hair. Bright and red-gold, the sight of it made Devon lean forward, his forehead touching the cooler glass of the windowpane. She had beautiful hair, thick coils knotted at the base of her neck.

Devon had a sudden vision of burying his hands deep in that hair and shook his head to clear it. Thoughts of making love to widows were depraved . . . even for him.

"Do you think you might?"

Devon reached for his white linen jacket. "Might what?" He looked back at Lil as he fished a gold piece from his pocket.

"Might come back tonight?" Lil swung her legs over the side and slid off the bed. She faced Devon, hands on ample, naked hips. "Have you heard a word I said?"

"Who bothers listening when they can feast their eyes on this?" Devon tilted his head to indicate

Lil as he slung his jacket over his wide shoulder. In three long strides he was across the room, leaning over her. He meant the kiss to be brief but she wrapped her arms around his neck, her leg around his hip.

"Tonight?" she purred as he slowly pushed away.

"I can't be sure. Don't count on me." With that Devon unclasped her hands from behind his neck, where they'd tangled with his hair. Before stepping back he settled the gold coin in Lil's palm.

"I told you, there's no charge, sweetie."

"I know what you said." Devon folded her fingers over the money. "But we all have to make a living, especially with times like they are."

"Business has never been better for me, and from what I hear, for you either, sugar."

When Devon jerked around as the sound of commotion on the street below drifted through the open window, Lil said, "That is nothing. Just some of the soldiers acting up. Happens all the time."

But Devon ignored her words and strode to the window. He scanned the street below with the eyes of a man used to searching out trouble. "Damn!" His curse was punctuated by the heel of his hand slamming against the wooden sash. Racing across the room, he grabbed the brass handle and yanked open the door.

"What is it honey? What's wrong?"

Devon was down the spiral staircase, heading for the front door before the last of her question was out. The stairs below were empty this time of the morning—most patrons of Lilian McAbee came calling after the shadows fell. Closed shutters kept out most of the sun's rays and the noise from outside, so that the shock of both hit Devon as he hurled himself out into the street.

From the brick stoop Devon looked around, then leaped off and elbowed his way through a group of soldiers. He didn't take time to question what the dirty, scraggly-haired sailor was doing before he grabbed him by the arm and spun him around. The burly man stared at Devon gape-mouthed, surprised enough to let loose his tug of war with the young widow over her carpet bag.

She gasped, the momentum sending her backwards against the rough bark of a palmetto. Devon glanced to the side in time to see her hat fly askew. The veil separated to show wide blue eyes set in a pale as ivory face. He was right about the hair. Strawberry blond curls sprang out in all directions as she grabbed hold of her hat brim with one hand. The other stayed firmly attached to the handle of her bag.

Devon turned, ready to offer assistance but the blind-side blow made him fall backward instead. "We'll teach ye to stick your snooty nose in where it ain't wanted," a rough voice said from behind him as Devon whirled around. His punch caught his assailant in the stomach, eliciting a loud "oof" sound as he doubled over.

"Son of a bitch." The man looked up with hatred in his eyes, then hurled himself forward, catching Devon's knees in his brawny arms.

They rolled onto the dusty street, first the sailor on top, then Devon. Curses flew like rockets as the pedestrians swerved to make way for the brawling men. Devon's fist slammed into a bristle covered jaw, stinging his knuckles. But in the next instant his opponent connected with Devon's mouth, smashing his lip against his teeth. The blood that spewed over his shirt could have come from his lip or the sailor's nose when Devon flattened it with his next punch. Devon lifted his clenched hand to land another blow, but the sailor just lay there. Straddling him, Devon grabbed hold of his filthy jacket.

"In Charleston we don't treat ladies like that." Devon jerked the man's head off the street. "Now apologize."

Devon twisted his head around only to find that the lady in question no longer stood beneath the palmetto fronds. Then shattering pain exploded in his head. Black dirt came rushing up to meet him. Devon lay, facedown, the smell of puff mud strong in his nostrils. Even if he'd anticipated the heavy booted kick to his ribs, or the groan of pain that came through his split lip, he could do nothing to stop either.

"That's what ye get for foolin' with true blooded sons of these here Confederate states," one of the men laughed as he helped his fallen buddy to his feet.

Devon tried to lift his head, but it wasn't until a strong arm braced him under his arms that he could pull himself up. His rescuer was Saul, Lil's man. The black man, for all his rippling muscles and broad face, was gentle as he helped Devon to his feet.

Lil stood on the porch, marginally covered by a silk wrapper. "Bring him on over here, Saul," she said, smiling cheekily to a well-dressed man who commented on her attire. "Stop by tonight if you've a mind to see more," came her reply before she led the way inside the dim interior of her establishment.

"I can walk on my own." Devon pulled away from Saul, embarrassed by the beating he took.

"Sure you can." Lil motioned to Saul, who backed away as Devon collapsed onto the horse hair settee in the front parlor. "And I suppose you could handle all three of those ruffians by yourself too."

Devon raised up on his elbows. "There were three of them?"

Lil sent Saul to fetch some water, shaking her head as she reached down to unbutton Devon's shirt. "Don't you even consider the odds anymore before you jump into a fight? Why I remember a time when Devon Blackstone had the advantage worked out every way to Sunday before he so much as answered a question."

He remembered those days too. As a matter of fact, Devon still considered himself a cautious man . . . at least for a blockade runner. He wasn't sure why he ran off half-cocked, so to speak. Actually, he did. "What happened to her?" He nudged aside Lil's hand and sucking in his breath, peeled the linen shirt from his body. His left side was turning an ugly molted purple. But it didn't look half as bad as it felt.

"The lady?" Lil arched her raven brow and sloshed a rag into the basin Saul had set on the floor. "That's what this was all about? Playing the chivalrous southern gentleman for some woman?"

At Devon's scowl she leaned over and wiped the blood from his lip. The front of her wrapper gaped open but she didn't bother to cover her breasts. "The lady ran off before the fight even started." Lil chuckled. "She probably didn't realize she was supposed to stay around and pick up the pieces of her knight in shining armor."

Trying to catch her breath, Felicity leaned against the whitewashed stucco in the alley behind Tradd Street. She'd run, dodging people and clutching her valise, all the way from the wharf. All the way from those terrible men.

Felicity sniffed, resisting the very strong urge to slide down the side of the building and give into a fit of tears. Her legs ached, her arm felt like it was going to break and she'd never been so hot in her entire life.

"Lord, how does anyone stand it here?" she muttered as she fished in her reticule for a hand-kerchief. Lifting the black veil she dabbed at the perspiration on her face.

She had half a mind to fling the blasted hat off. After all, posing as a widow hadn't protected her from those men who tried to steal her carpet-bag. Felicity squeezed the leather handle to assure herself that it was indeed safely in her possession.

With a sigh she straightened the heavy veil, effectively cutting off even the tiniest wisp of a breeze. Maybe those men down by the dock hadn't respected her widowhood, but they were obviously the lowest form of humans. But the truth was, most people she met on the train ride south were very solicitous of her.

Uncomfortable as she was, Felicity had to admit her plan to masquerade as a widow had been inspired. Almost as inspired as traveling to South Carolina to bring back Esther's children. Felicity consoled herself by imagining the expressions of admiration and love on the faces of her father and Jebediah when she returned to New York, with the three children by her side.

As pleasant as those thoughts were, Felicity didn't have time to indulge in them. She was hot and tired and more hungry than she ever remembered being. But all that would be taken care of as soon as she reached her cousin Louise's house on Meeting Street. Felicity sighed, thinking of the cool, lavender scented sheets that awaited her. And she'd rid herself of this awful hat and gown. Once she reached Louise and her husband Cyrus's house she wouldn't have to concern herself with ruffians again.

Looking both ways to get her bearings, Felicity stepped out onto the street. Charleston wasn't at all the way she remembered it. She knew there'd been fighting around the city, but she never expected to see so many signs of the war. The conflict left very few marks in New York City. Parades of soldiers, black draping over a few doorways and the tiresome political discussions were about the only indications.

But here . . .

The people she saw on the street were nothing like the genteel ladies and gentlemen who promenaded the oak lined avenues on her previous visit. These were coarse women and soldiers who seemed to have never heard of military discipline.

Felicity kept her eyes straight ahead beneath the veil and followed Tradd Street till it crossed Meeting. Turning right she headed toward St. Michael's Church, blinking back tears of relief when her cousin's house came into view. The shutters were closed against the sun and Felicity could almost feel the shadowed cool of the large, high ceilinged rooms.

Despite her fatigue Felicity practically skipped up the stairs to the front door. Lifting the dolphin-shaped knocker she let it drop with a loud bang.

Nothing.

Felicity knocked again, thinking Louise should speak with her servants about answering the door in a timely manner. It wasn't until the third time she used the knocker that tiny tendrils of doubt began inching through her. But she wouldn't panic. Wentworths didn't panic. Instead she stepped back, squinting through her veil at the shuttered windows for some sign of movement.

There was none.

The windows she thought merely closed against the heat, on closer inspection, were boarded up. Lifting up her skirts, Felicity raced off the porch. The garden bore signs of neglect; roses had been let go to seed and weeds were clogging the once neat walkways. Still Felicity refused to believe the obvious. She pounded on the servants' entrance, mumbling a prayer under her breath that someone would answer.

When she heard a voice, Felicity thought her prayers were answered. She whirled around, one hand flattened against her heart, the other still clinging to the heavy valise.

"They's gone."

Felicity stared down at the wizened black man who stood at the bottom of the porch steps.

"Gone? Where are they?" Could everyone possibly be out for the day?

He shrugged, his scarecrow shoulders outlined beneath a tattered shirt. "Ain't sure."

"When . . . when will they be back?"

The old black man shook his grizzled head. "Ain't comin' back, least ways not till all them Yankee devils be pushed off South Carolina soil."

"Yankee devils?" Felicity swallowed. She had the most uncomfortable feeling she was going to faint. "But I'm their cousin. I came all the way from . . . from Richmond for a visit."

Before he ambled away, the black man's expression said he thought that a particularly stupid thing to do. And the way she felt now, Felicity had to agree with him. Slowly, not caring if anyone saw her or not, she sank down on the porch step and yanked off the black bonnet.

What was she to do now?

All her plans hinged on finding Louise in Charleston. Louise would help her, Felicity was certain of it. She would understand what had driven Felicity to come to South Carolina. She would know where to look for Esther's children.

But Felicity had no idea where to look for Louise. Her husband's family was from Columbia, but there was no guarantee that's where they were. Besides, Esther had said her children were on a plantation near Port Royal, and Columbia was in the opposite direction of where she needed to go.

Wiping her hand across her forehead, Felicity leaned her shoulder against the porch rail. She could think better if she weren't so hot and tired and blasted hungry. But she knew one thing. She *was* going to find those children. "Even if I have to do it by myself," she muttered slowly, pulling herself up. She brushed the dust from her skirt and looked around, deciding which way to go. She'd come this far on her own—she wasn't going to give up now.

The first step was to get some rest and food. If she couldn't stay at Louise's she . . . Why she'd stay at a hotel! If she remembered correctly The Charleston Hotel was near here. She'd rent a room, take a nap, then decide the best way to handle her problem. Stepping out onto the brick sidewalk, she began trudging up Meeting Street.

The air was thick and off to the east, over the bay, she heard the rumblings of thunder. She needed to hurry to shelter before it stormed.

She paid little heed to the traffic in the street until a voice called to her. Felicity looked up to see a handsome coach stopped beside her.

"Young woman, come here." There was no mistaking the aristocratic authority in those words, but Felicity couldn't decide if it was a man or woman calling her. She squinted her eyes trying to see into the darkness of the coach, but couldn't make out a thing. Facing ahead, Felicity marched on only to have the carriage nudge forward beside her.

This time it was the black man holding the reins who spoke. "Miz Blackstone ain't gonna hurt ya none."

"I never thought she would." Felicity swallowed, trying to keep her composure.

"Then come over here. I'm much too old to chase after you."

The black man climbed off the box and opened the coach door. Cautiously, Felicity approached the conveyance. It was big and shiny black, much like the one she used when they went calling in New York.

"Come closer. Though some would argue otherwise, I'm not in the habit of devouring young women."

Felicity could now see the voice belonged to an elderly lady. She sat very straight, her gnarled hand rounding the top of a gold tipped walking stick which she tapped impatiently on the floor of

30

the coach. "Yes, yes, that's it," she said when Felicity was as close as she could get. "Now tell me young woman, who are you and what are you doing here?"

"I hardly think I owe you an explanation." Felicity turned, stopping herself from walking away when she heard the gravelly chuckle. But when she looked back there was no smile on the wrinkled face.

"You have a mind of your own. I like that," Eveline Blackstone said. "But that doesn't change the fact that you shouldn't be out and about all alone."

"I'm perfectly fine."

Eveline didn't dignify that with a response. Instead, she leaned forward on her stick, assessing the girl from a closer vantage. She was rumpled and not entirely clean, but obviously of quality. "Where are you from, child? I know everyone from hereabouts, and you aren't."

"I'm from Richmond." Felicity notched her chin higher and tried to shade her speech with some of her cousin's slow drawl.

"Richmond, eh?"

Felicity couldn't tell if the woman believed her or not. Though her face was heavily lined her eyes were bright and intelligent. They held Felicity entranced when she would have turned away. "Yes. I've come south to visit my cousin."

"Visiting?" The woman put so much disbelief into that one word that Felicity grimaced. It did sound ridiculous considering the circumstances.

And she had only to glance around to be reminded of those circumstances. The war was real in Charleston. Frighteningly so.

Felicity licked her suddenly dry lips. She couldn't let fear overwhelm her. And she couldn't go home empty handed. Not after the note she left for her father and Jebediah. She *would* find Esther's children and take them to their mother.

But first things first. Ridding herself of this overbearing woman took priority. And the simplest way to do so seemed to be to satisfy her curiosity. Felicity cleared her throat. "Actually I came to stay with her."

"Are you a widow?"

"I'm . . ." Felicity realized she'd left her hat and veil behind. "No."

"Then why do you wear that dreary garment?" Eveline pointed her stick toward Felicity's gown.

"I really don't think that's any of your concern." Felicity noticed the older woman's dress was well tailored but made of a jewel tone silk.

The woman seemed to take no offense at Felicity's words. She simply launched another question. "Who is this cousin of yours? I told you, I know everyone."

Felicity didn't doubt it for a moment. She was such a nosey old harridan. But luckily this part of her story wasn't a fabrication. She would tell her, then move on. "My cousin is Louise Fraser. She resides in Charleston with her husband—"

"Cyrus. I know them well. At least I did till

they up and ran off at the first sign of a Yankee. Feckless lot," she mumbled.

"I resent your reference to my cousin as—"

"I'm only speaking the truth, young lady. How are we supposed to deal with the problems brought on by this war if everyone goes running off?" she asked reasonably.

"I . . . I don't know."

"Of course you don't. Climb in here. I'm getting a crick in my neck from looking down. And besides, it appears we're in for a storm."

"Oh, I don't think I should." The words were barely out of her mouth before a nod from the elderly lady had the black man handing Felicity into the coach. Struggling seemed useless, and besides, Felicity couldn't believe the woman, for all her abrasive ways, was anything but harmless. And it was so nice to get off her feet and sink into the soft leather seat.

"Much better. And you didn't waste your time fighting Lucus. I like that. Conserve your strength for the important battles, I always say. I'm Eveline Blackstone, by the by. Now, where can we take you?"

The change of topics was so swift that at first Felicity only blinked. Then her manners surfaced and she nodded. "Felicity Wentworth, and I am quite capable of walking."

Eveline paid no heed to Felicity's remark. She simply glanced out the window to her servant. "Lucus, are we holding up traffic on the street?"

"Yes'm, I do believe we is."

The look from the older lady's sharp green eyes told Felicity she felt her personally responsible for the backlog . . . perhaps even for the traffic itself. Besides, the sporadic patter on the coach roof announced the rain had begun. With a sigh Felicity clutched her valise handle tighter. "Very well, the Charleston Hotel."

Eveline shook her gray head. "We can't have you staying there by yourself. Take us home, Lucus."

"But I . . ." Before she could protest, the coach lurched forward, throwing Felicity back against the seat. "I don't even know you."

"I'm sure Louise Fraser would vouch for me . . . if she were here, that is. Since she's decided to high-tail and run, our introduction will have to suffice. I can't in good conscience let a young thing like you wander the streets of Charleston. My daughter says I don't realize that times have changed. But I realize, all right. And the city isn't safe. Besides," she wrapped her other hand around the head of the walking stick and peered at Felicity over it, "I have plenty of room and you can keep me company."

Felicity wasn't at all certain she wanted to keep the woman company even if she had the time—which she didn't. But before she could figure out how to respond, the coach stopped in front of a large house, grander even than Cousin Louise's. Lucus opened the door and reached in for Mrs. Blackstone.

Having no apparent alternative, Felicity followed,

bending her head and hurrying through the now steady downpour to the portico. Brushing rain droplets from her hair, Felicity stood beside Mrs. Blackstone who seemed not to be wet at all. The older woman was much smaller than Felicity had assumed—perhaps because her voice suggested someone of larger stature. She seemed to bristle under the care of her servant who quickly let go of her elbow.

"Getting old is the price we pay for our sins," Eveline said when she noticed Felicity watching her.

"I'd say old age is preferable to the alternative," Felicity quipped, then wished she hadn't. Before she died, her mother warned her repeatedly that she spoke too often without thinking. When she glanced toward Mrs. Blackstone the woman's expression was stern.

"You have an impertinent mouth, young woman." Eveline pursed her lips. "Perhaps that's what I like about you."

The door was opened by a black woman who looked every bit as old as her mistress. Speechless, Felicity followed her into the house. The foyer was wide and open, beautifully appointed with murals and mahogany.

From the top of the wide spiral staircase came a high-pitched voice. "There you are, Mama. I've been ever so worried."

Felicity watched as a plump woman in billowing skirts floated down the steps. When her feet

35

landed on the marble parquet floor she rushed to Mrs. Blackstone, enveloping her in a gigantic hug.

"Are you trying to suffocate me, Judith?" Eveline extricated herself from the encompassing arms and stepped away.

"Why no, Mama." Judith sounded sincerely upset by her mother's remark. "You were just gone so long, and you know I don't like you driving around Charleston unescorted."

"I've been driving around Charleston since before you were born." Eveline tapped her walking stick on the floor to emphasize her point.

"Of course you have, Mama." Judith's tone was condescending. "But times have changed."

"I'm well aware of that. Felicity." Eveline turned toward her. "This is my daughter Judith Fenton. Judith, Felicity Wentworth of Richmond. She's Louise Fraser's cousin. Miss Wentworth will be staying with us for a while."

Was it Felicity's imagination or did the older woman hesitate before she said Richmond? In any case she didn't have time to worry about it. Mrs. Blackstone hobbled off into the large room to the right. After a quick assessment of their guest and an even quicker greeting, Judith followed.

"But Mama, we're not in the position to have visitors. Besides," her voice lowered, "you never liked the Frasers."

"Whether I do or do not like the Frasers is immaterial." Her tone never dropped so much as a decibel, and Felicity had to smile at the way Judith tried to hush her. "And the day you bury me,"

Eveline continued, "is the day this house won't have room for guests." She settled onto the edge of an elaborate winged chair that dwarfed her diminutive frame. "Come, come, Felicity, don't allow my daughter's manners to offend you. Leave your bag in the hallway. Lucus will get it for you."

Felicity gripped the handle tighter, lugging the valise as she entered the parlor.

"I certainly didn't mean she wasn't more than welcome." Judith's lips curved into a smile. "I merely meant—"

"Yes, yes, Judith. We are aware of what you meant. Now do ring for some refreshment. It's devilish hot out. Oh wait, here's Ruth."

The same elderly woman who opened the door entered the room bearing a tray that seemed likely to topple her forward at any minute. She set the silver on the tea table in front of Eveline. Her mumbled, "Of course it's hot out there, it's June ain't it," brought a chuckle from Mrs. Blackstone; a scowl from her daughter.

"Mama, you really shouldn't encourage Ruth to . . ." Judith began, but when she noticed her mother paid her no heed, stopped. With a muttered noise, she sank into the chair across from Eveline and snatched a sweet off the platter.

Felicity sat on the settee, her carpetbag nestled on the cushion beside her and longed to do the same. The sight of food made her salivate and she swallowed, trying not to show how hungry she was.

It seemed to take forever for Mrs. Blackstone

to pour the tea and Ruth to pass it. When the platter of cakes was finally offered, Felicity's hand shook as she reached for the largest. She nearly sighed as her teeth sank into the sugary confection.

"Well, I guess ye heard the news." Felicity paid little heed to the black woman's announcement until she caught a glimpse of Judith's expression as she reached for a second cake.

"I'll tell her Ruth. You may leave now." Judith's lips thinned when she noticed the black woman didn't move.

"Tell me what? What is it Judith?"

"I would have preferred to relay this to you after you rested." Judith scowled at Ruth, who was still in the room. "I know how tired you must be."

"Stop chattering away and get on with it. I'm not the least fatigued."

Well, if she wasn't, Felicity certainly was. She almost asked if she could be shown to her room, but Eveline's annoyed voice stopped her. "Whatever are you searching for, Judith?"

Looking up from the drawer she'd opened, Judith shook her head. "I know my smelling salts are here somewhere. Ruth, did you take them?"

"Of course she didn't," Eveline answered for her servant. "You're the only one who ever needs them, Judith. Now will someone please tell me what's going on?"

By this time Judith found the small bottle and Felicity's curiosity was piqued.

"It's Devon," Judith began and paused.

"Devon?" Felicity glanced toward Mrs. Blackstone when she said the name. Perhaps she'd need the smelling salts after all. Her face was ashen. "Has . . . has something happened to him?"

"Oh, Good Lord no." Judith brushed the thought aside. "Your grandson has the proverbial nine lives. It's just that according to Ruth he's back in Charleston."

For the first time in their short acquaintance Felicity saw the sharp-tongued Eveline Blackstone actually smile. And though she was still tired and uncomfortable and had no idea how she was going to accomplish her goal, Felicity smiled too.

"Yes ma'm," Ruth said when Eveline questioned her. "Heard 'bout it this mornin'. That boy done ran through them Yankee ships again."

Two

Hazy sunlight slanted across the counterpane when Felicity opened her eyes. For a moment she thought she was back at Wentworth House, resting after a taxing afternoon of visiting. With a sigh she remembered where she was . . . and why.

She was in the Charleston bedroom of a woman she barely knew. Turning her head into the pillow she swallowed, trying not to feel utterly over-whelmed. Certainly things weren't going exactly as she'd planned them from the security of her bed-room in New York. But there *was* a war. That should account for certain problems—like her cousin not being in Charleston.

Felicity sat up, determined not to dwell on that setback. She was safe, and rested, her hunger pangs gone—though she could have eaten more than the two small cakes. Now all she had to do was figure out a way to reach Magnolia Hill plan-tation near Port Royal, south of Charleston.

She could solicit Eveline Blackstone's assistance, though Felicity didn't think it wise to tell her why she wished to go there. The elderly lady seemed committed to the Confederacy and wouldn't take kindly to a Yankee in her midst, much less an Abolitionist Yankee. No, she'd have to come up with another reason for going to Magnolia Hill.

Any excuse would probably do. Mrs. Blackwell had seemed so obsessed with the idea of *Devon* being in Charleston she barely glanced Felicity's way when she asked to be shown to her room.

Sharp rapping at the door interrupted her musings about who this Devon might be. Felicity glanced up as Eveline Blackstone hobbled into the room.

"You're awake. Good." She motioned for Ruth to follow. "We've been going through Celia's clothespress—Celia's my granddaughter, Judith's daughter—and have picked out several gowns that might do. I assume you have nothing with you but that black thing?"

"I do have one other gown," Felicity said, glancing toward the chair where she'd draped the *black thing* before climbing into the bed. It was gone. Quickly her eyes dropped to where she'd left her valise, relief flooding her when she saw it. Brushing aside a tangle of red-gold hair, Felicity scanned the room for her gown. "Where is my dress? And do for what?"

"It's being brushed, though I doubt it will help. And for the ball, of course."

"Ball?" She didn't have time for balls. Balls were all Jebediah and her father thought she was

41

good for. She'd come south to prove them wrong. "I have no intention of attending a ball."

"Ruth, which hue do you think goes best with that red hair?" the elderly woman asked her servant, as if Felicity hadn't spoken.

"Not the pink, for sure. The green is good. But I think this here dark blue goes with her eyes."

"My thoughts exactly. She can wear my sapphires. I assume you've no jewels of your own?"

Felicity just sat there, her legs dangling over the bed, her mouth agape, listening to the two women discuss her as if she were invisible. With Eveline's question Felicity's mouth clamped shut and she blinked. "Of course I have jewels." Her father used to be extremely generous and jewelry was a favorite way he indulged his wife and daughter.

"But not with you?"

"No, but . . ." Felicity slid off the mattress. "But it matters not since I'm not going to any ball. Now if you'll simply return my dress, I'll . . ." Since neither woman paid her the least attention— they were discussing among themselves what adjustments were needed in the ball gown—Felicity paused. Hands on hips, she advanced on the two women. That she was a head taller than either gave her added courage.

"Perhaps you didn't understand me before. I'm not going to a ball."

They looked up as one. Eveline's lips pursed before she shook her head. "Devon sent word he shall meet us there," she announced, her tone most reasonable for her.

Felicity extended her hands. "But I'm not interested in meeting this Devon, whoever he is."

"He's my grandson. Not Judith's offspring," she was quick to add. "And you certainly should wish to meet him. I'm counting on him to see you safely back to Richmond."

"But, I . . ." Whatever Felicity planned to say—and she wasn't at all certain what that was—didn't matter. The two older women simply walked out of the room, the issue closed.

The war might be very close to Charleston, but in the ballroom on the second floor of the Summerville home, it seemed far away indeed. Tall gilded mirrors reflected candlelight from hundreds of candles. The room was abuzz with lively voices and tinkling laughter, and Felicity felt swept away to another time and place. Before her brother died . . . when it was still acceptable to have fun.

The recollection brought a twinge of guilt but she quickly dismissed it aside. She was in her element. The shimmering gown with its low cut bodice decorated with pink, silk roses looked gorgeous on her. As long as she brought Esther's children back to her, what difference did it make how she accomplished it? Jebediah would never know she went to a ball.

And it certainly wasn't as if she had a choice. Mrs. Blackstone and Ruth had come to her room as the time for the ball approached. While her mistress supervised, Ruth fluffed the wide, ruffled skirt and curled Felicity's hair into long curls that hung over one shoulder.

Besides, Felicity rationalized, now that she was in Charleston, and unable to find her cousin, she needed help. Perhaps a gentleman she would meet tonight might be willing to take her in his carriage to Magnolia Hill. Maybe even Eveline Blackstone's grandson would do it.

She needed to smile. She needed to cajole. Those two techniques never failed her. Without warning, the image of Jebediah's stern face when he rejected her flashed across her mind, but she dismissed it. Everyone was entitled a slip now and then.

But she wouldn't fail this time. There was too much at stake.

When a handsome young soldier, introduced to her as the son of William Edwards, Cyrus Fraser's second cousin by marriage, asked for the first waltz, Felicity accepted graciously. The music floated around them, a nebula of happier times, as they swirled around the ballroom.

Franklin Edwards smiled down on Felicity, his eyes blinking rapidly when she returned the gesture. His uniform was new, a gift from his mother, he explained. Unlike most of the soldiers present tonight, he was not a member of Major General Pemberton's force sent to protect the city. Franklin was home on leave.

Which meant he had time to drive her to Magnolia Hill. Once they got there she'd think of some way to smuggle the children back with her. Perhaps she'd just buy them outright. "What? I mean, I beg your pardon. I was just so carried away by the music. Strauss isn't it? I'm afraid I didn't hear you. I do apologize." Felicity took as deep a breath as her corset stays allowed. She needed to pay attention.

"Please, don't concern yourself. I admire a woman who appreciates the melodious strains of a waltz. It was inconsiderate of me to allow my prattle to interfere with your enjoyment."

"Oh, how you do go on." Felicity slanted him a look through her lashes. "Why if I simply wished to listen to the music I could have settled myself next to the orchestra. What did you say earlier?"

"I only wondered why Cyrus never mentioned his beautiful cousin from Richmond."

Felicity forced her smile to remain bright. "You mean he didn't? Why wait till I see him again. He'll wish he only had to deal with those dreadful Yankees." This brought the laugh she hoped, and Felicity relaxed a bit. Several minutes passed in banal conversation before she swallowed and pushed forward.

"I was wondering, Lieutenant Edwards . . ." She glanced down shyly. "Oh, no. I shouldn't ask."

"Please, Miss Wentworth, what is it?"

"No." Felicity shook her head delicately. Her curls shimmered on her shoulder. "It's too much of an imposition." Her eyes met his. "And I barely know you."

"But my dear Miss Wentworth, we're practically kin."

Felicity blinked. "Oh, we are, aren't we. Well, in that case. Do you suppose you could escort me to Magnolia Hill plantation? I realize it's a dreadful imposition and all, but . . . What's wrong?" The music was beginning to crescendo. The dance would be ending soon and Felicity didn't like the expression on the young lieutenant's face.

"Why, Magnolia Hill is near Port Royal."

"Is it?"

"Yes ma'am, it is. And Port Royal is in Yankee hands. It would take someone as slick as a blockade runner to escort you to and from Magnolia Hill."

"There you are, you scoundrel."

"Hello, Grandmother." Devon leaned forward to kiss her paper thin cheek, hesitating when she reached up and touched his lip.

"What happened to you?"

"Nothing much." Devon smiled, wincing. "A slight altercation with some of the South's finest."

"A brawl? My dear boy, it's the Yankees you're to be fighting."

"I'll try to remember that. Besides, it wasn't exactly a brawl. You're looking splendid this evening."

"I am not. I'm old and wrinkled and this damn hip is giving me a fit. And don't change the subject."

46

Devon glanced out over the ballroom. Here at least, the ladies of Charleston wore their best silks. But then it was for a good cause. "I didn't realize there was a subject to change," Devon said lightly when his grandmother tapped his arm with her fan. "How much money was raised for the Volunteer Aid Society tonight?"

"Not enough." Eveline's shoulders slumped. "And I fear it shall only get worse."

Devon squeezed her hand. At the moment she looked everyone of her seventy-eight years. "We're still holding out against McClellen in Virginia. Perhaps . . ."

Eveline smiled, placing her other hand atop his. They'd had this discussion before, she and her grandson. "I consider you one of the few people of my acquaintance clever enough to understand the Pandora's box South Carolina opened when it fired on Fort Sumter. But there's no use discussing it here." Now it was Eveline who sought to change the subject. "I see your aunt coming toward us and before she arrives I want to tell you about a young woman I met today."

"Grams." Devon reverted to his pet name for her. "If this is another attempt to introduce me to the perfect woman—"

"Don't be an idiot, Devon. I gave up on that after the dreadful Chapman fiasco."

"I tried to refuse her advances, didn't I?" Devon's green eyes danced with amusement.

"Yes, but—"

"And when she came to my room unescorted didn't I send her away immediately?" he teased.

"Would you hush! I've had a hard enough time living the entire incident down."

Devon threw back his head and laughed. "You don't give a damn what other people think. So don't tell me that."

"Would you listen!" Again she whacked her grandson's arm with her fan. "The young woman I speak of needs help."

"You're the saint in the family. So help her. Why, hello Aunt Judith. How absolutely radiant you look tonight." Devon knew just being around him annoyed his aunt, so he gave her a robust kiss. She visibly shuddered, extracting herself as quickly as possible.

"I came over to make certain you were all right, Mama."

"Of course I am. Stop hovering, Judith. Why don't you—Devon, what is it? I demand to know where you're going."

But Devon didn't stop to answer as he strode across the ballroom while the final strains of a waltz drifted away. He kept his eyes fixed on a couple near a fluted column. The man was tall and lanky, handsome in a boyish way, and dressed in butternut gray. But it was the woman who first drew his attention.

They started toward him, no doubt the soldier was returning the beauty to her chaperone, but Devon never gave him the chance.

48

"I believe this dance is mine," he said, reaching for the woman's mitted hand.

She looked up at him, her blue eyes wide. "There must be some mistake." She glanced down at the dance card dangling from her wrist. "This waltz is promised to a Captain Jamison."

Her smile was dazzling.

"There's no mistake." Devon pulled her into his arms as the orchestra began another song. "Captain Jamison extends his regrets. He sent me in his stead."

"Sir, I'm going to have to ask you to unhand the lady." The young soldier drew himself up, to his full height. "She obviously doesn't know you." His hand played on the hilt of his dress sword.

"It's all right, Lieutenant Edwards. Truly it is." Felicity's words came in a breathless rush. The insufferable man was holding her too close for comfort or propriety, and she'd like nothing better than for her young swain to throttle the rogue. But even her limited experience with fighting told her the lieutenant was no match for this man demanding a dance.

If he wished her as a partner that much, so be it. But she certainly wasn't going to be charming. And when she returned to Mrs. Blackstone she'd be sure to point out the boor.

The full rhythmic strains of the waltz filled the room and Felicity was swept even tighter into the stranger's arms. She dared not look up at him . . . it might be perceived as flirting. But she sensed that he studied her. For a boor he danced well, and now that she complied with his wishes, he held her only slightly closer than good taste dictated.

Forced by her refusal to meet his gaze, Felicity found herself staring at a white shirt and frock coat that covered a wide breadth of chest. He swirled her around the room, billowing her skirts, and she almost forgot to be offended—until he spoke.

"You've recovered from your grief quickly enough."

"I beg your pardon?" Felicity couldn't help glancing up . . . and gasped. She hadn't noticed before the deplorable condition of her partner's face. His left eye was a mottled purple, swollen, like his lip. It caused the smile he gave her to appear lopsided and rather endearing.

"I merely commented on your lack of widow's weeds tonight."

His eyes raked down lingering on the swell of bosom above the flower-trimmed decolletage and Felicity cursed the flush that spread to her face. "I . . . I don't know what you're talking about. And would you please stop . . ." Felicity's words trailed off. She couldn't explain exactly what she wished him to stop doing. "You really look like you'd be better off in bed."

"Precisely where I spent the majority of my day." The waltz was ending and Devon maneuvered them toward the open doors leading to the second-story of the piazza. "If you think my face is bruised you should see my ribs."

"I'm sure I'd rather not." Her partner chuckled devilishly, his hand tightening on hers at the same time he sucked in his breath. She felt slight stirrings of compassion that were quickly squelched as he danced her out into the moonlight. Her back stiffened. "What are you doing?"

"Insuring our privacy while you answer some questions."

"I have no intention of—Would you let go of me?" He did, suddenly. But by this time Felicity was backed against the railing. Though he didn't touch her with his big body, his arms braced on either side of the banister effectively held her prisoner.

Felicity considered screaming, but by this time another song, a spirited country tune filled the air with riotous sound. She doubted she'd be heard above the din.

Raising her chin, Felicity tried to remain calm. She'd handled overzealous suitors before. "If it's another dance you wish," she began, but stopped when his laughter exploded around her.

"You do have an inflated opinion of yourself, don't you?" Actually, under different circumstances waltzing with her would be quite pleasant. But he ached like hell where Lil had wrapped his ribs, and, unless he was mistaken, a few of them were cracked. All because of the woman haughtily staring up at him.

His words struck her as reminiscent of Jebediah's rejection, but at least her true love hadn't laughed. Before she even thought of the conse-

51

quences she balled up her fist and hit the man in the side. All signs of humor faded as he groaned. His strong hands gripping her bare shoulders brought the reality of what she'd done crashing down on her.

"Let me go or I'll scream."

"Why you little . . ." Devon sucked air through his clenched teeth, fighting back waves of nausea. If he'd had a bull's eye marked on his coat she couldn't have done a better job of hitting the spot where he was kicked this morning.

Light splashed through the open door, adding brightness to the full moon and he could see her fear. Her eyes were wide in her pale face. And she should be afraid. For as much as he wanted to protect her this morning, he wanted to shake her now.

But he resisted the urge. Instead his fingers slid up the curve of her shoulder, catching momentarily on the sapphire necklace that looked vaguely familiar. She stiffened as if expecting him to snatch the jewels from around her neck. But instead he slipped his thumb to the side, snagging a ringlet of fiery gold that shone brighter than the gems.

"I'd recognize this hair anywhere, even if I hadn't caught a glimpse of your face. Neither should be kept hidden." He twirled the silken strands absently, catching a faint scent of jasmine.

"I don't know what you're talking about." Felicity pushed forward, expecting . . . hoping he would do the gentlemanly thing and move aside.

He didn't.

Instead the hand that had only toyed with her hair now rested flat against her skin. The pad of his finger brushed across her pulse at the base of her neck and Felicity hoped he couldn't tell how rapidly it fluttered. She was frightened, yes. But there was something else that had her blood pounding. Something primitive, and erotic . . . and wild.

Felicity looked up and swallowed, trying to understand her reaction. Her flesh burned where he touched her. It was difficult to ascertain what he looked like—not that that sort of thing was important to her anymore, Felicity reminded herself. But with his eye bruised and swollen and his lip cut, she couldn't tell.

He was tall of course, broad of shoulder and chest. And though he wasn't garbed in the accepted dress of the day, Confederate gray, his form was certainly one to have the ladies drooling behind their fans.

Not that Felicity would drool. No, she was too concerned with a man's mind, with his commitment to others, to have her head turned by such things as powerful arms and slender hips.

She didn't know how long she stood like that, pressed between his body and the banister. His palm flattened above her breast. A strange lethargic feeling swept over her and her lashes began to drift shut. It took all her will to snatch his hand away. Felicity wondered if the print of his palm was branded into her flesh.

"You, sir, are no gentleman."

His reaction, a tilting of his head to the side, and a devilish grin, made her lean back, her waist pressed into the rail. He didn't seem the least upset by her words, but she made a discovery that had her pulse racing anew. With the souvenirs of whatever brawl he was in turned away and hidden in the shadows, he was a devastatingly handsome man.

Dark hair dipped over a forehead wrinkled in amusement. His eyes were light . . . green or blue, she couldn't tell in the moonlight, and crinkled at the edges. Somewhere along the way he'd broken his nose, no doubt in another brawl, but the resulting imperfection gave him a roguish air. But it was the mouth that really gave him a rakish expression. The side that wasn't swollen by someone's fist was generous and sensual. The dimple in his cheek deepened as he laughed softly.

"I don't recall saying I was one. But then, Red," Devon flicked the burnished curl behind her shoulder, "I'm not sure *you* qualify as a lady."

Indignation straightened her back. Felicity glared at her tormentor, all thoughts of his handsome face and form forgotten. "My name is Felicity Wentworth. No one calls me *Red*. And I most certainly *am* a lady."

"Felicity, huh?" The cad seemed to find the name amusing. "Well I don't know where you're from Miss Felicity, but—"

"Richmond. I'm from Richmond . . . Virginia," she added as an afterthought.

His dark brow arched, but he didn't question her

lie, though Felicity knew her accent had slipped. He simply continued his statement. "Around these parts a lady is grateful when a man saves her honor."

"The only person who's compromised my honor is you, sir. Now would you kindly step aside?"

He hadn't expected hugs and kisses, though standing this close to Miss Felicity Wentworth, Devon decided he certainly wouldn't mind, but this was too much. The little lady was entirely too haughty, and ungrateful for her own good. "Perhaps you enjoyed the attentions of those men this morning?"

"What men?" Felicity had an uncomfortable feeling she knew exactly what men he was talking about. Her eyes narrowed, as she examined her tormentor more closely.

"That's right," he said, folding his arms over his impressive chest. "I'm the one who foolishly came to your rescue."

Felicity thought back but she couldn't remember the person standing before her . . . as her rescuer or otherwise. She didn't even recall being rescued. Some awful man had grabbed at her valise, then she was knocked aside. When she regained her wits she lost no time gathering up her skirts and running as fast and as far as she could.

Drawing on her inner resources of charm, Felicity gave the man before her a brief, radiant smile. "I'm afraid you all have me confused with someone else. I . . ."

Felicity's words, spoken in her most authentic

fake accent trailed off as he slowly shook his head back and forth. The illumination of the two sides of his face, one bruised and swollen, the other incredibly handsome, fascinated Felicity. "I told you, Red, that hair of yours is hard to miss. Though why you wanted to cover it in black is more than I can understand."

"Apparently there is much that you don't understand." Felicity had enough of the boorish man. At this very moment she could be looking for someone to help her find Esther's children. A blockade runner, perhaps. And what was she doing? Being held against her will by someone from the docks. For all she knew this man was one of the ruffians who attacked her.

"Such as?" he asked as he again tilted his head to a rakish angle.

"Such as the fact that I do not wish to converse with you or be in your company."

This time when she shoved her mitted hands against his chest Devon stepped aside. In a flutter of deep blue ruffles she slipped by him. He caught the glint of candlelight in her red-gold hair before she disappeared from view, swallowed up in the crush of dancers.

The scent of her perfume lingered on the piazza as Devon watched her go. He shook his head and laughed. God, what had gotten into him? It was obvious from the beginning . . . hell, it was obvious this morning . . . the woman wasn't in the mood to be grateful. Not that he wanted much from her. But a simple "thank you" would be nice. Maybe make the ache in his side a little more palatable.

But she wasn't interested in his pain, or anything else about him for that matter. And Devon wasn't the type to push where he wasn't wanted. Unless it was on the high seas.

He leaned back against the baluster and drew a cheroot from the slim silver holder. The Lucifer burst into flame as he scraped it across his thumbnail. He lit the thin cigar, then examined the tip's red glow. One thing he did know was that the woman he danced with, the woman who denied any knowledge of him, was the widow from this morning.

There weren't two women in Charleston, hell in the entire South, with hair like that . . . or those blue eyes. For whatever reason she didn't want to admit they met this morning . . . when she was dressed in widow's weeds.

Taking another draw, Devon savored the sting of fine tobacco, trying to put the incident out of his mind. But it wouldn't shake loose. "Now why would she pass herself off as a poor, grief-stricken widow?" he mused, turning to look out over the moon kissed garden. Stately oaks, their gossamer veils of Spanish moss swaying in the soft breeze, stood guard over the grounds. Why would she indeed?

His suspicious nature, that served him well in the business of running the blockades, didn't overlook that there was a war going on. And people who pretended to be what they weren't were often called spies.

Devon shook his head. Miss Felicity Wentworth couldn't be a spy. She was too beautiful and . . . And she sure as hell wasn't from Virginia either. More like Pennsylvania or New York, unless he missed his guess.

With a flick of his fingers, Devon sent the cheroot in a glowing arc toward the ground below. He was being fanciful and stupid, making more out of the situation than it warranted. Maybe she was running away from her husband, or maybe. . . . Hell, he didn't know what she was up to. But he did know it wasn't any of his damn concern. Period.

Devon flexed his shoulders, cursing under his breath when his ribs cried out in protest. He was going to seek out his grandmother and give her his regrets that he couldn't stay longer. The *Intrepid* needed repairs after her last foray with the enemy, so he'd be in Charleston for a while, plenty of time to get reacquainted with Grams.

But for now he needed a stiff drink, not the weakly laced planter's punch he tasted earlier, and a soft bed.

Felicity pleaded a headache as soon as she saw Eveline Blackstone. But the sharp-tongued woman insisted they stay to meet her grandson. "Isn't it possible for me to see him some other time?" Felicity said as she stood, swishing the stuffy, perfumed air with her fan. It would be pleasant to go outside. Her eyes shot to the veranda doors. But *he* might still be there.

"You can never count on his being in one place long enough to chance meeting him again."

Which didn't really seem so awful. Mrs. Blackstone might think her grandson wonderful, but it was obvious to Felicity that his aunt held a different view. "I really don't think—"

"Oh, there he is now." Eveline took the younger woman's hand and practically dragged her, the cane playing a staccato beat on the polished floor, toward a group of people.

Felicity had no choice but to follow. She tried to see where they were headed, but the ballroom was packed with people. Then she caught sight of the man from the piazza, and tried to swerve away. Her skirts billowed out around her as she did.

"Would you stop sashaying so," Eveline ordered as she used the gold cane head to tap on a broad shoulder.

He turned, his brow lifting in surprise as he spotted Felicity. Even before Eveline made the introductions Felicity had a sinking feeling in the pit of her stomach.

Devon Blackstone grinned, wincing from the pain in his lip. The injury he received helping the chit. "Well, if it isn't Red," was all he said.

59

Three

"What *are* you talking about?" Eveline used the cane handle to regain her grandson's attention. "I want to present you to Miss Wentworth. Felicity, this is my grandson Devon Blackstone. Please don't allow his wounds to effect your perception of him."

"By all means Miss Wentworth, think nothing of my scars of valor." Devon bowed low despite the ache in his side.

Felicity snapped open her fan. "Indeed." Why did she have to encounter this man again? And why did he have to be Mrs. Blackstone's grandson? "I'm sure you received your wounds for a good cause."

"I thought so at the time."

Felicity straightened her back. "But you don't now?" Perhaps she hadn't thanked him properly, but then she didn't recognize him as her savior; truthfully, wasn't certain she had a savior. Surely he understood that. Besides, after his brutish actions on the veranda she wasn't sure he deserved her gratitude.

He didn't even answer her. The insolent man only grinned, that lopsided grin—oddly attractive despite the cuts and bruises—and turned toward his grandmother. "May I fetch you a cup of punch before I take my leave?"

"I was hoping you would stay longer. Perhaps partner Miss Wentworth."

Felicity gritted her teeth, thoughts of waltzing yet again with this man, repugnant. He would hold her close, and if she weren't careful, try to get her alone. A chill ran down Felicity's spine when she thought of his body against hers. Of course *she* could refuse to dance, but Mrs. Blackstone had been very nice to her, and she didn't wish to appear rude.

The grandson's laughter interrupted Felicity's musings. He looked at her, his eyes twinkling as if he knew exactly what she was thinking. "I imagine Miss Wentworth's dance card is full. Besides," he said, bowing first over his grandmother's hand, and then Felicity's, "I fear I've had my fill of dancing tonight."

He was declining to dance with her. Felicity couldn't believe it. She'd never been to a ball in New York or anywhere else that men weren't clamoring to be her partner. Why, at the ball held for the Prince of Wales in New York, his highness had personally requested she dance with him. Even here the invitation outweighed the spots on her dance card. Felicity longed to shove the list in his face to show him just how many men *did* want to dance with her.

But he wasn't paying her the slightest attention. Devon Blackstone was bent over his grandmother, kissing her cheek and giving her a hug that made the elderly woman actually giggle and slap at his arm.

"You behave yourself, Grams," he said, "and I shall call on you in the morning."

"Not too late," she ordered, though her voice had lost some of it's harsh edge. "I'll be visiting the hospital later. As a matter of fact, you might accompany me."

"I might." He could deliver some of the medicines he smuggled into Charleston. "Don't worry, I'll be there early."

With the briefest of nods toward Felicity, he turned and walked away. Out of her life for good, Felicity thought with a sigh of relief. For she'd already formulated her plans to quit Mrs. Blackstone's home long before the grandson paid his visit . . . dawn if necessary.

For now she only wished to settle her tired aching body into a feather bed and sleep. Her nap this afternoon hadn't near made up for the sleepless nights she spent sitting on cramped trains as she made her way south. Hopefully she wouldn't have to make the return trip by rail. Especially with three children. The idea of going by ship, spending her time in a comfortable cabin, appealed to her. She'd enjoyed the trip she and her mother took to England several years ago. Yes, the idea of finding a blockade runner to help her seemed perfect.

Now all she needed to do was find a blockade runner and offer him some of her gold. From what she'd read in the papers, they were a cunning, disreputable lot who'd do anything for money.

Eveline Blackstone was still watching her grandson as he made his way through the crowd. It was obvious the old harridan thought the sun rose and set on him.

"He's a fine boy," Mrs. Blackstone said. She glanced over at Felicity and seemed almost embarrassed by her pronouncement. Felicity wondered the words weren't hard for her to say with her razor sharp tongue. Felicity also wondered if she knew how rude her grandson could be.

As he disappeared through the double doorway it struck Felicity that there was something different about him—other than his good looks and imposing stature. Nearly every man in the room unless they were Mrs. Blackstone's age wore some sort of Confederate uniform.

Except Devon Blackstone.

His attire was very much what Felicity remembered the men wearing when she last visited Charleston . . . before the war. White linen molded casually to his large frame. His shirt was cotton, white, with only a black cravat to add any contrasting color.

The clothing of a gentleman. But that's where the parallel seemed to end. For beneath the civilized garb there was something wild and untamed. It made Felicity shiver just thinking about it.

"What's wrong with you, girl? It's hot as blazes in here, and you act as if you've taken a chill."

Felicity should have realized the old harpy was watching her. No one was safe from those bright probing eyes. Fluttering her mitted hand to her cheek, Felicity managed to shiver again. "I'm afraid I shall have the vapors," she said in her best imitation of Cousin Louise's drawl.

"The vapors, eh?" Those all-seeing eyes narrowed.

"Why yes. I get them quite often." Not entirely a lie. She learned the symptoms at her mother's knee . . . Mama was especially prone to them. And though Felicity wasn't certain she'd ever had them, there were times, when her corset was tight, that she felt short of breath.

Thanks to Ruth's arthritic hands, Felicity's corset strings were plenty loose. But she did have a headache, and longed for a chance to be alone and think.

"I suppose it is time we took our leave. This blasted hip is bothering me. Where's that daughter of mine?" Eveline thumped the cane on the polished floor.

"I'll find her." Felicity started off, then paused. Mrs. Blackstone *was* very old, and no doubt ached a lot more than Felicity—even if she was a shrew. Spotting a deserted chair beside a bunting draped potted plant, Felicity rushed toward it before someone else could sit in it. She dragged it toward

Mrs. Blackstone, who was leaning heavily on the rounded gold handle. She glanced over sharply when Felicity positioned the chair behind her.

"What's this?"

The acidity of her voice coupled with the stupidity of her question made Felicity blink. "Why, it's a chair. So that you might rest your hip," she continued when the crotchety old woman just stared at her.

"I don't recall asking you to fetch me a chair."

Felicity tried to remember the manners her mother drilled into her . . . she really did. But it was hard to think of simpering words when what she wanted to do was kick the chair. In light of that Felicity considered it the height of restraint when she turned away with a blunt, "Don't sit in it then."

Judith was huddled with two other ladies who resembled her in form and style of dress. All three wore black, as did most of the mature women in the ballroom. A grim reminder of the lives lost. She seemed reluctant to leave her friends but came willingly enough when Felicity mentioned Mrs. Blackstone's complaint about her hip.

"Mama just won't listen to reason," Judith said with a shake of her head. "I keep telling her she should stay at home. Why, someone her age just never knows what could happen! Especially with things the way they are."

"I suspect Mrs. Blackstone listens to no one." As soon as the words were out of her mouth Felicity was sorry. But instead of defending her mother, Judith agreed.

"Oh, you are so right. She won't even mind Doctor Bateman. If truth be known," Judith leaned toward Felicity, her black enamel fan spread as if she were sharing a large secret, "I think he's frightened of her."

"The doctor, you mean."

"Oh, not just him . . . everyone." Judith extracted her arm from Felicity's when she saw her mother. With a great show of haste she hurried to the older woman's side. Felicity noted with some amusement that Mrs. Blackstone had opted to sit after all.

Judith dropped to her knees and tried to grasp Eveline's hands. She was unceremoniously pushed away. "Oh Mama, Miss Wentworth told me of your problem. Let me call for a litter and we'll have you home in no time. I think I saw Doctor Bateman by the punch bowl. Perhaps he—"

"Would you get up and stop making such a spectacle of yourself? I don't wish to see that old quack Bateman, and when I ride in a litter, it will be on my way to the family plot. Now get out of my way so I can stand." She did so, refusing any help from her daughter, though Judith stood, her plump hands outstretched.

After the stuffiness inside the house, the breeze off the bay felt wonderful. At least it would have if the caress of it across Felicity's flushed cheek didn't remind her of Mrs. Blackstone's rude grandson. The idea that anything would bring back memories of their encounter on the veranda was unsettling.

With a conscious effort, Felicity put him firmly from her mind. As the coach rattled along the cobbled street she reviewed what she would do on the morrow. The first thing on her list was to leave the Blackstone house before the grandson showed up. Then she would find someone willing to take her to Magnolia Hill. A blockade runner.

She was so deep in thought she barely noticed the conversation going on around her. The voices buzzed about the outskirts of her consciousness; Judith's whining, Eveline Blackstone's harsh tones. It wasn't until the words "blockade runner" were spoken that Felicity paid any attention.

"What did you say?" Felicity sat straighter and inclined her head toward the shadow shape beside her. Since the night was brightened by a full moon, the coach lamps remained unlit. In the confines of the coach it was dim.

"I was simply expounding on the virtues of those men brave enough to tweak the nose of the federal blockaders."

"Now, Mama, I never said he wasn't brave. I simply wondered why he didn't offer his services to the Confederate government is all."

"The government is run by a passel of incompetents."

"Mama! How can you say such a thing?"

Felicity could almost feel Judith's eyes roll toward her. As if she was going to go about repeating Eveline Blackstone's views on the Confederacy.

"I shall say anything I blasted like, Judith. To Jefferson Davis himself if he were here. We weren't prepared for this war. And now everything is crumbling down around us."

"Oh Mama, you're wrong. Why Harry says—"

"I don't give a hoot what that husband of yours says."

"But he has President Davis's ear. Why just the other day I received a letter in which he said that the President is certain victory will eventually be won. I told you about that."

The older woman's snort was very unladylike and Felicity would have been tempted to laugh, but the conversation was drifting away from the original topic. Blockade runners.

"I know you never believed in Harry, but he's a brilliant man. And I think his appointment has proven that. You just don't like him because he married me."

Judith's voice was laced with tears and Felicity thought she'd be sobbing into her handkerchief any minute. Why she cared what Eveline Blackstone thought of her husband was beyond Felicity. Obviously the old harpy didn't like anyone . . . with the possible exception of her grandson. Which only proved her ineptness at judging character.

"Poppycock Judith. Stop your sniveling. The fact that he married you has nothing to do with my contempt for Harry."

Judith gasped and Felicity decided to step in before she became hysterical. "About blockade runners . . ."

"What about them?" Eveline's question cut through the backdrop of Judith's sniffles like a knife.

Felicity swallowed. "I'd love to meet one sometime. They seem ever so brave and romantic."

"There's nothing the least romantic about risking life and limb," Evaline snapped.

Felicity said nothing. She had no illusions about the romance of running the blockade. She just didn't want either woman to suspect the real reason she was interested.

"As for meeting a blockade runner," Eveline continued. "You already have."

"I have, but—"

"Don't interrupt, girl." The coach swayed to a stop and before another word was spoken the door was opened. Mrs. Blackstone's hip must have been truly bothering her, for it took an inordinate amount of time for her to descend to the street in front of her home.

Felicity could barely contain her curiosity. Who could be the blockade runner that she met? Who had the daring, the kind of reckless soul needed to defy the navy of the United States?

The answer came to her like a splash of cold water on a wintry morning. "Mrs. Blackstone." Felicity leaped from the coach, catching up her skirts and rushing after the older woman who hobbled up the porch steps beside her daughter.

"What is it, young woman? Goodness I haven't heard so much racket since those fools fired on Fort Sumter."

"The blockade runner? It's your grandson, isn't it?"

"Well, of course. Devon Blackstone is the most famous and successful of all the runners."

Felicity followed mother and daughter into the house. Though silver sconces lined the walls, few candles were lit. The front hall seemed cavernous, draped in shadows. The Blackstones had very few servants and those they did have were elderly. None of them were about to greet their returning mistresses. Even Lucus, who drove them back from the ball had disappeared around the side of the house after opening the door.

Judith handed one of the candlesticks to Felicity. The other she lifted high as she led her mother up the wide, winding staircase. Mrs. Blackstone followed meekly behind without a caustic word to anyone.

As Felicity opened her bedroom door, light from the candle splashed into the room, blending only with the silvery spill of moonlight shining through the windows. At Wentworth House the lamps were always aglow, shimmering off the flocked walls.

And there was always Addie, her lady's maid, to greet her when she returned from a party. Addie would unhook her gown, loosen the stays and comb out Felicity's curls, all the while asking questions about the ball. "Who did you dance with, Miss Felicity? Were the gentlemen handsome? Did everyone just love your gown?"

Felicity sank onto the bench and set the candle on the dressing table. Leaning forward she cupped her chin in her palms and stared into the beveled mirror. How could she have traveled such a short ways and come so far from her world?

The face that stared back at her had no answer. Except that this is what she wanted. A chance to prove herself worthy. To Jebediah. To her father.

Felicity sighed as she searched through her hair for the hidden hairpins that tamed her curls. One by one she pulled the silver pins and dropped them on the mahogany surface, dulled by a fine layer of dust.

If her quest for Esther's children was easy it wouldn't be much of a test of her convictions. But why . . . why did Devon Blackstone have to be a blockade runner? A spark of hope came to her. She could find another one. Certainly he wasn't the only blockade runner in Charleston. But his grandmother said he was the best. And he was the only one she knew of. Finding another would take time. Time she didn't have.

Standing, Felicity struggled with the hooks fastening the gown. She moaned in relief when the stays fell open. Leaving both on the floor, topped with her hoops and petticoats, Felicity sank to her knees and reached beneath the bed. She tugged her carpetbag across the Aubusson carpet, relieved that it seemed as heavy as ever. After she fumbled with the leather straps the bag yawned open. The green plaid dress . . . the only one she had left after the rest of her luggage was lost on the train . . . was folded on top. Felicity pulled it out and spread it across a chair. She needed it for tomorrow.

The shifts and stockings she brushed aside until she found the two leather pouches that lent their weight to the valise. The gold coins gleamed in the candlelight as she scooped several out into her hand.

The gold too would be needed on the morrow.

Felicity stuffed her belongings back into the carpetbag, shoved it under the bed and blew out the candle. Tendrils of smoke rose, floating in the breeze that drifted in the east window.

Thoughts of what she had to do tomorrow filled Felicity's head long after she climbed onto the billowy, feather mattress and arranged the netting. Tomorrow would be a real test of her mettle.

Felicity's eyes popped open to bright sunlight streaming in through the mullioned panes. She flung back the counterpane and netting and leaped from the bed. How could she have slept so late? Her plans hinged on rising early.

The night had cooled the water in the pitcher. Felicity quickly splashed some in the bowl and washed herself. Her fumbling fingers couldn't manage the corset and she had no desire to awaken the rest of the household . . . if they still slept. Finally, in disgust she flung the whalebone and starched fabric aside and stepped into her petticoats.

Her dress was simple but becoming, and thankfully fit nicely without the aid of her stays. Felicity smoothed the double flounced skirt down and straightened the puffed sleeves of the under blouse. Then she grabbed up the silver-handled brush on the dressing table.

Her hair seemed curlier than ever. Felicity could barely drag the bristles down through her thick tresses. She twisted her hair into a chignon, holding it in place with one hand while she jabbed pins into the golden mass with the other.

Glancing up she caught sight of herself in the mirror . . . and grimaced. Ever since she decided to marry Jebediah Webster this simple coiffure was the way she styled her hair. But instinct told her Devon Blackstone's taste was very different than Jebediah's.

And like it or not, it was Devon Blackstone she needed to impress today. The hair came tumbling down in a cascade of shimmering red-gold. A few more swipes of the brush smoothed the ringlets, and a dark blue taffeta ribbon that matched the trim on her gown, held the curls off her face.

Leaning forward, Felicity peered into the mirror. She looked tired, but since she saw no rice powder about there was nothing she could do to cover the mauve crescents beneath her eyes. A pinch to each cheek pinkened her pale face. She tried an experimental, flirtatious smile, scowling at the result.

Well, there was no time for anything else. The infamous blockade runner might already be here. Stepping into her slippers, Felicity hurried out of the room.

The tall casement clock in the hallway showed it was barely past eight, earlier than she'd thought. As quietly as she could, Felicity crept down the stairs. No one appeared to be about, and Felicity thought she was the first one up until she heard voices coming from the parlor.

She listened long enough to ascertain that it was Eveline and the servant Ruth talking. No deep baritone joined in the conversation.

Good. He hadn't arrived yet.

Her feet whispered across the cool marble, and she was out the wide front door without a backward glance. Coaches rattled by on the cobblestone street as Felicity scooted around the side of the house. She settled on a bench beneath the glossy leaves of a magnolia, and heaved a sigh of relief.

From her vantage point she could peer through the wrought iron fence to see if anyone came to the house. She spread her skirts, folded her hands and waited. And waited.

Where was the blasted man anyway? Didn't he recall promising to call on his dear sweet grandmother early? Well, maybe no one could accurately describe Eveline Blackstone as dear and sweet, but she was his grandmother.

The morning was warm and Felicity leaned back, relaxing her stiff shoulders. The hypnotic buzz of a fat, fuzzy bee caught her attention. She watched intently as it circled a fragrant blossom overhead, hovering momentarily before swooping in for the sweet nectar.

"Miss Wentworth, isn't it?"

The firm, male voice made Felicity jump. She jerked her head around and stared at the man *she* had hoped to surprise. He stood, hat in hand, leaning lazily against the garden gate. His grin was devilish, as if he enjoyed catching her off guard, and Felicity had to remind herself how much she needed this odious man's help.

"Why Mr. Blackstone . . . or is it Captain Blackstone? You did startle me." Felicity gave him her best smile, wondering if the accent wasn't a bit thick. His eyes narrowed slightly. The injured one looked a bit better this morning. The skin around it was still a mottled blue-green but the swelling had gone down.

"My apologies, Miss Wentworth." Felicity noted he didn't take the trouble to ease himself away from the fence to accompany his regrets with the appropriate bow. He just continued staring at her with his sharp, green gaze, so like his grandmother's.

Felicity swallowed, then widened her smile. Before she decided to devote her life to Jebediah and the abolitionist movement, her smile was known to send many a male heart to flutter. Devon Blackstone didn't look as if he had a heart, let alone experienced any flutters. His jaw tightened, and Felicity wondered why she didn't pick him out as a "nerves of steel" blockade runner from the beginning.

"I'm curious, Miss Wentworth," he began while Felicity found it difficult to keep her smile in place.

"Yes, Captain Blackstone."

"What are you doing in my grandmother's garden?"

"Why waiting for you, of course." At least *that* was the truth. The statement threw the rogue off balance, which lifted Felicity's spirits. She glanced at him through her thick lashes, then dropped her gaze to study her folded hands. "I feel just awful," she murmured.

"Why, pray tell, is that?" After all, he was the one who'd been beaten up.

"Because of the way I treated you last night, of course."

"Of course."

Felicity looked up quickly. He wasn't taking her apology in the spirit in which it was offered. "I mean, I treated you dreadfully. And after you risked your life to save me from those awful, awful men." She tried to appear sincere, but she still couldn't be sure Devon Blackstone wasn't after her carpetbag for himself.

His stance remained the same though his arms now were folded across his wide chest.

"You really were wonderful. I was simply so frightened, I didn't recognize you." Another truth whether he cared to accept it or not.

For what seemed like minutes he continued to stare at her, then he shifted, crossing his ankles. "The question remains, what are you doing here, at my grandmother's."

"I told you. Waiting to apologize." Felicity strove to keep him from noticing her gritted teeth.

"No, Miss Wentworth. I mean how did you get here?"

"Why I'm staying here. With your grandmother. I thought you knew that." But obviously he didn't because he straightened immediately.

"Since when?"

"Yesterday." Felicity realized she'd forgotten her accent and simpering ways, and snapped open her fan to try and camouflage the omission.

"Does she know of your chameleon personality?"

The fan flicked back and forth, stirring the lazy summer air. "Whatever do you mean?"

"I'm speaking of your quick change from struggling widow to belle of the ball."

"I . . . I can explain that." Felicity rose, her skirts swaying gently around her as she turned away from the captain. Lying was not something she did well, and she'd just as soon not face those steely green eyes when she did it. With studied indifference Felicity traced the waxy, white petals of a low hanging magnolia.

"I wore the mourning because I was frightened. Traveling to Charleston alone was . . . well, certainly something I'm not used to." She peeked up with a small smile.

"Then why do it?" Last night, lying in bed at his Tradd Street home he'd come up with several thoughts about the "widow." Most of them centered on the lovely Felicity Wentworth being a Yankee spy. If that accent hailed from farther south than the Mason Dixon Line he'd give up gambling for life.

"Why?" Felicity pulled a pristine handkerchief from her sleeve. "A promise. You do believe in keeping promises, don't you Captain Blackstone?"

"What promise did you make that would precipitate a journey to a war torn city?" he asked without answering her question.

Felicity sniffed. "It was to my Mammy. On her deathbed," she added, and couldn't help peeking up to see his reaction. He didn't appear the least moved. "In Richmond. Mammy was very dear to me, but she grieved for her children."

"What happened to them?" Devon couldn't help egging her on with this poignant story. A smile itched at the corners of his mouth but he kept his countenance sober.

"Sold south." Felicity did remember some of Jebediah's lectures on the evils of slavery.

"Tragic."

Felicity whirled around and caught his eye. The blackguard's tone wasn't what she hoped for. But there was no choice but to proceed. "I promised to go to South Carolina and buy them back for her."

"But she's dead. You did say it was a deathbed promise, didn't you?" Devon's brow arched.

"Dying," Felicity corrected. "That's why I must hurry." She sobbed into the handkerchief, her body shivering delicately. That is until she felt the strong arms circling her shoulders. Then she stiffened.

"There now, Miss Wentworth." The words were

comforting but she couldn't help wondering if he was grinning. She didn't dare lift her head to find out. "Everyone passes away eventually."

"I know that, of course, but . . ." She wished he'd let go of her. His large hand was rubbing up and down her back, leaving a trail of heat. And she wondered if he could tell she wasn't wearing a corset. "I simply must find her children." Felicity resisted the urge to push from his embrace.

He was taking advantage—shamelessly. And Devon didn't care. She was lying. And though a few innocent caresses wouldn't make his ribs hurt any less, it felt good nonetheless. Devon took a deep breath, the scent of her hair filling his nostrils. He dreamed of that hair last night. Of burying his hands deep in the luxuriant gold and watching the red highlights catch fire.

"I must find her children," Felicity repeated when he made no comment. His hands continued to touch her, her hair, her back. And a strange lethargy began spreading through her limbs. She almost wished she could forget this quest of hers and sink into the comfort of his strong arms.

Her neck grew lax as his fingers spread up under her hair to exposed skin. A sigh escaped Felicity's lips as her head fell back.

He wasn't smiling at all.

Felicity found that as surprising as the expression she did see in his vivid green eyes.

"Mr. . . . I mean Captain . . . I mean I don't think—"

His mouth was firm and hot when it swooped

down on hers. Felicity barely had time to realize what was happening before a buzzing sound in her ears blocked out all else. Her eyes drifted shut. Her arms, which till this point hung limply at her side, reached up to grab hold of him . . . to keep herself from melting to the ground.

She'd been kissed before, of course. It was something her beaus seemed to covet, and Felicity allowed them the honor as if she were a queen handing out royal land grants to her subjects. In the past she found kissing pleasant enough, but nothing had prepared her for the sensations overwhelming her now.

And then it stopped—abruptly.

Devon tore himself away, the pain in his ribs where her arms squeezed him had finally burned through the haze of his desire.

His hands cupped her shoulders as he held her at arm's length, and Devon had to admit she was a much better actress than he first thought. Perhaps her accent needed polishing and her sobbing could be improved, but she could pretend passion beautifully.

At the moment she appeared dazed.

By a kiss.

Certainly a woman as adept in the art of flirting expected as much, if not more. Especially if she was what he suspected . . . a spy.

Felicity swallowed, and stared into the face of Devon Blackstone. He studied her closely as she worked to control her breathing. A breeze blew in off the bay, soothing her fevered skin and blowing a lock of sun lightened hair across his forehead. It made him look rakish and handsome despite the bruised eye and cut lip.

Twisting away, Felicity made a spontaneous decision. She couldn't deal with this man as if he were one of her beaus at home.

Besides, she didn't need to. He was a blockade runner. Everyone knew they were a greedy lot.

Facing him, making certain she was out of reach of his arms, Felicity began, "I want you to help me."

"Find your Mammy's children," he said and that sardonic smile was back on his face.

"Yes." Felicity crossed her arms. "And I'm willing to pay you."

"Pay me?"

"Yes. Quite a large sum of money actually." She felt smug as he raised his brows.

"What exactly would I have to do to earn this . . ." he hesitated just a fraction of a second, ". . . large amount of money?"

He was interested. Felicity could see the avarice shining in his eyes. "All you need do is accompany me to Magnolia Hill plantation and bring the children back here."

Her complacency evaporated like morning fog when he threw back his head and laughed.

Four

"What are you laughing about?" Felicity balled her hands, planting them squarely on her hips. Her mouth set in a grim line, she faced him, calmly waiting for him to stop.

He didn't.

"What's so funny?" He was holding his side now, his breath coming in gasps, tears leaking from the corners of his eyes. He was obviously having a grand time at her expense.

Felicity's patience snapped.

Her fist whipped out, but before it could connect with the hard muscles of his stomach a vise-like grip manacled her wrist. "Not again, Red." His voice was firm. The dimples Felicity found so intriguing disappeared, leaving only slight indentations, shadows of the mirth that had filled his face.

His steely hold made struggling appear useless, but Felicity tried anyway. "Let go of me, you brute."

"Brute, is it?" Her skirts billowed around him

as Devon pulled her closer. His breath fanned across her cheek, as soft as his words. "What happened to the honey and magnolias of moments ago? Or even the hard-edged business woman offering to pay for my services?"

Felicity bit her lip and turned her face away from his mocking grin. She'd allowed a temper she barely knew existed before meeting Devon Blackstone to get the better of her. If there was ever any hope of him helping her it was gone now. And she had only herself to blame. With difficulty she softened her expression. Her eyes were wide when she turned them on him. "I didn't mean to hit you, not really."

"Give it up, Red. Nothing you do or say will convince me to take you to Port Royal." Devon let loose her wrist and brushed the stubborn lock of hair off his forehead.

"Why not?" Felicity braceleted her released wrist with her other hand, trying to wipe away the heat of his touch. He didn't answer. He only turned his back, ignoring her. Clutching the pointed finials on the iron gate, he stared out of the garden.

A woman labored by, dust from the road marring the ebony perfection of her skin. Her shoulders were hunched and she looked neither left nor right as she carried her cloth covered basket. Devon shut his eyes. Just watching her made him weary.

"Are you going to answer me? I told you I'm

willing to pay." Felicity waited, then said the words she hoped would buy his help. "In gold."

It got his attention. He glanced over his shoulder, slowly meeting her gaze. "As a result of helping you I have broken ribs, a black eye and cut lip." He shook his head when Felicity would have interrupted. "So you see, Red, I'm not inclined to offer my assistance even if I could."

"But . . ."

"As it is, neither of us can have what we want at Port Royal." He turned and after crossing his arms resumed his stance leaning against the fence. "The place is swarming with Yankees."

"That's what I'd be paying you for . . . to help me through them." Actually, Felicity felt she might be safer with the Yankees than with Devon Blackstone, but she didn't say it.

"You're not paying me for anything, Red."

Felicity let out her breath, annoyed with herself for wondering what he wanted in Port Royal. "Fine." Folding her arms in imitation of him, she pretended interest in the pears plumping on the tree beside her. "I'll find someone else." Certainly he wasn't the only blockade runner in Charleston. Besides, she wasn't certain she needed a blockade runner. If Magnolia Hill was in Yankee hands she could simply go there and ask for the children. Why hadn't she thought of that before?

Felicity glanced around to see Devon studying her intently, his green eyes narrowed. "What's going on in that pretty head of yours?"

"Nothing that concerns you." Felicity turned to

walk away, her hair drifting over her shoulder when she tossed a look back at him. "And don't call me Red."

"Why not?" Devon reached out, catching a curl between his thumb and forefinger. "No one has more of a claim to the name than you." He tugged gently, smiling when she reluctantly faced him. "And what you do while staying at my grandmother's house most certainly *is* my business."

Whatever retort Felicity planned was interrupted by a sharp rapping sound. Devon and Felicity twisted around to see Eveline Blackstone framed by the side window peering through the panes. She beckoned with the gold tip of her cane in a way that brooked no argument.

Devon waved, realized he still held the sun-splashed curl, and dropped it. "I think she wants us to join her inside," Devon said before offering his arm. Felicity laid her hand on his sleeve, mumbling something about bossy old harridans. She didn't realize the captain heard her until he chuckled.

"Better not let Grams hear you or she'll have your head."

"I'm not frightened of her," Felicity said. But as Devon Blackstone opened the door and bowed her into the hall she wasn't sure how true that was. Eveline stood, impatiently tapping her cane on the cold marble floor.

"I thought I was going to have to send the local militia after you. You seemed ready to ignore all my pounding."

"We came as soon as we heard you." Devon bent down to kiss her cheek. The reassuring scent of lavender drifted up from her red silk gown as he whispered in her ear. "And you know very well we did."

"Humph." Eveline pushed him away with her palm and turned to face Felicity. "And what were you doing out in the garden with my grandson young lady?"

"Well, I . . ."

"She was outside when I arrived a few minutes ago . . . contemplating nature. I simply paused to bid her good day."

Eveline's green gaze snapped back to Devon. "I'm old, not blind."

The tick ticking of the tall case clock was the only sound that followed her remark. Felicity was having a hard time not wringing her fingers. She glanced toward the captain, who shrugged like he hadn't a care in the world. To make matters worse he winked—his black eye no less—before turning on his heel and walking into the parlor. Leaving Felicity alone with his grandmother.

His grandmother who could have seen them kissing.

Felicity's cheeks burned with embarrassment but she refused to do any explaining, even though the older woman's expression clearly indicated she expected one. Instead, Felicity excused herself with a crisp curtsey. "I shall pack my things and leave. Thank you very much for your hospitality." With

86

that she hurried up the stairs as if she imagined Eveline would toss her cane aside and give chase.

Instead, the cane clumped across the hallway and into the parlor. Eveline shut the door behind her, studying the handsome profile staring out the window a moment before speaking. "What's between you and that girl? And before you answer remember I always could tell when you were lying."

Devon dropped the heavy silk curtain, watching the tassels fall into place. "That's because you ask when you already know the answers."

"Don't get impertinent with me young man. Remember, I haven't died and willed the Blackstone fortune to you yet."

Chuckling, Devon turned back to the room. "That old ploy never did work, and it sure won't now. For one thing, you don't have anyone else to leave your money to. And don't think for one moment I'd believe you've had a change of heart about Aunt Judith and dear Uncle Harry."

Eveline folded both hands on the gold handle and leaned heavily onto the stick. "Don't be insolent about your kin."

Devon shook his head as he left the window to help his grandmother to her chair. "I also think we both know that thanks to this war, my personal fortune is greater than yours—"

"How vulgar to discuss one's worth," Eveline interrupted. But even if her grandson didn't know her well enough to understand her, the sparkle in her eyes would reveal she enjoyed their verbal sparring.

"Yes, isn't it," Devon countered, his dimples showing. Then his tone sobered as he sprawled on the horsehair settee across from his grandmother. "Besides, I doubt the Yankees would consider your claim on Royal Oak valid."

Eveline's snort was unladylike and brought on a fit of coughing. With a casual motion that he hoped masked his concern, Devon stood and ambled toward the mahogany server. From a decanter he poured two tumblers of brandy. She was wiping tears from her eyes, an act Devon pretended not to notice, when he handed her the glass. She quickly took a sip, then leaned back against the cushions.

Devon studied her over the rim of his glass. "Has Doc Bateman been around lately?" he asked in the most nonchalant tone he could summon.

Even then Eveline jerked forward. "That old quack! Why would I want him around? Besides, there's nothing wrong with me that an end to this foolish war wouldn't cure."

"Maybe so." Devon took a swig of brandy, relieved, at least for the moment, that Gram's breathing was steadier. "But I wouldn't count on that happening soon."

"Blasted fools," she mumbled, then tapped her cane on the carpet for emphasis. "And as far as Royal Oak is concerned, it's been in the Blackstone family since before Gentleman Jack the pirate retired there. Who has greater claim to the property than we do?" She lifted her cane, pointing the tip toward Devon. "Than you do? The

Blackstone blood runs thick through your veins. The blood of brave men and women . . . Her voice trailed off. "Royal Oak was a legacy, Devon. A legacy I held for you. And now it's gone."

"The hell it is." Devon leaned forward, elbows on knees. His grandmother's sharp tongue he could handle . . . if truth be known he enjoyed sparring with her. He could even accept the coughing fits and infirmed hip on a logical level. Age brought such evils. But the melancholy that sometimes swamped over her he fought with a vengeance. "The Yankees might hold Royal Oak now, but it won't last. Remember the British in 1778? They occupied Charleston and all the area around Royal Oak. Jared Blackstone didn't give up then." Devon pointed toward the portrait of his great grandfather that hung over the fireplace. "And neither shall we now."

"But don't forget Jared Blackstone had himself a British wife." The woman beside him in the painting.

How could Devon ever forget? His grandmother was a great storyteller. She'd reared him on tales of his ancestors. Of Gentlemen Jack the pirate and the woman he kidnapped and later married. Of Jared Blackstone and his wife Merideth. Of all the Blackstones who'd come before him. Of the legacy passed down to him through generations. The legacy slipping through his fingers.

Taking another swig of brandy, Devon forced off the mantle of despair. "Perhaps I'll find myself a Yankee wife," he quipped. Glancing up, he noticed his words had the desired effect on his grandmother. She shook her head, laughing softly under her breath.

"You do and your Aunt Judith will positively swoon from embarrassment."

"I thought she did that when I stood up at the convention and voted against secession."

"Those men who pulled us from the Union will live to rue that day." Eveline leaned against the cushion. "How are things with the blockade? So few ships seem to get through anymore."

"They're tightening it, Grams. Like a noose around our neck." He set the tumbler on the tea table. "I can't be sure how much longer I'm going to be able to squeeze through."

"It's that bad?"

"I was attacked and boarded this run."

"But how . . . ?"

"The prize crew grew nervous when I threatened to toss a lantern into a hold filled with gunpowder. They all jumped overboard."

"My God, Devon." Eveline's fingers tightened around her cane. "You would have blown the ship up? Yourself?"

Devon shrugged. "There was little chance of that since the hold in question was full of shoes."

The laughter drew Felicity toward the open parlor door. When she came down the winding staircase, packed valise in one hand, parasol in the other, Felicity hadn't planned to do anything but slip quietly out the front door. There was nothing to be gained by another confrontation with any of the Blackstones.

Yet the laughter was like a lodestone. She recognized the captain's voice, and the other she assumed to be his grandmother's though she certainly hadn't heard her do anything but bark commands before.

Almost to the doorway, Felicity decided she didn't care why they were laughing, or anything else about them. She turned on tiptoe to make her escape just as Ruth came through the door from the dining room.

"Where ye be off to so early? And without even a good breakfast to keep ye goin'."

Felicity's gestures to quiet the woman didn't work. If anything she became more insistent.

"Don't ye go shushing me up. Does Miss Eveline know youz leavin'?"

"I'd be willing to bet she doesn't," came a deep masculine voice.

Felicity whirled around to see Devon standing in the doorway. He wore the same infuriating grin she'd learned to expect. Felicity squared her shoulders as best she could, given the weight of her valise. "I'm sure you'll be happy to inform her for me."

He was into the hallway and by her side before Felicity realized he was moving. "Actually," he said, circling her shoulders in a motion that prevented anything but compliance, "I think it best if you tell her yourself." He snatched the carpetbag, raising his brows as the full weight became apparent to him. "Stealing the family silver, are we?"

"I am not!" Felicity grabbed for the handle but he easily held it out of reach. "Give that back. You have no right."

"Your things will be returned. And I told you before, what you do while in my grandmother's home is of great concern to me. Now shall we pay our respects?"

Felicity had no choice but to go with him. But she didn't like it, and the expression on her face showed it as they marched together side by side into the parlor.

"What in heaven's name is going on, Devon?" Eveline was on her feet and met them before they got through the doorway.

"Miss Wentworth is leaving us, Grams."

"Your brutish grandson stole my bag."

Their words were spoken simultaneously, causing Eveline to look from one to the other, her mouth pursed. Devon dropped his hold on Felicity's shoulders and she yanked the sleeve of her plaid gown into place. But when she reached for her valise, Devon kept his body conveniently in the way.

"Give it back!"

"What are you doing with Miss Wentworth's carpetbag, Devon?" Eveline pointed her cane in his direction.

"Just holding it for her, Grams."

"Don't lie to me, boy. You never could," she complained, shaking her head as she retraced her steps to the chair.

"Well aren't you going to make him give it back?" Felicity was incensed.

"Oh, he won't keep it." Eveline motioned impatiently for them to take a seat.

"But I—" Felicity clamped her mouth shut and sank onto the chair. It was obvious she'd have to endure whatever the older woman and her grandson had in store for her before she could collect her belongings and leave. Oh why had she hesitated even a moment before quitting this house?

"That's better." Eveline leaned forward, her hands folded over the gold knob of her cane. "Now, kindly explain to me where you're going?"

Felicity took a deep breath, deciding it was no use to explain that her destination was none of the other woman's business. Both she and her grandson seemed bent on making it so. "I'm going to Magnolia Hill, to fetch some children. Some slave children. I shall buy them and take them back to . . . to Richmond."

"She promised her dear Mammy who is dying . . . or dead. Which is it Miss Wentworth?"

Felicity only glared at him in response.

"Hush up Devon. Let the girl finish."

Devon sat back, arms crossed prepared to enjoy another performance by the lovely Miss Wentworth. He wasn't disappointed. Her blue eyes clouded up till they reminded him of rain-kissed periwinkles. She studiously ignored him, focusing all her efforts on his grandmother. And her speech, which had lost most of its drawl, was now bottom creek slow and twined with jasmine and honeysuckle.

"What he said is true. My Mammy is dying and I promised to find her children and bring them back to her."

"Didn't anyone tell you there was a war on child?"

"Well . . . yes but . . ." What could she say? In New York the war seemed very far away? That she had no idea what it was like to be close to the fighting? None of that seemed appropriate. Instead, she pulled a handkerchief from her sleeve and sobbed into it delicately. "I promised her."

"For God's sake." Devon sat up, his elbows resting on his knees. "Can't you see this is all an act?"

"It is not!"

Devon ignored Felicity's outburst. "You asked about my relationship with her earlier. She's the reason I have this black eye. I stupidly ran to her rescue. Only yesterday she was garbed as a widow."

"That has nothing to do with going to Magnolia Hill." Felicity stood. "Now if you'll excuse me, I'll be on my way." Reaching for her bag, Felicity noticed the obnoxious grandson had opened it. He peeked inside, apparently assuring himself she hadn't filled it with candelabras and forks, before looking up and grinning.

Felicity jerked the valise from under his nose and snapped it shut. Damn him. And damn his harridan of a grandmother too. Felicity didn't need either of them. If truth be known the Blackstones had caused her a day's delay. They were lucky she *didn't* run off with the silver the way she felt right now.

With head held high and lugging the carpetbag, she marched toward the parlor door, determined to leave, no matter what. She would have made it too if Eveline Blackstone didn't say the one thing that could make her hesitate.

"Why don't you take her to Magnolia Hill, Devon?"

"What?" Devon was on his feet, glaring down at his grandmother. Felicity stood by the door, hardly daring to breathe. "My God, has senility set in?"

"Don't talk to me like that. I'll—"

"I know. I know. Disown me. Set me adrift in the world. Which is exactly what I'd be in Port Royal."

"I have more faith in you than that, Devon."

"The place is crawling with Yankees, Grams."

"So is the Atlantic Ocean, but that doesn't seem to stop you."

"She's lying, Grams," Devon said after catching his grandmother's eye.

"Well, of course she is." Eveline looked around toward the door when Felicity made some sound to contradict her. Felicity clamped her mouth shut. "But that doesn't mean she hasn't a legitimate need to reach Port Royal. Besides, it would give you a chance to visit Royal Oak and see how it's faring."

Devon brushed the lock of hair from his forehead. His expression was somber. "I'd already decided to go to Royal Oak. But on my own. The only place I'll accompany Miss Wentworth is to the rail station to place her on a train for Richmond and points North." He glanced around to see how Red took that news, but she was gone.

Felicity hurried along the brick walk, occasionally casting a glance over her shoulder. Devon didn't appear to be following her. "Thank heaven for that," she mumbled as she turned the corner onto Broad Street. She didn't need his help. And more importantly, she didn't want it.

Certainly it would be nice to push this responsibility off on someone else. But that someone else wasn't Devon Blackstone. Besides, if Magnolia Hill was in Federal hands she had nothing to worry about.

The Charleston Hotel was more crowded than she remembered from her last trip, but she rented a room without any difficulty. That night her sleep was interrupted only by vague dreams of a dimpled, mocking smile and a kiss that woke her. Felicity pounded her pillow, taking great pleasure in imagining it Devon Blackstone's face . . . or better yet, his cracked ribs.

Up with the dawn, Felicity rushed through her toilette, and dressed in her green plaid gown. She repacked her carpetbag, checking to make certain the pouches of gold coins were still there, pulled on her kid gloves and tied the satin ribbons of her bonnet under her chin. Then she went down to the lobby.

Renting the buggy was easy enough, especially when she was less than truthful about her destination. She bribed the stableboy into giving her extra oats for the horse and bought some fruit and bread from a black woman on Market Street.

Feeling smug about her progress, Felicity headed south out of Charleston.

Every turn and twist in the road that followed the river was familiar. For years, ever since he could remember, Devon road north to Charleston, and south to Royal Oak along the same pine-lined dirt road. He'd never really appreciated the monotony of the landscape, the moss drenched limbs and red-tailed hawks circling overhead. He never appreciated it—until now. Until the peace and solitude of the ride could be shattered at any moment by the enemy.

By Yankees who'd taken over his land.

Devon reined in his horse, a sway back mare with more heart than breeding, and slid from the saddle. Royal Oak was once known for her stables, but what good animals hadn't been sold to the local militia were commandeered by the Federals when they took Port Royal. After yanking the felt hat from his head he backhanded the sweat from his brow and led the horse to the side of the slow-running river.

His pocket watch, a legacy from his great

grandfather, Jared, marked the time at minutes past eleven. He was two hours from Charleston—two hours from learning Miss Felicity Wentworth rented a buggy and was seen leaving town, heading south.

He'd been all for letting her go off by herself. He planned to go to Royal Oak, but not today. Besides, he didn't believe a word of Felicity Wentworth's story about dying Mammys and children. If she wanted to go to Port Royal it was probably to meet up with the Yankees. And he wasn't inclined to help her with that.

But Grams, for all her sharp tongue, was a humanitarian. "A damn good Samaritan," Devon mumbled to the horse as he pulled on the reins. It was hot and muggy and though the *Intrepid*'s need for repairs had him momentarily land-bound, there were a lot more interesting things he could be doing with his time.

Even though he couldn't help wanting to know why the woman was so set on reaching Magnolia Hill. It irked him that he couldn't stop wondering. And it worried him because Magnolia Hill was the plantation that adjoined Royal Oak.

Devon remounted with grace not normally associated with a sea captain. He rode south at a steady pace, his eyes narrowed and ever watchful for Union soldiers.

When he heard the snicker of a horse from around the bend in the road, Devon leaned forward, patting his mount's shoulder to keep her quiet.

He was on the ground, melting into the vegetation along side of the road by the time he heard a female voice raised in anger.

Miss Felicity Wentworth was yelling. At her horse, a wheel, someone named Jebediah, and fate in general. Shaking his head, Devon lifted a branch and peered through the hole he made in the foliage. Felicity, her red hair loose and flowing over her shoulders was marching back and forth in the road. Beside her, one wheel off and lying on its side, was the buggy.

Devon couldn't help grinning as he stepped into view. "Having a bit of a problem, are we?" She whirled around, her hand pressed to her chest, her mouth open.

"What in heaven's name are you doing here?" Felicity swiped a strand of perspiration dampened hair off her face. "Did you . . . did you follow me?"

"Actually . . . yes. But it wasn't my idea. My grandmother thought—"

"I don't care what she thought. I asked for your help, and you refused." Hands on hips she glared at him, wishing she could slap that insolent smile from his face. "Well, I've decided I can handle this on my own."

"So it would seem." Devon let his gaze drift to the lopsided buggy, then back to meet hers. Color rose in her cheeks, but she didn't break the stare.

"A temporary setback. I was going to—" Felic-

ity was spared saying what she planned to do . . .
she actually had no idea . . . when Devon rushed
forward, grabbing her around the waist. "What are
you—"

"Shush." He turned her, his arms crossed beneath her breasts. His mouth was so close to her
ear his breath tickled. "Listen."

"But I don't hear—" This time his hand covering her mouth, blocking off the words.

"Horses," he mumbled more to himself than her.
"Lots of them."

Five

Pressed to his body, Felicity could feel the tension in his muscles as his strong arms surrounded her. He hesitated, then pulled her, Felicity's feet hurrying to keep up, back toward the side of the road. His palm still covered the lower half of her face and Felicity could smell a mixture of leather, salt and him.

"Run into the woods." Devon's voice was a hoarse whisper as he abruptly let her go. Before she could answer he leaped over the wheel and raced toward the horse still harnessed to the buggy.

Reeling, Felicity fought to regain her balance. She cast a quick glance over her shoulder toward the dark, mysterious woods behind her, then down the sun-dappled road now filled with the echo of horse's hooves. There was no doubt in her mind that Devon Blackstone thought those horses belonged to Federal troops.

He just didn't know that she'd been hoping some Union soldiers would come along. And it was just her luck that they came *after* Devon Blackstone showed up.

"Did you hear what I said?" Devon hissed. He jerked at the buckle, then with a slap to its rump sent the horse galloping north along the road. With not so much as a backward glance, Devon advanced on Felicity, grabbing her hand and dragging her along behind him as he ran for the concealing thicket off the side of the lane. "Come on," he said, only to come up short when Felicity latched onto a sapling. "What the hell . . . ?"

Wriggling, Felicity yanked her arm free. "My carpetbag," she yelled, gathering up her skirts and starting back toward the buggy. How could she have neglected to get *that?*

"Forget it." Again the captain had her in his grasp. Again Felicity fought him.

"No! No, I can't leave it. Just let go of me." Dust thrown up by the advancing troops clouded the road to the south. If she could only manage to stay away from Captain Blackstone until she was seen. But she underestimated the captain's quickness.

"Like hell," he growled before giving her a shove toward the underbrush. He grabbed the satchel, and was back to her before she even recovered her balance.

Then carpetbag in one hand, her wrist in the other, Devon darted into the woods. The ground was spongy and the vegetation thick and leafy, making their headlong flight difficult. Not ten rods off the wagon rutted road the terrain sloped downward abruptly. The captain didn't slow his steps—or hers. Slipping and sliding, Felicity managed to keep her footing, only to be knocked to the ground at the bottom of the ravine.

Spitting dirt, Felicity rolled to her back just as the captain flopped down on top of her. "How dare—" His hand covered her mouth again, cutting short her protest.

The pungent smell of damp earth and the musky smell of Devon Blackstone filled her lungs as Felicity tried to catch her breath. The weight of his body blanketing hers didn't help matters. But struggling was useless. With every movement she made, his hand tightened about her jaw. To keep her feet still he threw his thigh across her legs. In resignation Felicity sank back, shutting her eyes.

When she opened them again his face was inches from hers. The chords of his neck strained as he peered toward the slope. And he now held a pearl-handled revolver, pointed toward the road. While he searched for signs of Yankees, Felicity studied him. His bruises were now a mottled greenish-gray, not nearly as noticeable as before when his eye was swollen. The swelling had subsided from his lip also. Not that it mattered to her, and certainly not as she was lying in a muddy ditch. But he *was* a handsome man . . . for a despicable Rebel.

Devon dropped his gaze, grinning despite the circumstances when she immediately looked away. He considered lifting his hand, but an acquired sense of survival kept it in place. He had a sneaking hunch Miss Felicity Wentworth would be only too glad to get them found by the Yankees. The soldiers had halted by the buggy, and Devon could hear one of them order several men to dismount and look about. There was some speculation that someone might be in the woods, and Devon felt Felicity stiffen as they discussed a possible search. But the commander of the group decided against wasting time with whoever abandoned the buggy.

"They won't last long in the swamp," he said before ordering his troops forward.

Felicity's eyes drifted shut as she heard the hooves and clanking of reins moving on down the road. The hand covering her mouth slowly loosened till it was no more than cupping her chin. Her captor let out his breath and settled his cheek on the rumpled lace above her breast. His hair fell forward, brushing her face and Felicity lifted her hand. For one foolish moment she considered sifting her fingers through the unruly sun-kissed locks.

At that instant he lifted his head. His green eyes met hers and Felicity's arm fell to her side. Now was the time to scream. There was a chance the soldiers were still within earshot. But an inexplicable lethargy swept over her. It was either caused by the danger of the moment or the hypnotic spell of his eyes, but irregardless Felicity could do nothing.

She couldn't even turn her head away when she knew he planned to kiss her. In her mind Felicity was certain she didn't want it to happen. But logic seemed no match for the strange feelings overwhelming her.

By the time his lips actually touched hers, Felicity thought she couldn't stand it if he didn't hurry up. Her sigh sang sweetly through the humid air as her mouth opened for him. His taste was erotic and delicious. Intoxicating enough to alter her perception of reality.

Where less than a minute before, his weight was a binding, unwelcome burden, it now felt wonderful. The kiss deepened and Felicity forgot such mundane things as mosquitos and heat. Suddenly heat was good. And wildly consuming.

Her hands lifted, fingers ruffling through his cropped hair as his lips tore away from hers. Felicity's breath came in gasps as he trailed his mouth down the curve of her chin. This time her sigh sounded sultry, a prelude to surrender. Her body arched off the ground, drawn to him by some unexplainable force, aching for his touch.

When it came, soothing her breasts through the layers of fabric, Felicity's fingers tightened in his hair. He squeezed, flicking his thumb across the sensitive nipple and she moaned.

Devon muffled the sound with his mouth as it again ravaged hers. She was hot and sweet. He could barely keep his hands from searching beneath the skirts and frilly white petticoats to find the liquid fire he knew was there. If they weren't lying in a ditch in the middle of Yankee infested territory he'd have her naked and wrapped around him faster than he could whistle Dixie. As things were he was having a hard time . . . a really hard time not following this to its natural conclusion.

Devon flattened his hand over her breast, groaning as he felt the torrid tip in the center of his palm. He'd never been with a woman who responded so quickly, with such utter abandon. Perhaps he'd just never been with a woman so practiced. Which, considering his background, was saying a lot.

Slowly, because he was having a difficult time making his body obey his mind's commands, Devon lifted his head. Her hands wrapped around his neck, trying to pull him back, and Devon came close to complying. Only the surety that this, like so much about Felicity Wentworth, was an act kept him from forgetting the mud and the Yankees and the entire damn war.

He'd kissed her because she looked like she wanted kissing . . . needed kissing. And because the thrill of escaping the enemy just seemed to call for such a primal act. But he hadn't expected to like it quite so much, or to come close to losing control. He prided himself on his control, as well as the easygoing facade that camouflaged it.

As the dark auburn lashes lifted over blue eyes filled with unrequited passion, Devon knew both would be tested. He smiled, that lazy grin that ladies seemed ill equipped to resist, and snuggled deeper between her spread skirts. The latter was definitely a mistake. That part of him he would swear couldn't get any harder did.

His quiet laugh was at his own expense, but it

was obvious the young woman beneath him didn't see it that way. Her eyes, which moments ago were wide with wonder, narrowed. There was still some disbelief in their depths—whether it was because of what happened or because he stopped—Devon wasn't sure. The only thing he was certain of was that spy or no, he planned to have Felicity Wentworth. He'd choose the spot and the time, and they'd finish what they began.

But it wouldn't be now. Anger sparked in her eyes as he rolled away. "I don't think this is a good idea . . . now," he said, pushing to his feet. Extending his hand, he offered her assistance, not surprised when she ignored it.

Not a good idea *now!* Felicity couldn't keep her eyes from blinking. What did he mean it wasn't a good idea now? It wasn't a good idea ever. As a matter of fact, Felicity would have to say kissing Devon Blackstone, Rebel and blockade runner, was about the worst idea imaginable. Then why had she done it . . . and enjoyed it so much?

Even now, with her anger at a fever pitch, Felicity couldn't completely shake the sensual euphoria. That was perhaps the worst rub of all. Especially because she knew the captain was the one who'd put a stop to the madness.

Shutting her eyes, Felicity couldn't imagine what had gotten into her. She shook her head, cringing when dirt trickled from her hair onto her shoulders. "Look what you've done to me!" she said, then wished she hadn't. This was no time to lay blame, but she couldn't seem to help herself.

She shoved a wayward curl from her face and scrambled to her feet, slapping at her mud encrusted skirts. "I can't believe how you dragged me down here." Felicity swatted a giant mosquito buzzing brazenly around her ear.

"I considered it the lesser of two evils." She acted as if the kiss hadn't happened. Which was fine with him . . . as long as they both knew it had.

"That's your opinion," Felicity mumbled. "I doubt those Yankees would have done anything to us. After all, we're not Rebel soldiers." Lifting her skirts, Felicity attacked the side of the bank. The curse that slipped out as she slid back down would have shocked Jebediah. Devon Blackstone seemed to find it amusing.

Felicity shot him a look over her shoulder. "Are you going to help me or not?"

Devon shrugged. "We'll be better off following the stream a bit."

"To where?" Felicity threw her hands up, then scurried after him as he ignored her and strode along the branch parallel to the road. "The buggy is up there," Felicity insisted as she caught hold of his arm.

"And it's not worth a tinker's damn without a horse."

"Which reminds me. Why did you let Peaches loose?"

"Peaches?" Devon lifted his brow.

"I named her that . . ." Felicity scowled at the

108

captain's expression. "Well, I had to call her something."

Devon just shook his head, and continued on, pausing when her gown tangled on a thorn bush. "I let . . . Peaches go so she wouldn't end up a bona fide member of the Yankee cavalry."

Exasperated with trying to untangle the decorative netting on her skirt—and since Devon gave no indication of helping her—Felicity gave it a tug. She cringed as the fabric tore. With a sigh she trudged on. "Well the horse . . ." Not for anything would she call her Peaches again, ". . . isn't doing *us* much good, is she?"

Devon didn't respond to that. He did however stop and stare down at the carpetbag he held. "What in the hell is in this?" He hefted it up. "I know I teased you about taking the family silver, but—"

"That was teasing?" Felicity stared at him haughtily, not realizing the dirt smeared across her face did much to ruin the effect.

Devon dropped the bag. "Maybe not entirely." He bent to unbuckle the leather straps. Before he could, Felicity snatched up the carpetbag.

"I'll carry it," she said, stalking off along the stream bank. The blasted thing was so heavy, she half hoped he'd insist on taking it back, but when she glanced over her shoulder he only shrugged and followed.

Felicity took three more steps before dropping the carpetbag and sinking down on top of it. "Where are we going, anyway?"

"This should be far enough." Devon began scaling the slope. "Stay there for a minute."

Stay there! He had nerve telling her to stay down in this bug infested ravine. Felicity glanced around. Behind her a stream slithered by. Dark and slow-moving it mirrored the oak branches overhead in its murky depths. Tall grasses stood sentinel, their swaying the only indication that a breeze moved the heavy air.

Felicity groped for her handkerchief, using the back of her hand to wipe at her brow when she couldn't find it. Her knuckles came away wet and dirty. The sob that followed her discovery was involuntary. How could she have gotten herself into this mess?

How could any of this be happening to Felicity Elizabeth Wentworth?

She didn't—Felicity looked down at her hand and grimaced—sweat. And she certainly never got dirty. But there on her hand was proof of both. In disgust she wiped her hand down one of the few clean spots on her gown and sighed.

If Jebediah only knew what she endured for him. A familiar itching sensation made her slap at her wrist. She was too late to keep the insect from biting. A tear trailed down Felicity's cheek, mingling with the sweat and dirt.

She needed to go home.

It was as simple as that. Neither Jebediah nor her father would want her to go through all she'd been through. If they knew her predicament, they'd be the first to demand she return to the world of quiet strolls in the garden and sleeping till noon. They probably were sitting in the parlor right this minute wondering where she was and whatever possessed her to embark on such a foolish undertaking.

Just her absence was probably enough to make Jebediah realize how much he loved her. And her father . . . Felicity scooped up her hair in hopes of catching a whisper of air on her neck. Of course her father loved her. It was just Arthur's death that caused him to act so . . . so uncaring.

Felicity shivered, despite the suffocating heat. Her mind made up, she gathered her skirts, snatched up her satchel and began to climb. With every slippery step her resolve deepened. She would go home. She would take the longest most soothing bath imaginable and lie upon her silk sheets and forget this terrible experience ever happened.

She would explain what she tried to do to her father and Jebediah and they would pat her hand and tell her what a brave girl she was. The very thought made Felicity smile as she struggled to lug the carpetbag up the embankment. And of course Esther would understand—

Felicity stopped in her tracks, the heavy valise making her lean to one side. She'd forgotten about Esther and her children. A wave of guilt washed over her. How could she forget about Esther? Shutting her eyes only made it worse.

"You don't follow orders very well, do you Red?"

Felicity's head jerked up to see Devon Blackstone standing on the road above her. The sunlight formed a bright aura around him and Felicity shaded her eyes to get a better look. "Why . . . why you have a horse."

"I was hoping I'd hidden him from the Yankees good enough." Devon rubbed the animal's neck. "He's not much, but I think he'll get you back to Charleston." His head cocked to the side. "I assume you know the way."

Felicity struggled up the remaining few feet to the road, ignoring his last remark and the hand he extended toward her. "As it happens," she said, straightening her skirts as elegantly as if they weren't torn and dirty, "I'm not returning to Charleston at the moment. My original plan was to visit Magnolia Hill, and visit I shall."

Hands on hips Devon stared at her, but she didn't back down from returning his gaze. "You're going to Magnolia Hill," he finally said.

"That's correct."

"Despite the Yankees?"

"Yes."

"And the broken buggy wheel?"

Felicity glanced down the road imagining the bone jarring ride astride the horse . . . or worse, the hot, tiring walk. She clenched her teeth. "Yes."

"To fetch your Mammy's children?"

His voice held such a patina of disbelief that Felicity squared her shoulders. "I believe that's what I told you earlier."

112

"Oh, that's what you told me all right . . . among other things."

"Then as long as we understand each other, I suggest we get started."

"We?"

The arched brow seemed to indicate his southern journey was at an end. Which was fine with Felicity. How long could it be until she again encountered some Federal troops? This time she could elicit their assistance without interference from the Rebel. Felicity smiled sweetly, deciding his last view of her would make him sorry to see her go. "It was such a pleasure meeting you, Captain Blackstone," she purred. "Do give my regards to your grandmother when you reach Charleston."

That said, she yanked up the leather handles and started down the wheel-rutted road with as much dignity as she could muster.

Resolve and noble intentions buoyed her for the first ten rods or so. Then the weight of the satchel, the heat of the day and the unfamiliar length of the road before her settled in. Pride kept her going. Pride refused to let her glance back when she heard the clop clop of horse's hooves behind her. Foolish pride.

As much as he annoyed her, the sound of Devon Blackstone's voice was oddly comforting . . . even though his tone was steeped in mocking humor.

"Do you have any idea where you're going, Red?"

Admonishing him to refrain from calling her

that despised nickname seemed an exercise in futility. Felicity simply lifted her chin. "To Magnolia Hill Plantation." The gentleman at the hotel had given her fairly accurate directions . . . she hoped.

Tilting her head to the side—he was now beside her, riding the poor sway-backed horse—Felicity said, "You seem to be the one in need of directions. If I'm not mistaken Charleston is that way." Shifting to point was a mistake for she tripped over a torn section of skirt. It was lucky for him that he didn't laugh.

"I'm not returning to Charleston. At least not yet."

"Oh, really?" Felicity's tone was one of boredom with the conversation.

"I've decided to check on Royal Oak. It's been in my family for generations."

"How utterly fascinating." Felicity turned her face away to cough. The silly horse was churning dust up on the road.

"It neighbors Magnolia Hill."

Felicity stopped, furiously fanning at the dust that sprayed up around her as the captain reined in his mount. "What are you trying to say Captain Blackstone?"

Devon leaned forward, his wrists crossed over the pommel. "Simply this, Miss Wentworth. That since we are both headed in the same direction, perhaps we should travel together."

"Don't you think your mount might tire of such a slow pace?"

Devon grinned as he ran his hand down the

114

shaggy mane. "I figured we could share Blueberry's services."

"Blueberry?"

The dimples in Devon's cheeks deepened. "Seems a fitting name for a horse, don't you think?"

Eyes narrowed, Felicity turned on her heel and started down the road again. "I'm sure I don't care if we travel together or not." When she felt the tug on her carpetbag she yanked it forward, stumbling in the process.

"I just thought it might be easier if I hooked this on the saddle," Devon said. He'd dismounted, and with a flourish pointed toward the horse.

Her suspicion that the blockade runner would jump on the horse and gallop away with her money was strong. But not as pressing as the pain in her arm. Reluctantly, Felicity handed over the satchel.

Devon tied it to the back of the saddle, then turned back to Felicity. She was dirty, with untamed curls straggling down her shoulders, and obviously bone tired. Not exactly at her best. But she still held her chin at a stubborn angle. Despite himself, Devon had to admire her determination to go to Magnolia Hill. Regardless of the real reason.

He motioned toward the horse. "I don't have a sidesaddle, but you're welcome to ride."

"That's very kind—" Felicity began, then stopped. "Where are you going to be?" A memory flashed through her mind of entwined limbs and straining bodies. As tired as she was, Felicity

115

thought walking preferable to snuggling up to the captain again. But apparently that wasn't going to be a problem.

"Though Blueberry gives it his all, I don't think he's up to carrying both of us. You ride, I'll walk for a while."

Perhaps not the most gallant offer she'd ever received, but at the moment it was the most welcome. She even allowed him to help her up into the saddle.

Riding had never been something Felicity particularly enjoyed. Sitting astride the woebegone horse in the middle of nowhere did nothing to change her opinion.

But an hour later when they stopped for water, and the captain suggested they both walk for a while to rest the horse, she felt differently. At least she didn't have to lug the carpetbag.

"How much longer till we get to Port Royal?" Felicity was doing her best to keep up. She didn't even bother to swat at the mosquitos any more as they walked down the pine and holly lined road.

"We might make Magnolia Hill by dusk if we keep moving."

The captain's meaningful stare made Felicity realize she'd slowed her pace. Defiantly she quickened her step to match his. He didn't seem to notice the improvement.

Of course *he* didn't seem to notice the terrible conditions of their journey. The only concession he'd made to the heat was removing his frock coat and untying his cravat. His shirt was soiled and plastered to his skin by perspiration, but somehow he didn't look as bad as she felt.

He wasn't wearing his brimmed hat anymore, but that was because he gave it to her some miles back. Though Felicity hated to take anything from him, she could feel the sun burning her face before the hat offered some shade.

But it was still hot. Trudging along behind him, Felicity tried to determine how long it was until the sun set. She considered asking the captain, but held her tongue. They would get there when they got there.

Felicity tried to fill her mind with thoughts of Jebediah. Of the expression on his face when she returned triumphantly with the children. But as she tramped one foot in front of the other, it was the man in front of her that occupied her thoughts.

Bareheaded and with his white shirt open he reminded her of the pirates of old. She almost expected him to turn about, cutlass in hand, gold earring dangling.

When he did turn it was to suggest Felicity remount Blueberry.

"I know what you're doing," she said, putting her foot in his cupped hands.

"And what is that, Red?"

"Making fun of me for calling my horse Peaches."

His chuckle caused the horse to skitter to the side and Felicity stood back while the captain calmed him. Then he grabbed her around the waist, hoisting her into the saddle before she could slap his hands away. "I wouldn't make fun of a fine southern lady like you, Red," was all he said before nudging Blueberry into a walk.

"Well, this is it."

Felicity jerked awake, clutching at the saddle to keep her seat. Devon stood off to the side, staring down a narrow two wheel lane that meandered through land, swampy in some places, dry in others. *"This* is Magnolia Hill?" It didn't appear at all like her perception of a rice plantation.

"It's a back entrance through the fields." Devon admitted. "I thought this might be the best way to approach the main house." He reached up and lifted Felicity down. "I also think we should give Blueberry another breather. We might need her later . . . in case we have to make a quick departure."

"For heaven's sake. You act as if you expect to find the place infested with vermin." Felicity stuck strands of hair up into the hat, which was the best she could do to tidy up under the circumstances. This wasn't how she planned to look when she met Esther's children. But some things couldn't be helped.

"If you're finished primping, Red, we'd best be moving on. Clouds are gathering, and it can get pretty dark out here with the moon hidden."

Ignoring the primping remark *and* the deplorable nickname, Felicity started down the path. The captain was right about one thing. Twilight was falling, shading the landscape in a soft magenta. Frogs croaked from the unplanted rice beds, cloaking the clop of horse's hooves on the packed earth.

Anticipation quickened Felicity's feet. She was almost there. First thing she'd do was order a bath, then a meal. Nothing heavy, though she was very hungry. Some cold chicken would do. Then to bed. In the morning she'd inquire about the children, buy them if necessary, and start the hard trek home. The prospect of starting another journey so soon after ending this one wasn't appealing, but she didn't want Jebediah and her father to worry any more than necessary.

"We'll tie Blueberry here." The captain's voice interrupted Felicity's musings. They'd come upon some outbuildings, surrounded by spreading oak trees.

"It's up to you," she said, shrugging. "But you'll only have to send someone back after him." She couldn't see his expression in the dim light, but he tied the reins to a branch and motioned for her to follow. "What about my carpetbag?"

"Will you forget the carpetbag?" Devon said, grabbing her hand and pulling her away from the horse.

"But it has—"

Her words stopped abruptly when he yanked her against his body. His face was close to hers and she breathed in his scent on her gasp of surprise. "I don't care what it has in it. We can't go creeping up on the house lugging that thing."

"Creeping up? But why would we do that?"

119

That wasn't at all what she'd planned to do. But the captain didn't seem in any mood to explain. He simply pulled her closer.

"Now, unless you wish to be left behind too, you'll follow closely and keep your voice down."

He didn't give her time to respond. He simply let her loose and rounded the dilapidated building. After skirting it he headed toward the thicket of trees to the east. Felicity followed, even mimicking his crouched over stance.

By the time they reached the pines, Felicity could hear voices and the faint strains of a harmonica. She opened her mouth to question the captain but he put his finger to her lips. As they crouched even lower, Felicity noticed he drew the revolver from his belt. They made their way to a fence. It was in serious need of repair but offered some cover.

And they needed that. For as Felicity peeked over the splintery wood rail she saw the elegant grandeur of Magnolia Hill. And the Yankee soldiers sprawled in tents all over the yard.

Six

Only Devon's strong arm kept Felicity from standing and walking toward the campfires that dotted the lawn and circular carriage drive. One of the soldiers crouched by the flames would surely escort her into the white columned house. Instead, she was jerked back behind the fence, her face so close to the captain's that she could make out the green prisms in his eyes. "What in the hell do you think you're doing?" His voice was low and threatening.

All she could do was stare back at him, her breath coming in gasps as the mist settled over the grass. She'd done it! She'd reached her destination despite the war only to be stymied when her goal was in sight. She sank into the dirt behind the rails, her mind racing with possibilities.

One loud scream and the Yankees would be upon them. Devon might be holding her arm, but he hadn't covered her mouth.

Once she explained who she was and what she was doing here, the Federal troops would embrace her cause. She could go in the house, whose windows shone bright with light, have her bath, and her much needed sleep. The commanding officer would help her find the children; perhaps even see her safely home.

. It was obvious what she should do.

Felicity sucked in her breath to scream. But in that instant the Rebel's face swam before her closed eyes: his green gaze and no nonsense nose; the cocky grin that infuriated her even when she found it disarmingly sensual; the subtle shades of lavender marring his handsome countenance.

The bruises he earned protecting her.

Air escaped through her lips, but no piercing sound came. Could she take a chance that the soldiers wouldn't harm the captain, even if she lied about who he was?

The decision was wrenched from her as Devon yanked her up, towing her behind him as he zigzagged through the stand of loblolly pines.

"Where are we going?" Felicity kept her voice low.

"Well we sure as hell aren't staying here." Any minute Devon expected to hear a shouted order to halt . . . or worse, the whine of a Minny ball sailing past his ear. God, the Yankees were everywhere.

As soon as they cleared the shadows of the tall trunks, Devon tore off toward the crop of outbuildings, Felicity at his heels. With his back against the rickety shelter, Devon shut his eyes and sucked in a calming breath.

Intellectually he knew the Yankees were in the area. Christ, he'd run across them on the road, and slipped through their damn blockade enough times. But to actually see them sprawled across the grounds of Magnolia Hill, to know that he might find the same thing when he got to Royal Oak . . .

Devon forced those thoughts from his mind. He had more immediate problems—like Felicity Wentworth.

Devon opened his eyes almost expecting the red-haired beauty to have disappeared. He knew she would just as soon ally herself with the Yankees as him. She'd most likely prefer it. But she hadn't deserted him yet. The clouds parted and he could see the shimmer of starlight in her hair as she huddled near his feet.

"We need to fetch Blueberry and be on our way."

Felicity looked up, though she couldn't see much other than the outline of his white shirt. "But . . . but I need to find the children."

His snort of laughter stiffened her back. "What children? Did you see any little Negro children frolicking about? There are none of Abner King's people left here."

"Well, where are they?" They couldn't have simply disappeared. Not after she traveled all this way.

"I don't know." Devon heard the tone of defeat in his voice and did nothing to correct it. "I just don't know." He straightened. "There's a place I think we can stay tonight." He hesitated a moment. "At least I hope it's still there."

The place was a dilapidated shed near the river. Devon and Felicity had carefully worked their way to where the horse was tied. Then, keeping a lookout for sentries, Devon led the way south.

When Devon saw lamplight filtering through the cracks in the wall of the small building he was relieved . . . but not entirely worry free.

"Stay here," he whispered, then before Felicity could respond, slipped into the darkness.

Felicity stood, her arms wrapped around her waist, Blueberry's reins dangling loosely from her fingers. She kept her gaze trained on the cabin, its windows a beacon of light in the darkness. Night sounds surrounded her . . . unfamiliar night sounds. To the left she could hear the river's lazy passage between ill defined shores. Something brushed against her skirt and Felicity stopped breathing.

"Devon." The word was a soft plea, that went unanswered. "Captain Blackstone." Felicity swallowed and dared to raise her voice.

The only response was a screeching that carried on the still night air and hatched goose flesh all over Felicity's body. The noise came again, an answering call, and suddenly the door of the small cabin burst open.

Light spilled out, surrounding a bent-over old man. He lifted a kerosene lamp and peered about before calling out the captain's name. Felicity watched as Devon stepped into the circle of brightness and embraced the man.

They talked quietly for so long that Felicity felt

she'd been forgotten. Dead tired and frightened as she was, she still hesitated to march forward and intrude upon the reunion scene.

Even when the captain turned and beckoned she was reluctant to move, only walking toward the cabin when he came forward to take her hand. The old man whose long frizzled hair hung limp and straggly about his naked shoulders, only stared at her as he slipped out into the darkness.

"He's going to hide Blueberry," Devon explained as he led her through the cabin door. He set the battered tin lamp on a table that Felicity was surprised could bear the weight.

She glanced around quickly at her surroundings, shivering despite the stagnant heat. The furnishings were spare and as rickety as the table. Despite the need to sit, Felicity doubted the only chair was safe. In a corner on the floor was a pile of blankets. Jars and crocks filled most of the other available space. The mosquito netting draped over the walls gave the interior a ghostly presence.

Felicity swallowed, moving across the dirt floor toward Devon, who was running his finger down the front of a tall case clock that looked as out of place in the small cabin as Felicity felt. "Who is he?" she whispered, the catch in her voice exposing her fear.

"The Swamp Man," Devon said with a shrug. "No one knows for sure. Some say he's descended from Indians who roamed the area hundreds of years ago."

"An Indian." Felicity swiped hair from her face

and looked toward the door. "I thought he was a slave."

Devon laughed. "He wouldn't like you calling him that . . . though I don't doubt there's some Negro blood flowing through his veins." Devon closed the door of the clock, shutting off the empty interior—no weights, no pendulum. "Of course, I imagine there's a goodly amount of white blood in him too."

"But how do you know him? What are we doing—"

"I take timepiece."

Felicity jumped, turning toward the door where the old man stood, staring at the captain from deep set dark eyes. His hand rested on the hilt of a knife strapped to his thin frame.

The captain didn't seem to notice the threatening gesture as he ran his hand over the clocks smooth finish. "I thought this looked familiar."

"You rather I leave for Yankees?"

"Hell no." Devon turned to face the old man. "I never begrudged you anything. But it won't tell time without the inside workings."

"What I need time for?" he asked logically, pulling the door shut behind him. "Just like shiny part." He pointed a bony finger toward the brass face before settling in front of a cracked pottery bowl.

"You hungry?"

Felicity began salivating at the mention of the word. She was less enthusiastic when he began scooping gobs of something out of the bowl. Devon accepted the proffered food gratefully, handing some to her before taking a bite of his own. Felicity smiled wanly at no one in particular and nibbled. It was rice mixed with some meat flavoring she couldn't place and figured she was better off not trying. But it was surprisingly good, and by the time she'd finished Felicity had eaten three clumps handed her via the captain.

The old man didn't look her way or acknowledge her presence during the makeshift meal. It wasn't till later that he made any indication he even knew she was there. After they ate he headed for the door.

"I give you time," he said. "For her." His gnarled finger arched toward Felicity then toward the heap of blankets on the floor. "But make it quick."

Felicity glanced up. "I don't understand."

"Time for . . ." The old man grunted and made an undulating movement with his lower body that made the color drain from Felicity's face. She didn't meet the captain's eye as she began to protest. "How dare you—"

Her words were cut off by the captain's hearty laugh. "Thank you, but that won't be necessary. I'm too tired tonight."

"Tired?" the old man grunted as if he found that a stupid excuse.

"Maybe in the morning," Devon said, then wrapped his arm about Felicity's waist and dragged her toward him to keep her quiet.

The old man seemed to find that an acceptable

answer. He bent over, grabbing up one of the torn blankets and blew out the light. Felicity, standing with her mouth agape, listened as he scratched his way to the far side of the cabin and flopped down. Then she turned on the captain. It was so dark she could barely make him out, but that wouldn't stop her from telling him what she thought of his plans for her.

"What do you mean, 'maybe in the morning'? Nothing—"

The rest of her words were cut off by his firm mouth as it settled over hers. Felicity felt herself hauled up against his hard body. When the kiss ended, the captain's hand replaced his lips.

"Now sugar, I said we had to wait till morning," he said, ignoring her struggles to pull his hand free. He nudged curls away from her ear, which despite Felicity's anger, caused shivers to race down her spine. His whispered words were little more than a breath of air. "Behave yourself. I'll explain later." He paused a moment before adding, "Trust me."

Trust him? That was the last thing she should do. What had trusting him done for her so far? Gotten her in a run down shack in the middle of a swamp with an old Indian who was willing to give then privacy to . . . to do all manner of unmentionable things.

But, crazy as it seemed, she did trust him. At least she would until he explained himself—and it better be good.

The heat must have gotten to her. That was the

only explanation Felicity could come up with as she allowed herself to be lowered onto the blankets. The captain removed his hand, and in the darkness she could feel his breath brush across her cheek as he asked if she was all right.

Wonderful, Felicity wanted to respond. Just absolutely wonderful. How could he even ask such a question? The air was so still and heavy it made breathing difficult, the blankets were lumpy and if they weren't home to a plethora of vermin she'd be very surprised. She was dirty and despite the rice, hungry, and the worst thing was that she was lying beside a rebel blockade runner.

Felicity gritted her teeth, deciding she would never fall asleep.

The next thing Felicity knew sunlight streamed through a crack in the wall, hitting her in the face. She squirmed to get away from the bright light and realized she no longer lay on the blankets. She blinked and stared directly into Devon Blackstone's green eyes. He stared at her as her head lay on his chest. The rest of her was sprawled over his body.

"Oh my heavens." Felicity tried to jump up but Devon's arms surrounded her.

"Shhh."

"Don't shush me." As Felicity jerked her head around red gold curls spilled over Devon's face. "Where is that . . . that man?"

"Natee is more than likely giving us the privacy he promised."

"Ohhh," Felicity drew the word out in frustration. "Let me up."

"I will. Directly."

"If you think I'm so grateful to you for these accommodations that I'd . . . that I'd . . ."

"Relax, Red." Devon loosened his hold, sitting up after Felicity slid off him. "Nobody expects anything from you. I've been on the beholding end of your gratitude before, remember?"

Guilt made Felicity fold her arms and lift her chin. "As long as we understand each other."

His stare was long and intense. Felicity refused to look away. "I believe we do," is all he said before leaning back down on his elbow. A grin played around the corners of his mouth. "I just don't know about Natee."

"What do you mean by that?" With a flick of her wrist Felicity flipped curls over her shoulder. She didn't want to look at him again. It was too easy to notice that devastating smile, or the way his hair fell across his brow.

"I mean, it's better if the old man thinks we're lovers."

The snort was involuntary and none too ladylike. "Better for you, you mean." Devon's chuckle made Felicity swing her head and glare at him.

"Actually, I was thinking of you."

"Humph."

"Natee isn't much for strangers. Which Red, you are." Devon stretched his long body. "He also doesn't have much use for women . . . except for the obvious."

"Which is?" Color drained from Felicity's face when his grin turned wicked. "No, never mind. Don't tell me."

"Of course he is passably fond of Grams," Devon continued. "But then most everyone is."

Felicity shot him a look of disbelief before scurrying to her feet. She brushed off her skirts, regardless that the act didn't do much for the mud encrusted fabric, and tried to tidy her hair. Then she started across the packed earth floor toward the door.

"Leaving so soon?" Devon arched a brow when she paused to glance around. "Natee won't have much respect for my ability to please you."

"You're disgusting." Felicity reached for the crude latch only to have it jerked from her hands as the door opened from the outside. She swallowed a scream as the ancient Indian stood before her, his wrinkled face wreathed in a toothless grin.

"I have fish," he said in his guttural voice. He shoved the string of three glassy-eyed catfish toward Felicity. She had no choice but to take them. "Keep his strength up." He jerked his head in Devon's direction while Felicity held the still squirming creatures at arm's length.

"What am I supposed to do with these?" Felicity glanced over her shoulder. The captain was barely containing his mirth. Mirth at her expense. She wanted to throw the stupid fish in his hand-

131

some face, and leave this awful place. But . . . she didn't know where she was.

"Go cook," the Indian ordered her, accompanying his words with a shove out the open doorway.

In his defense, Devon did stand when this happened. But Felicity thought his movements slow and he didn't say anything to the old man as he ambled across the cabin.

Felicity stood in the leaf-filtered sunlight, clutching the filthy string, expecting at the very least an apology—which she wasn't about to accept. Instead, the captain grabbed her arm as he walked by her, pulling her farther away from the cabin.

"What are you doing? Let go of me!" Felicity swatted at him with the limp fish.

"Keep your voice down. And get those things off me." Devon snatched the string from her hand and sent the fish sailing onto the ground. They landed with a plop.

"I'm so tired of you telling me to be quiet," Felicity complained, but her voice was low, drenched in defeat.

"Now listen." Devon wrapped his arm around her soft shoulders, knowing how downcast she must feel since she didn't even fight him. "I'm going to have a talk with Natee. See what he knows about Royal Oak. I don't want any more surprises like we had last night." He gave her a squeeze. "Why don't you cook up these fish?"

"Are you insane?" The spark was back in her blue eyes. "I don't know how to cook fish."

"There's nothing to it. Look, Natee already started a fire."

He turned her and sure enough on the small patch of sandy soil a low smoky campfire burned. But Felicity ignored it as she scanned the rest of the clearing. There were no buildings except the one where they'd spent the night . . . if you could call the ramshackle pile of rotting boards a building. It looked as if the next high tide would take it swirling into the dark, murky river.

Actually there was nothing in the clearing but a pile of bones and the fire.

"Where's Blueberry?" Felicity demanded. "And my carpetbag?"

"Hidden," Devon said succinctly. "And don't worry, Natee didn't steal your gold. Money doesn't interest him."

Felicity's mouth dropped open. "How did you know about the—I mean I don't know what you're talking about. I don't have any gold."

"Give it up, Red. The thing weighs a ton. You won't let it out of your sight. And not even a woman like you cares that much about a few ribbons and doodads."

Felicity wrenched away from his loose embrace. Swallowing, she turned to face him. "What do you know about a woman like me?"

Devon stared down at her. He could swear there were tears shimmering in those beautiful eyes. *And* he would swear her distress wasn't an act. With his finger he traced the high curve of her cheek. When she tried to turn away his hand cupped her jaw. "You're right. I don't know anything about you."

She could barely breathe. The heavy, sweetly scented air seemed sucked away, leaving a vacuum where they stood. A vacuum that shimmered with invisible forks of lightning. He was going to kiss her. Felicity was certain of it. And as much as she knew she shouldn't let him, she longed to feel the firm heat of his lips. He was dirty and rumpled and yet she ached for him. Her eyes drifted shut, she leaned forward in anticipation.

"Blackstone, come smoke." The crusty old voice rang into the clearing.

Felicity's eyes jerked open to see that stupid cocky grin. What was in her mind?

"I guess I better . . ." Devon nodded toward the cabin. "Why don't you cook these?" He scooped up the fish and handed them to Felicity.

Surprise made her take them. "But I don't know how," she called after his retreating form.

"Just clean them and throw them on the fire," he tossed back.

She glanced down at them, then let the string slip from her fingers. She'd done worse things on this journey. The important thing was to remember why she came.

Felicity caught the captain's arm just before he entered the cabin. "Wait. Ask him about the children."

His brow arched. "Your Mammy's children?" He couldn't believe after all that they had been through, she was sticking to the same ridiculous story. But she seemed adamant.

"Yes. Yes." Her fingers tightened in his cotton sleeve. "I must find them. Please."

Again Devon had the strange impression she wasn't acting. He needed to watch himself. Obviously he was vulnerable to her beauty and charms. Though right now he had to admit she wasn't at her best. Her glorious hair was dull and tangled, and she looked like she'd rolled in the mud flats off Charleston harbor at low tide.

"Please," she whispered again, and Devon nodded. Her smile was the first genuine one she'd offered him. "Their names are Ezra, Sissy and Lucy. I don't know their ages exactly, but the oldest is almost a man. Oh, and they lived at Magnolia Hill."

"I'll see if he knows anything about them."

"Thank you."

Because he could feel himself being sucked into the depths of her eyes, Devon pointed to the fish lying in a heap on the ground. "Better cook those," he said and watched the gratitude in her expression fade. But she didn't rebel, and as he entered the cabin he cast one last glance her way. She was holding the fish in front of her, a grimace on her pretty face. Devon was chuckling as he met Natee.

Goodness they were disgusting looking creatures with their flat eyes and long whiskers. But at least they'd stopped struggling as if they could escape the line and jump back into the water.

Felicity was fond of fish; poached salmon and flounder almandine were two of her favorites. But she never imagined those dishes started like this. Arthur had fished when he was younger. He'd even offered to take her along. But Mama insisted it wasn't an activity suited to ladies. And now Felicity knew why.

Clean them he'd said. Felicity looked at the fish, then toward the only water around, the river. With a sigh she marched forward. Her mud encrusted shoes slid on the slippery shore, but she pushed on through the tall grass. What difference did a little more dirt make? Heaven's, she hoped her father and Jebediah appreciated what she was doing for them.

Holding the string in her outstretched hand she dunked the fish into the water. Once. Twice. They still didn't look clean to her. They needed a good scrubbing, but she wasn't about to touch them any more than necessary. So she swished them around in the water, only stopping when one of them started flapping his tail.

"Oh my goodness." Felicity dragged the fish out of the river and holding them as far away as she could returned to the clearing. With a plunk she dropped the fish on the smoldering fire. Sizzling sparks shot up, forcing Felicity to jump backwards. As she moved closer to the fire, fanning the smoke with her hands she caught sight of the fish. They seemed to be staring up at her with accusing eyes.

The smell of something burning was strong as

Devon stepped out of the cabin. Inside the acrid smoke of Natee's pipe had masked the odor that fouled the air. Devon's gaze shot first to the fire where the fish charred, then to the woman sitting complacently on a nearby log.

"What in the hell are you doing?"

Felicity glanced up from her contemplation of a raised welt on her arm and blinked. "Why, I'm cooking the fish." Hadn't he told her to do as much? She jumped to her feet as he squatted by the fire, dragging the fish from the flames with a long stick. "I hope you don't think I'm going to clean them again." Felicity watched as each catfish landed in the dirt beside the fire.

"Again?" Devon sat back on his heels. His expression was a study in confusion when he looked up. "You didn't clean them before."

With a flick of her hand Felicity sent her curls flying over her shoulder. "I most certainly did. Admittedly I didn't scrub them. Well, I didn't have a brush," she said when she heard the deep chuckle begin in the captain's chest. "What is so funny?" she demanded, hands on hips. When he didn't answer, only laughed harder, Felicity took a step forward. Then another.

By this time tears were seeping from his eyes. "Stop it." Felicity swatted at his arm, but the booming laughter continued. "Stop it, I said. Oh, I hate you!" Not caring about the consequences, Felicity plowed into him, knocking them both over. Her fists pummeled his chest as she landed on top of him on the packed ground.

"Hey." Devon grabbed for her hands, missing the first time, but finally managing to manacle her wrists. "Don't," he managed between guffaws. "That hurts."

"I don't care." She struggled against his superior strength, fighting also the tears that burned her eyes. "I—"

"I know, you hate me." Devon jerked her arms out to the side. Her breasts flattened against his chest. When she sucked in a breath, Felicity stopped her wriggling. She shut her eyes, but it was too late. A crystal drop of moisture escaped the confines of her thick lashes.

"Don't cry." Devon was no longer laughing. He reached up to touch her cheek, to follow the path of the tear down her dirty face, but she tried to jerk away. His hands in her hair brought her face back to his. His eyes narrowed as he studied her expression. "What's wrong, Red?"

"Nothing." Felicity sniffed and tried to look away. He tightened his fists. "Let me alone."

"I can't do that. Now tell me." His leg flipped over her skirts when she tried to kick at him. "Tell me."

"You're a brute."

His laughter was swift and short-lived.

"And a cad. And a rogue."

"True enough, but that's not what made you cry."

"You laughed at me," Felicity spit out, then immediately wished her words back. She let out her breath. "You laughed at my cooking."

138

Devon arched his neck and stared at the hazy blue morning sky. Overhead a red-tailed hawk drifted on the air currents. When he dipped his head, Felicity was staring at him. "I'm sorry. I shouldn't have laughed."

"You're still making fun of me."

"No, I'm not." Devon kept his expression sober. "You probably never cooked a fish before."

"Of course, I haven't."

"Or cleaned one either."

Felicity didn't think that even required an answer.

"I should have explained better."

"Do you mean that?" Felicity wrinkled her brow. Her face was mere inches from his, and she searched for any signs of his devilish grin. But his well-shaped mouth remained uncurved, and there was no hint of his dimples. "Are you sure you aren't making light of me?"

"I swear. It was my fault. And I apologize."

Felicity sighed. "All right then. I accept your apology."

"Good." Now was the time to let her up. But Devon couldn't bring himself to loosen his hold on her hair. The golden-red curls fell around them like liquid fire and he tightened his hold. She squirmed and Devon wondered if she could tell through her mud encrusted skirts how hard he'd become.

"I think . . ." Felicity swallowed. She didn't know exactly what she thought, but she recognized the gleam in the captain's eyes. She could feel her own body respond to it. "Don't." Her voice was a whisper.

"Don't what?" He hadn't done anything . . . yet.

"Don't kiss me."

"Why?"

"Because . . . because I don't want you to."

"Liar." Devon proved his assertion when it took no more than a nudge for her lips to drop to his. God, he loved the taste of her. Devon's tongue shot into her mouth, drinking of the sweetness and honey inside. He moaned as she responded in kind.

It was happening to her again. Felicity's body seemed to melt and mold itself around him. She couldn't stop herself from responding to his touch . . . from wanting more. Her fingers dug into his hair as the kiss deepened.

He was ready—hell, more than ready—and she was ready. Devon rolled them over, settling himself between her legs. It didn't really matter to him that they were again lying in the dirt. Somewhere in the back of his mind, he knew it should. But at the moment, his desire easily overpowered his reason.

She arched into his palm when he covered her breast. He squeezed and she moaned, the sound almost covering the gruff cough from overhead.

As if someone had poured cold water on him, Devon jerked around. He let out his breath on a string of curses. "Damnit, Natee," he said to the

140

old Indian looming over them. "You scared me to death."

Natee only smiled . . . or grimaced. It was very hard to tell the difference. "I'm going hunting," he announced before looking pointedly at the charred fish. With a shake of his head that sent his gray braid flopping, he turned and hobbled out of the clearing.

Devon was still watching the spot where he'd been when he felt the shove to his chest.

"Get off me. Get off me this instant!" With each word her voice got louder.

Devon complied, rolling to the side. "You're as changeable as the currents off Devil's Creek."

"What's that supposed to mean?" Felicity demanded, then wished she hadn't. She had a pretty good idea what he was referring to, and she didn't want to discuss it. To try and dismiss the captain she began brushing at the dirt covering her skirts. Despite her best attempts very little of the caked on mud fell away.

Devon didn't bother with an explanation. Pushing to his feet he stretched. His movements were tentative at first, then more vigorous when he realized his ribs weren't hurting as bad today. Ignoring Felicity he toed off one boot, then bent to tug on the other.

Felicity caught sight of his actions out of the corner of her eye. But it wasn't till he shucked his shirt that she forgot about her skirts and looked up, mouth agape. "What are you doing?" His chest was broad and tanned. If he was bent

on raping her she would fight him. She *would,*
Felicity assured herself.

"Taking a bath," was all he said as he strolled
off around the side of the cabin.

"A bath? A bath!" The very word sounded heav-
enly. Felicity scurried around the corner just in
time to see the captain, naked as the day he was
born, step into the dark waters of the river.

Seven

The short squeal caused Devon to glance over his shoulder as he sank into the cool water. He couldn't help smiling at the sight Miss Felicity Wentworth made, standing amid the cord grass, her hands splayed over her face.

"Come on in," he called. "Rinse off some of the mud from yesterday."

"No, thank you." Felicity's voice was muffled by the heels of her hands.

"Suit yourself. But I can tell you it feels good to be clean."

"I'm certain it does." Felicity spread her fingers the tiniest bit when she heard splashing. The captain was nowhere to be seen, but his clothes, shirt, pants and underdrawers floated near the shore line. She waited, watching for him to reappear. The Vs in her hands spread.

"Captain Blackstone." Felicity stepped closer to the water, her shoe slipping in the mud. Nearby a turtle slid in the dark river. "Devon," she called again, her hands now on her hips. "Where—"

The captain's head and shoulders appeared above the surface in a burst of foam. He was laughing, his hair dark and slicked back, his skin shining in the sun.

"That wasn't funny."

"What? Don't tell me you were worried about me?" He shook like a great golden panther, water droplets showering out across the river.

"Hardly." Felicity watched as he reached out, grabbing up his clothes and dunking them beneath the water. "Do we have time for such games?" she said, her delicate brow arched. "What did your friend have to say?"

"No Yankees at Royal Oak." Devon rubbed the fabric between his knuckles. "At least there weren't yesterday."

"What about the children?" Felicity stepped forward in her desire to hear his answer.

"There are some people there." Devon shrugged. "Natee didn't know who." It still surprised him that she kept up this farce of searching for children. But then, a lot of things surprised him about the lovely Miss Wentworth.

"When can we leave?" Felicity paced along the shore, not even bothering to keep her skirts out of the mud.

"You sure you don't want to join me, Red? Clean yourself up a bit?"

Felicity lifted her chin. No one had to tell her how filthy she was. Or how uncomfortable. "I'll wait until I can bathe in more . . . private surroundings."

144

Devon merely shrugged. Then, gathering up his shirt and pants, he started walking toward shore. The water lapped about his chest, then gradually receded to his waist and she didn't move. She only stood there watching, her eyes wide in her dirty face.

"Speaking of privacy," he began as his feet came to a stop on the soft bottom. "I'm not a man who requires a lot." The breeze fluttered a lock of her hair but she remained as if fixed in the mud. "However," Devon continued, "I think it only fair to warn you that I haven't a stitch on."

"I'm well aware of that." Felicity's voice held a hint of contempt.

"Then you must also know if I take three more steps your way, I shan't have any secrets from you."

Heat flooded Felicity's cheeks as she comprehended his meaning—and as she realized how long she'd been standing there, staring at his naked chest. Without a backwards glance at the breadth of sun-darkened flesh, Felicity turned and marched away. She could hear his chuckles over the sound of splashing water as he climbed out of the river.

And Lord help her she was sorely tempted. Jebediah and her father would never forgive her if they knew, but once she passed the curtain of hollys she had the strongest urge to pivot and peek through the leaves.

To see if the intriguing patches of dark brown hair that covered his chest, trailed lower. To see how the corded muscles tapered to his waist and hips. To see what caused the long hard ridge that she felt whenever he lay on top her.

But conscience prevailed over curiosity, so she didn't slow her pace until reaching the clearing by the cabin. Then she bent over, throwing her hair over her head and vigorously finger combing the tangles and dirt from her curls. After that she tore off the cleanest section of petticoat she could find rubbed vigorously at her cheeks.

"Water would help," Devon said, from behind her.

Felicity glanced over her shoulder. *"You* were in the water."

"I'm not now." Devon dropped the carpetbag on the ground. It was followed by his saddlebags. "I traded Apple Dumpling for a boat."

"Apple Dumpling?" Felicity stared at him, wondering how he could look so good when she felt so awful. His clothes were clean and damp, but obviously not the same ones he'd rinsed in the river. His hair was brushed back, curling up at his nape.

"The horse," he said as he disappeared into the cabin.

"I thought the horse's name was Blueberry," Felicity said, following.

"Blueberry . . . Apple Dumpling. Not much difference. Do you want some rice since the fish are—" Devon paused, not wishing to bring on another flood of tears, real or contrived.

Felicity accepted the glutinous rice, amazed at the things she willingly ate when she was hungry enough. "Anyway," she said, munching on a bite, "why did you trade your horse away?"

"River's easier traveling. And a sight safer, too."

The boat was old, looked barely able to float, but the captain was right about one thing, it was easier traveling. At least for Felicity. She sat at one end and watched as Devon rowed them through the murky waters. Sometimes they glided through terrain that seemed more swamp than river, with tall grasses forming mazes, swaying with the currents. Salt marshes, the captain called them as he navigated through them with little difficulty.

"If we had time, I could fix you a feast from here," he said, motioning with one of the oars. "Crabs and shrimp." His smile was crooked as he smacked his lips. "Alligator."

Felicity turned her face away, watching the Queen Anne's Lace sway in the breeze, but she couldn't help laughing. "I'll bet you never ate alligator in your life."

"That's one bet you'd lose, Miss Wentworth. Natee and I used to hunt them."

Felicity slanted him a look through her lashes. She didn't know whether to believe him or not. But just as a precaution she pulled the fingers trailing in the water up into the boat.

"How long until we reach Royal Oak?" Despite her lack of cleanliness and the gnawing hunger that the rice hadn't erased, Felicity was finding the lazy journey through the sun-dappled marsh pleasant. Too pleasant. She had to remind herself of the reason for being here in the first place. And it wasn't to enjoy watching Captain Blackstone's muscles as he rowed.

"We've been on the plantation for a while. Natee camps at the edge of our land." Devon guided them into another narrow channel. "If you look carefully you'll be able to see the main wharf to the right."

Felicity squinted, catching sight of the deserted wharf when they cleared a stand of pines. "It looks in disrepair."

"I've no doubt of that." Devon pulled the oars through the water. As foolish as he knew it was, he let the view slip away without looking. "There hasn't exactly been a pressing need to export anything from Royal Oak since the Yankees came along."

Felicity could think of nothing to say to that. It certainly wasn't as if she weren't glad the Union forces had captured the area. She wanted them to drive the Confederates forces from the South . . . anything to put an end to the war and free the slaves. Yet she couldn't help feeling pity for the captain. What was it like to lose one's home?

But a few minutes later when she looked around her, the pity evaporated to be replaced by the more familiar mistrust. "Where are we going?" They'd slipped by the entrance to the wider channel leading to the wharf, and were now in an area where low lying branches canopied the water and the cord crass swished the hull of the boat.

"I think we'll come in through the back door."

"But why?" It would have been so much easier, and quicker to step out of the boat onto a wharf, even if it was rickety.

When he said nothing Felicity resumed the argument. She leaned forward. "Is it because of the Yankees? You said yourself they aren't here."

"Natee said they weren't here yesterday," he replied, and Felicity slumped back in a huff.

Sure enough the place where he finally pulled the boat aground was tangled and marshy. If there'd ever been a path it was gone now, reclaimed by the swamp. Felicity's shoes oozed into the spongy earth as Devon handed her ashore.

"Don't forget my carpetbag."

"Your gold will be safe enough here, till we scout out the area."

"I'm not interested in scouting," Felicity said, digging in her heels. "I want my—"

Her words were cut off when the captain turned abruptly. He was so close she had to tilt her head to see his eyes. His voice was low, but brooked no argument. "I don't give a damn, Miss Wentworth, what you want. No doubt you'd enjoy running into an entire regiment of Yankees." He lifted his hand in silent protest when she opened her mouth to argue. "On the other hand, I don't wish to meet up with even one." Devon let his breath out slowly. "Now unless you come along quietly, I will leave you here alone to guard your precious carpetbag."

She wanted to scream at him. To tell him what a bully she thought he was. But the expression in the depths of his green eyes preached prudence. He no longer appeared the amiable southern planter, the rogue whose smile made her stomach quiver. He was still breathtakingly handsome, but there was a sharpness to his features, an untamed gleam in his eyes.

He didn't wait for a response from Felicity, but then she assumed he knew she would agree to his terms rather than stay here by herself. When he started back through the reeds, Felicity followed, not even giving a backward glance to the boat and her carpetbag.

The air was heavy and insects droned lazily around Felicity's head as she crept along behind him. Discomfort was becoming something she expected, and she tried to console herself by imagining the pleased expression on Jebediah's face when she returned home with the children.

But to her dismay, Felicity realized she couldn't conjure up an image of Jebediah's face. She shut her eyes, thinking of his angular features, his grim mouth, but no picture came to her. She did however, stumble against the captain's broad back. He reached around, catching her under the elbow. His brow arched quizzically and Felicity straightened her back and jerked herself free from his touch.

What difference did it make that she couldn't remember what Jebediah Webster looked like? That wasn't important. She loved him. She did. And soon he would love her.

"Would you watch where you're going?"

All thoughts of Jebediah vanished from her

mind when Felicity realized the captain had stopped. Before them were the grounds of the once manicured plantation. To the left the long carriage drive curved along, its alley of oaks dripping with wispy moss, hauntingly beautiful.

Felicity's gaze followed the drive till it reached the house itself. Sprawling, yet graceful, it shimmered in the late afternoon sun. And Felicity, used to the splendor of Wentworth House, was awed.

But Devon saw not the fluted columns or tall gabled portico. Instead, he focused on peeling paint and the deserted, broken windows. The forlorn skeleton of his family's home for generations.

Intellectually he knew it would be like this. He'd known, and he thought he was prepared. After all, Royal Oak had been no more than a place he visited and infrequently at that, for nearly a decade. More than a decade, if you counted the years he was away while at the Academy. But he always knew it was there. The home of the pirate, Jack Blackstone, and so many others.

Grams never questioned his desire to become a seaman. "It's in your blood," she said before he went away. "But so is the plantation. When you are ready for it, Royal Oak will be there for you."

But it wasn't.

Devon swallowed and glanced around. His vision was blurred and he blinked several times to clear it. He'd stepped from the cover of the trees without thinking of the possible consequences. But he saw no sign of Yankees, or anyone else for that matter.

Careful now, regardless of the apparent desertion of the place, Devon drew his pistol from its holster. He skirted the outbuildings, the stables where thoroughbred horses once pawed the ground nervously, the smokehouse now empty of hams. The closer he got to the house the more destruction he saw. He'd decided to travel to Royal Oak to assess the war's damage and now he knew.

Weeds choked the crushed shell drive. He bounded up the steps of the landside porch, a second set of footfalls reminding him he was not alone. A glance over his shoulder showed him Felicity rushing to keep up. The door hung lopsided off its top hinges. Devon peered through the opening, motioning for Felicity to stay behind him.

Inside shadows vied with filtered rays of sunlight streaming through the dirt encrusted windows. Devon's heels clicked on the chipped marble as he strode across the entryway.

"Where is everyone?" Felicity's voice echoed through the house, and she didn't need the captain's scowl to tell her she'd spoken too loudly.

Devon glanced in the west parlor. The only furniture that remained was a horsehair settee, and that had the stuffing billowing out. The walls were bare, only the lighter patches of wallpaper giving any hint of the paintings that once graced the room.

Turning on his heel, Devon examined the other front room. He could almost hear the ghostly strains of violins and piano as he glanced around the scarred ballroom.

Back through the hallway, toward the river entrance, he noted the furnishings remained in the dining room and east parlor.

"I don't think anyone is here," Felicity whispered. She decided the captain must agree with her for he lowered his pistol. He started to slide it into his holster when a soft whine sounded from the back of the house. Rushing forward, Devon pushed open the door to the butler's pantry, leveling the barrel of the pistol.

"Don't shoot. Oh, please don't shoot," came the muffled plea from one of the people huddled in the corner.

"Hattie?" Devon squinted to see into the darkened room.

"Mast'a Devon, is that you?" The tone was tentative at first, then more assured. "What ye doin' here, scaring a body to death?"

"Sorry. But what in the hell are you doing hiding back in the pantry?" Devon holstered his pistol as Royal Oak's housekeeper marched her ample girth past him into the hall. She was followed by two women Devon didn't recognize.

"Well, just how was we supposed to know it was you?" she asked logically. "Ain't been nothin' but Yankees and no goods hangin' round here since Miz Eveline up and went to Charleston." She shooed at the two younger women with her apron. "You all run along. See if'n ye can't find somethin' for Mast'a Devon to eat. Ye is hungry, ain't ye? Never knowed a time when ye weren't."

Before he could answer, Felicity stepped from

153

behind him. "Please, madam, do you know anything about three motherless children?"

Hattie's turbaned head sunk lower into her chins as she studied Felicity with a wary eye. "Three chillen? What's she talkin' 'bout, Mast'a Devon?"

"This is Felicity Wentworth, Hattie. She's looking for her Mammy's children."

"She doin' what?"

Felicity threw the captain a scowl when he shrugged his shoulders as if her guess was as good as his. "I've come south to find three children," Felicity repeated in her most no nonsense voice. "There names are Ezra, Sissy and Lucy. They are of the Negroid race and the last I heard were slaves at Magnolia Hill."

"Are they here, Hattie?" Devon couldn't believe Felicity Wentworth was keeping up this farce, but she seemed intent upon getting an answer.

"Now I don't rightly know. There's a passel 'a chillen stayin' in the cabins. But I ain't sure 'a their names."

"Is there food for all of you to eat? Wait a minute. Where are *you* off to?" Devon turned away from Hattie as Felicity started toward the front doorway.

"Why to the cabins, of course." She paused. "Where exactly are they?"

"You're not going anywhere alone." Devon shook his head, then brushed the stray hair off his forehead. When he redirected his attention toward Hattie, he heard a toe tapping on the plank floors. He shut his eyes, took a deep breath and faced

154

Felicity. "All right. We'll go." The sooner he found out the real reason the redheaded beauty wanted to come to Royal Oak, the better.

"Now stay behind me," he ordered as they stepped out into the sunlight. The slave quarters were off to the side of the big house. They were in as much disrepair as the rest of Royal Oak, and Devon was glad his grandmother wasn't here to see. She always prided herself on treating her people right.

A few heads peeked around doors as Felicity and Devon walked through the dust down the narrow alley between the two rows of cabins. Devon recognized a few people and called them by name.

"Mast'a Devon?" A tall man with skin the color of polished ebony stepped into the roadway, blocking their way. Felicity instinctively grabbed hold of the captain's hand.

"Eb." Devon squeezed the small hand nestled in his, then stepped forward to clasp the other man's shoulder. "I was hoping to find you here."

"Aw, Iz here, all right. Ain't nowhere else to go. Miz Eveline, she here?"

"No." Devon shook his head. "Her hip is giving her fits, though she's the last one to admit it." As he spoke more people wandered out of the double row of cabins, some hesitantly, others more boldly. Devon greeted them all in turn.

"Is this all of you that are left?" Devon asked Eb. He lifted his hand to indicate the thirty or so people. Once Royal Oak had been one of the largest rice plantations in South Carolina. And where

Hattie had ruled the house servants with her efficiency and bossy ways, Eb was second only to the overseer, Tom Smith, with the field hands. And even Tom had admitted the workers listened better to Eb, then to him.

Eb glanced around, then shrugged his powerful shoulders. "There's a few more, I reckon. Some of the no 'counts runned off when Miz Eveline, she leaved for Charleston. Then them Yankees come through. They took Mast'a Tom and most a the young bucks." He shrugged again. "I ain't heard nothin' more of 'em."

Devon listened with a heavy heart. "How are you all managing?" Slavery was the one issue where Devon and his grandmother disagreed. She blamed his stint in the navy where he rubbed elbows with "those know nothing Northerners" as she called them, for Devon's opinions. But it had always been his intention to manumit Royal Oak's slaves one day. But he never planned to simply set them adrift as they were now. He'd thought to pay them wages to work the land.

It had been a grand design that filled his head on many long nights staring out at the open sea under a canopy of stars. The question had been was he willing to give up the life he loved, the life of a seafaring man, to go home to Royal Oak and put his plan into effect?

Ironic how a war made decisions for you.

Mentally shaking off his melancholy Devon caught the thread of Eb's explanation. "Hattie, she done seen to it that most everythin' was hid when

156

them Yankees came. They sure was in a takin' mood. But they didn't find much food here," he said with obvious pride.

Devon couldn't help smiling thinking of Hattie foiling the Yankees. "So none of you are going hungry?"

"Oh, no siree. We alls doin' okay."

Meanwhile, Felicity couldn't wait another minute. It wasn't as if she hadn't given the captain every opportunity to ask about the children. She had. But he simply didn't seem inclined to bother with her concerns. So Felicity stepped forward. Despite her feelings of trepidation.

It wasn't as if she hadn't been around Negroes before. Her father didn't employ any but Jebediah often brought them to his meetings. But here, in the heart of the South, surrounded by them, Felicity faltered. She wished for the ease with which the captain spoke to them, but lacking that she steeled herself.

"I'm looking for three children," she began. Then because all eyes seemed focused on her, she rushed on with her sketchy descriptions. At first no one said anything, but then the captain nodded and the man, Eb, cleared his throat.

"Sounds to me like they might be here."

"Where? Where are they?" Felicity couldn't contain her euphoria. When she began this quest Felicity had no conception of the trials she'd endure. The danger, the heat, the dirt—Devon Blackstone. There were times . . . many times . . . she wished for nothing more than to be back safe and sound at Wentworth House, having tea with friends, chatting about the latest styles in Goody's or lamenting about the lot of the poor slaves in the South.

Abolitionism had become one of her favorite topics after the slavery cause began consuming her father's life, and thus hers. Most of Felicity's friends listened politely, thought she was so very knowledgeable, and changed the subject at the first opportunity.

But she hadn't known anything—not really.

And now she was afraid her knowledge was more than she wished.

But she followed Eb, walking side by side with the captain through the gathering of people. The slaves parted for them, closing in behind and following, forming a small procession headed toward a cabin near the end of the row.

When they stopped, Felicity's mouth went dry. She tried to swallow, but couldn't. The cabin was similar to the others in design. They were all small, with two front windows and a door. The walls were formed from some sort of stucco that contained pieces of shell. Felicity heard the dry hacking cough before she even approached the open doorway.

She glanced up at the captain. He watched her with that part amused, part mocking expression on his face. She knew he didn't believe her story about finding her Mammy's children. Since some of it was a lie, the rest rather unbelievable, Felicity didn't think she could blame him. He probably wondered what she planned to do now.

The cough came again, a deep grating sound, and chills raced down Felicity's spine. She knew she should take the final steps, and enter the small cabin. She'd come so far, endured so much. What were three more steps?

Would she know if these were Esther's children or just three other lost souls displaced by the war? And what would she do if that were so? Go home empty handed? Continue her search? Neither seemed acceptable.

If these children weren't Esther's she was really at a loss for what to do.

And she couldn't face her father and Jebediah a failure. She just couldn't.

Felicity swallowed and forced her feet forward, almost tripping over a tear in her gown. Inside the cabin the light was dim. Dust motes danced in the thin stream of sunshine slanting through the door. The windows were covered with ragged stretches of burlap bags.

It took a moment for Felicity's eyes to adjust to the shadows. When they did she slowly glanced around the room. The only piece of furniture was a lopsided table. There were no chairs to sit on and no cupboards. If there ever had been a bedstead it was now replaced by a tumble of blankets—where three people huddled.

One of them stood as Felicity approached. He was a boy of perhaps twelve years, with a thin frame and long gangling legs. He carried a spindly rooster in the crook of his arm. The boy stepped forward, blocking Felicity's view of the cabin's other occupants.

"Are . . . you Ezra?"

His eyes narrowed and his angular chin lifted but the boy didn't answer . . . not at first. Then in a voice that belied his belligerent stance he said, "Yes'm, I am."

A small pig-tailed head peeked around one of his legs but Felicity barely noticed. She was basking in the thrill of achieving her goal. She wrung her hands with excitement as she stepped toward him. "I've come to take you away from here." Her message was delivered with such enthusiasm Felicity wondered at the children's lack of response— until it came.

One child shrieked, "No," then started crying. The coughing started again. And the boy standing in front of her shook his head and backed up. Bewildered, Felicity glanced around.

It was then she realized she hadn't entered the cabin alone. Captain Blackstone was by her side.

Eight

"Hush up, all of you." Devon's voice was not unkind, but firm enough for four mouths to shut and four pairs of eyes to look his way. "I never heard such carrying on."

"Well, I just don't understand," Felicity began but stopped when his narrowed gaze met hers.

"I meant you too, Miss Wentworth."

Felicity bristled under his admonishment. Her glare however was lost on the captain as he turned his back on her and studied the children.

The youngest, a girl of four or five was staring at him with big, black eyes and doing her best not to sniffle into the ratty piece of cloth she held to her damp cheek. Another girl was still just lying there on a mound of blankets. She seemed barely able to support herself on bent elbows.

Then there was the boy. He looked hungry, dirty, and yet ready to jump on Devon if he made a move toward either of the others. Still finding it difficult to believe there actually were three children—he would have bet all he had the story was

161

a fabrication—Devon motioned toward the girls, directing his question toward Ezra. "Are these your sisters?"

"Yes'sur."

"Where's your mother?"

"She's dead."

"No, she isn't." Felicity leaped forward, ignoring the annoyed line of the captain's mouth. "Your mother is alive and well, living in . . . in Richmond." Felicity bit her lip, then continued. "And I've come to take you to her." Again her announcement wasn't met with the kind of enthusiasm she'd hoped. Felicity took another step. "Don't you want to see your mother?" For the life of her, Felicity couldn't understand why there was no response. Her hands which moments before reached out, fell to her side. If there had been a chair in the cabin she would have slumped onto it.

"What makes you think your mother is dead?" Devon asked, not missing Felicity's anguished expression.

"She just is, that's all. We ain't seen her for . . ." The boy seemed at a loss to describe when he last saw his mother. "She just is," he repeated.

"And you're certain these are your *Mammy's* children?" Devon turned on Felicity.

The skepticism in his voice was not lost on her. She notched her chin higher. "I am." Sinking to her knees, her skirts billowing out in the dirt, Felicity held out her hand toward the youngest child, who immediately stuck a dirty thumb in her mouth. "Your mother's name is Esther."

The little girl said nothing but her brother stepped between her and Felicity. "Her name ain't no secret."

"Perhaps not." Felicity stood. "However she did send me to find you."

"A lady like you?" He sounded completely incredulous.

Felicity was saved explaining by a fresh outbreak of dry coughs coming from the girl who now lay flat on the rumpled blanket.

"Sissy sick," came the pronouncement from the youngest child, the first sound she'd made other than a whimpering cry.

"Yes, I can see that." Felicity stepped closer. She had very little experience with sickness. Always healthy herself, she couldn't even remember her parents or brother being ill.

Taking one more glance around the cabin, Felicity said, "This is no place for these children. The main house is better I should think." Ignoring the children's shocked expressions and the feeble attempt by Ezra to block her way, Felicity knelt beside Sissy. She meant to help the girl to her feet, but the captain was there also. Reaching down he lifted the child, blankets and all.

Felicity imagined they made an odd looking procession as they wove their way along the tree lined path, Captain Blackstone in front, carrying the sick Sissy; Ezra, following close behind clutching the youngest child's hand; and Felicity bringing up the rear. Despite her dirty and raggedy appearance, Felicity kept her chin high and her eyes straight ahead, resisting the urge to meet the curious stares she knew followed them.

As she trudged along, Felicity couldn't help wondering if Jebediah had ever traveled south. Had he ever seen for himself what he preached so vehemently about? When she returned to New York she would ask him.

"What ye think yur doin', Masta' Devon, bringin' them chillen in this house?" Hattie stood in the doorway, her arms akimbo, her stance defiant.

Felicity expected the captain to deliver a lambasting to the woman—which she thought she deserved. But instead he only proceeded forward, forcing her to step aside. "Are there any beds upstairs?"

"Yankees didn't bother themselves with takin' stuff 'ceptin' down here in de front rooms."

"Does the west bedroom have clean linens?"

"Well now ye know Miz Eveline always insisted on clean linens," she said, puffing her way up the stairs as she climbed after Devon. "But I ain't gonna be responsible for what she's gonna think of this."

"Don't concern yourself, Hattie," Devon said as he kicked the door open. Felicity rushed forward to turn down the bed. The sheets did indeed appear clean, though a musty smell drifted up from the pillow.

Devon settled the girl on the bed, hearing her soft sigh as the feather mattress billowed around her. He straightened and tilted his head toward Felicity. His expression, the arched brow and widened green eyes, clearly asked what was to be done now.

From her vantage point near the doorway where Felicity had retreated to keep the other children company, she returned his stare. The truth was Felicity didn't know what else to do for the child. It wasn't until she glanced down at the gaunt face by her side, that she had an idea.

"Food," she said. "I think these children need something to eat. And some water. Lots of it." They could all use a good scrubbing—as could she.

After a nod from the captain, Hattie bustled out of the room. The intervening silence was broken by Sissy's coughs. Felicity rushed forward, not knowing exactly what to do until she thought to prop pillows beneath her head. The raised elevation seemed to help.

Felicity was draping the coverlet around the girl's shoulders when she noticed the captain walking toward the door. "Wait," she called out. "Where are you going?"

Devon turned. "I thought I'd leave you with your ministrations. I know nothing of treating the sick."

"Well neither do . . ." Felicity stopped herself from speaking the truth. She wouldn't beg him for assistance. She didn't need it. "Neither do most men," she finished and reaching around continued fussing with the counterpane.

"Hattie will help."

"Fine." Felicity began draping the mosquito netting for want of something better to do.

"And Miss Wentworth."

"Yes?" She looked up, meeting his eyes, and that damned amused expression.

"I would appreciate the opportunity to speak with you . . . after you've done what you can for these children, of course."

"Of course."

Felicity let her shoulders droop after he left the room, closing the door behind him. She nearly flopped across the foot of the bed . . . probably would have if the youngest child didn't tug on her skirt. Felicity looked down into the dirty upturned face.

"Is ye really gonna take us to Mama?"

"No she ain't," came Ezra's reply before Felicity could answer.

Felicity pretended she didn't hear him. "Yes, I am, Lucy. I shall take you all." Her gaze listed to include the boy who still held onto that rooster. "And you won't be slaves anymore. You'll be free." A knock sounded at the door and Felicity gestured for Ezra to open it. Hattie stood in the opening carrying a tray laden with three bowls of something that smelled wonderful to Felicity.

Swallowing, she motioned for her to place the platter on the bedside table. "But first," she said, as another woman carried in a bucket of water and set it on the floor, "we need to get you all cleaned up and ready to travel."

* * *

She'd never been so tired.

Felicity arched, rubbing the small of her back with her hands as she stepped into the hallway. Behind her the three children slept; Sissy and Lucy in the big bed, and Ezra, with his rooster, on a cot Felicity insisted be brought to the room.

They were relatively clean, fed, and Sissy's cough seemed a little better.

Felicity was filthy, hungry, and exhausted . . . and she couldn't keep from smiling. That is until Hattie appeared at her shoulder.

"Masta' Devon he says he wants to see ye."

"I know," Felicity whispered as she closed the door to the bedroom. Luckily the black woman's voice hadn't awakened the children. "Where is he?" she asked, leading Hattie away from the spot.

"He's down in the library, but he done said yous to clean up in here first." Hattie turned the knob, opening the door into another bedroom.

Felicity stepped inside and could have cried at what she saw. The room was large with an elaborate carved marble fireplace, a high tester bed and a brass slipper tub full of water. How long had it been since she'd enjoyed the luxury of a full bath? How long since she'd taken such things as cleanliness and a full stomach for granted?

Felicity wasted no time stripping out of the gown she'd worn since she left Charleston. Was it really only two days ago?

Each mud stiffened piece of clothing she passed to Hattie was looked upon with disdain, but Felicity didn't care. She didn't even mind that the water was cool, or that the only soap was hard and smelled of lye.

She sank into the water, scrubbing first her hair, then her skin until at last she felt clean. After stepping from the brownish water Hattie dried her and pointed toward the gown on the bed.

"Masta' Devon done said ye was close to Miz Celia's size, so I found one of her dresses. Ain't real fancy, but least ways it's clean."

Unlike when Ruth had altered one of Celia's gowns for her in Charleston, this time there were no clever fingers to loosen the bodice or take up the hem. But Felicity was beyond thinking of anything but her growling stomach. "Do you suppose I might have something to eat?"

"Down in the library with Masta' Devon," Hattie said as she took Felicity's shoulders and forced her onto the bench facing the vanity. She "humphed" and scowled, her jowls settling into her neck as she brushed at Felicity's damp hair. She finally twisted the mass of curls on top her head sticking hairpins in at odd angles. "I ain't no ladies' maid," she declared as she stepped back to survey her work.

"It's fine." Felicity jumped up from the seat. It wasn't as if she were seeing anyone but Captain Blackstone, and he had certainly seen her looking worse. She gathered up the skirt of the yellow silk gown and headed for the door. "Where is the library?"

"Down the stairs and to the . . ."

Felicity didn't wait to hear what else Hattie said.

She decided if there was food there she would smell it. But the downstairs was larger, with more rooms than she originally thought, and it was the aroma of tobacco smoke rather than food that led her to the open door.

Devon Blackstone stood, his back to the door, his elbow propped on the mantel. He held a cheroot in one hand, a wineglass in the other, and his eyes were fixed on the portrait above the fireplace. Felicity slipped into the room unnoticed.

Though she opened her mouth to announce her presence, Felicity hesitated. Her gazed traveled to the painting, to the man captured in oil with lifelike splendor. It was an old portrait, Felicity could tell by the style of dress, but that wasn't what caught her eye.

It was the man himself.

He was large, with long blond hair that almost but not quite hid a gold loop that hung from his ear. His features were bold, and though he too was very handsome, he didn't look like Devon Blackstone. Except for his eyes and for the way he seemed to fill the canvas with his presence. The same way the captain dominated a room.

Deciding he must be an ancestor of some sort, though perhaps an unsavory one, Felicity didn't notice Devon turn until he said her name. Actually, it wasn't her name.

"Well, Red." He lifted the glass in salute. "You're looking mighty fine."

Felicity's mouth tightened into a straight line as she recognized the unmistakable slur in his voice.

169

"You've been drinking," she announced as she made her way toward the tray of food.

"See, I told you she was a clever wench," Devon said, glancing up at the portrait and winking. "I was just telling my great, great, great, great . . . Hell, I don't know how many greats of a grandaddy he is. Anyway," he turned back to face Felicity, "I was just telling the pirate about you."

"You have a grandfather who was a pirate?" Felicity eyed the painting with renewed interest. No wonder the captain reminded her of a buccaneer.

"Sure do." Devon gulped down his wine, and reached for the decanter on the mantel. "He sailed the Spanish Main, terrorizing the good folk and stealing their daughters."

Dressed as he was with his white shirt open at the neck low enough to see the beginnings of curling chest hair and his pants snug, Devon looked as if he could easily terrorize the area. And Felicity had only to remember the kisses they'd shared to know how easily he could capture the daughters. How enjoyable it might be to be captured.

Felicity forced that thought from her mind as she sank into the chair pulled up to the small table by the open window. Outside twilight softened the harsh edges of neglect Royal Oak suffered from. But Felicity was more interested in the food on the table than the warm June evening. She lifted a piece of cornbread to her lips, salivating before she even bit into it.

"He kidnapped his wife, you know," Devon continued as he watched her chew. It was almost as enjoyable to study the curve of her jaw line as the succulent spill of creamy breasts.

Felicity glanced up. "No," she said calmly. "I didn't know." She wasn't certain what kind of fish was on the plate in front of her but she was too hungry to care.

"Miranda was her name." Devon pointed his glass toward the portrait at the opposite end of the room and Felicity followed the motion with her eyes. "Beautiful, isn't she?"

It only took a glance to see that the woman in the painting was lovely. Her gown was of the same vintage as the pirate's. Her hair was dark, twisted high with a lace fontange. And she seemed to be smiling at the pirate across the room. Felicity shook her head at such a silly notion.

"They came to Royal Oak after Jack . . . that was his name. Gentleman Jack Blackstone they called him. Anyway, after his pardon, he and Miranda came here. They added onto the original house, flooded the fields and made it a profitable rice plantation. Helped make it what it is today." Devon paused and glanced around at the faded drapes and the threadbare rug.

"Not what it is today," he said after slugging back the brandy. "Bringing Royal Oak to her knees was left to my generation."

She felt sorry for him.

As strange as it seemed that she could feel anything like compassion for him, she did. The fork stopped midway between the plate and her mouth, while she searched for something comforting to say. The captain was facing the hearth now, but she could have sworn she had seen tears in his beautiful green eyes before he turned away.

"The war won't last forever." Felicity touched his sleeve. She'd abandoned her meal, rising and moving up behind him so quietly he jerked with the contact. If she expected a weepy expression when he turned to face her, she was wrong. His eyes were hard and narrowed, like gleaming emeralds, as he let them rake over her.

"Don't tell me you're another damn ostrich with its head buried in the sand?"

"What?"

"You aren't convinced we're going to win this war and kick the damn Yankees off our sacred soil, are you?"

"No." Felicity dropped her lashes. "No, I don't think that."

"Good." Devon reached to refill his glass. "Because it won't happen. Oh, I know what you'll say. What of Manassas? One good southern boy is worth ten of the enemy."

"Actually, I wasn't planning to say . . ." Felicity began but the captain cut her off. Apparently his argument wasn't so much with her as himself.

"Well it isn't true. I know the Yankees. Hell, I went to school with them. Did you know I went to the Naval Academy?"

Felicity shook her head. Her hair was drying and several curls escaped the tight chignon and wisped around her face.

"Hell, yes. Graduated second in my class. Destined for great things, I was." His glass went up in a mock toast before he emptied it and back-handed the amber liquid from his mouth. "That was before the war though."

"You were in the United States Navy?"

"That I was, Miss Wentworth. Fastest rising young officer in the whole damn thing."

"But why did you . . . why didn't you stay?"

"And fight against my native land?" His incredulous expression was made slightly comical by his drunkenness. "Surely you jest. Do you have any idea how many Blackstones would roll over in the family plot if I betrayed the family name?"

"But if you don't believe in the cause . . ."

"But Red." The mocking smile returned. "Did I say I didn't believe? Hell, I advocate a state's right to look out for their own welfare. I'm not in favor of tariffs that choke our economy or fat-bellied politicians telling us—"

"What of slavery? Do you support that institution?" Felicity sucked in her breath when he turned his gaze on her. Suddenly all signs of his drinking were gone.

"No," he said, his voice flat. "I don't believe it's a good thing."

"Yet you fight to keep men in shackles."

"Shackles?" Devon threw back his head and laughed. "Have you been reading *Uncle Tom's Cabin?* Where in the hell do you get shackles?"

"No. I mean . . ." Jebediah had given her a copy of the novel, but she hadn't read it. However, she did know where she'd gotten her impassioned accusation. Jebediah used the line often in his sermons against the evils of slavery.

"And besides, you're a fine one to be preaching against slavery. You with your dying Mammy."

"I wasn't preaching," Felicity insisted. But she knew she was. She also knew how pompous she sounded. Ignoring his arched brow she reseated herself beside the table and took a bite of fish. The room was quiet for a moment, only the evening sounds of frogs and crickets floating in through the open window.

"I'm not fighting, you know."

Felicity twisted around in the chair. "I beg your pardon?"

"You accused me of fighting to keep men in shackles. I'm nothing more than a lowly blockade runner. Hell, I don't even shoot at the blockaders. That's not the way it's done. I just sail quietly through the darkness." He walked to the window, lifting the drapes with one hand. "This would be a perfect night. No moon. Plenty of mist off the river. Just right for slipping through the net." He glanced over his shoulder. "Do you know that we sometimes sail so close to the enemy that I can hear them whistling on deck?" He chuckled, "God, we could whistle a duet if I wanted to."

"It sounds dangerous."

Devon laughed again. "Don't act so concerned," he said as he dropped the fringed curtain and took the chair across the table from Felicity. "Remember, I was the fastest rising officer in the fleet.

When it comes to sailing I know my stuff. Hell, all us Blackstone men do. The pirate, the privateer. But I didn't tell you about him, did I?"

"No, just the pirate."

"Well, it's a good thing I'd rather talk about you. Once you get me started on the Blackstones, I can go on forever." He pointed her way. "It's Gram's fault. She thought our family more interesting than fairy tales, so when I was young and couldn't sleep . . ." He shrugged. "But enough about me. I'd rather discuss you . . . and those children."

Felicity took a quick bite of corn bread. "What about me?"

"You can start by telling me why you risked coming down here."

"I told you. To collect my Mammy's children." Felicity tried but she couldn't meet the captain's gaze.

"So you said. But then, I never believed you."

Felicity's eyes flew to his. "Well, now that you've seen them—"

"I admit their presence here makes me wonder about my original opinion of you."

"Which was?"

"That you are a spy."

"A spy!" Felicity couldn't help laughing. "Certainly you never thought—"

"Why not? You certainly are beautiful enough to separate a man from his secrets." His hand reached across the small, oval table to touch the curls resting against her cheek. "And your hair. I've been fascinated by it since the moment I first saw you."

Dusk had settled, filling the room with deep shadows that seemed to cocoon them. No one had lit the lamp on the desk or the sconces over the fireplace.

Pulling back from his touch was the logical thing to do, but Felicity seemed unable to move. She could only stare at him through the grainy darkness, the food on the table forgotten. She swallowed, though her mouth had suddenly gone very dry.

When his hand curved to cup her cheek, Felicity knew he would kiss her, and the thought alone sent emotions surging through her body. He tilted her face up toward him as he leaned across the table. Their breaths mingled. His smelled of brandy and desire, a heady potion.

Even before their lips met Felicity's eyes drifted shut. She couldn't believe this was happening to her again. But her entire being seemed to center around him.

His tongue wet the seam of her mouth and she opened for him, moaning when he gently bit her lip. He toyed with her, nibbling, testing, teasing, everything but deepen the kiss as Felicity longed for him to do.

She clutched the edge of the table to keep from grabbing his shirt and pulling him toward her. She ached and still he played, dipping his tongue into the sultry cavern of her mouth only to withdraw it quickly.

His fingers filtered back through her hair, cupping her head with a force just short of pain. Felicity's lashes lifted and she stared into his intense green eyes. Then suddenly his mouth was devouring hers and she was swept up in the dizzying passion. She matched him kiss for kiss, standing in her desire to get closer to him.

Felicity could scarcely breathe. The room, which had been cooled by a breeze drifting through the window, was now suffocatingly hot. She arched forward, still clutching the table, as his mouth left hers and traveled a molten path toward her ear.

"Why can't I believe you?" His words were whispered, no more than a husky breath really, but Felicity heard them. Felt them. Like an icy wind from off the sound slapping her in the face.

She jerked back, struggling to regain a composure which wasn't as quick to respond as her emotions. He leaned forward. On either side of the platter piled with fish his palms lay flat on the table. And he stared at her, his eyes heavy lidded and probing.

Part of her wanted to fall back toward him. To forget everything but the way he made her feel, the sensations that exploded through her with no more than the touch of his lips.

But she couldn't.

The old Felicity who shopped and spent her time at balls and soirees might. But there were too many people depending upon her now. Her father, Jebediah, Esther, and the children. There was no time for her old self-indulgence.

Besides, the captain was looking at her now as if he knew the battle waging inside her. And found it amusing.

Felicity's spine stiffened. "I do believe I've had enough to eat for now." She smoothed her skirt, resisting the urge to straighten her hair where his strong fingers had dislodged the pins. "I'll bid you good night."

With all the dignity that she could muster, Felicity turned and walked toward the door. Her hand slipped over the smooth, brass knob as his soft chuckle sounded in the background.

"Sweet dreams, Red," was all he said before she forgot dignity and fled the room.

"Hell's fire." Devon mumbled the words under his breath as he listened to her retreating footsteps. Why hadn't he kept his mouth shut? What did it matter whether he believed her or not? He wanted her. More than he'd ever wanted a woman. He ached with wanting her.

What the hell did he care why she came to Royal Oak? She couldn't cause the plantation any more trouble than the Yankees already had. Even if she were a damn spy, it didn't mean he couldn't tumble her to the floor and relieve some of the tension they both were feeling.

Because she might be fighting it, but Devon knew she experienced the same desire that had him wishing he could run out and take a plunge in the river.

But instead he pulled his hands down across his face, trying to scrub away some of the effect of the brandy. He'd drunk too much, feeling sorry for himself and all the Blackstones to follow. Getting nostalgic and maudlin in the process. And that wasn't why he came to Royal Oak.

After lighting the lamp on the desk, Devon sank into the leather chair behind it. He unlocked a mahogany drawer and reached inside, extracting a thick packet of papers.

He had them drawn up before the war. Grams hadn't approved but Devon was adamant, though he agreed not to do anything at the time. Royal Oak did after all belong to Eveline Blackstone. But she'd long ago expressed her desire to bequeath the plantation to her favorite grandson. She'd gone so far as to give Devon her power of attorney. Devon used that power now as he began signing the letters of manumission freeing the slaves.

"Damn his sweet dreams," Felicity mumbled as she punched the feather pillow beneath her head. It might as well be filled with rocks for all the rest it brought her. She was restless and fidgety. What little sleep she'd managed *was* filled with dreams.

But they hadn't been sweet.

They'd been erotic and sensual. Filled with visions of Devon Blackstone, his smile, his rumpled, sunlit hair, his strong body and magical hands. And always his eyes.

Even awake, Felicity had only to lower her

lashes for his vision to appear. With an unladylike growl she yanked back the mosquito netting and slid off the bed. Her skin was so sensitive the soft cotton of the sleeping gown Hattie found for her was irritating. Felicity crossed her arms over her breasts as she padded across the floor. Her nipples ached, and she hated Devon Blackstone for making it so. Before she met him she never felt like this. Never even knew she *could* feel like this.

The sky was barely tinged with the first pinks of dawn as she looked out the window, but already there were people in the yard below. Several slaves leaned against a fence. They were listening to Devon Blackstone who stood among them, holding the reins of the horse he brought from Charleston. Apparently Natee had decided to trade back the animal for the boat. While she watched, Devon mounted and rode off at a canter down the long oak lined drive.

Well, at least she wouldn't have to face him this morning. Felicity hurried and dressed, foregoing the stays. When she peeked in the room beside hers where the children were she found them already awake. Sissy seemed improved though she still coughed often and appeared weak.

"I'll see about getting us all some breakfast," she said. "Ezra, come with me to help carry it." The boy made no reply, but he did follow along behind Felicity as she walked out into the hallway.

Hattie was at the bottom of the stairs, her pose, hands on hips, one Felicity was learning to expect.

"Masta' Devon done rode out. He didn't think you'd be about so early."

"I see." Felicity knew he was gone. And as far as being up, maybe she didn't normally witness sunrise, but he didn't have to act as if she slept the day away.

"He done said to tell you he'd be back tonight, and to give you this."

'This' was a revolver that Hattie pulled from her apron pocket and handed toward Felicity. She merely stared at it. "What am I supposed to do with that?"

"I ain't sure. But Mast'a Devon done said you was to take it." Which seemed to be next to a proclamation from God in Hattie's eyes. She nudged Felicity's hand with the gun.

Not knowing what else to do, Felicity took it, holding the butt gingerly and wishing Devon were here so she could tell him what she thought of his order. "Wait here," she told Ezra before heading back into the hall toward the library. She crossed into the room and placed the pistol on the desk. As she left she couldn't help glancing first at the portrait of the pirate, and then at his wife.

While she and Ezra arranged bowls of cornmeal on a tray, Felicity talked to him about his mother. "She's very anxious to see all of you again. We'll stay here today to let Sissy rest and then start north. I'm not certain how we'll get to New York, but I'll think of something," she said more to herself than him. "After all, I've gotten this far, haven't I?"

181

Felicity didn't expect any response and she received none as she started up the wide, winding stairway. She would find a way to get the children to their mother.

They were near the top riser when Felicity heard a commotion outside. She turned just as the front door banged open. Eb stood in the doorway, his beat up hat in his hands. "They's comin' " he yelled to no one in particular.

"Who's coming?" Felicity shoved the tray into Ezra's hands and retraced several steps.

"The Yankees! They'z comin' up the lane."

"The Yankees!"

It was obvious the black man thought it the worst possible news. But Felicity couldn't help smiling.

Nine

"Take the tray on upstairs," Felicity said as she brushed back a straggling curl from her forehead. "I'll be up directly."

"But Miz Felicity . . ."

"No arguing now." As she descended the stairs, Felicity pointed toward the black man who still stood in the hallway. "Eb, I'd like you to shut the door please."

"Yes'm."

"You may open it again when the Yankees knock. I'll receive them in the east parlor."

With that, Felicity marched back down the wide central hall, past Hattie who stood with her fists firmly planted on her ample hips. When she reached the open parlor door, Felicity turned. "Hattie, do you suppose you could find some refreshments, please?"

"Ye mean for them Yankees?"

"Why yes. I do believe it's the sociable thing to do."

"I ain't sure Mast'a Devon gonno like this."

Felicity doubted he would either. But Devon Blackstone wasn't here . . . and hopefully she and the children would be gone before he returned. If nothing else, that should please him. Without another word Felicity entered the parlor, keeping the door ajar so she could hear when the Yankees knocked.

As it turned out, that was a useless precaution for they didn't so much knock as pound. The noise startled Felicity, who was sitting calmly in a dusty winged chair thinking of how she would broach her request to the Yankee commander.

In the hallway the voices were loud and crude as someone demanded entrance. Felicity forgot her plan to greet the soldiers in the room and went to the doorway in time to see four men push past Eb, knocking him back against the wall.

"What do you think you're doing?" Felicity rushed forward, stopping abruptly when the four turned toward her, their pistols drawn.

"Now, would you looky here. If it ain't one of them sweet Southern belles comin' to the aid of her darky."

"That will be enough, Sergeant. Are you Mrs. Blackstone?" one of the men asked, addressing Felicity.

She was so shocked by their behavior and appearance she couldn't speak at first . . . couldn't even deny the sergeant's contention. These men weren't anything like she'd imagined they'd be. Arthur and all the other young men she'd seen march off to war were clean and mannerly, handsome in their pressed blue uniforms.

"I asked you a question, ma'am."

Felicity swallowed. Of the four this man, their lieutenant, appeared the closet to a gentleman. She would deal with him and ignore the others. "No, I'm not Mrs. Blackstone. I am Felicity—"

"Where is she?" The young officer's voice showed signs of strain, but it wasn't unkind, despite his interruption.

"There is no Mrs. Blackstone here at present." Felicity smiled, forcing herself to continue even after it became obvious her charms did not affect the lieutenant. The burly sergeant however stepped forward, and rubbed his hand down the front of his tangled beard.

"Do you suppose we could discuss this in the parlor?" Her words were for the lieutenant, but it was the sergeant who responded first.

"There ye go lieutenant, the little spitfire wants to get ye all to herself."

"That will be enough Sergeant Poole. Take the men and search the house."

"Search the house? But I told you. . . ." Felicity's protest was drowned out by the sergeant's surly response and the clomping footfalls of the men as they tramped down the hall.

Reholstering his gun the lieutenant turned toward Felicity. "After you," he said, motioning toward the parlor.

Not knowing what else to do, Felicity started walking . . . stopping only when she heard a loud crash from the rear of the house. It was followed by a scream. "What are they doing?" Felicity pivoted, but her rush toward the sound was cut off by the lieutenant's hand clamped about her arm.

"There's no need for anyone to be hurt. Not as long as you cooperate."

"Cooperate with what?" Twisting and pulling only made him tighten his grip.

"We're a foraging unit from Hilton Head. You Southerners have to learn you're in a Federal occupied area and stop—"

"But I'm no Southerner." The lieutenant's brown eyes narrowed in disbelief but Felicity continued. "I'm from New York. My name is Felicity Wentworth and I—" Felicity stopped when she saw one of the soldiers forcing Lucy and Ezra, with his rooster, down the stairs. "What are you doing with those children?"

"Found this contraband upstairs, lieutenant. There's another sick one up there."

"These children are not contraband." Felicity eluded the lieutenant's hand and swept over to Lucy, lifting the child in her arms. "They are my wards and I will not have them bullied."

"The little spitfire's got her a temper to match her hair. I like that in my women." The sergeant came into the hallway, a disgruntled Hattie in front of him.

"Go outside and see how many men the others have been able to gather up," the lieutenant said. "And leave those people here."

"Gather up for what?" Felicity marched back toward the officer. "I demand to know what's going on here."

"There was a pistol back there on a desk. It's loaded." Another of the soldiers stomped up the hall carrying the gun Devon left for her.

"This yours?" After examining the weapon handed to him, the lieutenant glanced up at Felicity.

"No. . . . Not exactly. It belongs to the owner of. . . . Who it belongs to isn't important. He's not here and I am. And I want to know what you all are doing here."

"I told you Miss. . . ."

"Wentworth."

"Miss Wentworth. We are a foraging party sent to collect food stuffs for the army and men to work at the naval yard at Hilton Head."

"Well, I haven't been here long, but I don't think there's any food to spare, or men either for that matter . . ." Felicity's voice trailed off when she realized the lieutenant wasn't listening to her at all. Instead, he went to the front door and swung it open.

"It appears you are misinformed about the state of Royal Oak," he said as he motioned toward the activity in the front yard. Several wagons were lined up across the crushed shell drive. Soldiers, mindless of the flowers they crushed, formed in a line. They hefted burlap bags on their shoulders, passing them from one man to the next.

"Found this rice under the smokehouse floor," the sergeant yelled. He spit out a stream of tobacco. "These Rebels ain't as smart as they think."

To the side of the house other soldiers prodded a group of perhaps ten black men, including Eb.

"You can't do this," Felicity whispered to no one in particular. "It isn't right."

But right or wrong didn't stop the soldiers from invading the house a second time. They pulled curtain's from the windows and pictures from the walls, spreading their destruction beyond the two front rooms. The sound of breaking china echoed through the house.

Felicity could do nothing but stand back and watch, a sick feeling in the pit of her stomach. She held Lucy in her arms and sheltered Ezra and Sissy as best she could. At least the lieutenant had allowed her to bring the sick child downstairs. But he'd refused to listen to any of her pleas to stop the carnage going on in the house. Not even when she'd pointed out the silver stuffed pockets of the soldiers.

A loud whoop sounded from upstairs and Felicity watched in horror as a soldier exploded down the stairs clutching her carpetbag. "Looky here what I found me," he yelled.

"Oh no you don't." Felicity shoved Lucy into Ezra's arms. "That is mine!" The pleasure on the soldier's thin face turned to surprise when Felicity launched herself at him. She yanked on the handle, almost managing to loosen his grip before he swung his arm. The back of his hand connected with Felicity's cheek, sending her flying against the stairs. She reached out and clutched the banister.

"That's not necessary, Corporal Sowers," the lieutenant said as he came through the front door.

"Damn woman came at me," Sowers offered up in defense of his actions.

Tears stung Felicity's eyes, and she wanted nothing more than to give in to a fit of anguished sobs. Instead, she swallowed, trying her best to ignore the pain in her jaw and moved forward toward the lieutenant. "That bag is mine," she said, surprised at the firmness of her voice under the circumstances. "I'm Felicity Wentworth of New York, and I came south to rescue those three children. I'm appealing to you as a gentleman to make certain we are returned home."

The lieutenant stared at her, appearing to see her for the first time. And Felicity had a moment of hope. But it was dashed when he shook his head. His mouth below the bushy blond mustache was a tight line. "I'm sorry ma'am if what you say is true—"

"It is true," Felicity said rushing forward and grabbing his hand. "My father is—"

"Unfortunately," he continued, "there's nothing I can do for you." He glanced down toward the corporal who was busy stuffing his pockets with gold coins. "Put the money back. We'll take the satchel with us to headquarters."

"But it's mine," Felicity repeated even though she knew they paid her no heed. Her shoulders slumped and she had another urge to give into those tears. With a sigh she sunk down on the bottom step as the corporal and lieutenant clomped out of the house. Whatever would she do now? She was stuck in South Carolina with almost no money, surrounded by Yankees who wouldn't help her. And totally at the mercy of a man who neither trusted or liked her . . . and *he* was Lord knew where. Maybe Devon Blackstone was lying dead someplace, the victim of a Yankee bullet.

The thought made her catch her breath and wring her hands. She was so distraught she didn't notice Hattie tapping on her arm at first. "What *do* you want?" she finally demanded of the rotund woman.

Hattie scowled at Felicity's sharp tone, but it didn't stop her from speaking out. "Them Yankees say they's takin' our slaves."

"Yes, I know." Felicity rubbed the area between her brows. She, who never suffered from ill health, had developed a terrible pain in her head. "There's nothing I can do," she said, explaining what she considered obvious. If she couldn't save herself or her belongings how could she possibly help Royal Oak's slaves?

"But they ain't."

"Ain't . . . aren't what?" Why didn't the woman just let her alone so she could think? Somehow she had to figure out a way to get herself and the children to the North.

"Ain't slaves. Them Yankees iz treatin' 'em like slaves and they ain't. None 'a us iz."

190

"What are you talking about?" Felicity stood and faced the black woman.

"Mast'a Devon, he done freed us all . . . last night. He done told us this mornin' 'fore he left for de fields."

"You're no longer slaves?" Felicity cupped Hattie's ample shoulders.

"No ma'am we ain't."

"The papers?" Felicity's hands tightened. "Did he give you papers that said this?"

"Yes'm but we done gives em back for him to keep. He done put them in the library."

Before Hattie finished her sentence Felicity was rushing toward the back of the house. The library was a mess with papers and books strewn everywhere. A quick glance showed that the pirate and his wife were pulled from the wall, but the portraits themselves seemed to be unscathed. And though they were thrown helter skelter at opposite ends of the room, Felicity couldn't help thinking they still appeared to be smiling at each other.

Shaking her head to dislodge that foolish thought, Felicity grabbed up a handful of papers. They were plantation reports and she quickly tossed them aside. Like a madwoman she searched through the littered floor for the papers freeing the slaves. But she could find them nowhere.

"Come on Devon. Where did you put them?" she murmured as she stood, hands on hips surveying the destruction of the room. Her gaze caught on the painting of Miranda, on the smiling blue eyes. They *were* looking at the pirate, and they seemed to be sharing a delicious secret.

"Of course." Felicity lifted her skirts and bolted toward the portrait of Gentleman Jack Blackstone. The gilt frame was heavier than she thought but Felicity managed to move it aside. There, tucked in the back of the frame, was a bundle of papers.

Scanning them quickly, Felicity assured herself they were the ones she sought. Then with a whoop of her own she raced through the house. The lieutenant was mounted, just lifting his hand to start the procession of wagons and men forward when she burst through the front door.

"Lieutenant, stop," she yelled, holding the packet high and waving them in the air.

Twisting in his saddle, he looked back at her. "I told you there's nothing I can do. I'm sparing the house because of who you say you are. Don't expect anything else."

"But this isn't about me." Felicity marched forward till she was beside the nervously prancing chestnut gelding. She shaded her eyes from the sun with her hand as she stared up. "It's about those men."

"What about them?"

"You can't just take them."

"They are contraband. I agree with General Butler at Fort Monroe. South Carolina doesn't consider herself part of the United States so she can no longer expect Federal laws to apply."

"But these men are not slaves. They are free men of color and as such cannot be hauled away against their will. These papers prove it." Felicity held up the packet. After a moment's hesitation the lieutenant took it. Looking inside he quickly scanned one of the letters of manumission.

"Interesting," he said tossing the papers back at Felicity. "But it makes very little difference. These men are accompanying me of their own free will." He leaned down. "Ask them if you don't believe me."

Not giving the Federal officer time to change his mind, Felicity hurried back along the line. She recognized Eb, the only person she knew, in the second wagon. "Are you leaving because you want to? You can tell me the truth," she added because he seemed uncomfortable that she'd stopped in front of him.

"Ain't nothin' here for me Miz," he said. "The soldiers promise to pay me good money. Ain't never had that before. Mast' Devon, he done set me free, but I needs more than that. I needs some money." He pulled a battered straw hat down over his eyes. "Ye tell Mast' Devon Eb's sorry."

"I shall." Felicity stepped back as the wagon started rolling. "I'm sure he'll understand," she said, though, of course, she had no idea how he'd feel about any of this.

And she had no time to ponder Devon Blackstone. The dust hadn't settled on the wide allee of majestic oaks before Lucy was by her side, tugging at her skirts. "What is it, honey?" Felicity reached down to touch the child's tangled braids.

"It's Sissy," came the small voice.

Felicity rushed into the house to see the older girl on the floor, struggling for breath as coughs seized her slender body. Grabbing her by the shoulders, Felicity pulled her to a sitting position, holding her while the attack subsided. With a sigh of relief, the child rested her head against Felicity's breast. Closing her eyes, Felicity tightened her arms around Sissy's frail body, trying to impart to the child some of her own waning strength.

But when she finally lifted her lashes, Felicity realized there were more battles to be fought. Perhaps a dozen people stood in the hallway. And all eyes were on her.

"What you plannin' to do now?" Hattie asked, her hands on their customary perch at her waist.

"Do . . . ?" Felicity swallowed. "I don't know."

Her answer apparently wasn't satisfactory for the Negroes, all women and girls except for Ezra, appeared surprised. They looked at each other, and mumbled under their collected breath.

"Well, I suppose we should wait for Captain Blackstone." Felicity had an awful vision of him never returning. Perhaps he just decided to leave after granting his slaves their freedom. After all, he never had promised to do anything for Felicity. Maybe he was on his way back to Charleston right now. And she was stuck here.

Or . . . Felicity tried not to think about the other reason he might not return. The area was obviously full of Federal soldiers. Soldiers who probably wouldn't think twice about killing a blockade runner. Of course they wouldn't know he

194

was a blockade runner, but they'd assume he was the enemy—didn't the lieutenant think as much of her?

Felicity pushed to her feet. She couldn't think about the possibility of Devon Blackstone being dead. Or even that he wasn't going to return.

And something had to be done now.

"Ezra." Felicity motioned toward the boy. "Take Sissy upstairs to bed. And mind, put some pillows under her head so she doesn't get to coughing again."

"Yes'm. You wants I should stay with her?" Ezra looked up from gathering his sister in his arms.

"No." Felicity swiped some strawberry blond curls off her face. "That will be . . ." she glanced down to the child standing at her side. "Lucy's job. Do you think you can handle that, sweetheart? Now you'll have to let us know if Sissy needs anything. Just like you did earlier."

The little girl's dark eyes were serious as her head bobbed up and down in agreement.

"Good." Felicity gave her a pat on her back as she followed her brother and sister up the stairs. One problem temporarily taken care of . . . and many more to go. Felicity took a deep breath and wished she had some experience handling things . . . anything. But her father and Arthur had relegated her to a position like her mother's. She was to look pretty and be sweet and sociable.

Not that Felicity had minded.

Before the war, before Arthur died and her father

turned to the abolitionist movement with the fervor of a zealot, Felicity had enjoyed her life. It was pleasant and simple. Nothing like the situation she found herself in now.

"Is there any food left?" she asked, putting her mind to the problems at hand.

"Some. Masta' Devon had us put some rice back in a shed near the swamp. But it ain't enough to feed everyone for long."

"We'll worry about that later. Are there any wagons left?" This inquiry was met by a shrug. "Ezra, go see if you can find a wagon, or cart, anything to bring the rice to the main house."

"Course, there's the boy's rooster. He be a tough old bird, but I guess I done eat worse."

"Ye ain't eatin' Mast'a Cock!"

Master Cock? She didn't know the rooster had a name. Felicity couldn't help smiling . . . until she noticed the stricken expression on Ezra's face. "We won't be eating Mr. Cock," at least not for a while, Felicity amended silently. "Now run along, Ezra. The rest of you come with me. We'll see what, if anything, is left."

By early evening the rice was brought to the house and some of it was boiled up with a slab of fatback the Yankees missed when they cleaned out the secret cache in the smokehouse. Several bags of cornmeal were also discovered in a cabin, and there were vegetables in the kitchen garden that the soldiers overlooked.

Felicity assembled Royal Oak's remaining residents in the dining room. The table was still intact, though several long gouges marred the polished mahogany finish. By looking through the house, enough chairs were found in one piece to seat everyone except Sissy and Felicity. They took their simple meal upstairs, Felicity helping the girl take bites between her coughs.

"We really gonna go to see my momma," Sissy asked after a sip of milk—Ezra had found a cow when he was searching for the wagon.

Felicity hesitated only a moment. "Yes, yes, we are. Just as soon as you can travel we'll be on our way north."

"Maybe y'all shouldn't wait for me."

"Nonsense." Felicity swallowed and tried to keep her voice steady. "We . . . I need a few days to rest anyway. By that time you'll be feeling more yourself."

Sissy didn't say anything to that, but Felicity didn't think the girl was convinced. She ate only a few more bites of the rice, though Felicity tried to persuade her to finish her plate. After that the girl drifted off to sleep.

Dusk shadowed the room by the time Felicity stood and walked to the window. Lifting the curtain that hung cockeyed from the rod, she stared into the night's grainy darkness. "Where are you Devon Blackstone?" she whispered, trying her best to suppress the sob that quivered her voice.

She just couldn't believe he left her here. Besides, she'd spoken with Hattie again, and the woman was certain Captain Blackstone said he'd return. And he hadn't. The later it became the more certain it seemed there was some reason he couldn't.

"Maybe he was only captured," she mumbled, but realized that didn't make her feel any better than imagining he was dead. She thought about his smile and the green eyes that often seemed bright with devilment. And she left the room and wandered to the library.

No one was about and she imagined they'd all gone to bed. After lighting a candle she found on the desk, Felicity sat down and looked over the fireplace. She'd propped the portrait of the pirate on the mantel. More and more the man with the flowing golden hair reminded her of Devon Blackstone. Her gaze drifted across the room. And more and more Felicity found herself wishing the captain would look at her the way the pirate looked at his wife.

But that was ridiculous. What did she care how Devon Blackstone looked at her . . . or if he looked at her at all for that matter. He was the enemy. A rebellious secessionist. A profiteering blockade runner and slave holder to boot. No, Felicity remembered. He wasn't a slaveholder. Not anymore. But he used to be.

Besides, none of that meant anything one way or the other. She loved Jebediah. *He* was good and pure, worthy of her love and admiration. *He* preached against the evils of slavery, *He* was strong and wonderful and . . . Felicity slumped back in the chair and shut her eyes trying to conjure up a picture in her mind's eye of her beloved.

Long, thin face, Adam's apple . . . Felicity's brow furrowed as she concentrated on the wavery image. She could remember the mouth. Tight and stern. Not like Captain Blackstone's.

"Oh my goodness!" Her eyes popped open and she sat up straight. It was the Rebel she saw. His handsome face and powerful body swam before her when she closed her eyes, blocking out any vision of Jebediah. "This can't be!"

Shutting her eyes Felicity tried again, but again it was Devon's crooked grin that greeted her. "No." Felicity shook her head. "I don't want to think about you. The Yankee soldiers probably killed you anyway."

Felicity didn't realize how sad that thought made her till the faint echo of a horse's hooves drifted in on the night air through the open window.

Pushing herself up, Felicity dashed away a silly tear that escaped through her lashes. She pressed her hand to her chest, trying to slow the racing beat of her heart and started for the door. "It's about time he got himself back here," Felicity mumbled to herself. "The entire Federal Army marches through, taking the food and harassing all of us and where is he?" Since she had no idea how to answer that question, Felicity just quickened her pace down the wide hallway. She'd let him do the explaining . . . and it better be good. How dare he just ride off and leave her like he did?

She could hear his spurs on the porch now and resisted the urge to brush back her hair and smooth the wrinkles from her skirts. Why should she care how she looked for the Rebel? Nonetheless, the fact that she did made her grab the brass doorknob with extra zeal.

Felicity yanked open the door. "It is about time you returned. I was—" Her gasp cut off the rest of her words.

"Well now if it ain't the pretty little spitfire comin' to greet me. And it looks like you was expecting ol' Sergeant Poole, wasn't ye?" This outrage was punctuated by an evil chuckle as Felicity tried to slam the door.

With all her might Felicity pushed and shoved. Her lungs burned and her arms strained with the effort, but against the burly sergeant who'd stepped into the opening, the door wouldn't budge.

"Help! Ezra . . . someone!"

"Now we won't be needin' anyone else, will we girl?" The sergeant gave a shove, then reached around the edge of the door.

"Get your hands off me. Help! No, don't!" The sergeant's hamhock hand curved around Felicity's mouth and jaw. He smelled of sweat and unwashed flesh, and Felicity thought she'd be sick. But she ignored the nausea. She clawed at the hand, kicking and wriggling until a smack connected with her cheek. The pain stunned her into stillness.

The Yankee wrapped his arm around her waist. His breath was fetid as he leaned his head over her shoulder, hissing in her ear. "We can make this hard or easy, girl. Makes no never mind to me." With that he dragged her onto the porch. Felicity's heels skidded across the bricks and through tear clouded eyes she stared hopefully back toward the dark house. But there was no sign that anyone even knew of her struggle.

The night air was heavy with moisture and the sound of frogs and cicada. The sergeant dragged her past his horse and toward the empty barn. Now that the ringing in her ears stopped, Felicity desperately tried to think. There must be something she could do. But nothing came to her as the Yankee kicked open the door and flung Felicity onto the straw littered floor.

Though bruised and battered, once out of his clutches Felicity felt a sudden surge of power. She scurried to her feet as he turned to slam the door.

"Ain't gonna do ye no good to run." The sound of his voice was accompanied by the scrapping of a Lucifer. Felicity glanced back to see the flame blossom in his hand. He held the match high and it sent flickers of demonic fire and shadows blotching across his jowls. "I see ye, girl," he said as he yanked a lantern off its hook.

He blocked the door.

The only escape was up.

Felicity's mind seemed unable to function beyond those simple truths. With speed she didn't know she possessed, Felicity lunged toward the ladder leading to the loft. Splinters dug into her palms as she grabbed hold of a rung and began to climb.

Her breath came in painful gasps as she reached ever higher. Her eyes came level with the loft, then her chin.

201

Then the hand clasped around her ankle.

"No! No!" Felicity screamed and kicked, but the iron grip never faltered. And it was pulling her backwards. Felicity tumbled down in a tangle of skirts and petticoats. The sergeant grabbed her around the waist, breaking her fall and jerking her away from the ladder.

"Ain't no way you're gonna win, girl." He hit her again as she clawed at his face. "And I'm gettin' tired of being nice." He threw Felicity onto the floor, falling on top of her before she could scramble away.

His weight forced the air out of her lungs. She opened her mouth to scream, but no sound save a shattered whimper came out.

"That's a girl," he said, reaching between their bodies to jerk up Felicity's skirts. "You're gonna' like this."

Ten

The sergeant swore as Felicity's nails clawed down the side of his face. He stopped groping and settled his weight more fully on Felicity's abdomen. With his free hand he wiped down the grizzled whiskers, pulling his fingers away and staring at the smear of blood. "Why you no good Rebel whore. I'll show you what happens to the likes of you when the Union army rides through."

He lifted his arm, his fist clenched and Felicity turned her face, shutting her eyes and steeling herself for the blow.

But it never came.

Instead, the disgusting weight of his body disappeared. Felicity's eyes flew open in time to see the shocked expression on the sergeant's flabby face as he was yanked backward. "Devon." Felicity no more than breathed the name when she saw the captain's fist connect with the startled sergeant.

But she didn't have time to savor her rescue. Felicity scurried back through the straw to avoid having the sergeant's rump land on her legs.

The sergeant might have been surprised from behind, but he regained his composure quickly. With a burst of strength and a yell, he propelled himself at Devon. They fell to the floor in a tangle of arms and legs. They rolled till Devon landed on top, straddling the broad body with his legs.

His opponent's face was an angry red as he flailed his arms. Devon avoided the beefy right and landed a punch of his own on the Yankee's jaw. Stunned, the sergeant fell back, and Devon followed up his advantage. He wished he dared pull out his pistol and kill the bastard, but he couldn't risk firing a shot. Who knew how many other damn bluebellies were around?

Another satisfying crunch to the side of the head and the sergeant flopped back on the floor. Grabbing the tunic of his uniform with both hands Devon yanked him off the floor. Since there was no sign of fight left in him Devon let loose his hold.

Jerking his head around Devon looked toward Felicity. She sat, leaning against a stall, her face pale in the flickering light. Bruises were starting to mottle the perfection of her skin and her large eyes just stared at him.

"Are you all right?" Devon's breathing was still harsh, his chest heaving. When he'd ridden up to the house, taking a path through the trees, and saw the horse with the Federal saddle he'd been furious. Apparently he'd been right about Miss Felicity Wentworth all along. She was a spy after all . . . a spy meeting her contact at Royal Oak.

He'd played that scenario out in his mind as he crept to the barn, following the stream of light shining through the windows. But it only took one glance into the interior to realize how wrong he'd been.

"Felicity?" Devon leaned toward her. "Did he hurt you?"

"No." Red-gold curls fell over her shoulder as Felicity shook her head. Not the way she could have been if the captain hadn't come along. "I'm all right," she added.

"You're sure?"

"Yes." Felicity's eyes narrowed as she took in the captain's appearance. "Are you?" His shirt was torn down the front, held together only by the waistband of his pants. He was dirty and wet and she could see fresh cuts on his arms and chin.

"I've been better." Devon stood. After claiming the Yankee's pistol, he hauled him up by his tunic. "I ran into a Yankee patrol about dusk who took exception to my being in the neighborhood."

"What did you do?" Felicity rose and worked at brushing the straw from her clothes.

"I ran like hell, of course," Devon said, forcing a grin he didn't feel. There was something about this woman that made him want to protect her. He felt it from the first time he saw her, and ever since he'd collected his share of scrapes and bruises doing it. He didn't want to think about what would have happened to her if he'd been just a little later.

Felicity smiled, grimacing slightly when the mo-

205

tion hurt her sore lip. Her gaze drifted to the sergeant who Devon held at arm's length, his own pistol aimed point blank at the protruding stomach. "What . . . what are you going to do with him?"

Devon shrugged. "We'll tie him up for now. See if you can find me some rope."

"I ain't alone, you know." The sergeant spit into the straw. "The rest of 'em will come lookin' for me soon."

"Do you think he's right?" Felicity glanced around the side of a stall.

"'Course I'm right, little girl. The Union army's gonna be down on this place like a bird on a June bug. You'll be sorry then you weren't nicer to ol' Sergeant Poole."

"Could be," Devon agreed, toying with the trigger. "But you aren't going to be around to see it." Devon grinned into the Yankee's suddenly pale face.

"Are you . . ." Felicity swallowed. "Are you planning to kill him?"

"Don't you worry about it." Devon motioned toward Felicity. "Did you find anything to tie him with?"

"Some twine." Felicity held out a tangled ball. "But I don't think we should just shoot him. I mean, I know he's despicable and . . ." She couldn't help shuddering as she walked toward Devon, thinking about just how despicable the Yankee was, of what he tried to do to her. "But I can't just kill him."

"You won't have to. I will. Now bring me the

206

rope, and for God's sake don't get to close to him!"

But the warning came an instant too late. Before she knew what happened the sergeant reached out and grabbed her around the waist. With a jerk he hauled Felicity in front of him. There was a glimmer of light on steel, then a knife pressed into the soft flesh of her neck.

"Drop that gun, Rebel, or the little spitfire here's gonna get awful bloody."

Felicity could barely breathe. Her head was forced back against the soldier's coat but she could still see Devon. He hesitated, and Felicity had an awful moment when she questioned whether he planned to give up the revolver. But in the end he let it go and she heard it plunk to the floor with deadly finality.

"That's a good Rebel. Now kick it over here . . . gently."

Devon kept his eyes on the knife, on the honed edge that pressed against the pale skin, as he nudged the gun across the straw with the toe of his boot.

"Get it closer! You know I can't reach it over there!" The sergeant hiked Felicity closer, ignoring her moan of pain. At the same time Devon kicked the pistol hard, sending it toward the Yankee in a shower of straw. The soldier tossed Felicity aside and grabbed for the gun, just as Devon dove at him.

Both men went sprawling. Arms and legs locked

as they rolled across the floor trying to gain the advantage.

The pain in her hip told Felicity she wasn't dead. Tentatively she tried to sit up. Tears stung her eyes but she kept pushing. She'd thought for certain the soldier had slit her throat. But her fingers only encountered a few drops of blood when she wiped them down her neck. She only had an instant to thank God for saving her.

To her right the struggle on the floor captured all her attention. Felicity looked around frantically for some weapon to use against the Yankee.

Then she spotted the pistol.

Half hidden in the straw, its wooden handle gleaming, it seemed to beckon. On her knees she lunged forward, grabbing the gun. She'd only held a gun once before . . . the one the captain left for her, and this one was heavier. Aiming was difficult, especially when her target moved constantly.

Could she fire the gun?

"Please Devon, please," she begged under her breath for the captain to be victorious. She didn't want to shoot. But the sergeant still had hold of the knife, and though Devon's hand manacled his wrist, trying to maneuver the point away, the Yankee was tenacious. Finally with a grunt he leaned back, yanking his arm from Devon's grip, and lunged.

The impact of the bullet sent him reeling backward. A blossom of red spread over his dark blue tunic as he caved onto the floor.

Felicity stood amid the wispy smoke curls from

the barrel, not yet comprehending what she'd done. It wasn't until a warm hand covered hers, gently prying the gun butt from her fingers, that she looked up . . . up into Devon Blackstone's handsome face.

"Oh . . . no." Reality struck her as hard as Sergeant Poole's fist had. She'd shot . . . probably killed a man. With an anguished cry Felicity collapsed against the captain's chest. Her sobs grew louder when his arms settled around her. "I didn't want to shoot him," she mumbled, trying to gain control of her voice. "But I thought he was going to . . . to stab you. Is he . . . is he dead?"

Devon didn't have to check to know the answer to that. Whether by design or accident her bullet hit the Yankee dead center in the chest. He'd seen the last of this war.

"Well, is he?"

Her voice held a slightly hysterical pitch, and Devon was tempted to lie. But she'd discover the truth soon enough. And as much as he'd like to stand here comforting her, there were things that needed to be done—and the sooner the better. In the end, Devon had no choice. "He's dead," he said, hesitating only a moment when he heard her whimper. "You did what needed to be done." Devon dug his fingers into her wildly curling hair. "He wouldn't have stopped with killing me. You would've been next. Then anyone in the house he came across."

Felicity pulled away enough to fix her watery

stare on the man who held her in the circle of his arms. "Do you really think so?"

"Yes, I do."

Devon watched as a level of composure settled across her face. He wished he could hold her longer, could caress her and tell her how frightened . . . how murderously angry he was when he saw what the Yankee was doing to her. He'd kiss her and love her and show her how different making love was from what that animal had in mind for her.

But there wasn't time. Every second he hesitated put Felicity and Royal Oak in more jeopardy.

"Where are you going?" Even though the night was warm and close, the loss of his strong body pressed to hers sent a chill through Felicity. She tried not to glance toward the lifeless form of the blood covered sergeant as she watched Devon go to the door. He peered out through the opening, then looked back. "He could have been telling the truth about not being alone."

"There were others with him this morning." Felicity kept her eyes trained on Devon's face. "They were here. They took all the food and most of the men. But I don't think they were like . . . him."

Devon ignored this last remark. "I'm not surprised they were at Royal Oak. Yankees are swarming all over the area."

"They were commandeering food and workers for their naval station at Hilton Head. Your men went with them voluntarily. I told the lieutenant you'd freed them, but he offered them wages. I suppose they . . . What are you doing?" Her eyes widened as she watched Devon lean over the Yankee.

"Getting rid of the body." Devon grunted as he heaved the dead weight over his shoulder. "Damn, he's bleeding like a stuck pig. Douse the—"

"Wait a minute." When her words had no effect, Felicity ran to the barn door and spread her arm across the opening. "You can't just . . . get rid of him. We need to contact someone. The authorities."

Devon arched his brow and hiked the sergeant higher on his shoulder. "You mean the Yankees?"

"Well . . . yes. The lieutenant was a fairly reasonable man. I'm certain if we explained to him what Sergeant Poole had in mind he'd. . . ."

"Sure he would, Miss Wentworth. I'm sure if he knew the circumstances he'd give us both a whole trunk full of medals, too. Now get rid of that damn light. We'll have the entire Union army down on us if we aren't careful." With that Devon pushed past her.

"Did you hear me?" Felicity picked up her skirts and raced after him. "What you're doing is wrong."

Devon stopped abruptly. Shifting the sergeant's dead weight he turned on Felicity. Starlight reflected off her golden hair but he couldn't see her expression. No doubt it was sincere. "Wrong? You pick this out to be wrong? Hell, everything is wrong. But it will be a damn sight more wrong if we don't get rid of this . . . this. . . . Never mind he'd been in the Navy half his life, Devon couldn't think of a term foul enough to describe the man weighing down on him. "Now do what I said, and hurry up about it."

She had no choice. For a split second Felicity stood still in the stable yard trying to decide what to do. But in the end, she raced back into the barn and extinguished the light.

A sliver of moon was playing hide and seek with the clouds. By the time Felicity ran back outside she could barely make out anything save the large shadowy shape of the main house. She stood, trying to catch her breath, looking about for some sign of the captain. Had he just left her?

"Devon." The name was softly spoken, but seemed to carry on the moisture laden air.

"Over here."

Her gaze followed the sound of his voice. She finally managed to make him out by the house. She hurried to the hitching post at the foot of the wide porch steps. Captain Blackstone stood by the tethered horse. With a flick of his wrist, he untied the reins and began leading the animal away from the house. The sergeant lay face down across the saddle.

"Get inside," he said. "I'll be back directly."

There was no room for argument in his tone, but that didn't stop Felicity. "Wait a minute," she said, when she caught up with him. "I . . . killed him." Felicity swallowed and forced herself to point to the man sprawled across the saddle. "I shall confess."

Her pronouncement didn't meet with the reaction she'd hoped. The captain just kept walking. He sounded tired as he again ordered her back to the house.

"I won't," Felicity insisted as they started along the path they used when they came to Royal Oak. Was it only yesterday? "Listen to me. Certainly the lieutenant knows what kind of man Sergeant Poole was. He'll have to understand."

"He'll understand one thing. His sergeant is dead and a Southerner killed him."

"You're wrong." Felicity batted at a vine that smacked into her face as she tried to keep up with the captain. "He'll believe me."

"You can't be that naive." Devon left the path, pressing ahead as much from memories of boyhood adventures in the swamps as any clear sense of sight.

"Naive." There was no path now, and Felicity struggled to keep close to Devon, fearing she'd be swallowed by the enveloping undergrowth if she left his side. "I am not naive." Oh how she wished her words were true, but Felicity had long suspected she was. Certainly her trip south seemed to corroborate his opinion. But after seeing Esther's three children Felicity couldn't believe she wouldn't do it all over again.

But did doing it over include killing a man?

Felicity pushed that thought aside. "You don't understand."

"It's you that seems unable to grasp some simple facts." The ground beneath Devon's feet became spongier with each step he took. "This is war, Red. And we're in the middle of occupied territory." The underbrush was reedy and cordgrass parted as he moved forward. "There wouldn't be any civilized questions or trial."

"So you say. But I'm still willing to take my chances." Certainly if she took a life there should be some penalty to pay.

"Maybe so. But I'm not willing to risk Royal Oak, or any of its people."

"But—"

Devon stopped abruptly at the edge of a waterway that snaked its way, dark and foreboding, through the marshy grasses. "If the Yankees even suspected one of their own was killed here they'd burn this place down. We're damn lucky they haven't already. Most of the plantations around here aren't as fortunate."

"And they'd terrorize anyone they found here . . . black or white." Devon reached up, grabbing the sergeant by his belt. "Now maybe you want that on *your* conscience," he said as he pulled. "But I sure the hell don't."

Felicity didn't either. Which is why she said nothing as he dragged the sergeant to the edge of the water and with a nudge, rolled him in. The body splashed into the dark water, sinking slowly beneath the surface.

Felicity wanted to look away, but she couldn't. She watched by the light of the new moon till there was not a ripple left. She took a deep breath. "Shouldn't we say . . . something?"

214

Devon stopped, his arms half out of his torn and bloody shirt. He met her gaze. "You want to say something, say it." He'd officiated over more burials at sea than he cared to remember. And he always felt moved to say a few words about each of his sailors. But he had nothing but contempt for this man. Apparently Felicity couldn't think of much good to say either.

A mumbled, "May he rest in peace," was all she offered. "What are you doing now?"

"Getting rid of this saddle." With a jerk he relieved the animal of the extra weight. Balling up his shirt he stuffed it in one of the saddlebags, tossing it all into the water. "We'll hide the horse till morning when we leave."

"Leave?" Felicity hurried after Devon, who was already leading the horse back the way they'd come. "But we can't go back so soon. Sissy is still very weak."

"Then we won't take her."

"Oh, but we—"

Devon turned so quickly Felicity ran into his chest. "Tomorrow those Yankees are going to be looking for their sergeant. Hopefully they'll think he deserted. But we can't count on that. If he bragged to anyone about what he planned to do, we can however count on them coming back here. It would be better for everyone and for Royal Oak if we were no longer around."

"You're right," Felicity said.

"What? Did I hear you correctly? Are you actually agreeing with me?"

215

Felicity couldn't see well enough to read his expression, but she imagined he was grinning. With an annoyed flounce of her head she marched ahead, starting off into the underbrush.

"Red." She heard the disgusting nickname and ignored him until she felt his hand on her arm. "The house is this way."

His breath was fetid and his weight suffocated her. No matter how she squirmed or pushed he wouldn't go away. Felicity begged, she pleaded, but he only laughed and continued to push her down further and further into a vortex of groping hands and tangled legs. "No. Oh, no, no, please don't!" Felicity cried over and over again.

Then suddenly she was lifted up against something hot and hard. Even in her fear she recognized the smell, the feel of the man who held her.

"Red. Red, wake up. It's only a dream."

His voice was strong and comforting, and Felicity reached out, clutching the arms that held her. "Don't let me go. Please, don't let me go."

"I won't, honey. Just hold on to me."

And she did, crying and sobbing while Devon rubbed her back and patted her hair. She'd come into the house with hardly a word to him after they'd cleaned up the blood in the barn. She'd insisted upon going directly to bed and that she was no longer upset about what happened this evening. Now he knew the truth. Her screams had awakened him as he lay sleeping in the next room.

"Don't let him get me," she sobbed.

"I won't. You're safe." As safe as he could make her surrounded by the Yankee army. But he didn't think she'd begrudge him the lie. Anymore than she'd question the way holding her made him feel. In the nether lands of night, nothing seemed real.

Yet her next words showed that she hadn't lost touch with reality. She pulled away enough to look into his face. "I killed him," she said, her voice calmer than he expected.

"You saved my life." Devon dug his fingers through her thick hair, framing her pale face with the heels of his hands. "You had no choice," he added, more forcefully. "No choice."

The new moon had risen, washing the room with the palest of silver glow. But it was enough light for Devon to see her eyes, large and fringed by tear-spiked lashes, her small nose and the generous mouth. Her bottom lip quivered and his hands tightened. "Tell me you understand."

"I do," Felicity whispered. "I do." He seemed pleased by her words but he didn't let her go. His hands continued to cup her face, his thumbs tracing an arc, brushing away the dampness of her tears. The moment lengthened, heightened, and still Felicity could not pull her gaze from his.

His face was inches from hers. Just as it was when he comforted and consoled. But his expression no longer offered either. He looked at her in a way that made her feel shivery and hot at the same time. It was as if the air between them was electrified, like the still before a summer storm.

217

His movements slowed and Felicity swallowed, though her mouth felt dry. Awareness swept over her. He sat on the side of her bed, naked to the waist. Nothing separated his muscled chest from her body except the thin material of her shift.

Her breathing slowed, matching his. Felicity was certain he could read her thoughts when she noticed the slight curve of his mouth as he angled her chin up. And she didn't care.

Her mind preached caution. But the message sounded stilted and oh so boring compared to the dimples deepening on Devon's cheeks. Her hands moved forward, past the strong rack of his ribs, up across his hair-roughened chest. Reality was sharp-edged and painful. Here surrounded by the gossamer sway of mosquito netting was the promise of sensual delight . . . a reprieve from harsh memories.

Devon sucked in his breath as her fingers caressed his skin. His body tingled and the will power it cost him not to pull her against him was something he didn't know he possessed. Her nail skimmed across his nipple, either by chance or design, and he moaned.

Then her eyes dropped to his chest and she jerked her hands away. "Oh, I hurt you?" Felicity felt her face flush and she wished the feather mattress would open and swallow her. She may have been the belle of New York, but she knew nothing of seduction.

"Felicity."

It sounded strange to hear him say her name.

He forever called her that annoying name, Red. Yet she didn't respond till he said it again.

"Look at me."

Slowly Felicity lifted her lashes. There was no mistaking the desire in his gaze. "What?"

"Touch me."

His words were like a key that unlocked her inhibitions. Without further prodding Felicity reached out, giving free reign to her passions. His skin was hot, slick with sweat and the feel of it did strange melting things to her insides. Felicity traced the curve of his collar bone all the while meeting his gaze. When her fingers drifted down over the hard nub of his nipple there was no doubt this time of her intention. Devon's eyes closed, then opened as he drew her face closer.

"Are you sure you know what you're doing?" he asked, his breath a warm mingle with hers.

She didn't know anything except if he didn't kiss her this instant she would shatter into a million pieces. Her fingers tightened in the hair on his chest and she tugged, pulling him closer in response. His lips met hers and any grasp she held on reality splintered away.

His mouth was hot and hungry, devouring her in a way that sent devastating desire singing through her veins. Felicity clutched at him, urging him closer. She didn't protest when he levered her down onto the pillow, his own body following to cover hers.

His mouth left hers, forging a trail of flaming kisses down her chin and neck. Felicity arched up long before he reached the tip of her breast. Through the thin cotton he bit and suckled, sending the spirals of passion spinning higher.

"God, I've dreamed of this." His fingers caught in the fragile fabric, tearing it aside till his eyes feasted on the rose-tipped splendor of her breasts. The rasp of his day's old whiskers sent shivers down her spine and Felicity writhed on the sleep-rumpled sheets.

"Tell me if I hurt you." Devon lifted his head to stare into her eyes. She looked passionate and wanton . . . far removed from the woman who had nightmares and cried in his arms. But he didn't want to do anything that would remind her of the Yankee sergeant. If anything, he wanted to erase that horrid memory from her mind. To replace it with the sensual delights he knew they could have together.

Felicity couldn't imagine what he was talking about. Hurt? Nothing he did hurt her in the least. She'd never felt so wonderful. Felicity filtered her fingers through his hair, bringing his lips back to hers. When his tongue plunged into her mouth, she greeted his flesh with equal fervor, demanding as good as she gave.

She was an eager student, especially with such an enjoyable game. Soon her tongue parlayed with his, flirting, and teasing till he ravished her mouth like a man possessed. With a flick of his wrist the rest of her shift was stripped away.

He jerked his mouth away from hers, heaving in a frantic gulp of air. Devon's eyes feasted on her naked beauty for a brief moment before he was rasping kisses across her breasts, from one puckered tip to the other, then down the smooth line of her stomach. The golden delta at the apex of her legs beckoned . . . enticed.

The first plunge of his tongue was aggressive. He felt her startled response, the push of her hands on his shoulders. But his hold on her thighs was firm. He touched her again, more gently this time. Then again. Back and forth across the sensitive bud. Her body relaxed, then tightened. Devon was conscious of her groans and they sounded like a siren's song to him, sending him ever higher.

The first waves of pleasure forced a cry from her lips. Her hands thrust out, first grabbing the sheet, then clawing at his shoulders. Hotter and harder, the ecstasy came until Felicity lost all sense of time or place.

Devon didn't think he'd ever been harder or more aroused. He fumbled with the front of his pants, finally freeing the part of him that most ached for fulfillment.

He could wait no longer.

Her orgasm was wild and unfettered and his body demanded the same. She was an accomplished lover and his one desire was to bury himself deep inside her. She was wet and ready. He slipped up her body, melding his mouth with hers as he guided her legs around his hips.

His first thrust was deep and hard. And he didn't realize until it was too late, that her passion did not come from experience. But the thin barrier of her maidenhead was no match for his ardor. He was through, expanding into her before he could stop himself.

She made only a slight noise, and then she was moving with him, milking him with her body. Devon's release was strong and complete. Drained and replete he collapsed on top her. He lay there trying to compose himself, trying to form an apology for the savage way he took her. If he'd known she was a virgin . . . If she'd told him.

But he had it in his mind from the beginning that she was a spy, or the very least a woman who used her body to gain favors from men. Well, if she was, he was the first and she'd asked for nothing.

Devon lifted his head and stared down at her. She looked sweet and innocent, with her wide blue eyes, and he felt like a cad. "Red . . . Felicity . . . I don't know exactly what to say."

"I don't either." It hadn't taken long for reality to come crashing down on Felicity, and with it the enormity of what she'd done. She blinked up at him. "I don't think Jebediah is going to understand."

"Well, this type of thing isn't easy to explain," Devon began before the entirety of her words registered. When they did he paused, and raised himself higher on his elbows. "Who in the hell is Jebediah?"

Eleven

"You heard me," Devon insisted because she just lay there looking at him, her eyes wide. "Who is Jebediah?" He rolled away and sat up, surprised by his own insistence. Why should he care so much that she had to explain their love making to another man? She was nothing to him but a woman who happened to be thrown in his path . . . repeatedly. A nuisance. A beautiful nuisance. But a nuisance all the same. He would see her back to Charleston and that would be the end of it.

Scrunching up higher on the pillow, Felicity swiped hair out of her face and yanked at the sheet. The cotton wouldn't budge till she gave Devon a pointed look. He arched his brow, then reluctantly shifted his weight. With a sigh of relief, Felicity pulled the sheet over her breasts. Once she had herself covered she felt some sense of decorum return.

However her torn shift was still in plain view and the captain seemed not the least modest as he sprawled beside her. Felicity tried to keep her eyes straight ahead while she sorted out in her mind what just happened.

But she didn't have the luxury of deep thought. The captain tucked his finger beneath her chin, forcing her to turn and meet his gaze. Oh, why had she mentioned Jebediah? Felicity took a deep breath and swallowed. "He's my betrothed," she said.

"Your betrothed?" The question ended on a note of disbelief.

"Well, sort of. He will be when I return."

"To Richmond?"

"Ah . . . yes." For some reason—perhaps the memory of the way they'd held each other—the lie seemed harder to tell.

Devon turned his head. The first hint of dawn paled the window, and the morning birds had started their chatter. So the woman he suspected of being a Union spy appeared to be anything but. There really were children that she seemed intent upon taking back to their mother. She was a virgin. And she was engaged to be married.

He should be pleased that she didn't have traitorous intentions toward the Confederacy. Relieved that she would be out of his life soon. But damned it what he felt wasn't a far sight from relief.

He took a deep breath. "It would probably be best if you didn't relate this . . . incident to your betrothed."

Felicity glanced his way. "I suppose you're right.

But . . ." She felt her face heat, but didn't look away. "Won't he know?"

She was earnest and so obviously embarrassed by her question that Devon couldn't help taking it seriously. After all, he was the more experienced of them. "Not necessarily. You ride, don't you?"

"Occasionally."

"Ever astride?"

"Not till I came down here."

"That's enough." Devon reached out to touch her cheek. "If he loves you . . . if he wants to marry you, I don't think he'll question it." He paused. "What's the matter?"

"Nothing." Felicity lowered her lashes. She couldn't believe she was having this conversation . . . or that the Rebel was being so understanding. And then there was what he said. The truth was Jebediah didn't want to marry her. Not now at least. But she couldn't tell Captain Blackstone that. She just couldn't.

When she looked back up a scowl had darkened his expression. "What's wrong?"

"This Jebediah. What in the hell is he doing letting you travel alone in the middle of a war? Doesn't he have any sense?"

"Of course he does." Felicity bristled. "He's very sensible. And intelligent. And good," she added, pulling the sheet to her chin. "And he loves me very much. Very much. So does my father." This she delivered with added vehemence.

"Well then why in the hell—"

"They didn't know I was going to come. No-

225

body did." Felicity tilted her head to look at him. "I wanted to do this by myself."

"Well it was a pretty dumb idea, if you ask me." Devon threw his long legs over the side of the bed.

"I don't recall anyone asking you," Felicity said, holding on to the sheet when he gave it a tug.

"Fine. Keep it." Devon let go of the sheet that he'd planned to wrap around his waist, and stood. "I'm not embarrassed by my body." He faced her, hands on hips.

"I'm not either." Felicity lifted her chin . . . but held onto the cotton fabric. She met his eyes with her own, staring him down, even when the one corner of his mouth turned up and his dimples appeared. It wasn't until he reached down for his pants that Felicity let her gaze drift—down. He was a fine looking man . . . all of him.

Felicity tried not to squirm, and by the time he looked back up her stare was fixed squarely on his face.

"It's getting light," he said, motioning toward the window where the morning rays streamed through the dusty window panes. "We need to be leaving soon."

"But—"

"We don't have any choice, Felicity. We can travel most of the way by boat. Sissy should do fine."

Felicity sighed. He was right about one thing. She seemed to have no choice. "I'll get ready . . . as soon as you leave."

Sitting on the edge of the bed, Devon yanked his pants on. "I'm going to go rouse Hattie and the others. We need to work out what's best for them. I'll be downstairs when you're ready."

Felicity sat staring at the closed door long after he'd disappeared through it. Everything seemed surreal—the early morning light filtering through the mosquito netting, the smell of magnolia and jasmine. And her in bed, naked beneath the sheet, still feeling satiated and replete from making love with a Rebel. How could her life have taken such a turn?

But a holler from downstairs reminded Felicity that she didn't have time to ponder the things that happened to her since she left New York. She jumped from the bed. Her shift was hopelessly torn and Felicity tossed it aside, trying not to think about how that came to be. After hurriedly searching through the lacquered clothespress she found some underclothes and a clean, serviceable gown that fit reasonably well.

Next she tied back her hair as best she could. Before she left the room Felicity reached beneath the mattress and found the few gold coins she'd secreted there before the Yankees came. They were a far cry from the amount of money she started her trip with, but that couldn't be helped.

The rooster was strutting around, crowing loudly and the children were already up. Sissy's cough seemed a little better and she smiled shyly when Felicity ask after her health.

"She done slept most all the night," Lucy offered, racing up to Felicity and giving her legs a squeeze. "Is we gonna see Mama today, Miz Felsy? That's what Masta' Devon done said."

"He was in here already?" Felicity scooped the child into her arms, smiling when she nodded her head vigorously.

"He said we was goin' on a trip . . . a boat trip."

"He was right." Felicity glanced over toward Ezra, who stood holding his pet rooster, his eyes trained at something out the window. He'd yet to say a word. "And how are you this morning, Ezra?" she inquired.

He glanced up, continuing to stroke the bird's red comb. "It don't seem right."

"What doesn't?" Felicity lowered Lucy to the floor, scooting her off with instructions to gather anything she wanted to take with her. Then Felicity joined Ezra across the room.

"You takin' us north. You bein' a white woman and all."

"Well, I can assure you it is right." Felicity took one of his hands in hers. "Once we reach . . ." Felicity hesitated, realizing it probably wasn't a good idea to tell him their final destination . . . since the captain didn't even know. "Once we reach your mother you won't have to worry about belonging to anyone again. No man will call himself your master."

The dark eyes looked up at her earnestly, but Felicity didn't think he completely understood. And she didn't have time to explain it to him now.

"Just trust me," she said, and gave his hand a squeeze. "For now, I need your help. Can you come with me? I have something for you to carry. And we must hurry."

Felicity wasn't certain when the idea had come to her, but she realized it was something she must do. So she lifted her skirts and rushed down the stairs, followed by Ezra and his rooster. Devon and most of the other servants were in the parlor and didn't notice Felicity as she hurried down the hall and into the library.

"What ye doin', Miss Felicity?" he asked as she lugged at the heavy gilded frame.

"I'm saving a pirate," was all she said, before motioning for him to help her.

"So there you are." Devon strode into the dining room where Felicity and the three children sat around the table. They were each finishing a bowl of rice. "Are we ready?"

"Yes. Oh, yes we are." Felicity jumped up, embarrassed because her response was too enthusiastic. It was difficult for her to look at the captain without remembering what it felt like to be in his arms. And that was a memory best forgotten. Like the sergeant. Which was why she knew Devon was hurrying everyone along. He wanted to be gone before the Yankees came snooping back, looking for the missing sergeant.

"Good. Let's go then. Here." He tossed a burlap bag of provisions—all he dared take from the meager supply left at Royal Oak—toward Ezra. The boy deftly caught it with the free hand not holding the scrawny rooster. At first Devon wondered how the boy had managed to keep the cock from the chopping block. But after closer examination it didn't look like there was enough meat on the bird to feed a flea.

After pulling out the chair Devon scooped Sissy into his arms. Felicity grabbed Lucy's hand and they were off.

Outside, several of Royal Oak's people still milled around, seeming not to know what to do with their new freedom. Devon wished he could do something else to help them. But their freedom and a share of what supplies where left at Royal Oak was all he could do.

Devon settled the girl under the first spreading oak of the allee. With hands on hips he turned to take a last look at Royal Oak. The gleaming white walls and stately columns seemed to be rising from the early morning mist off the river. He always loved this house. Always thought of it as home. Even after he'd been in the Navy for years, when he was at sea for long periods of time, he'd feel twinges of homesickness for the low country plantation.

"Royal Oak is in your blood," his grandmother always told him. "Just as surely as the scent of saltwater draws you away, the feel of low country mud between your toes will call you home."

Devon shook his head. It had been years since Grams said that but the memory was as clear and bittersweet as if she were at his side now. Well, it would take more than low country mud to get him back here again. He was probably getting his last look at the house that had been home to generations of Blackstones. It amazed Devon how deeply sad this moment made him.

"You'll come back." Felicity didn't have any idea what made her say that. Any more than she knew why she laid her hand on his arm. He looked down at her and Felicity had to stop herself from wrapping her arms around him.

"Do you think so?" A sad smile, so unlike his usual devilish grin, curved his lips.

"I do," Felicity said with more determination than she felt. How was she supposed to know what would happen? Nothing was as she imagined anymore. If the world was as it should be she would be asleep in her bed at Wentworth House. She'd be dreaming of all the beaux who'd begged for a place on her dance card the previous night. But that life seemed so far away . . . and so frivolous.

Felicity swallowed back the tears clogging her throat. If she didn't watch it she would burst out crying. She straightened her shoulders. "Don't you dare give up hope, Devon Blackstone," she said, surprised when he threw his head back and laughed. "What? What's so funny?" Here she'd tried to be supportive and he . . . he thought it was a joke.

"Nothing, Red." Devon sucked in his breath, and shook his head. On impulse he lifted her into a quick hug. Before setting her back on the ground he kissed her full on the lips. "It's that you sounded just like Grams when you said that."

Felicity tried to regain her composure. The kiss had been anything but passionate. Still, she felt flustered and tingly. Her hands flew to her cheeks, which Felicity was sure were bright red. And then she realized what Devon said. "Your grandmother?" Felicity's voice rose to a screech.

"Yep." Devon gave the house a cocky salute, then turned to lift Sissy.

"But she's an . . . an old . . ." Felicity couldn't think of how to describe the elderly lady—not to her grandson anyway. Especially to the grandson Felicity depended on to take care of her and the children.

But he didn't seem to take any offense at her sputtering. If anything he seemed to find it humorous. "Battleax," he offered. "Harridan?"

"Well, I didn't exactly mean that," Felicity protested, though in truth she'd thought of her as much worse.

"Really?" Devon glanced back and arched his brow as he led the way down the path to the side of the house. "Most people view her that way."

"Perhaps she *is* a little opinionated." Felicity grabbed Lucy's hand and followed.

"She is that," he chuckled. "Grams always says what she thinks. But she has a heart of gold. '

Felicity was just as glad the captain didn't turn to see her expression when he said that.

"And she's smart." Devon paused, shifting Sissy

higher against his chest. He glanced back at the house through the veil of gray wispy moss. "I think that's what made the Blackstone family so strong."

Felicity's gaze followed his as she waited for him to continue. As the sun rose over the tops of the stand of pine and hardwoods to the east of the house, it cast a glow on the whitewashed walls. For a moment it seemed as if the house beckoned her. The feeling was odd but undeniable. Why should she care anything for a Rebel's plantation house in South Carolina? Felicity swallowed and forced herself to look away.

"What made the Blackstones strong?" she asked, to help rid herself of the strange urge to race back to the house.

"What did you say, Red?" Devon shook away the pull of his home and met her gaze. "Oh, about our family's strength." She was staring at him, her eyes, wide and intent, the soft color of rainwashed flowers. His heart beat faster. "It's the women we marry," he said, wondering if it were possible to drown in her eyes. "The Blackstone men always choose exceptional women as their wives."

"Starting with the pirate?" she asked, her words unexplainably breathless.

"Aye." Sissy had fallen asleep against his shoulder. Devon had the strongest desire to place her on the pine tag covered ground and reach out to the woman standing before him. Instead, he took a deep breath. "They all married well. Enriched the bloodline Grams says. Of course she was one of the women who married a Blackstone so she might be a bit biased."

"And what of you?" Lucy pulled on her hand and Felicity let her go.

"What about me?"

"Are you planning to marry an exceptional woman?" Why she asked, Felicity didn't know. If he were, it certainly wouldn't be her—not that she wanted it to be. Although told enough times to believe it that she was beautiful, Felicity knew looks weren't the positive traits Devon spoke of. Intelligence, strength of character, intrepid spirit. Those were the things he would look for in a wife. The characteristics his grandmother would approve. And in those areas Felicity considered herself the most unexceptional woman around.

"I might," Devon said with a grin. But as the dimples faded, his gaze left hers and focused on the house. "Though I doubt it really matters."

Felicity opened her mouth to argue his opinion, though she had no idea how she'd do that. But she was saved by a giggle coming from the child at her feet. Felicity glanced down and saw the little girl holding a caterpillar. The wiggly worm squiggled and turned, trying vainly to escape.

"We need to be going," Devon said, all traces of emotion erased from his voice. He was turned and three strides down the path before Felicity could rid Lucy of her pet and follow.

But he didn't get far before he encountered a small group off the path near the smokehouse.

"Masta' Devon suh." An elderly black man stepped forward, his battered straw hat clasped in his hands. "Could we be speakin' to ye a minute, suh?"

"Certainly, Ben. How you doing, Gabe, Mercy, Hattie?"

"We ain't good, Masta' Devon suh," Amos answered for all of them. "It ain't like we be complainin' but we ain't anxious to be leavin' Royal Oak." Gabe, a man with hardly a tooth in his head, and the white-haired Mercy nodded in agreement.

"I understand," Devon said. "I told you earlier, I'm not forcing you to leave. You're your own master now. It's going to be difficult at first . . . for everyone. But I've divided up all I have. The land is yours to use." Devon glanced away. "I wish there was some money to give you but I—"

"Would money help—" Of course it would, money always made things better. That was one lesson Felicity learned at her father's knee. "There's no need to answer." Felicity dug into her pocket, then held out the coins. "Here," she said. "It's for you and the others."

Ben looked at the gold shimmering in her hand, then up at Devon, who merely shrugged.

"Take it," Felicity said, when he continued to hesitate. "Devon, tell him it's all right."

"I think she means for you to have it, Ben. And if I were you I wouldn't cross her. Miss Felicity can be a powerful force when she sets her mind to it."

Felicity shot him a scowl. He was making light of her—powerful force indeed—but at least it worked. Ben held out his hand and Felicity plunked the money into his open palm. "That should do you all for a while." Till this war is over she wanted to say, but since her journey south she wasn't so certain this conflict would be resolved soon.

Devon seemed more sure that it would be a drawn out affair. He folded his fingers over Ben's wrinkled hands. "Use it sparingly. I can't promise there'll be any more. Take care of the rice, and it will take care of you. There's plenty of game, and fish." Devon paused, and smiled. "Listen to me. You're the one who taught me to catch my first crab."

"Near took your toe off too as I recall."

"That it did." Devon clasped the old man around his narrow shoulders. "Take care, Ben. You too, Mercy, Gabe." He gave Hattie a hug. "And remember, for your sakes as well as mine, I haven't been here since the war started."

"Yes suh, Masta' Devon. We ain't seed hide nor hair of ye."

Ezra was waiting by a small sloop when Devon, Felicity and the children reached the river. He sat, a piece of cordgrass sticking out of his mouth, his bony knees doubled up to his chin, petting Mast'a Cock. The rooster ruffled its feathers and crowed, but Felicity was too impressed with the boat to notice.

"Where did you manage to find this?" Felicity shaded her eyes and admired the boat. It had a rakish cut even though it was in need of paint.

"You forget, I'm a man of the sea," Devon replied with a wink. "Natee helped me build this years ago. When I left Royal Oak for the Navy, I moored it in one of the small inlets near here. One the Yankees haven't discovered yet."

"Well, it's very nice," Felicity said as he handed her into the bow.

"It should get us where we want to go." The sun was showing the time to be near nine o'clock. "I'd hoped to get an earlier start," Devon said as he pushed the boat into the current.

"At least there's been no sign of Yankees." Felicity never thought she'd dread running into her countrymen, but after last night so much had changed. Felicity paused as she arranged blankets under Sissy's head and glanced around. Was this where she and Devon dumped the sergeant's body last night? She'd been so disoriented in the dark she couldn't tell.

Shaking her head, Felicity pushed the subject from her mind. Devon was right. It was self defense. The sergeant would have killed them both if given the chance. Still she couldn't help wondering what Jebediah and her father would think of what she'd done. They were so pure . . . so pious.

"Did you hear me, Red?"

"What? Oh." Felicity glanced toward the stern where Devon had raised a small triangular sail. "I was thinking about . . . never mind. What did you say?"

"Better keep an eye on Lucy, or she'll be overboard."

Felicity twisted around. At the pointed front of the small boat Lucy stood, her head and arms out of view, folded over the bow, her tiny bottom sticking up in the air. "Oh, for heaven's sake. Lucy," Felicity called. She moved forward, keeping her body low so she wouldn't dangerously rock the boat. With her arm she circled the little girl's waist, pulling her back onto her lap.

"What are you doing, trying to feed some hungry alligator?" Felicity asked as she flipped up her skirt and dried the child's fingers with her petticoat. As soon as she'd said it Felicity knew her mistake.

"Is alligators gonna get us, Miz Felcy?"

"No, honey."

"But ye said—" Fat tears spilled over Lucy's lashes and rolled down her ebony cheeks.

"I just meant . . . don't cry." Now the petticoat was used to wipe Lucy's eyes. Felicity's gaze shot toward Devon who was sitting in the stern, his hand on the rudder.

"I think the ladies on my boat are insulting the captain and crew," he said in a booming voice. "Wouldn't you agree, First Mate Ezra?"

Ezra glanced back from his perch in front of

Devon. His hands stilled on the rooster's back. "I ain't sure what you mean, Masta' Devon."

"It's captain. And I'm referring to the fair lady passengers thinking we can't protect them from something like a little ol' gator. Why it's down right insulting."

Felicity caught the twinkle in his green eyes and couldn't help smiling. "Why we never meant any disrespect," she said in her best southern drawl. "Did we Lucy?"

Lucy sat on Felicity's lap. Her crying was temporarily quieted as she looked from Felicity to Devon and back.

"Was that it, Lucy? Are you thinking Ezra and I can't take care of our womenfolk? 'Cause if that's the case, I'm going to be mighty sad."

"Goodness." Felicity lifted the little chin with her finger, and looked into the child's face. "We wouldn't want to make Captain Blackstone unhappy, would we?"

Lucy shook her head vigorously.

"That's good," Devon said, puffing out his chest. "But you have to remember on a ship, the captain is boss. Everyone must do as he says. So you'll have to keep fingers and toes out of the water."

"Do you understand?" Felicity asked, as she gently brushed back the child's tightly curled hair. After Lucy nodded, Felicity gave Devon a look of thanks. He smiled in return and Felicity was struck with how much he reminded her of his pirate ancestor.

Sitting in the hull with the sun turning his hair

golden and the backdrop of dark water and stately cypress he cut a handsome figure. He was dressed only in tight trousers, boots and a loose fitting white shirt, that because of the heat was open half way down his chest. Dark curls showed in the V'd opening, spawning memories of how it felt when that hair brushed across her breasts.

Felicity's mouth went dry.

"What?" Devon cocked his brow as her eyes flashed up to his.

"I didn't say. . . ." Had she said something? Had she moaned? Felicity looked away quickly, her gaze catching on the mud-bank shore. "I was just wondering where we are. You didn't explain how we're getting to Charleston."

"One thing this area has going for it is its waterways. We can travel from Port Royal to Charleston and practically never enter open sea or cross land." Devon smiled. "And its a hell of a lot faster and easier than riding."

"Why didn't you come down this way?"

"I was chasing you."

Felicity shifted around to look at him. "Chasing?"

"Following is probably a better word. I couldn't imagine what you wanted at Port Royal."

"I told you about the children." The sweep of Felicity's hand took in all three of them. Sissy was asleep, her head padded by blankets. Ezra was hunched forward, a straw hat covering his eyes, and Lucy rested her head on Felicity's shoulders. Felicity figured she was napping too. Every once in a while she could hear a sucking noise coming from where two fingers were stuck in her mouth.

"You told me," Devon agreed. "But I didn't believe you."

"But—"

"I said *didn't*. Obviously I do now."

They were sailing through a narrow waterway cut like a ribbon in the swaying cord grass of a salt marsh. To the left, standing like sentinels, Felicity could see tall loblolly pines. She watched as a hawk circled overhead, buoyed by currents of air . . . and she debated telling Devon the truth . . . the whole truth.

She swallowed. "Devon, I . . ."

"I'm glad you found your Mammy's children," he said and Felicity couldn't bring herself to tell him she was an Abolitionist from New York.

"Yes . . . so am I." After that Devon lapsed into silence, and so did Felicity. The landscape changed as they sailed between overhanging cypress that filtered the sun. Before she knew it Felicity's head was nodding to the side, and her eyelids grew heavy. She'd gotten precious little sleep the night before and now she couldn't stay awake.

How long Felicity slept she didn't know but when she awoke it was to a loud rumbling sound, reminiscent of the gunshot that killed the sergeant. Her eyes flew open and she clutched Lucy as the boat lurched to the side. A sudden gust of wind whipped hair across her face. "What's happening?"

241

Felicity sat up, patting Lucy's head as she began to cry again.

"A storm," Devon yelled over the next peel of thunder. "It came on us fast. We need to find some shelter." As he spoke the first splattering raindrops fell on the boat's passengers. Sissy woke, coughing, and Lucy cried louder. Only Ezra seemed unfrightened as he helped Devon trim the sail.

"Where can we go?" All of a sudden the sky was a dark purple and the trees on shore nearly doubled over with the force of the wind. The waterway that had seemed so slow moving and tranquil when she fell asleep now bubbled and boiled, dashing the small boat about. Water sloshed into the bottom of the hull and Felicity joined Ezra in bailing as Devon manned the oars.

"Is we gonna die, Miz Felcy?"

Felicity took a moment to touch the child's cheek. "Of course not, Lucy. Don't you remember what the captain said about taking care of us?" But as the rain quickened, coming at them in blinding sheets, Felicity wished she had more faith in her own words.

Twelve

"Where are we?" Felicity stumbled ashore, then quickly reached back into the boat for Lucy. Devon had managed to reach shore despite the wind tossed waves and pouring rain. With Ezra's help he hauled the small craft higher onto the sand beside a dilapidated wharf.

"Up there," he yelled. "There's a house." He tossed the wet provisions toward Ezra and scooped Sissy into his arms. Felicity was trudging along, Lucy snuggled close to her breast when Devon caught up with them. He passed, forging ahead through the rain toward the plantation house. The wind whipped through the oaks and pines, a plaintive background for the booming thunder.

Wet leaves slapped at Devon's clothes, the path, once wide and well traveled was now overgrown, nearly reclaimed by the vegetation. The hair on the back of his neck prickled and Devon jerked around. "Get down," he screamed over the anger of the storm.

"We're coming," Felicity shouted back, unable to

understand him, surprised when the captain came plowing back at her. They fell in the mud amid flying arms and childish screams just as an ear-splitting crash sounded overhead. The sky exploded with sparks as lightning seared into the top of a loblolly pine. Branches, laden with needles and cones crashed to the ground.

"Are you all right?" Devon lifted his head when it seemed no more debris was likely to fall. He was sprawled over Felicity, the two girls and Ezra's head, which was the best he'd been able to do considering the split second timing.

"What . . . what happened?" Felicity's face was smeared with wet dirt and she felt bruised and battered.

"Lightning," came Devon's succinct reply as he helped them to their feet. Sissy was coughing, the sound coming from deep in her chest and Devon knew he needed to get her to shelter quickly. "Come on," he said as he turned to hurry along the trail.

Though it couldn't be more than late afternoon, the heavy cloud bank and blinding downpour made seeing difficult. It wasn't until another zigzag of lightning illuminated the sky that Felicity got her first look at the house that would offer them shelter. It was large with a two story portico. Dual stairs wound up to the entrance. After Felicity managed to drag herself and Lucy onto the porch they gained a degree of relief from the driving rain.

Devon tried the door, cursing eloquently when

he found it locked. Handing Sissy to her brother, he stepped back and gave the portal a powerful kick. The door flew open with a bang. Any reservation Felicity may have had about breaking into a house disappeared when she entered the dry interior.

"Stay here," Devon ordered as he slammed the door against the storm. Within minutes he returned with a silver branch of candles held high. The tapers threw light across his rain-slicked hair and handsome face.

Felicity leaned against the foyer wall, trying to catch her breath. She still held Lucy, but the little girl was squirming to get down.

Devon moved the candlestick in an arch, amazed at what he saw. Unlike Royal Oak where many of the furnishings where battered or gone, from what he could tell, no one had disturbed this house. It was almost as if the inhabitants were off for the season in Charleston.

"Where are we?" Felicity pushed away from the chair railing and walked toward Devon. Her wet shoes squeaked on the floor.

"Sea View. It belongs to a man named Pinkney Doyle, who obviously named it with an optimistic outlook." Devon arched his brow and smiled. "Even on the clearest day you can't see the ocean from here."

"Where exactly is *here?*" Felicity followed Devon around as he poked his head and the candles into each room. As with the hallway, nothing seemed disturbed.

"We're on Edisto Island. It's one of the Sea Islands that lie between the mainland and the barrier beaches." He handed Felicity the branch of candles and headed back for Sissy. Her coughing had stopped for the moment but the storm had brought with it a drop in temperature. The girl needed to get out of her wet clothes.

"Follow me," he said, returning to Felicity and motioning her toward the double staircase at the rear of the hallway. "This place is where I was heading when the storm broke, but it caught us out on St. Helena Sound and I couldn't make land quickly enough."

He nodded for Felicity to open the first door at the top of the stairs, and followed her inside. Felicity swept the light around the room, taking in the high canopied bed and luxurious furnishings. The wood floor was covered by an Aubusson rug that they were all presently dripping on.

"Ezra, take one of the candles and see if you can get a fire started. It looks as if they left some wood in the fireplace."

Devon settled Sissy into a chair in front of a lace edged vanity. The wind howled down the chimney, but with the help of some balled up paper Devon found in the Queen Anne's lady's desk, Ezra got a fire going.

In the meantime, Felicity lit more candles and searched the clothespress for something dry to put on the girls. "Where is this man Doyle? Is he likely to come back and find us rummaging through his things?"

"I wouldn't count on seeing him tonight," Devon said as another bolt of lightning slashed outside the window. Devon paused and glanced around the room. "I don't know what happened to Pinkney and his family," he said, his voice somber. "When the Federals captured Port Royal last fall General Lee forced the residents to leave their homes. The battle lines fell right through this area." He ran his fingers over the gossamer thin mosquito netting. "This used to be Victoria's room."

Momentarily lost in memories, Devon pulled himself back, surprised to see four sets of eyes fixed on him. "Ezra and I will be in the next room. You think you can manage to get these girls into some dry clothes, Red?"

Since she was already seeing to just that and because she hated the nickname Red, Felicity didn't deign to answer. Once she dried and dressed not only Lucy and Sissy, but herself too, Felicity went in search of the captain. She held up the skirt of a gown she found in the wardrobe. Obviously, Victoria was a taller woman than she. She also seemed to have a penchant for ribbons and bows.

And Felicity didn't like her.

Which was completely unreasonable since she never met the woman and seeing that her home was supplying much needed shelter for her and the children. But something about the look in Devon Blackstone's eyes when he spoke of the missing Victoria raised Felicity's ire.

"What is Victoria Doyle to you?" she blurted

out when a freshly dressed Devon answered her knock.

"To me?" he asked, obviously surprised by her question. "She was . . . is, for all I know, Pinkney's wife."

"His wife?" She'd assumed Victoria was the beautiful, spoiled daughter of the family. "Oh . . . oh well. I just wondered how you knew her."

"Most everyone knew her . . . and Pinkney. How are the girls?" Devon asked, switching the subject.

"They're fine. I left them in bed, and they promised to stay awake long enough to eat. That is if we can find anything to feed them."

"We have the rice we packed if there's nothing else."

But they did find plenty to eat . . . a veritable feast after the famine of the last few days. The larder was full. Cheese, though the mold needed to be sliced off, and ham, and flour to make biscuits, which Felicity prepared after seeking Sissy's advice.

"Not bad," Devon said around a mouthful as he sat at a scarred table in the kitchen. They'd already fed the children and were now in the process of cleaning up. So far Devon's contribution to the tidying was devouring the leftovers.

"I thought we would eat those in the morning," Felicity scolded as she sloshed water into a large iron pot.

"There's still plenty, Red." Devon held up the platter amply piled with fist shaped biscuits.

Sissy's recipe obviously called for feeding more than five people. It also hadn't mentioned anything about keeping the bottoms from burning, Felicity thought as she watched Devon scrape charred crust off his next biscuit.

Well, she tried her best. Felicity tentatively stuck her hand in the dirty water and swirled the soap scum back and forth. She was exhausted and her shoulders ached from bending over the stove extracting the never ending stream of biscuits.

And she highly resented the captain's slouched posture with his feet crossed at the ankles and propped on the table. His trousers stretched tauntingly across the corded muscles of his thighs and . . . and everywhere. Obviously Pinkney Doyle wasn't as well endowed as Devon Blackstone . . . or else he was an exhibitionist.

"What's the matter with you?" Devon jumped to his feet.

"I don't know what you're talking about."

"You just sloshed water all over me and the floor."

Felicity glanced down to where the bricks had already absorbed the soapy water, then back at Devon. He still held a biscuit, well lathered with peach preserves. "Sorry," she said, smiling sweetly.

"Why do I feel that apology is less than sincere, Red?"

"I haven't the faintest idea." Felicity resisted shoving the entire contents of the kettle toward him. But the dampness across the front of his trousers made his manhood even more apparent and Felicity didn't know why she couldn't seem to get her mind off that fact. She swallowed. "Do you suppose you could refrain from calling me Red? It isn't my name, you know."

"Really?"

"Really." Goodness he was handsome when he smiled. If it wasn't for those dimples maybe she could resist him . . . maybe.

"I would think everyone would call you that." Devon stalked around the table . . . behind her.

"Well, no one *else* ever has." He made her uncomfortable when she couldn't see him. He was close. She could smell his scent, even over the aroma of burned biscuits.

"Don't tell me nobody ever commented on your hair."

"Of course they have." Felicity shrugged her shoulders to counter the chills brought on by his fingers in her hair. She'd gathered her curls, piling them on her head. "Most people find the color distinctive . . . pretty."

"And you think I don't find it . . . attractive?" Devon trailed a curl that hung down her slender neck. Part of him preached avoidance. The woman was betrothed to another for God's sake. And he more than anyone should know how unfair it was to use proximity to lure someone away. Hadn't *he* been the victim of such actions? Just being in this house was a vivid reminder.

But he couldn't seem to help himself. She smelled so good. And her skin was so soft. She dropped her head, leaving her neck more vulnerable . . . more exposed to him.

"I . . . I don't know *what* you think," Felicity said. She was trying to keep her wits about her, to concentrate on her task. But the water was growing tepid and she still hadn't started to scrub the pot.

"I think you're beautiful. I think I've never seen hair so dazzling, or eyes the color of spring flowers."

Felicity swallowed and her hands tightened on the edge of the kettle.

"I think you have this strange power over me that I can't explain," Devon continued. "And right now I'm not even interested in trying."

Felicity shut her eyes as his hands cupped her shoulders. She was barely breathing as he turned her to face him. Her hands dripped dishwater, but neither of them noticed, not even when she wrapped them around his waist.

Her lips parted and she waited for that moment when he touched his mouth to hers. He hesitated, almost as if he had the same doubts that plagued her.

This was wrong.

She knew it.

He knew it.

But neither seemed able to step back. Neither seemed able to stem the flow of desire that zinged between them.

"When we were out in the storm," Devon said, his voice as breathless and husky as it was then.

"Right before the lightning struck, the hair on the back of my neck bristled and my skin felt charged."

"I wondered how you knew it was going to strike that tree." She couldn't take her eyes from his. Every time she breathed her breast met his chest, barely touching. The fleeting caress was driving her insane.

"It was something Natee told me. Once when he was young lightning struck him. I was in awe of him, and I listened over and over as he described how he felt right before it happened." Devon paused and slid his hands up the side of her neck, hooking his thumbs beneath her chin. "That's how I feel now. Just like I'm ready to be struck by lightning."

Felicity moaned. His words dissolved any doubts that might have lingered. When his mouth finally pressed against hers she ignited. Her hands clutched at his back, yanking at the shirt he'd tucked into the tight trousers till her fingers encountered firm, bare flesh.

Devon's kiss was carnal and deep. His tongue thrust, attacking her mouth in a way that demanded surrender. He felt her shudder and reveled in how quickly he could fire her passion. But the flame was a double-edged sword. His own desire raged all consuming through his body with such savage power that he lost control completely.

When breathing became impossible his lips tore away from hers, and burned a trail down the side of her throat. His hands fumbled frantically with the tiny buttons that marched down the front of the gown. Several lost their hold on the garment and skittered to the brick floor, unnoticed in the heat of their passion.

At last her breasts were free and Devon feasted on one, then the other, suckling the dusky pink nipples, till they ruched hard and pebbly as a blackberry.

"Oh God, Red." Devon pushed her gown lower, untying the petticoat tabs with impatient jerks. He shoved everything toward the floor, leaving her standing, basking in his heated stare.

Felicity's breasts rose and fell as he looked at her. If not for the hands that clasped her hips she felt her knees would buckle and she'd melt to the floor. But he gave her no chance. He backed her up till her buttocks caught on the edge of the table. With a quick thrust he pressed his lower body against hers. The ridge of his manhood beneath the trousers was large and iron-hard. Of their own volition Felicity's legs spread, welcoming him into the flaming V of her body.

He ground against her. His mouth devoured. And he felt ready to burst.

A sweep of his arm sent the biscuits scattering. He lowered her back, tracing the contours of her body with his flattened palms. Her breasts with their torrid nipples, the crescent indentations of her waist and the delta of red-gold curls, all received his heated attention.

She was hot and wet when his finger found the fiery sheath that awaited him. She quivered, writhing as his finger found the tiny kernel of sensation. When his tongue took up the caress she convulsed uncontrollably.

Devon couldn't get rid of his trousers fast enough. He thrust them down over the glistening head of his manhood and spread her legs wider.

His entry was smooth and deep, eliciting a moan from each of them. Devon's elbows rested on the work-worn table, bracketing her head. Her hair was loose, flowing over the edge like molten gold shot with flames. Legs, soft and smooth wrapped around him. The rain had slowed to an incessant patter against the window panes as Devon thrust into her again and again. His open mouth melded with hers, as the rhythm grew more frantic.

Felicity grew tense as a tightly wound spring, shimmering on the verge. Her entire being centered where their bodies merged. Then with one final plunge he sent her spiraling off, shattered. She could barely breathe, and her fingers clawed at his sweat-slick back. Her cries were soon drowned out by Devon's as he arched up, spilling his seed in a climax that echoed hers.

The downward descent left Felicity exhausted. She stared up at the captain as he loomed above her. They both seemed unable to catch their breath. Felicity opened her mouth to speak, then closed it again when she realized she didn't know what to say. And still he stared at her.

They'd lit several oil lamps prior to fixing the food, so the kitchen was bright with light. But that didn't help her read his expression. When she could stand the force of his eyes no longer, she reached up, tangling her fingers in the thatch of dark brown hair covering his chest.

His hand covered hers, pressing it against his skin. She could feel the excited pounding of his heart. He held it there a moment, then levered himself up. When he reached for her, Felicity hesitated only briefly before taking his hand.

"The table must be hard," he said as he picked up parts of her clothing that were strewn across the floor.

"I didn't notice," Felicity answered honestly.

He smiled that devilish grin that made his dimples spring to life. "I doubt I would have either." He handed her a petticoat.

Feeling vulnerable and embarrassed, Felicity held it up to her breast, a move he seemed to find amusing. "We really need to talk about this . . . don't you think?" For the first time his voice held a hint of uncertainty.

"I don't know." Felicity looked away, uncomfortable with watching him step into his trousers. She still clung to the lace trimmed petticoat. "I'm not sure there's anything to say."

"We made love on the table, for God's sake." He quickly buttoned his pants, then ran his fingers through the tangle of hair that lay on his forehead.

"You think I don't know that?" What she didn't know was how it could happen so quickly. Turning away, Felicity pulled on the petticoat. Then she grabbed up the gown and tossed it over her head.

Without bothering to fasten it she hurried from the room. But she didn't expect Devon to follow her. He caught her by the arm before she reached the front hallway.

"What is it? Are you worried about 'what's his name'? Your betrothed?"

"Jebediah." Felicity tried to jerk her arm away. She gave up when he wouldn't let her go. "His name is Jebediah. And yes, I'm worried." Felicity hesitated. "I don't like doing this to him."

"I don't recall seeing him here." Devon tightened his grip. He was being irrational and he knew it. She was to marry another and he should leave it at that. But this certainly wasn't the first irrational thing he'd done where she was concerned . . . and it probably wouldn't be the last.

She sucked in her breath. "Jebediah is an honest, admirable man. He deserves better than to have me. . . ." She bit her lip, unable to continue with an explanation of what she'd done. Twice. Besides, there was no need to clarify matters to the man before her.

"Then he shouldn't let you go running around by yourself during a war, for God's sake."

"He didn't *let* me. And that's no excuse for my actions." Tears blurred her vision and she tried to blink them away.

Devon let his hand slide down her arm. "You want me to promise this won't happen again?"

She shot him a look that clearly asked if he could, a look Devon couldn't meet. "Listen," he said, sinking down on the bottom step of the stairs. "I don't know why this happens." He chuckled. "Actually I do, but . . . Never mind." He shook his head. "I'll try," he finally said. Devon moved over as she joined him on the riser. She still held the gown together with her fingers.

"It certainly isn't all *your* fault," Felicity conceded. "Perhaps if we didn't spend so much time together, alone." She glanced over and smiled. "After all, we'll be parting company as soon as we reach Charleston."

"It might work." But Devon noticed that neither of them moved. If anything she seemed to get more comfortable, leaning back and looking around. "Is this a rice plantation also?" she asked, and Devon had the notion she was proving to herself that they could sit and chat without ending up in each other's arms.

"Cotton," he said. "But not just any cotton. The black seed cotton that grows here is known throughout the world for its silky fibers. They call it Sea Island Cotton."

"Oh." Felicity tried to think of something clever to add but she couldn't. "Well, I suppose I'll say good night then." She tried to stand but Devon was sitting on the edge of her skirt. The pull tugged the ends of her bodice from her fingers and the top gaped open. Though less than an hour earlier she lay beneath him, wearing nothing, she couldn't handle the spark of desire that shot into his eyes.

Felicity jerked on the gown and freeing it ran up the stairs. Sissy and Lucy were asleep, so she quietly changed into a fresh shift and climbed into bed with them. But though she was tired, sleep was a long time coming. She couldn't stop thinking . . . of Jebediah . . . of Devon.

The next morning dawned bright, with only the mist off the waterway to impair the view. Devon was right. You couldn't see the ocean. But from the front porch Felicity could see the destruction done by the storm. Several tall pines were snapped off near their tops, and the ground was littered with leaves and Spanish moss.

When she saw Devon and Ezra coming up the path she was tempted to rush inside. Facing the captain was not something she wanted to do. But it was inevitable, and best done with as little fuss as possible. She shaded her eyes with the back of her hand. "How did the boat hold up?"

"Good." It was Ezra who answered. "Mast'a Devon says we can be on our way as soon as we eat somethin'." Ezra carried the rooster, Mast'a Cock, under his arm. He reached the bottom of the stairs and looked up at Felicity. "You got any of them biscuits left from last night? They sure was good."

Felicity couldn't help herself. Her eyes shot to Devon. He stood with one foot on the bottom step, his forearm braced on his knee. And he didn't say a word. "I baked some fresh this morning," Felicity told Ezra, then stepped aside as he bounded up the stairs.

258

"Doesn't take much to make him happy."

"And what is that supposed to mean?" Felicity raised her chin when she noticed his grin.

"Not a thing. Just commenting on how anxious to eat the boy is."

"Well, breakfast is inside if you want it."

"Oh, I want it." He smiled up at her. "Make no mistake about that."

Felicity wasn't sure if it was his smile, or the way he looked at her, but she felt herself growing warm. She turned abruptly and entered the house. She didn't turn around but could tell by his footstep that he followed her back down the hallway and into the kitchen.

When Felicity came downstairs this morning she noticed the captain had cleaned up the biscuits from last night. The table was cleared off and the kettle she'd been washing was rinsed and dry.

After they'd all eaten their fill—the biscuits were barely burned this morning—Felicity packed up as much food as they could carry. Sissy, despite the trials of the journey, seemed to be feeling stronger. She insisted on walking to the dock, smiling when she made it with nothing more than a helping hand from Ezra. Her improved health cheered Felicity, who was wondering how she could take the sick child north on the train. The trip from New York to Charleston was tiring enough for just Felicity. But if Sissy continued to recuperate, perhaps she could get the children to Esther soon.

The weather today seemed to be compensating for the havoc of the previous afternoon. Blue skies, with only a wispy hint of clouds and a soothing breeze from the east made the trip pleasant. From beneath the shade of a wide brimmed straw hat, Felicity viewed the changing landscape.

"It really is very beautiful here," she said, turning to glance back at the captain. "When it isn't storming, that is."

"Yesterday was nothing. You should see it when it really blows. Hurricanes come up from the Bahamas." He shook his head. "They can tear buildings apart."

"Still." Felicity let her gaze drift out across the water where a snowy white heron stood guarding the mouth of a small inlet. "It's so peaceful." She sighed. "It's hard to believe there's even a war going on." He was quiet for so long, Felicity wasn't certain he heard her. But when she slanted him a look, his eyes met hers.

"Most everyone who lived here before the war has been driven out. Their sons are either fighting or dead."

"I left them some money."

"Who?"

"The Doyles. We ate their food and took their clothing. I had one coin left. It only seemed right to repay them in some way."

Devon's smile was sad. "A pretty gesture but I imagine some Yankee bastard will profit from your generosity. Just because Sea View has been spared so far doesn't mean the Federals won't ransack the place before it's all over."

She hadn't thought of that. But then Felicity realized there were many things she hadn't thought of. Like what happened to the poor slaves after they were free. In all his lectures on the subject of slavery Jebediah had never touched on that.

And the people of the South . . . the slaveholders . . . Jebediah and her father portrayed them as fire breathing monsters, ready to do the devil's bidding. Hardly the way she'd describe Devon Blackstone.

"You planned to free your slaves even before the war started, didn't you?"

"We talked about it, Grams and I."

"You must have done more than discuss it. I saw the dates on those letters of manumission."

Devon shrugged. "I had our lawyer draw those up, but when you're in the Navy your time is not your own. I wasn't at home when the war started. And then it was too late to do anything about our people." Devon tied off the sail and called to Ezra, who sat in the bow of the boat with his sisters.

"Yes sir, Cap'n sir."

Devon smiled. "Spoken like a true sailor. Can you work your way back here past the ladies and steer this thing for a bit?"

"What are you planning to do?" Felicity pulled aside her skirts as Ezra scrambled by, obviously anxious to do anything the captain asked of him. He even left Mast'a Cock with his sisters.

261

"I, my dear Miss Wentworth, am in need of a nap."

"A what?"

"You heard me." Devon gave Ezra some simple directions and handed over control of the rudder. "Now if you'd be so kind as to offer your lap as a pillow . . . ?" Devon arched his brow toward Felicity, who couldn't help smiling.

"Oh, I suppose I must. We can't have the captain falling asleep at the helm." All three children seemed to think this was funny, and Felicity noticed the girls even lowered their chatter as the captain shut his eyes.

At first Felicity sat there, her back straight, trying to ignore the weight of his shoulders and head resting on her. Then, cautiously, as she noticed the even rhythm of his breathing, she glanced down. The lock of hair that he repeatedly shoved back rested on his forehead. She resisted the urge to brush it back.

His skin was darker than when she first met him. It was a deep bronze, except for the tiny white lines that radiated from his closed eyes. His nose was slightly crooked, as was his mouth. Felicity found herself growing warm when she thought about what that mouth could do to her.

"Miz Felicity. Miz Felicity."

Felicity looked up as her name was hissed a second time. "What is it?" She could tell from the tone of Ezra's voice that something was wrong, and she almost expected to find they were sinking.

"Over there," he said, keeping his tone quiet.

"On the shore, beyond them trees." He pointed and Felicity followed the line of his finger. "Them a powerful lot of Yankees."

Felicity's mouth dropped open. Ezra was absolutely right.

Thirteen

"Shouldn't we wake the cap'n?"

Felicity slammed her mouth shut, glanced down at the man who nestled in her lap, then at Ezra. "I don't think so," she said as she removed the straw bonnet from her head and dropped it over his face. "Steer slowly toward the opposite shore. I don't believe they've noticed us yet." The inland waterway was wide and the small boat sailed near the center.

"You wants I should dock, cause I ain't sure how to do it."

"I don't know where we are." She twisted around, taking in the cordgrass and swampy terrain. "Let's just move ahead as fast as we can. Girls," she said, addressing Sissy and Lucy, "just keep on doing what you were. Pretend they aren't even there."

"They ain't gonna shoot at us, is they, Miz Felcy?"

"No, Lucy. They have no reason to harm us." At least she hoped they didn't. Of course how the soldiers might react to Captain Blackstone was a different story.

The captain shifted in his sleep and Felicity nervously patted his hand while she watched the blue clad soldiers marching along the road, not a hundred yards away. They were partially obscured from view by a screen of holly and pine.

"How many ye think there is?"

"I don't know. They seem to be heading some-place in a hurry." They'd come up on the tail-end of the Federals, on the wagons and horse drawn guns, and were now sailing past the foot soldiers, marching four abreast—rows and rows of them.

Devon's head turned and he snuggled deeper against her stomach. "Hmmm, Red," he murmured, and the vibration of his voice sent gooseflesh up Felicity's spine.

"Hush now." She soothed the words over him while stroking his hand.

"Oh, Red," he mumbled, and Felicity wondered if she was going to have to knock him over the head to keep him quiet. But after burrowing deeper against her, he stopped his fitfulness and began to snore softly, and Felicity sighed with re-lief. She could see cavalry up ahead, presumably leading the troops. Perhaps she could sail by the army without them even knowing she and the chil-dren were there.

A whistle and holler from shore erased that hope. "Would you looky there?" came a crude shout that Felicity tried to ignore. "If it ain't a pretty little belle out for a sail with her darkies."

265

The words were followed by a sharp reprimand, and Felicity let out her breath till she heard an irritated, "You there."

Glancing across the waterway she saw a soldier standing beside his horse, motioning her closer.

"What should I do, Miz Felicity?" There was panic in Ezra's voice.

"Keep going straight."

"What if he starts shootin'?"

"He won't."

"What's going on?" Devon knocked away the hat and tried to raise his head. Felicity pushed him back into the pillow of her billowing skirts.

"Hush up and stay down," she hissed as the Yankee soldier called out again.

"I think he's gonna shoot," Ezra said again.

"He's not."

"Who's not? What the hell is going on?" Devon pushed against her hands when she tried to cover his mouth. "What is it?"

"Yankees," she answered succinctly. "Now stay down or I'll have Sissy and Lucy sit on you." Felicity scanned the river ahead, smiling when she saw a small waterway leading off away from the soldiers. "Can you steer into there?" she asked Ezra.

"I thinks so."

"Good. Do it."

"Not too sharp a turn," Devon said. "Or you'll swamp the boat." He lay low, whispering bits of advice as the boy took them beneath the feathery leaves of a cypress. "Are we out of sight?" he asked after they'd sailed behind a spit of moss-covered live oaks.

"Yes." And this time she didn't stop him as he sat up and looked around. "There were Federal troops," she said before he could ask. "Lots of them. Marching along the road."

"Hell."

"We got away," Felicity explained reasonably. "They can't get over here . . . can they?"

"Not unless they swim," Devon agreed. "But I'm more worried about where they're going." He shifted. "How many were there?"

"I don't know. A great many."

"How many, damnit. A regiment? A battalion?"

"I don't know." Felicity's tone was indignant. "They had wagons and cannons. What's wrong?"

"They're heading for Charleston." Devon impatiently wiped hair off his forehead. "Maybe the Federals have decided to forget a frontal attack by water and come in the back door."

"You mean a battle?" Felicity couldn't believe this was happening.

Devon didn't answer as he replaced Ezra at the tiller.

"What are you doing? We just came this way to hide." Felicity twisted her hands.

"This entire area is a labyrinth of waterways. I can keep us close to them and out of sight."

"But why should we want to stay with them?" Felicity tried to keep the panic out of her voice. Lucy had crawled back and was now settled in Felicity's lap. "Shouldn't we just get away?" The memory of Sergeant Poole was still too painful. She wanted to leave this land where danger lurked around every corner.

"I need to know exactly where they're headed, Red. And how many of them there are."

They traveled the maze of small waterways that wound their way through the thick cordgrass and cypress with seemingly no design for most of the afternoon. The girls grew cranky, quieting only when Felicity told them stories she remembered from her childhood. Her mother had been a society matron, and little else, but there were times she'd come to the nursery, usually with one of her friends, to see her golden-haired child. During those visits, Felicity would do whatever she could to seem the perfect child.

"Oh, she's going to be such a beauty. Just like a princess," Felicity's mother told her father on one of those rare occasions when they'd come together. Her father had agreed in that distracted way he had, and insisted that he had work to do in the library.

"But what of the Glesner's ball?" her mother had implored, looking up at him through her lashes. "You promised to escort me."

"So I did," Felicity had heard him say as they left the nursery. And she had wished with all her heart she could go with them . . . to be the little princess they wanted her to be. And when she grew older, she did. Between her good looks and her father's money, Felicity became the princess of the season. Her mother had died a few years before, but Felicity still had her father and brother, Arthur, to impress.

However her father didn't much care what his daughter did as long as she caused no scandal.

And Arthur, much to their father's annoyance, had taken up the abolitionist cause. When he should have been following in his father's shadow, learning the business of making money, he was off listening to the likes of Henry Ward Beecher. When Arthur announced that he'd enlisted to fight the holy war against slavery, her father had been livid. He'd held onto that anger until word reached them that Arthur died near a little town called Manassas.

From that moment on, her father changed. He no longer ignored the subject of abolitionism; he now embraced it. If his only son had to die, at least it would not be in vain. Instead of letting Felicity go on her merry way, breaking hearts and dancing till dawn, her father insisted she join him at the prayer meetings and sermons espousing the evils of slavery.

That is how she met Jebediah Webster.

And how she ended up deep in a South Carolina swamp, with three children and a Rebel blockade runner for company, Felicity thought.

"What happened to de princess then," Lucy asked, an annoyed edge to her voice.

"Oh." Felicity realized she'd let the story she was telling hang while her mind wandered back over her childhood. Felicity smiled at the child who was busy sucking her fingers. "She met a

269

prince and lived happily ever after," Felicity finished.

"But what happened to the dragon?" Sissy insisted.

"He ran away and decided to be good."

"Fascinating story," Devon said, and Felicity shot a look back over her shoulder.

"I wasn't aware you were listening." He only grinned, and she turned back to the children.

"Tell us another," Lucy begged and Felicity's shoulders sagged. She was hot and tired and wondered when they'd ever get to Charleston, or wherever they were going.

"I will in a bit," she told the child. Then she looked back at the captain. "Where exactly are we going?"

"North," he said, then steered them around a huge cypress root that stuck out of the water like a giant's knobby knee. "The soldiers will stay on the road, especially if they have horses and cannons. I'm following, but keeping my distance while I'm doing it. Come dark we'll slip back into Secessionville Creek."

"And then?" Felicity's expression showed bewilderment. "Are we going to race them to Charleston?"

"Then, Red, I'm going to do some reconnoitering."

"Reconnoitering what?"

"The Federals."

"But they'll see you." Hadn't she done her best to keep his presence a secret from the soldiers?

"No, they won't. It'll be dark. And I'll be careful."

"But . . ."

"Don't worry about it, Red."

But she did worry about it . . . a lot.

As darkness draped itself like a smothering blanket over the countryside, they reentered Secessionville Creek. Devon trimmed in the sail and using one of Felicity's petticoats to muffle the oars, rowed up the creek, staying to the east side of the waterway. Everyone kept their voices down, but it wasn't until Devon saw campfires ahead that he insisted upon quiet.

"They're camping on the old Lewis place," he whispered, before lifting his finger to his lips.

As they skimmed past the soldiers, they clung to the deep shadows thrown by the shore line trees. At one point Felicity could hear the plaintive wail of a mouth organ and she shut her eyes tight. She realized it didn't matter if she could see them. It was whether or not they could see her that counted, but it was still comforting to pretend she was invisible.

Felicity didn't realize anyone noticed her tactic until Devon's voice sounded close to her ear.

"We're by them. You can open your eyes now."

Felicity sucked in her breath and stared at him hard, though she doubted he could see her in the darkness. Lucy, who'd been nestled in her lap, lifted her head, and Felicity pushed the child back against her chest. "I don't know how you can take this so lightly. Sneaking by them like that was awful. I thought for sure they'd hear my heart pounding."

"I hear'd it Miz Felcy."

"I'm sure you did, Lucy."

"This is what I do all the time. Did you think blockade runners just sail on by all those blockaders and beg them to take up the chase?"

"Of course not. I . . ." Felicity realized she didn't know exactly what a blockade runner *did* do. But it didn't seem like the captain was waiting around for her to come up with an answer. He rowed round a spit of land and into a small cove. The skeins of Spanish moss hanging off the trees looked eerily gray in the wane moonlight.

"You all stay here. I'll be back soon," Devon said as he checked the shells in the revolver he'd taken off Sergeant Poole. He handed it to Ezra, seeming to know intuitively that Felicity wanted no part of the weapon.

"Where are you going?" Felicity couldn't stop herself from grabbing his arm.

"I'm going to scout around, like I told you."

"Oh." She took a deep breath, clinging to him tighter when she heard a noise. "What was that?" She was certain they would be overrun by Yankees at any moment.

"An alligator." Devon yanked off his boots. "But you all will be safe enough here."

Felicity glanced around. "What about the alligators?"

"Just stay in the boat. I won't be long."

"How will you get back there?"

"Swim," he said and Felicity could see the flash of his teeth.

"But—"

"Don't worry, Red. I'll be back." He gave her a quick kiss and slipped over the side of the boat.

"Are we gonn' be eaten by gators?" Lucy wanted to know. She tugged on Felicity's hand.

"Of course not. You heard the captain. We'll be fine." Hoping against hope that was true, Felicity settled Sissy more comfortably and cuddled Lucy against her side. Ezra seemed intent upon proving himself a man. He took up the revolver and stared into the darkness.

She shouldn't be so frightened. At least that's what Felicity kept telling herself. She'd been through so much since she left New York. For heaven's sake she'd even killed a man.

But the terror wouldn't go away.

As she sat huddled in the small boat, trying to act brave for Sissy and Lucy, and Ezra too, Felicity realized it was just that . . . an act.

Her hands tightened in the fabric of Sissy's shawl and she offered a silent prayer. The fact that she implored God for her own safety didn't surprise her. Nor that she was very concerned for the children. After all, she had started this entire undertaking for their sake.

What did bewilder her was that her most ardent appeal was for Captain Blackstone. Felicity tried to tell herself it was because he was in the most

273

imminent danger, or that her life and those of the children's depended upon his safe return. *She* certainly had no idea where they were.

But neither of those reasons was valid. She cared about him. Cared about him deeply.

And the very idea was absurd.

Felicity had no idea how long they waited.

The moon rose above the tree tops, a glowing sliver of white in the sky and still the captain did not return.

"Where ye think he iz?" came a nervous voice from the stern of the boat.

"I don't know Ezra. But I'm sure he'll be along directly."

"It ain't good," he countered. "Him gone so long."

"The captain knows what he's about." Felicity paused. "I'm sure he's fine."

Sissy's cough took Felicity's mind off whether or not she believed what she told Ezra. The girl sipped at the water Felicity gave her, then fell back asleep, her head in Felicity's lap. Lucy lay on the bottom of the boat, her arm hooked around Felicity's ankle.

"Why don't you get some rest, Ezra? I'll keep watch for a while."

"Beggin' your pardon, Miz Felicity, but the cap'n, he told me to watch out for y'all."

"That's very admirable, but you're just a boy. I can—"

"If it's all the same to ye, Miz Felicity, I'll keep up the watch."

"All right, Ezra." Felicity didn't add that she too would keep the vigil.

As she sat slumped in the gently swaying boat, Felicity's senses attuned, she became aware of the myriad sounds of the lowlands. The occasional alligator roar sent shivers up her spine. But most of the night noises were more subtle . . . and pleasing to the ear.

The lapping water, the broom grass and pine needles rustling in the slight breeze off the ocean, even the incessant drone of nocturnal insects could be soothing, if one forgot the aggravation of their bite. Now and then Felicity could hear the forlorn call of an owl.

And the smells. With nothing to do, but sit and worry, Felicity tried to distinguish the varied odors. The pluff mud she knew. At first the salty tang was offensive, and upon reaching Charleston where the mudflats reeked of the odor, Felicity kept a perfumed handkerchief pressed to her nose. But now . . . well, she must have grown used to it.

Together with the jasmine and magnolia, the Cherokee rose and the subtle scent of Spanish moss, the pluff mud formed a tapestry of scents she would always associate with this place.

Felicity would have thought herself too nervous to nap, however the ebb and flow of the tide must have rocked her to sleep for when Devon Blackstone emerged from the water beside the boat she was startled awake.

"Oh, where have you been?" she demanded, though knowing enough to keep her voice low. She twisted around and couldn't stop the hand that reached out to touch his wet, whisker covered cheek.

"Did you miss me?"

His lips tasted of salt water when he leaned forward, rocking the boat to give her a quick kiss. "Certainly not," Felicity insisted, but he paid no heed to the lie. He rolled into the boat, and started pulling on the anchor rope before she could even chastise him for getting her wet.

"What is it? What's wrong?" she asked, because his movements were uncharacteristically fast. "Are they after you?" She suddenly had a vision of the five of them rowing for their lives, fighting off the entire Yankee army.

"They never saw me," he answered as he stuck the revolver Ezra handed him in his waistband. With practiced ease he rowed them toward the center of the narrow creek.

The sail caught the breeze as he unfurled it, billowing out, a beacon even in the dim light from the crescent moon.

"Aren't you afraid they'll see us now?"

Devon swiped wet hair from his forehead. "I scouted out their sentries. They're all well downstream. But it wouldn't matter anyway. We have to get to Fort Lamar."

"Fort Lamar? I thought we were going to Charleston?"

"I was able to sneak up close enough to hear some of the officers talking—"

"My heavens! They would have killed you if they caught you."

"Why Miss Wentworth, you sound as if you'd be truly devastated if they had."

Felicity stiffened her spine. Even in the near darkness she could see his devilish grin. She couldn't let him know she had feelings for him. He might lust after her, but that was all. And she wasn't about to let him think she worried about him.

"I was simply concerned for the children's safety if you didn't return."

"But not your own?" His brow lifted.

"Well, that too."

He chuckled then, a deep, rich sound that made Felicity smile. She hid the reaction from him by turning to fiddle with Sissy's blanket. But his next words had her looking back at him.

"They're going to attack the fort in the morning."

"Are you sure?" Felicity shook her head. "Of course, you're sure if you heard them." She paused, as she twisted her fingers. "What are you going to do?"

"Warn them," he stated succinctly.

It was near eleven o'clock at night when they reached the landing at Secessionville. Devon handed Felicity and the children out of the boat, settling Sissy on a blanket Felicity spread on the ground before racing off toward the fort.

There were troops camped in the fields between Secessionville and the fort that defended the town. Devon grabbed hold of the first officer he saw, a clean shaven Georgia boy from Atlanta.

"I'm not certain we should just burst in on Colonel Lamar like this," he mumbled as they approached the M shaped fort.

"Believe me, he'll be glad we did."

The fort loomed up on the flat landscape, its yellowish brown sides of dirt sloping to four parapets. Devon was glad to see the cannons mounted on each. And even happier to note the mortar inside the fort.

Colonel Lamar, for whom the fort was named was in his quarters, enjoying a cigar and whisky when Lieutenant Baxter knocked on the door.

"Enter."

After hearing the colonel's tone, Baxter tossed Devon a look that clearly said this better be good. "I have a civilian here, sir, who says he has some intelligence about the enemy."

"Show him in, Lieutenant." Colonel Lamar took a quick swig, grimaced slightly, then straightened his tunic.

"Colonel Lamar." Devon entered the room and came straight to the point. "I've sailed up the Folly River and parts of Long Island Creek today and I saw myself a powerful lot of Yankees."

Lamar scratched at his side whiskers. "That's hardly news. The enemy is entrenched on the southern tip of the island." He paused a moment. "What was your name, sir?"

"Blackstone, Captain Devon Blackstone."

"I've heard of your exploits, Captain Blackstone, but this—"

"Is going to be a catastrophe if you don't listen. Those Yankees are no longer entrenched. They're marching this way. At least they were until dark. Right now they're bivouacked some five miles away, and they plan to attack at dawn."

The colonel's face blanched beneath his gray whiskers. "Are you certain of this, Captain?"

"I heard two of the officers talking with my own ears. Their ultimate target is Charleston but they plan to take Fort Lamar out on their way."

The colonel rubbed his chin. "How many?"

"Two divisions. Each with perhaps three brigades."

"Over six thousand men." The colonel shook his head. "To our five hundred." He hesitated only a moment. "Lieutenant, assemble my staff, tell them to report to me in five minutes."

"Yes sir." Baxter backed out of the room and took off at a run.

"I appreciate your patriotism, Captain, and I'm hoping your assistance will continue."

"I'm at your service, sir. But I have a personal matter to attend to first."

"Personal matter?"

"I was not traveling alone. There is a lady with me and three Negro children. I had to leave them by the dock when I came here." And now that the alarm was sounded Devon was anxious to get back and see them to safety . . . or relative safety. The odds of stopping the blue tide of soldiers at Fort Lamar didn't look good.

"By all means see to your lady. Then hurry back. I gather you're familiar with the area?"

"Born and bred, sir."

"Good. You'll be able to get through to General Evans at Fort Johnson then. We need reinforcements."

Fort Johnson was located some five miles away, and Devon had no doubt he could reach it quickly, after he saw to Felicity and the children. They were probably scared to death after the way he just rushed off. Thinking of their anguish made him quicken his pace as he crossed the cottonfield, traveling against the flow of soldiers who were hurrying toward the fort.

Devon was running by the time he reached the dock. "Red," he called out, looking around for some sign of her. "Felicity?" He searched the area, then started down the path toward town.

"Captain Blackstone!"

Devon turned as his name was called again. An apple cheeked young soldier trotted up to his side, pulling a chestnut mare by the reins. "I'm Private Burns, sir. The colonel sent me with this horse and to give you this letter for General Evans. He also asks that you hurry. We need those reinforcements, sir."

Devon took the leather pouch that contained the communication from Colonel Lamar. He glanced down the road toward Secessionville, where lights glowed from the windows of several houses, then back at the young soldier. He hated to leave without finding out what became of Felicity and the children, but he had no choice. If those reinforcements didn't get to Fort Lamar in time, it wouldn't matter where the woman was.

"Tell Colonel Lamar I'm on my way," he said, gathering up the reins. He reached up to the saddle, preparing to mount, but looked back at the private instead. "Do you suppose you could do something for me? I seem to have misplaced a lady and three Negro children. If you could check in these houses, I'm sure you'll find them. Just tell Miss Wentworth what I'm doing and—"

"Sorry, sir, but my orders are to get right back. We need to drag cannons off the floating battery moored next to the wharf."

Devon thrust his left foot into the stirrup. "I understand." He pulled himself into the saddle, patting the animal's neck when she started to prance. The best thing . . . damn the only thing he could do was leave, gallop off as fast as he could. Gritting his teeth in resignation, Devon slapped the reins. "Good luck to you, private."

"And to you too, sir. And to your lady friend," he added, but Devon was already out of ear shot.

She waited as long as she could. But it was dark and the mosquitos where droning about and there was no sign of Captain Blackstone.

And not more than one hundred yards down the road the town beckoned. With clean sheets and water and perhaps even a bite to eat. Not that she couldn't do without any of those things. Felicity found she'd become very accustomed to the hardships she was living under. But Lucy was crying softly, and the sobbing was punctuated often by Sissy's coughing.

"Do you think you can walk a ways?" she asked Sissy after she slumped back from her hacking fit.

"Yes'm, I's can walk."

"Where's we goin', Miz Felcy?"

"Into town." She held up her hand, palm out when Ezra protested. "I know Captain Blackstone said to stay here, but I think he's been detained. And he couldn't really mean for us to just remain at the dock all night."

So they started out. Felicity held Lucy, who'd fallen asleep. Ezra's arm supported his sister . . . and she held the rooster.

The first house they came to was two storied with a sagging front porch. The man who answered the door reminded Felicity of Jebediah. He was tall and spare with a narrow face and deep set eyes. Felicity couldn't help smiling. "I'm Felicity Wentworth," she began, edging her body forward when she sensed he wanted to shut the door. "These children and I are . . . well, we have no place to go, and I was hoping—"

"Be on your way, woman."

This time Felicity lifted her hand to stop him

from shutting the door in her face. "You don't understand—"

"No, Missy. *You* don't understand. We don't cotton to strangers around here."

"But—" Her voice drifted off when she realized there was no one to hear her.

The woman at the next house was not as rude but the result was the same. She didn't want them in her home.

Down the road, set back from the street behind a fence of boxwood stood another, more affluent looking house. When Felicity approached this dwelling she decided a change in strategy was needed. She left the children at the bottom of the porch steps. Flicking her hand over the skirt of her gown she brushed as much dirt away as she could. After she tidied her hair she marched up the steps intent on doing battle. These people didn't like strangers. Well, she'd give them as close as she could to one of their own.

"How do you do?" she asked the frail woman dressed in black who answered the door. "I'm . . ." she hesitated only a moment. "Mrs. Devon Blackstone. Perhaps you know my husband, the blockade runner?"

"Yeh?" The woman cupped her hand funnel-like to her ear. "Did you say you was married to the Blackstone boy?"

"Yes," Felicity raised her voice. "Yes, I am."

"He's a rascal, that one," the woman chuckled. "And too handsome for his own good. Is he still such a handsome devil?"

"That he is," Felicity admitted. "I was wondering if—"

"Where is he? I haven't seen the Blackstone boy for ages."

"That's what I need to speak to you about. Devon . . . I mean, that Blackstone boy is at the fort. And I was wondering . . . I mean he was wondering if I could stay at your house and wait for him?"

"You want to come in?" she asked and Felicity nodded. "Well, why didn't you say so. Any Blackstone is welcome here."

"Oh, I am . . . ? I mean, thank you." Felicity glanced around. "I have three of our people with me."

"There's quarters out back." The woman, who said her name was Mrs. Hawkins . . . the Widow Hawkins, arched forward to peer around Felicity. "They's been empty for a spell, but I imagine your Negros will find them good enough."

"I'm sure you're right, but I'd really appreciate it if I could keep them with me. Devon would be ever so grateful too."

It had taken no more than the mention of Devon Blackstone's name to get the four of them ensconced in a front bedroom. Felicity insisted Ezra tie Mast'a Cock in the barn . . . there was no sense pushing their luck. Widow Hawkins offered them sliced ham and cornbread, but the children ate little, they were so tired.

Felicity only picked at her food too, wondering if she should tell Mrs. Hawkins about the advanc-

284

ing Yankees. But what could she do? She was obviously too old and infirm to leave. Felicity was sure she only heard a fraction of what was said to her.

In the end she decided there was no need to upset the elderly woman . . . especially when Felicity didn't know for sure what was going on.

Which was why she couldn't sleep. At least that's what Felicity tried to tell herself as she lay in the big feather bed between Lucy and Sissy, while Ezra slept on a pallet spread on the floor. Felicity didn't fidget for fear of waking the girls, but she couldn't even shut her eyes.

"Where is he?" she mumbled softly. What on earth had happened to Devon? Felicity prayed that he was safe, then cursed him for not returning. Surely he could find them if he tried. There weren't that many houses in the town. He just didn't—

The terrifying roar of a cannon made Felicity sit straight up in bed. Her hand flew to her mouth. Oh God, Devon!

Fourteen

He didn't wait for the foot soldiers.

Devon changed horses and galloped back through the predawn darkness.

He shouldn't have left her.

It didn't matter that she wandered off from the wharf. As he rode along, the haunting sounds of night creatures his only company, Devon decided he should have taken Felicity and the children to the fort with him.

"Oh, what am I worried about?" he wondered aloud, causing the bay to prick up his ears. Felicity Wentworth was a grown woman. She traveled from Richmond to Charleston by herself . . . and managed to get accosted on the day she arrived, Devon reminded himself.

Devon lowered his head to skirt a swaying skein of Spanish moss. And that's when he heard it. Gunfire. Artillery. Coming from the direction of Fort Lamar. Apparently the Yankees hadn't waited until dawn. It couldn't be much later than four or four-thirty.

Kneeing his mount into a gallop Devon reached the open back of the fort that blocked the Secessionville Peninsula just as the firing stopped. Jumping from the horse he sent it with a slap of his hand back toward the town, then raced toward the raw earth walls.

Spotting Colonel Lamar near the eight inch columbiad on the right parapet, he pushed his way through the soldiers lining the redoubts. General Evans hadn't bothered to send a written response to the request for reinforcements. "They're on their way, Colonel Lamar," Devon said after the older man spotted him.

"Ah, Blackstone. Thank God." The colonel's benediction was interrupted by several frantic cries from the wooden observation tower.

"Here they come again!"

Grabbing a rifle from a pile "requisitioned" from the dead Union soldiers that littered the outside slope of the fort, Devon aimed over the dirt wall and fired. And fired. He no sooner pulled the trigger—the enemy was so thick there was no need to aim—than he tore open a cartridge with his teeth and reloaded.

Still they kept coming.

Line upon line of blue clad men climbed the slope only to be rebuffed by rifle and bayonet. When at last they retreated, Devon slumped over his gun. The air was heavy with saltpeter and sulphur, and though there was a lull in the shooting, the pounding still sounded in his ears.

A third attack closely followed, bringing the

Federal troops all the way to the parapets. They advanced, seemingly impervious to the hot fire rained upon them by the battery. Impervious, that is until they fell, one on top of the other.

Devon had no idea how many he killed that morning. He only wished they'd stop coming so he could stop mowing them down. But by the time the main advance slowed, and took shelter behind trees and cotton furrows running perpendicular to the fort, he was glad it was he behind the barricades.

But moments later the protection of the fort proved futile. From across the marsh a Yankee flank opened fire. The shelling forced the Confederates from their guns. Devon fell back with the other men, firing as he went. If the main force attacked now, they'd find little resistance. They could plow over the fort, take Secessionville, and their way would be clear to attack Charleston from the rear.

But then, from the marsh, Devon heard more firing. A cheer went up from the battery when they realized the reinforcements had arrived. The Federal riflemen now had to turn their attention to the Confederate troops storming across the footbridge linking the peninsula with the James Island shore.

Firing, sometimes heavy, sometimes light, continued till about nine o'clock. By then the Yankees withdrew, though no one knew if it was an attempt to reorganize or a full-scale retreat.

By late morning word came back. The scouts

sent out to reconnoiter reported that the Yankees were on their way to their camp on the southwestern tip of James Island.

While the battle raged, Devon had little opportunity to think of Felicity or where she might be. But now as the grave diggers went about their grim job, he could think of little else. Stopping only long enough to splash water over his face, Devon tramped out of the fort, crossing the fields toward town.

He was tired and hungry. His throat burned raw from the smoke and the sun beat down on his head and shoulders, making him wish for a patch of shade and a cool drink. He glanced longingly toward a canvas awning set up beneath the spread of a giant oak. The townswomen were ladling up clear cool water and offering squares of cornbread to the soldiers who straggled out of the fort.

Devon considered stopping. Surely wherever Felicity was, she'd be all right for a few more minutes. Or maybe she wouldn't. With a grunt, Devon turned back on the path, and almost missed the crown of golden-red curls on the woman carrying two buckets of water balanced in either hand.

"Red?" Devon took a tentative step forward. "Red!" he called across the intervening field.

Felicity dropped the buckets, not caring that water sloshed over the rims. She wanted to cry. She wanted to laugh. Yet she could only stand rooted in the cotton field staring at the man hurrying toward her.

All last night and this morning she worried

about him, sending up short, fitful prayers when she had a chance, and now here he was.

Her gaze flew over him, from the top of his wind tossed hair to the tip of his boots, looking for any sign of injury. The breath she hadn't realized she held whooshed out when she saw he was unharmed.

He was dirty, his whiskered face and hair covered with streaked grime, and his usual cocky stride lacked its usual energy. But he was still the most handsome man she'd ever seen.

He stopped within five feet of her, and Felicity swallowed. Throwing herself into his arms seemed so melodramatic, yet she could barely keep herself from doing just that. At first Felicity thought he would initiate a kiss or at least a hug. But like her, he hesitated, and the moment was lost.

"You seem to be all right," he said, lifting a lock of hair that dangled down her cheek. "A few more freckles, perhaps."

Goodness, she hadn't even considered how she must look all hot and mud stained. Was she always to appear her worst around him? "I seem to have misplaced my hat." She couldn't take her eyes off him. "And you? There was word of many dead and wounded." Felicity couldn't keep the quiver from her voice.

"Safe and sound." Devon arched his brow. "Were you concerned for me?"

"Well, naturally I . . . We are acquainted, and . . ." Felicity glanced down before she poured out her heart and soul to him. And wouldn't *that* be embarrassing? Especially when it seemed he hadn't given her a second thought. "Would you like a drink of water," she finally asked, remembering the buckets, on either side of her that she'd dropped. With a flourish she scooped up the ladle.

She held it toward him and he stepped closer. Which was a mistake. Felicity could smell him clearly, the gunpowder and sweat, the salty fragrance of his skin. It was a poignant reminder of what he'd been through . . . of how fragile life was.

His hand covered hers as he tipped the ladle bowl toward his lips. His first sip was tentative, then he lowered his head and gulped the clear, cool liquid. Felicity resisted the urge to place her other hand on his sun-kissed hair.

"Where are the children?" Devon drank his fill then looked up, backhanding the moisture from his mouth.

"Ezra's over there." Felicity pointed to where a group of people were slicing meat from a roasted pig. "Sissy is at the Widow Hawkins's house with Lucy."

"Tilly Hawkins's?" Devon cocked his head to the side.

"I believe she said her first name is Matilda, yes." Felicity also knew the lie she'd told the elderly woman. "She appears to be acquainted with you."

"More my grandmother than me," Devon said as he took a step back. Taking her in his arms was too tempting standing this close. "But I was always fond of her. And as I do recall she made excellent molasses cookies."

"She seems very nice." Felicity swallowed. As a matter of fact I need to tell—"

"There she is now." A smile was in Devon's voice.

Felicity glanced up, shading her eyes with the back of her hand, in time to see the widow coming their way. She leaned heavily on her carved hickory cane, but her step was lively . . . and determined. Devon started out to meet her until Felicity grabbed hold of his arm.

"I have to tell you something."

"What's wrong?" Devon stared down at her. "Sissy's all right, isn't she?"

"Oh, yes. It's nothing like that. It's just—"

"There he is. I told you he'd be all right," the Widow Hawkins said, directing her words to Felicity who could only smile weakly and nod. "Still as handsome as ever." She gave Devon a shove as he leaned over to kiss her cheek. "And still as ornery. I would have thought Felicity would settle you down."

Devon only had a chance to toss a questioning glance toward Felicity who seemed absorbed in studying the tips of her shoes before the Widow Hawkins was slapping at his arm.

"Don't tell me you're losing your hearing too? I asked about your grandmother. How is the dear woman?"

Felicity nearly rolled her eyes at the widow's description of Mrs. Blackstone as a "dear woman," but Devon didn't seem to find it unusual. He answered, bending his head toward the older woman, and using tones loud enough for her to hear.

"Well, I suppose I should get this water over to the tent," Felicity said, when there was a lull in the conversation. When the word "wife" came up she would just as soon not be there. She shrugged away Devon's attempt to help her with the buckets. "I can manage. You get some rest. You look . . ." The rest of her sentence was mumbled as she scooped up the handles and made her getaway.

She expected to hear the captain's laughter at every step. Certainly he'd think it the most amusing thing that she told Mrs. Hawkins they were married. He'd probably think since they'd been intimate that she desired such an arrangement. Felicity snorted as she emptied first one bucket, then the other, into the water barrel. Imagine her married to a Rebel. Preposterous. Felicity had to laugh at the very thought.

"Somethin' funny, ma'am?"

Felicity glanced up to see a soldier, his arm wrapped in a bloody bandage, standing before her. He looked no older than Ezra. "No. . . . I'm just so glad the battle's over."

"And that we whupped 'um."

Felicity smiled. "Yes, that too."

She didn't think she'd ever worked harder.

Of course, seeing that until her trip south she'd

never worked, made that an easy assumption. Still, by late afternoon, there were blisters on her palms and her lower back ached. Tendrils of damp hair hung down her neck and she was certain her face was one gigantic freckle.

And she felt good.

The soldiers she fed and offered water were profusely thankful. And the other women, some camp followers, whose husbands were in the Fourth Louisiana Battalion, but mostly residents of Secessionville or hereabouts, appreciated her help.

Of course they all thought she was Mrs. Devon Blackstone.

The Widow Hawkins might be old and hard of hearing, but she was a devoted gossip. She related stories of the Blackstone family to everyone within listening distance.

"Where did you say you were from, dear?" she wondered as Felicity carved a loaf of bread still warm from the oven.

"Richmond." She might as well keep that lie going, especially surrounded as she was by southerners still exuberant from a Yankee rout.

"Wentworth? You did say that was your maiden name, didn't you? Sometimes my hearing isn't what it should be."

Felicity merely nodded, then wiped her hands down the front of the towel she had wrapped about her waist.

"I don't recall any Wentworths when I visited Richmond. But then that was a long time ago. At any rate I'm so glad Devon Blackstone found you." She reached over and patted Felicity's hand. "That King girl never was any good for him."

"King? Ouch!" Felicity stuck the thumb she'd just cut into her mouth.

"Oh dear, did you hurt yourself?"

"It's nothing." Felicity pulled the digit out of her mouth and wrapped it in the toweling.

"Come over and sit in the shade a minute. You've been working too hard."

"No. I'm all right, really."

"Come on, dear. If you won't do it for yourself, do it for an old woman who needs a rest."

With a smile, Felicity gave into the coaxing. They both found a seat on a bale of cotton. The Widow Hawkins lifted a palmetto fan that hung from her waist and swished it back and forth through the humid air. "You did know about Victoria King, didn't you? I didn't mean to cause you any pain. I just figured since she was once betrothed to your husband he'd mentioned her to you."

Here it was. The perfect opportunity to recant and own up to the truth. 'I am not married to Devon Blackstone.' That was all she had to say to end this entire farce. Felicity even opened her mouth to do it. Instead, "Yes, I knew about her," came out.

"I'll be frank." Tilly leaned toward Felicity. "I never liked the girl. Oh, I know, she came from good stock. The Kings, you know have been around these parts forever. And Lord knows she was beautiful." Tilly patted her hand. "Not that

295

you aren't, dear. But there was just something about her. Do you know what I mean?"

"Not exactly." Though Felicity's curiosity was certainly piqued by now.

"Well, it doesn't matter. Water under the bridge, as they say. The truth was, Devon was madly in love with her. And everyone thought she felt the same way. But . . ." The narrow shoulders lifted in a shrug that promised no explanation.

"But what?" Felicity insisted.

"Why he went away, dear. To join the Navy. My, he did look handsome in that uniform. Of course, I never went on like this when Mr. Hawkins was alive. But then he was a handsome devil himself."

"I'm sure he was." Felicity paused, waiting for the widow to continue her story. When she didn't, Felicity decided a little prodding was in order. "So, what happened? I mean I know, but . . ."

"Well, of course he told you about how she broke their engagement, and to marry a man old enough to be her father. But rich as Midas."

"Sea View."

"That's right. She married Pinkney Doyle. All that money from sea island cotton. Of course, Devon Blackstone was hardly a pauper. The Blackstones have been one of South Carolina's most influential families for years. Why Devon's grandfather was a senator. And you know about his uncle by marriage, Harry Fenton. He's one of Jefferson Davis's most trusted advisors." She sighed and swiped the fan past her nose a few more times.

"But Devon wanted to be a sailor. And I suppose Victoria didn't think that was prestigious enough for her. Word was they argued about it before he left, but I assume your husband thought it was settled for he was sure surprised when he came back to Charleston and heard about her wedding."

"I can imagine." That wasn't the only marriage he'd be surprised about. Their own would leave him speechless. A fly droned around her head and Felicity absently swatted at the insect. "So is that it? I mean, she married someone else without telling him."

"Goodness, isn't that enough?" The widow's narrow eyes spread. "But even if it were it isn't all. There's the duel, of course."

"The duel?" Felicity's voice rose in surprise.

"Gracious sakes, he didn't tell you any of this, did he? I'm surprised word of it didn't reach Richmond. It was all the talk in Charleston and down this way." Tilly pushed to her feet, her joints groaning in protest. "Anyway, it's not for me to tell you."

"What?" Felicity couldn't believe her ears. The woman who'd chattered about everything and everybody since she met her, was now—now that the topic was compelling—going mum. "Mrs. Hawkins." Felicity jumped up and raced after her. "Tell me what happened. I have a right to know." Actually she didn't, not really, but the words just spilled from her mouth.

"You do at that, my dear." The widow paused and took Felicity's hands in one of hers. The gnarled fingers closed around Felicity's. "But your husband's the one who should explain it to you."

"But he won't."

"Goodness dear, you obviously haven't been a wife very long if you don't know how to get information out of your man. Just sweet talk him a bit, and he'll come around."

Sweet talk. Somehow or another Felicity didn't think her sweet talk worked on Devon Blackstone. Unlike the flock of beaux who seemed to hang on her every word in New York, the captain was impervious to her smiles and honeyed words.

Not impervious to her, of course. He was very attracted to her, just as she was to him. But the explosion that occurred when they let that attraction get out of hand didn't lead to talking. An involuntary shiver ran up her spine.

"Come on, dear, there are hungry soldiers that need to be fed."

Felicity glanced up at Mrs. Hawkins' words, realizing she'd been daydreaming about kissing Devon Blackstone. Shaking her head, she trudged over to where the town's women and soldiers vied for space under the spread tarpaulin, and resumed slicing bread.

Felicity was tired but beginning to think she

might get away with her lie. Word had filtered through the residents that the Yankees had been shoved back to their camp on the southeastern tip of James Island.

"Wouldn't surprise me none if they get into one a them boats they keep down there in Hilton Head and get the hell off the island altogether." The soldier who told her that quickly apologized for cursing, then sunk what few teeth he had into a hunk of bread covered with ham slices. He looked more like he should be settled in a rocking chair than carrying a gun.

"There aren't any more Federal troops around here then?" Felicity handed him a dented tin cup full of water.

"Naw. We done showed them what they was up against," he bragged. The old man eyed the liquid in his cup. "Ye don't have somethin' with a little more bite, do ye?"

"Sorry." Felicity shook her head. All the available liquor was turned over to the army surgeons. With a grimace, he threw back his head and drained the cup, then backhanded his mouth. "Them Yankees found out about us Rebs, they did. Also got themselves a lesson on pluff mud," he said with a chuckle. "Learned ye just can't march no army through it."

"Is that what they tried to do?"

"Yep, heard the colonel talkin' about it meself. Tried to flank us but got stuck in the mud." The soldier guffawed so hard Felicity feared he'd choke on his food.

Well, she wasn't crazy about the Union army losing a battle, and she certainly regretted all the blue clad bodies buried in front of the fort. Over three hundred, she'd heard, trying not to imagine her brother as one of them.

But hopefully they wouldn't run into any more Union soldiers on their way back to Charleston.

And as soon as Felicity spotted Devon she was going to suggest they pick up the children and resume their journey. There seemed to be nothing else they could do here.

Unfortunately the Widow Hawkins saw Devon before Felicity did. She glanced up to see the tall blockade runner, leaning over to hear something the withered old lady said. He laughed and Felicity's heart sank. She must be telling him about Felicity's claim to be his wife. Well, she would face that square on.

True, she was hoping to avoid owning up to her lie, but now that it was out in the open she'd explain why it was necessary . . . and endure the captain's insufferable grin.

But though she was steeled to take whatever ridicule came her way, there was none.

When Devon came closer Felicity noted he'd cleaned himself up some, though he still needed a shave. "You must be tired," he said. "You've done enough. Most all the soldiers are back in the fort anyway."

Felicity thought she detected a hint of pride in his voice, but that was ridiculous. She hadn't really done anything. Besides, she meant nothing to him.

Felicity quickly pulled off the makeshift apron. She was tired, but that wouldn't stop her from doing what needed done.

"I'm ready," she announced, stuffing hair back into her lopsided chignon. "Ezra must be with the girls. We'll pick them all up and be on our way. Thank you so much for taking us in, Mrs. Hawkins," Felicity said, turning toward the older woman. "I shall be eternally grateful."

"It was my pleasure, dear. And you were so very helpful. But we'll have plenty of time to talk later."

"I only wish we did." Another lie. "But Devon and I really need to go." Felicity flashed her "husband" a quick smile.

"Not so fast, Red. Tilly asked us to stay the night, and I think it's a good idea."

Well, she didn't! Felicity swallowed and looked from one to the other. "What about Charleston?"

"We'll be much better off getting a good night's sleep and starting fresh in the morning." Devon pulled Felicity's hand through his elbow. His other arm he offered to the Widow Hawkins.

Felicity wanted to dig in her heels and refuse to go, but in the end she had no choice.

Dinner was a nightmare.

Mrs. Hawkins obviously didn't get much company, times being what they were. She made the most of having two pairs of young ears to soak up all her gossip. There wasn't much to eat, but

301

then no one was particularly hungry. At least Felicity wasn't. She'd had her fill of handling food today.

When Mrs. Hawkins suggested they retire to the parlor, Felicity excused herself to see to the children. Through the entire meal nothing had been mentioned about her "marriage" to the captain. And Felicity could barely stand the tension of anticipating when it would happen. Several times she opened her mouth to confess, only to shut it again. Maybe, just maybe, she could get away without anyone knowing.

Sissy wasn't good. She'd fallen asleep soon after drinking some broth and eating the milk-soaked cornbread Felicity had brought her earlier. Lucy, after being reassured that they were safe and the battle was over, cuddled down contentedly by her sister. Ezra, looking as tired as Felicity felt, sprawled on the pallet by the unlit fireplace.

"I'll come back soon," Felicity murmured as she left the room. At least she hoped she would. If Mrs. Hawkins didn't throw her out. But she seemed a kind soul, Felicity told herself, and surely the captain wouldn't allow it. Of course, she didn't know how he'd feel about her passing herself off as his wife to old friends.

She couldn't believe the subject of their relationship hadn't come up. Except that the conversation—mainly between Devon and the Widow—centered around mutual acquaintances, and what had happened to them since the war began.

But not a word about Victoria and Pinkney Doyle.

The one subject Felicity longed to know more about was completely ignored. Ask your husband about it, Tilly had said. Felicity snorted as she descended the stairs. She was certain *that* would do her no good.

Stopping before the Chippendale mirror in the hallway, Felicity placed the candle on the table and patted her hair into place. She leaned toward the looking glass, sighing at what she saw. Even in the gentle glow of candlelight she looked awful. Her skin was no longer porcelain white, and the captain didn't exaggerate about the sunspots that freckled the bridge of her nose.

Mauve tinged the crescents beneath her eyes, and her clothes, though stylish and of good quality, didn't fit well. Not to mention the fact that they were travel stained.

Felicity touched a freckle, then let her fingertip trail down her cheek and neck to the scooped decolletage of her gown—Victoria's gown. *She* probably never went outside without her bonnet, or spent the afternoon feeding soldiers, or . . . or any of the other myriad things Felicity had done since she left home.

But it didn't matter. Soon she'd be back in New York. She'd sleep till noon if she chose and spend the rest of the day shopping or visiting friends. And this would all become an unpleasant memory. A week or two of rest and she'd look and feel as good as new.

Besides, what difference did it make now? What difference did it make how she appeared for Captain Blackstone. A Rebel. A blockade runner. A slave holder.

It was with a great deal of self disgust that Felicity pinched her already sun pinkened cheeks and moistened her lips before entering the parlor.

The captain stood when she entered, and smiled. And heaven help her Felicity's knees felt weak. "How's Sissy doing?"

For a former slave owner he seemed genuinely concerned for the children's welfare. "She's asleep. I imagine they all are now."

His dimples deepened as he offered her a glass of wine.

"It's wild plum," Mrs. Hawkins informed her as Felicity took a sip. "My late husband, bless his soul, made it himself, from the tree out back. Every evening we'd sit in here and . . ." Her voice trailed off and she blinked her rheumy eyes. "Anyway, I rarely drink it anymore, but thought this occasion called for a bit of a celebration. Devon was good enough to fetch a bottle from the cellar."

"It's delicious." Felicity took another drink. She'd drink the wine, then excuse herself. No one was likely to awaken her with accusations about her lies. And tomorrow, after some rest she'd be better able to ignore any of the captain's comments. And besides, perhaps everyone would go to bed and Mrs. Hawkins and the captain would never discuss his marital status.

"I propose a toast," the widow was saying. "To our glorious defeat of the Yankees."

Felicity gave an inward shrug and took a sip.

"And goodness!" Mrs. Hawkins fanned the air with her palmetto leaf. "How could I have forgotten the most important thing to toast?" She raised the small crystal goblet again. "To Devon Blackstone . . ."

Felicity touched the rim to her lips.

"And his lovely bride."

Purple wine sprayed out of Felicity's mouth. Over her gown and the leg of Captain Blackstone's pants as he sat on the settee beside her.

"Oh goodness. Oh, goodness, is she all right?" The elderly lady bent over Felicity and dabbed at her bodice with a lace edged handkerchief. "Whatever happened?"

The captain was behind her, pounding on her back and Felicity was trying to catch her breath. And she wished she could just swoon away. She shut her eyes, waiting for Devon to expose her for the liar she was.

Seconds ticked away on the steeple clock gracing the corner of the mantel, and he said nothing. He stopped drumming between her shoulder blades and Felicity stopped coughing. And waited.

"I think she swallowed wrong," he said, leaning around to look her in the face. "Is that what happened, my darling wife?"

If looks could wound, the captain would have toppled to the carpet. As it was, he only grinned.

"It's been a long day, Tilly," he said. "And an eventful one. I better take my *wife* to bed."

"Oh, of course. I was just chattering on, not thinking about how tired everyone is." She started to rise and Devon leaned over to help her. "Why, I do believe I'm fatigued also. Do run along and have a good night. I had my maid open up the bedroom at the top of the stairs for you both."

"That won't be necessary," Felicity blurted out, then grimaced as two sets of eyes looked her way. "I mean, Devon can sleep there, of course. But I think I better stay with the children. Sissy could—"

"Nonsense." This from Devon who moved toward her, draping his arm around her shoulders. "Sissy will be all right." He turned, pulling her effortlessly toward the doorway. "We'll see you in the morning, Tilly," he called back over his shoulder.

At the bottom of the stairs Felicity grabbed hold of the newel, and gritted her teeth. "What do you think you're doing?" She kept her voice low as they watched Tilly hobble to her first floor bedroom and shut the door.

"I'm taking my *wife* to bed," was all he said before scooping her up into his strong arms.

Fifteen

"Put me . . . down." The last word ended with a thump as he did just that—in the bedroom at the top of the stairs. He shouldered the door shut. Felicity stood, her composure sorely strained, leaning against the paneled wood.

She tried to calm her heaving breast and regain some composure. But that was difficult when the captain stood, grinning down at her.

There was a candle on the commode. It didn't offer much light, but certainly enough for Felicity to know that Devon was enjoying her discomfort. She took a deep breath and swallowed. "How long have you known?"

"That we're married?" His dark brow arched.

Felicity grimaced. "That I was forced to tell that falsehood to provide shelter for myself and those children."

He watched her a moment, his eyes narrowed. "Are you telling me that Tilly Hawkins, the sweetest, most caring woman alive, save Grams, refused to take you in unless you lied?"

"Well . . . no. But," she paused, then added quickly, "I didn't know what kind of person she was. *And* several other households had turned me away." She lowered her gaze. "It just so happens this was when I decided to use another tactic." She glanced up. "I didn't think I had a choice. How was I to know you were friends?"

Devon shrugged. "I guess you just have to be more careful whom you lie to."

"Perhaps so." What would he think if he knew of all the lies she'd told? There was a part of Felicity that wanted to find out ... . to simply tell this man the truth about everything. But baring her soul didn't seem the wisest choice at the moment. Not that she knew what the wisest course of action was. "What are you going to do now?"

Devon lifted his shoulders again. He was so close she could smell the soap he'd used to shave the whiskers from his cheeks. Smell the sweetness of the wild plum wine.

"I suppose I'll go to bed," he said, though he didn't move away from where he pinned her to the door.

"I won't sleep with you." The words, blurted out, seemed to amuse the captain, and Felicity could easily imagine why. After all, she'd done it before—twice—with apparently not even a second thought. "I mean . . ." Felicity tried to think of some explanation for her behavior. She wished he wasn't standing so close to her. A deep breath would brush her breasts against his chest. She could feel her nipples tighten with the realization.

308

Lifting her chin, Felicity fought her body's reaction and stared him in the eye. "Don't you think we should tell Mrs. Hawkins?"

"She'll be heartbroken."

"To find a liar in her midst?"

"Well, that probably wouldn't please her. But she thinks we're perfect together."

Felicity's eyes widened. "Well, we're not! I mean, well that is simply ridiculous."

"I didn't say *I* agreed."

"I should hope not." And if he'd only move away from her, Felicity could stop thinking about how wonderful it felt in his arms.

"After all, you have what's his name . . . your betrothed."

"Yes," Felicity agreed. "I do. And his name is Jebediah Webster."

"Ah, that's right." Devon nodded sagely. "Jebediah. Is he in the Confederate army?"

"Certainly not." Felicity tamed her indignation when she remembered her lie about being from Richmond. "He's a minister."

"You're going to marry a preacher?"

Felicity flattened her spine against the door. The distance between them didn't increase, and she wondered if he moved toward her. "What do you mean by that? Why shouldn't I marry a minister?" Suddenly Jebediah's arguments against their marriage came flooding back and she expected a reaffirmation of her unworthiness from the captain. Instead, he reached out and touched his fingertips to a ringlet framing her face.

"Because you have too much spirit to marry some musty old minister," was all he said before bending his lips down toward hers.

Felicity's heart pounded in her ears as he hesitated. Their breaths mingled. "Who said he's musty?"

His nose brushed hers as he angled his head to look at her. "Isn't he?"

What a time to have an overwhelming desire to be honest. Feeling guilty and liberated at the same time, Felicity nodded, admitting the truth about Jebediah to Devon . . . and herself. "Insufferably so," she breathed and her candor was rewarded with the touch of his lips.

The kiss deepened, and Felicity's senses swam. His tongue, his teeth, the way he moved his mouth, all seemed to make her bones soften. It happened every time he touched her, and she seemed unable to fight the reaction. At least not without a heroic effort.

His large palms were flattened on the door, bracketing her head. And his body was pressed to hers. Felicity could feel the proof of his desire, strong and hard, and the spring of passion tightened.

But when his lips left hers to forge a burning path down the side of her neck she summoned her strength and shoved against his chest. "Don't . . . don't you think we should tell Mrs. Hawkins?"

"Tell her what?" Devon couldn't get enough of her. Last night when he was riding for reinforcements, today during the battle, he thought of her. And he'd yearned.

"Tell her I lied. Tell her we're not married." Felicity stretched her neck to give his magic lips more access.

"Not now." Her breasts were firm and so very responsive. He drew his fingers across the tips and the nipples tightened. He wanted to taste them. To see if they were as sweet and sensual as he remembered.

"Oh . . ." Felicity could barely breathe. She writhed against him, catching her breath when he inched up her skirts. The night air kissed her skin. "She's bound to find out."

He didn't answer and Felicity knew she should be more concerned, but his hand found the sensitive skin of her thigh and she wrapped her arms around his neck to keep from swooning to the floor.

His lips were hot and demanding when they returned to hers. And she was lost. Kissing him back with the expertise he'd taught her. With the abandon she could not explain. With the spirit he said she possessed.

"Oh God, Red." Devon yanked up her skirts, wanting, needing to feel the moist heat of her body. He should take her to the soft feather mattress, not a dozen feet away, but he didn't think he could get his feet to move. He kissed her, open-mouthed and passionately, while his hands roamed at will. Her buttocks were rounded, and he molded them to his hands, swallowing her sigh when his fingers shifted forward, skimming the moist crevice between her legs.

She was on fire. Felicity could barely stand the torment of wanting him as she did. Her hands tore at his shirt, longing to feel the bunched muscles beneath his sweat slick skin.

"Touch me."

At first his words held no meaning for her. She *was* touching him. As much as she could. Then as he moved against her, his body hard and arching toward her, she knew what he meant. Her hand dropped, inch by aggressive inch down the front of his shirt. At the waistband to his pants she hesitated . . . but only for a moment.

His groan, long and deep, was her reward as her palm traced the rigid length of his manhood. And then she was fumbling with the buttons, anxious as he to feel him inside her. But her fingers trembled, and the simple task, didn't seem so simple.

For his hands were also busy, caressing her tender skin, searching for the sensitive center of her sexual being. Turning her bones to jelly.

His kiss sent her head spinning. His touch, the sensual slide of his fingers, shattered her completely. Her knees buckled and her mouth beneath his went limp. His hands joined hers, frantically unfastening the front buttons of his pants.

Free at last Devon shoved the broadcloth pants and drawers down over his hips and grabbing Felicity's buttocks lifted her up.

"What . . . are . . . you . . . ?" Each word

312

was reluctantly asked as she tore her mouth away from his, only to arch back for the contact.

"Your legs . . . put them around me."

"What? Oh . . ." Felicity sighed as her body seemed to move by instinct and wrap around him. Slowly she sank onto his straining staff, taking him completely.

For a long moment Devon could do nothing. He felt weak and strong at the same time, ready to slide with her to the floor, ready to climb the highest mountain. She felt so wonderful, so incredibly right.

He lifted her slightly, then arched, watching her beautiful face as his movements intensified. Her breathing was as ragged as his, her kisses as frantic. And then he rocked forward and felt her stiffen.

The waves of pleasure washed over her again and again, drowning her in pleasure. Her cry of ecstasy was captured by his mouth.

His own release was long and shattering, leaving Devon drained and satiated as only this woman could make him. Her breasts heaved against him as he lowered her. But her feet barely touched the floor before he scooped her up in his arms and headed for the bed. Devon nearly tripped on his pants, but thankfully, he managed to sprawl Felicity and himself across the mattress.

"Are you all right?" Devon lifted his head, and her giggle was his answer. He grinned in reply and kicked at his pant's legs, managing only to entangle them more. "Damn." Leaving the warm soft pillow of her body, he twisted around and sat up. His boots were first to go, then he shed his trousers and shirt.

When Devon turned back, she looked up at him with wide blue eyes. Her hair was tangled, caught up with pins in some places and spilling over the coverlet in others. Rucked up around her hips, her gown was wrinkled and soiled. And Felicity Wentworth didn't seem to even notice any of it. She was watching him.

He smiled, ready to make an amusing comment, one that might ease the tension of the moment. But before he could say anything, his expression sobered. "I can't explain why this happens between us, why I'm here in your bed," he said, answering the question in her beautiful eyes. "All I know is that I'm tired in body and soul. Today was hell . . . for both of us. Let me sleep beside you . . . and try to forget."

He would leave if she said to. Felicity was certain of that. No more teasing and taunting about her lie to Mrs. Hawkins. He would leave and in the morning he would either reveal the truth or allow the elderly woman to believe the untruth. But he would bother her no more tonight.

Except that she wanted him with her. No matter what happened on the morrow. For tonight she wanted to feel his strength. And she didn't care if it was right or wrong.

He studied her, the cords of his strong neck standing out in relief as the weight of his body rested on his arms. When she slowly, deliberately, raised her arms, the emerald of his eyes seemed to melt. He sank into the cradle of her body, his face buried in her hair.

Felicity held him like that, giving as much comfort as she could. She thought of the horrors of the battle and her arms tightened. At first she'd tried not to look at the wounded that were brought by wagons into Secesionville, but when she realized one of them might be Devon, she forced herself. Now, feeling him warm and alive . . . safe in her arms . . . made her remember the prayers she'd offered.

He lay there so long Felicity thought him asleep. Just when she would have shifted, to counter his weight, he lifted his head. His eyes found hers, and his smile showed no sign of its usual arrogance.

"I'm sorry," he whispered. "This can't be very comfortable." He shook his head when she started to protest. "And you're still dressed in this too tight gown." With that he raised himself up and gently turned her over. He began unfastening the row of buttons down the back.

He undressed her with infinite care. Felicity knew she should be embarrassed, but she wasn't, not even when he skimmed the shift down over her breasts and hips and she lay naked in the shimmering candlelight. His gaze was hot and admiring. But though he brushed his fingertips over her exposed flesh he made no attempt to kiss her.

One by one he removed the remaining pins from her curls, then fanned her locks into an arc across the pillow. "I love the color of your hair," he said, and Felicity felt it the most wonderful compliment she'd ever received about her looks.

But more important than praise of her beauty was the way Devon made her feel. Cherished. Protected. And important to him.

It was all a ruse, of course. He didn't cherish her. And his protection was but temporary, while they were forced to travel together. As for whether or not she was important to him, Felicity doubted he usually gave her more than a passing thought.

It didn't matter. Not tonight. This was what she wanted. Felicity forced from her mind the reality of the situation. She didn't even wonder if she were falling in love with him. Because she knew that couldn't be true. She loved what's his name . . . Jebediah. Didn't she? Devon kissed her brow and she sighed. His smile was sweet as he reached across to the commode and doused the candle.

With a flick of his wrist he flipped down the mosquito netting, cocooning them inside the starlit bed. Felicity cuddled to his side as he wrapped his arm around her. Within minutes he was asleep. As she lay there, breathing in his smell, enveloped in his warmth, Felicity felt the sting of tears behind her eyelids. She drifted off to sleep wondering why.

Charleston seemed to have changed even in the short time they'd been away.

Felicity couldn't decide what made the city look

316

different, she just felt the increased tension in the air. Even before they docked and stepped ashore.

It didn't take Devon, the children and her very long to travel from Secessionville across Charleston Harbor to the city. She could see the blockading squadron out beyond Fort Sumter. But Devon paid them little heed, so she didn't either.

Their relationship was on very tenuous ground. Which seemed strange after the night they'd spent together. But as the small sloop sailed toward the Ashley River dock, Felicity could barely meet his eyes.

It wasn't like that last night. After sleeping soundly in each other's arms, they awakened before dawn to make love again, this time more slowly. But that didn't mean Felicity was any less shaken by the experience. It still amazed her how he could set her heart pounding and scatter her senses with a touch . . . a look.

Which was probably why she avoided his stare now.

And had for most of the day.

This morning she'd been alone . . . and lonely, in the big bed when she awoke. After quickly dressing and pinning up her hair she hurried in to see about Sissy, Ezra and Lucy. They were still asleep, but she woke them, helped the two girls ready themselves, while Ezra ran to the barn to check on Mast'a Cock. Then she headed downstairs.

If the Widow Hawkins knew the truth, and she couldn't imagine that Devon didn't tell her this morning, Felicity wanted to be ready to leave. Especially now that Mrs. Hawkins knew she'd spent the night with the captain. As she descended the stairs, supporting one of Sissy's arms—Ezra had the other—Felicity cringed, imagining what the elderly woman must think of her.

But it was with a warm smile and kind word that the widow greeted her. "Devon is out doing some chores for me. He's such a dear," Mrs. Hawkins said. Nothing was mentioned about her relationship to Captain Blackstone. And they parted at the widow's door with kisses and promises to keep in touch and visit when the hellish war was over and the Confederates had driven the hated Yankees off their soil.

"Why didn't you tell her?" Felicity could stand it no longer. The steeple of St. Michael's loomed ahead. Soon they would separate, probably never to see each other again, and she had to know.

Devon tacked into the wind blowing off shore. He considered pretending he didn't know what Felicity was talking about, then thought better of it. She'd done everything but ignore him all day, and he didn't want her returning to her silent ways. But he had no good answer for her. He merely shrugged. "What would have been the point?"

"I don't know." Felicity turned to face him, hoping the children either wouldn't understand her conversation or that the stiff breeze would carry her words away from their ears. "Honesty. I know," she added, holding up her hand. "I'm a fine one to talk. But she's your friend. Surely she'll discover the truth."

"Perhaps."

He didn't seem to want to expound upon it so Felicity didn't push. "Anyway, I'm thankful. It would have been . . . embarrassing."

Her face was shadowed by the large brimmed straw hat she had pulled low on her head, so he couldn't tell if she was blushing. It was too bad, for Devon decided he liked to see her cheeks flush with color. Clearing his throat to stop the sentimental bend of his thoughts, Devon leaned forward. "Have you thought about how you're going to get to Richmond? I mean, with them." Devon notched his chin toward the three children huddled in the front of the boat.

"Richmond? Oh, by train, I suppose." She actually had a much larger problem than getting to Virginia. One that troubled her night and day. She had to take them to New York. But of course Devon didn't know that.

"I've been thinking." He swiped the unruly hair from his forehead. "If you think you can wait a week or two, I might be able to help."

"Help?"

He shrugged. "I need to run a load of cotton down to Nassau and bring back supplies, but after that, I might be able to do something about getting you home. Or you could stay in Charleston with my grandmother." Devon hurried on before he lost his nerve. "I realize you want to reunite the children with their mother, but . . ." Devon let his

319

words drift away. What was he saying? Hell, what was he thinking?

The woman was engaged to another. And just because she looked at him with large innocent eyes, and made love with him, didn't mean she was ready to settle here in Charleston to be near him. Hadn't he learned his lesson from Victoria? A woman was much more willing to give her body than her heart.

And what in the hell was he doing thinking of hearts and flowers anyway? There was a war on. A war that the South was losing, regardless of how a few land battles had gone. The blockade was squeezing the life blood from its people, and some of them didn't even know it yet.

But he knew it. His years in the Navy had taught him the necessity of open ports. He might be able to sneak through the line of Federal ships, but the odds were getting worse as the Yankees strengthened their hold on Port Royal.

At any rate he had no right to be thinking the things he was thinking about Felicity Wentworth.

"Never mind," he said, fooling with the sail. "It was just an idea."

"I have to get home." What else could she say? Felicity swallowed and looked toward the shoreline. "I . . ." What would he say if she told him the truth . . . all of it? That she wasn't from Richmond, but New York. A Yankee. A Yankee who'd come south to free three slaves.

She wanted to. She almost did. But then he

320

called to Ezra to help him furl the sail, and the moment passed.

When they went ashore Devon rented a coach to carry them to his grandmother's house. Word had preceded them about the battle at Secessionville and the Yankee rout. As soon as they crossed the threshold of the large house the questions started.

"Well, there you are finally. Where have you been?"

"Hello to you too, Grams." Devon settled Sissy on to a chair and crossed the hallway. He kissed her wrinkled brow and gave her a quick hug.

"I was worried," was all she said before changing her tone and demanding to know what had happened.

"The Yankees visited Royal Oak, though thankfully the place is still in one piece." Devon didn't add he thought that was only a temporary situation.

"And what of those letters of manumission?"

"Delivered." Devon brushed his fingers up through the stubborn lock of hair across his forehead. "I did the best I could for our people under the circumstances." He turned toward Felicity, taking her hand and pulling her forward. "Miss Wentworth was very generous with her time and money."

This comment brought a nod as if Mrs. Blackstone expected no less . . . and from a virtual stranger. She leaned onto her cane, stacking her hands over the rounded hickory knob, and pursed her lips. "I don't know what we're all standing in here for. Devon, help your old grandmother into the parlor." As she said this, Eveline's gaze fanned the hallway, coming to rest on Ezra—and the rooster.

She jerked her head up straight. "Young man," she said, her voice aristocratic. "Would you mind explaining why you saw fit to bring a farm animal into my house?"

"That's Mast'a Cock." Felicity stepped forward, placing herself between Devon's grandmother and Ezra, who was practically shaking in his shoes.

"Mast'a Cock?"

The rooster threw back his head and crowed, seemingly in protest to Mrs. Blackstone's strident tone. Ezra's spindly arms wrapped around the bird as he flapped his wings.

"He's really a sweet animal," Felicity assured, though at the moment the rooster seemed crazed. Felicity looked to Devon for help, but he was leaning against the banister, arms folded across his chest, that maddening grin upon his handsome face. He merely lifted his brows slightly as Felicity scowled at him.

"Ezra," Felicity ordered. "I think you had better take Mast'a outside. Put him in the stables, but make sure to keep him hidden." They both knew what would happen to the bird if some hungry Charlestonian got a hold of him—and it didn't matter there wasn't enough meat on the old bird to feed a flea.

When he'd taken the noisy bird outside, Felicity

turned back to face Mrs. Blackstone. "I have three children with me," she said, refusing to be cowed by the woman's haughty stare. "I would appreciate it if they could stay here."

Eveline Blackstone didn't say anything at first. Her narrowed gaze settled first on Lucy, who'd come up behind Felicity and clung to her skirts, then on Sissy. She took several steps closer, her cane making a stiletto sound on the marble floor. Felicity resisted the urge to throw her body between Sissy and the nasty old woman. "This child appears to be ill," Eveline announced after examining the sunken eyes and the gaunt cheeks.

Felicity's spirits plummeted. She'd hoped the issue of Sissy's health wouldn't come up until Felicity could figure out a way to remove the children from the Blackstone home. "Well, yes she is," Felicity admitted. "But—" Felicity never got the opportunity to reveal what she planned to say. Mrs. Blackstone, who didn't seem to be paying her any mind anyway, interrupted.

"Then what is she doing down here? Devon, take her upstairs and put her to bed. You." She pointed an arthritic finger toward Lucy, who cowered further behind Felicity's skirts. "Are you this child's sister?"

Lucy peeked around the petticoated gown and nodded.

"Then follow my grandson upstairs and turn down the bed. You can do that, can't you?"

Lucy took a hesitant step, obviously torn between following a direct order and seeking safety.

The decision was taken from her when Felicity bent down and gave her a hug. "Of course you can do that, can't you Lucy? Now run along with Sissy."

Felicity thought Devon's grandmother might resent her interference, but when she straightened, she realized the woman wasn't even watching her. She'd summoned Ruth, and had set about giving her a list of instructions which included fetching a doctor.

"And don't let him tell you he's too busy to come here," Eveline said. "Remind him who pays for most of the supplies he uses if need be." She thought a moment, then shook her head. "Remind him whether he balks at coming or not. And before you leave, tell Lucus I want my tub filled with hot water."

"If you're plannin' on takin' a bath, I better stay to help ye."

"It isn't for me. You know I only bathe in the evening. Those children look as if they've been dragged through the swamp." Her dark eyes rested on Felicity.

She would not be intimidated. Raising to her full height, Felicity swallowed and linked her fingers. "They have been through the swamp, as have I." She knew her own appearance wasn't much better than their's. "If we're dirty, it was the least of our worries, what with the Yankees and the heat and—"

"Yes, yes, well, they're safe now, aren't they?"

Felicity wasn't certain about that but she agreed,

and followed Mrs. Blackstone into the parlor. She sat on the edge of her chair, nervously wishing Devon would return and talk to his grandmother so she wouldn't have to.

"Word is that there was a battle at Fort Lamar?"

"Yes. We were there at the time."

"I figured you might be." Eveline settled back in her chair. "So did we defeat the Yankees?"

"They turned back, yes."

Eveline sighed and leaned forward, hands clasped on her cane. "They'll be back. They always come back."

"Now Grams, don't be so pessimistic." Felicity turned, relieved to see Devon standing in the doorway, his booted ankles crossed. He pushed off from the doorjamb and crossed the carpet, stopping behind Felicity's chair. "I sent Ezra upstairs. I imagine he's being scrubbed raw about now."

"Maybe I should go see about him." Felicity jumped to her feet, only to sink back into the chair as Mrs. Blackstone spoke.

"Nonsense. The boy isn't going to want you up there, while he's bathing. And as for you, Devon, listening in on conversations isn't polite, but since you did, I might remind you that we are of the same mind when it comes to the eventual outcome of this war."

"Perhaps, but that's no reason to frighten our guest."

"Poppycock, our guest, as you call her, doesn't

frighten easily. I should think you'd discovered that by now."

Devon merely shrugged and settled into the winged chair beside Felicity. He ignored his grandmother's thinned lips when he placed his boots on an embroidered footstool. When he'd made his long body comfortable, he swiped at his hair and faced both women. "It doesn't look good. From what I can tell the Federals have themselves a real stronghold at Hilton Head. They can fuel their blockades and cover most of the South Carolina coast with little difficulty."

"What of the *Intrepid?* Are you going to be able to slip out of the harbor?"

"Oh, I'll get out." Devon blew air through his teeth. "I'll probably even be able to bring supplies back into Charleston . . . this time. But without a steady supply of goods, the Confederacy is sunk."

Felicity couldn't believe that she, a northerner, was sitting here while the Blackstones discussed the fate of the war. They even seemed to include her in the conversation . . . as if she had anything of import to say. And as for Mrs. Blackstone's comment about her fearing nothing . . . well, nothing could be further from the truth. She was afraid of everything.

Of not getting the children home safely. Of encountering Yankee soldiers. Of encountering Rebel soldiers. Goodness, she was even frightened of Mrs. Blackstone. Which is why she was annoyed when Devon announced plans to visit the docks and check on the *Intrepid*'s refitting. Luckily, though, she didn't have to remain with the older woman.

"I think I'll take a nap before dinner," Eveline declared. "And by the looks of you, a rest would do you good, too," she said to Felicity before hobbling from the room.

Dinner that evening was a strained affair. Partly because Devon hadn't returned from the docks. Felicity realized she missed his presence, and not only as a buffer between herself and his grandmother.

Actually, it wasn't Mrs. Blackstone who bothered her this evening. It was Devon's Aunt Judith. She was incensed that her mother was allowing three Negro children to stay in the house as guests.

"It's not that *I* care," she insisted between bites of cornbread. "But what will people think? I mean, Harry has a position where it's important how people view us. I can't believe you don't understand that."

"Harry's an underling trying to ingratiate himself to a fool," Eveline mumbled, though she changed her words when Judith asked her to repeat herself. "It's foolish of us to care what other people think, times as they are."

"What do you mean by that? Why, the Confederacy just won a great victory, and Harry assures me many more will follow." Judith turned her attention to Felicity for the first time since they sat down. "I just envy you so, being there to actually see Colonel Lamar send those Yankees running."

"A lot of them didn't run. They died." Felicity didn't know what possessed her to say that except dying was what that battle had been about. Dying and fear of dying.

"Felicity's right," Mrs. Blackstone said, shocking Felicity. "Your nephew was there and he could have been one of the men who were killed."

Judith stiffened. "Well, you act as if I don't understand that. After all my own son, James, is serving the cause."

"On his father's staff."

"And just what is wrong with that? Honestly Mother, people would think you didn't admire our great President and what he's up against in this war."

Judith continued espousing the virtues of Jefferson Davis until her mother nodded off over her soup. The activity of getting Mrs. Blackstone to bed gave Felicity the opportunity to excuse herself, pleading exhaustion.

But she couldn't sleep. Long after she heard Judith come upstairs to bed, Felicity paced the confines of the large airy bedroom. What was she to do?

Thank goodness Mrs. Blackstone didn't feel the same as her daughter about Esther's children, for the doctor had proclaimed Sissy ill with pleurisy.

"She can't possibly survive a trip by train," he said, when Felicity suggested they must get home. "Rest is what she needs. Time in bed."

From her experience traveling by rail on the trip south, Felicity knew how tiring it was for a well person. She couldn't risk Sissy's life by subjecting her to that. But what? The only means of transportation that supplied a bed was by ship, and that was something she couldn't do with the war.

Felicity crossed to the window and parted the lacy curtains. Pressing her forehead to the glass panes she tried to think what she could do. She was so deep in thought that at first she didn't notice the solitary figure walking up the street.

Devon.

Felicity couldn't help the wave of excitement that swept over her. It wasn't until he nearly reached the house that she realized how wobbly his steps were. He grabbed hold of the wrought iron fence posts and looked up. Felicity jerked back but she couldn't tell if he'd seen her or not. But one thing she was certain of.

Devon Blackstone was drunk.

Sixteen

Had he seen her in the window?

Devon swiped at the annoying lock of hair hanging over his brow and laughed. Felicity Wentworth, woman of red-gold hair and blue eyes, was either fast asleep or looking after her charges. Her interest in him was limited to how he could help her. Or sex.

"Ah, sex," Devon mumbled to himself. There was that. Strong and overpowering. "And mind consuming . . . don't forget mind consuming," he muttered, then glanced around to make sure no one was witness to his display of drunken blubbering.

He wasn't *that* drunk.

Not that he hadn't tried.

After checking with his chief mate, Andrew MacFarland, and discovering that the *Intrepid* was not only repaired, but loaded with cotton, he visited several dockside taverns. And he drank.

At first he didn't know why. It wasn't like him to tip more than a few tankards of ale. But the further into his cups he became, the clearer his mind became, a paradox in itself.

Felicity Wentworth.

It all came down to her, and Devon wasn't the least bit happy about it. He was leaving tomorrow, and damnit, he didn't want to.

Because of her.

Devon blew out his breath and pushed open the front door. It was late, but someone had left a candle burning for him on the hall table. He grabbed the silver candleholder and headed for the stairs. He needed sleep and he probably should have gone to his own house, but he couldn't stop thinking about her, and he was drawn here.

Somewhere along the line he'd fallen in love with her. Devon snorted and nearly tripped over his own boots. He still wasn't used to the idea. When it first hit him, sitting amid some of his crew at the Rusty Pelican, he stopped in mid-swig and slammed the mug onto the scarred table top.

"What the hell is the matter with you, lad?" Andrew had asked, eyeing his captain cautiously.

"What? Oh, not a thing." He'd smiled, trying to ease his mate's mind. But he hadn't taken so much as another sip before he'd taken his leave with a mumbled excuse about sailing the next night.

So here he was, standing outside the bedroom where his "true love" slept. Devon was still drunk enough to find that amusing. His *true love* was betrothed to another. She was also the kind of woman he'd vowed never to tangle with again. Hadn't Victoria taught him not to trust beautiful, flirtatious women who cared only about themselves?

Except he didn't think Red's thoughts were purely selfish. She'd surprised him with her care of the Negro children. She'd surprised him about a lot of other things, too. Which was exactly why he was standing here, fighting the demons that urged him to knock on the door.

She couldn't stand it another second.

Felicity clutched her fingers together and stared at the door. After Devon moved out of view from the window she heard him enter the house. By the sound of his bootsteps she followed every step— even his stumble—as he climbed the stairs and strode the hall.

Then he stopped. Right outside her door. She swallowed and waited for the knock that never came. Her initial reaction, to turn him away with a polite but firm chastisement, faded. Curiosity turned to concern as she held her breath, attuned to the slightest sound coming from the other side of the paneled wood.

She could feel his presence. Her fingertip skimmed over the smooth surface separating them, and it was almost as if she were touching him. Her lashes drifted shut and she could see him, standing tall and powerful.

Before she could stop herself, Felicity yanked open the door. The expression of surprise on his face matched hers. And now that she had opened the door, Felicity couldn't think of a thing to say.

He stood, his forearm braced on the doorjamb, his head leaning into the bunched muscles of his upper arm. Staring at her. He hadn't knocked, but he'd been standing there for what seemed like an eternity, and she had to know it.

Felicity swallowed, and dropped her gaze. "What do you want?" Her voice was no more than a whisper.

The grin came slowly. "I'm not sure you want to know the answer to that."

Her eyes shot up to meet his, and she was instantly lost in their sea-green depths. Felicity wet her suddenly dry lips with the tip of her tongue. "Perhaps you're right." And perhaps she should shut the door and forget this nonsense. She'd fallen into his arms before and no good had come of it. Well, no long-term good. But then he said something that made her instinctively open the door wider.

"I'm leaving tomorrow evening."

"So soon? But I thought your ship was damaged. You said . . ."

"The *Intrepid*'s repaired," he shrugged. "And loaded with cotton. I can't wait any longer or the moon will be too bright." Devon's hand slid down the green-painted woodwork. "Besides, I'd say the goods I bring back are sorely needed."

"I'm sure they are. . . . I just didn't think you'd be going away so quickly." Felicity's breath caught as she looked into his eyes, as she saw the raw desire there. She didn't say a thing as he stepped into the doorway, moving ever closer. His arm snaked around her waist, catching a handful of delicate white nightrail as he dragged her up against him. Her unfettered breasts pressed into his chest.

"I'm going to miss you, Red." The words were murmured against Felicity's mouth, and then his lips sealed with hers.

She wanted him, right there and then. Forget that the door was open to the hallway and his grandmother or aunt might walk by at any moment. Forget that she'd vowed never to let herself be vulnerable to him again. None of that mattered now that she was in his arms again. Again for the last time.

Devon managed to hang onto his senses long enough to edge the door shut with the heel of his boot, but he didn't let loose of her mouth, or body. She felt so wonderful to him. Earlier he'd haunted the taverns convinced that he was the victim of another doomed love affair, though his feelings for Felicity were much stronger than he'd ever felt about Victoria.

He'd cared for Victoria, certainly, and planned to marry her. The match was practically preordained by their families. But when she'd wed another, his anger had overshadowed any heartache he felt. So when she came to him, suggesting her situation didn't preclude their having a loving, intimate relationship, all he felt was disgust.

Devon could never have those feelings for Felicity . . . he was certain. Even knowing she was betrothed to another man didn't cool his ardor.

"I want you." Each word was punctuated by a scattering of kisses as he lifted her higher. Her bare toes skimmed above the floor as he backed toward the bed. He flopped them both across the quilted counterpane, sliding slightly to the side so his hands trailed down across her breasts.

Felicity moaned, her body alive, her senses reeling. He twisted to sitting, quickly shucking his boots. Then, while she fumbled with his shirt and pants, he stripped off the borrowed nightrail. At last, naked chest to breast, he settled on top of her. The forest of curling hair skimmed across her nipples, distending them, tightening the spring of desire.

He kissed her: the side of her neck, the tender valley between her breasts, her mouth. He tasted of whiskey, smooth and sultry, and of the passion they shared. When he tore his lips from hers, Felicity arched up, wrapping her arms around his neck to guide him back. But he was stronger physically, and resisted the tug. He did appease her with a short deep foray into the sweet recesses of her mouth before leaning up on his elbows.

Felicity's eyes fluttered open when she realized he stared down at her. Pale moonlight gilded his strong features, and Felicity spread her fingers to sift through the dark waves of his hair. "What is it?" she whispered, for the night was soft and his expression was tender, at odds with the hard, long ridge of masculinity that pressed into her stomach.

"I love you." Devon watched as Felicity's eyes widened. He touched the corner of one with the pad of his thumb. When she said nothing, he shook his head, sending a lock of hair tumbling over his forehead. "I don't suppose you expected to hear that from me, did you?"

She tried to swallow, but couldn't. "I. . . . Well, I . . ." Felicity fumbled to find the right words, finally answering his question as honestly as she could. "No, I never imagined you felt anything for me at all."

His grin was devilish. "Aw, come on, Red. You must have suspected I had some feeling for you." With his knee, Devon spread her legs, sliding down into the cradle of her body.

Felicity sighed. She could feel him hard and hot, poised at the entrance to her body, and she could hardly resist thrusting down over him. Yet there was a remnant of rational thought about her, enough anyway to marvel at his revelation.

He was being unfair. What did he expect from her? Though a declaration of undying love would be nice, it evidently wasn't forthcoming, at least not now. He shouldn't have blurted out his feelings. And if his wits hadn't been dulled by whiskey and the scent of her, he would have known better. "Don't say anything." Devon's finger traced over her lips. "I just thought you should know." With that he plunged into her, sending them both on a wild and frenzied climb to the peak.

* * *

When Felicity woke she was alone. Except for his scent still lingering on the pillow and the radiant satiation of her body, she might have thought the night was only a beautiful dream. As it was, she couldn't deny the reality, any more than she could decide what it meant.

Life had always seemed very simple to Felicity. She learned at her mother's knee to prize her beauty. And though at times her existence bordered on boring, her way was clear, marked by the many parties and soirees she attended, and reigned over. The war brought changes, but even then she understood what was expected of her. Hadn't she shown as much by proposing to Jebediah?

But ever since she came to Charleston . . . ever since she met Devon Blackstone . . . her life was no longer simple. There was no straight and narrow path that led to acceptance and love.

"Oh, what am I to do?" Felicity threw her hands up over her head, and pushed down into the pillow, but there was no time for soul searching. After a timid knock, the door inched open and Lucy poked her head inside.

"Miz Felcy?"

Immediately alert, Felicity sat up, holding the counterpane to her chin. "What is it? Is something wrong with Sissy?" How could she lie abed selfishly pondering Devon's love when these children were her responsibility?"

"No ma'am, she okay." The child stood, studying the tips of her shoes.

337

"What is it then? Is something wrong with you or Ezra?"

"We's fine. It's Miz Blackstone."

Felicity brushed hair out of her face. "What about her?"

"She's wonderin' if yous gonna sleep the day away?"

"Oh, she is, is she?" How dare the old harridan send Lucy upstairs to awaken her! Felicity bristled with indignation until she caught a glimpse of the mantel clock.

"Twelve thirty!" Felicity started to jump up, then remembered her state of undress, and clutched the blanket higher. How could she have slept so late? The reason was all too obvious to Felicity. "Lucy, honey, would you please go downstairs and tell Mrs. Blackstone I'll be there directly. Oh, and Lucy?" Felicity called the child back into the room. "Is Captain Blackstone at home?"

"I ain't seen him, Miz Felcy," she said before shutting the door and skipping down the hall.

Why did a mantle of sadness fall over her just because the child hadn't seen Devon? She certainly didn't have to be around him all the time. When he left she'd *never* see him again. Felicity sighed and slowly climbed from the bed.

But thoughts of Mrs. Blackstone lurking below stairs, wondering why she slept so late, hurried Felicity through her toilette. She tried to act as if she always slept till noon—which before the war had actually been very common—as she descended the stairs. Better that than letting the old harpy suspect the real reason.

Felicity took a deep breath when she reached the wide central hallway, and patted a wayward curl behind her ear. She took a step toward the parlor, stopping dead in her tracks when she heard it.

"Oh, my goodness!" Only one rooster that she knew crowed that loudly . . . or that insistently. Mast'a Cock. What in the world was Ezra thinking to bring that bird in the house when Mrs. Blackstone told him specifically not to?

Hurrying into the parlor, Felicity spotted Ezra sitting cross-legged on the floor. He had a small cylindrical object in his hands and he stared intently into it. Felicity didn't see the rooster, but she was sure Ezra knew where he was.

"Where is it?" she whispered after gaining the boy's attention. "Ezra, you heard Mrs. Blackstone. She doesn't want your rooster in here."

"But . . ."

"No buts about it, Ezra. Mrs. Blackstone is not a woman you want to cross."

"You'd do well to remember that, young lady."

Startled, Felicity jumped and looked around. Her hand flew to her heart. Her mouth opened, but not a sound came out.

"Miz Felcy!" Lucy clutched at Felicity's skirts. "Miz Eveline's tellin' us stories. 'Bout pirates!" she added, her high pitched voice nearly squealing.

"That's . . . wonderful." Now that Felicity glanced around, she could hardly believe her eyes.

The parlor looked like a combination sick room, nursery, and barnyard. She spotted Mast'a Cock, who at the moment was resting comfortably and quietly, in a wooden crate.

Felicity skirted Ezra, who was absorbed by the brass object he held, and taking Lucy's hand went around the chair to where Devon's grandmother sat. If Mrs. Blackstone was as angry about the children as Felicity thought she was, all four of them—plus Mast'a Cock—could find themselves out on the street. And Felicity had given the small amount of money that the Yankees didn't *liberate* to the freed slaves at Royal Oak.

Forcing a smile on her face Felicity faced the older woman. "I apologize for the children." Her smile faded slightly. "And the rooster." The expression on Mrs. Blackstone's face, the narrowed eyes, the thinned lips, caused Felicity to pause. But Felicity hadn't been through all she had, or overcome all she had, to be cowed by this woman. Straightening her spine . . . and forgoing the smile, Felicity continued. "However, if someone would have simply awakened me, I would have taken care of them." Felicity let out her breath slowly, never allowing her gaze to waver from the older woman's hard stare. If she and the children were tossed onto the street, she'd simply find somewhere else for them to go.

"I do very little unless I wish to do it." Eveline's expression softened as she glanced toward the child clutching Felicity's hand. "Now where were we?" she said, motioning with her cane for

Lucy to sit down. "You too, Miss Wentworth, unless you'd rather be doing something else."

"No . . . I mean, I'd enjoy listening." Felicity settled into a chair across from Eveline Blackstone's.

"The pirate done 'napped the purty lady," Lucy chimed in.

"It is *kid*napped and yes I do believe that's where we stopped."

"Gentleman Jack." The words slipped from Felicity's mouth before she could stop them. Eveline Blackstone looked up and something about her expression reminded Felicity of Devon.

"You know about Jack Blackstone?"

"Only what your grandson told me. I saw the portraits at Royal Oak."

"Ah, yes, Jack and Miranda. They were fascinating people, as I'm certain Devon told you. But did he mention Jared Blackstone and his wife Lady Merideth? Their portraits are in the library. You must see them later."

After that the older woman related a fictional—Felicity assumed—and very entertaining story about the pirate and his true love. Lucy was enthralled, and Sissy, nestled against some pillows, was animated. It was obvious Ezra enjoyed the "pirate" parts but he went back to studying the brass instrument otherwise.

It turned out he had the microscope that was so prized by the pirate's wife, Miranda. "It still works?" Felicity asked, moving toward Ezra and joining him on the Aubusson carpet.

341

"So I'm told. Of course, we replaced the lens after finding it in an old crate in the attic. Look through it if you like."

She did, and that's how Devon found her, sitting on the floor, her gown spread around her in a graceful circle, when he entered the parlor a few minutes later. He stood, leaning against the door-jamb, thinking how right she looked in this house.

"Devon." Felicity felt his eyes on her and glanced up. Her heart beat faster and she struggled to her feet, accepting his hand when he pushed off from the doorway and offered his help.

"There you are." Mrs. Blackstone's tone had a tendency to sound accusing. "How are things aboard the *Intrepid?*"

"Just about perfect." Devon's gaze lingered on Felicity's face for a moment before he let go of her hand. "I see no problem with sailing tonight. The clouds should obscure what moon there is. Do you have your letters finished?"

"Most of them." Eveline leaned forward on her cane. "Well young man, aren't you going to help me as gallantly as you did Miss Wentworth? Or aren't my eyes a deep enough blue?"

Devon grinned cheekily. Leave it to his grandmother to notice the longing looks he was giving Felicity . . . and to comment on them. "Now Grams, you know your eyes are brown, not blue. And if you gave any indication you wished to rise, I'd be more than happy to assist you."

"Poppycock," she said, though she allowed him to take her arm and help her to her feet. "And

342

my eyes happen to be hazel. At least that's what my beaux used to tell me."

"Beaux," Devon laughed. "Did grandfather know about them?"

"My suitors were before your grandfather as you very well know. Now be a good boy and entertain these children while Miss Wentworth accompanies me to the library. And mind, make certain Sissy gets her medicine at one o'clock. The bottle is on the table. Goodness knows I had to browbeat Doctor Bateman before he gave me anything."

Eveline reached out her large knuckled hand to Felicity and there was no choice but to take it and walk with her from the room.

"Don't worry about them. They'll be fine," the older woman said when she noticed Felicity glance back over her shoulder. "Now I wanted to show you the portraits of my husband's father and mother."

The room was large and book-lined. It smelled of old leather and tobacco and Felicity could imagine Devon sitting in here, his feet planted on the mahogany desk top, a cheroot clamped between his strong white teeth.

"There they are." Eveline Blackstone settled into a winged chair and pointed to the paintings. Like the ones of the pirate and his wife, these were on opposite walls, facing each other. "My husband was the spitting image of his father. Dark. Handsome. Devon has their good looks, though his hair is a bit lighter." Her gaze clouded. "The Blackstone men have always been too handsome for their own good. Attract women like flies to honey." Her eyes narrowed on Felicity and she felt her cheeks darken.

But she refused to be intimidated by the old woman. Felicity raised her chin and returned her stare. Eveline didn't back down, but Felicity thought her expression softened. "Of course, they make good husbands once they find the right woman."

"Oh, really?" Felicity changed her tack, trying to appear uninterested in the subject. "I understand from a Mrs. Hawkins in Secessionville that your grandson found the right woman once . . . at least he thought he did."

"Victoria King was never destined to be a Blackstone. That was the one time in my life when I should have spoken up and didn't. Not that Devon would have listened, but he *should* have." She folded her hands over the cane's knobby end. "So you're concerned about Victoria, are you?"

"No!" Felicity protested adamantly, then clamped her mouth shut. Sitting in a chair directly across from Eveline, Felicity faced her squarely. "Don't read a happy ever after ending for your grandson and me." Felicity swallowed as Devon's words from last night came back to her. *I love you.* She let out her breath slowly. "I'm betrothed to another." Not exactly a lie. Felicity was certain when she returned with Esther's children, when she'd proven herself worthy, Jebediah would want to

344

marry her. She just wasn't so sure now that she wanted to wed him.

"Does Devon know about this?"

"My engagement? Yes."

Eveline lifted her shoulders in a gesture that belied her age. "Then he shall have to find a way to overcome it."

"But it isn't something that can be overcome." Anymore than she could forget her feelings for the Rebel.

"All in good time. All in good time," was all she said before telling Felicity she had to write her letters for Devon to take. "I'm afraid I must count on blockade runners to deliver my mail to England and the North."

"The North? I don't understand?"

"Devon sails to Nassau, as do vessels from the North. It's a simple matter of transferring a mail pouch from the *Intrepid* to another ship."

Transferring something from Devon's ship to one heading north. It sounded so simple, Felicity didn't know why she hadn't thought of it before. Nassau. A slight detour to be sure, but certainly one she and the children could handle. All she needed was a cabin with a comfortable bed for Sissy.

The plan was perfect . . . except for one thing. Felicity didn't think Devon would go along with it. He spoke of blockade running as if it were dangerous. But staying in Charleston was out of the question. If Felicity didn't get Sissy home soon she might never be reunited with her mother. The doctor wasn't optimistic about her recovery. Besides, it was obvious Devon thought the Yankees were an increasing threat to Charleston.

She had to do this. She just had to.

After leaving the library, Felicity leaned against the wall in the hallway and closed her eyes. She *would* do it. And not for Jebediah Webster. Not even for Esther and her children, though she cared dearly about the children. Somewhere along the way, Felicity realized it was important for *her* that she take Ezra, Sissy and Lucy to their mother.

"There are more comfortable places to nap," Devon said, slipping up beside her and curving his palm around her cheek.

Felicity lifted her lashes and smiled into his sea-green eyes. She was glad they would be together longer . . . even if he wasn't likely to be. Not at first anyway. "I wasn't sleeping, only thinking."

"About me?" His brow arched in a way Felicity found endearing.

It was on the tip of her tongue to offer him a flirty response, but somehow she thought he deserved better from her. "Not right at the moment. But I was earlier."

His grin was devilish. "I suppose that will have to do." Devon's expression sobered. "I wasn't so drunk last night that I don't remember what I said to you."

"I remember too."

His fingers splayed through her hair and he pressed closer. "This isn't the place, and damnit, I don't have the time right now. But I'm asking you to wait for me." He paused to take a deep

346

breath. "I shouldn't be gone long, and when I get back we can settle this." His brows drew together. "You aren't still in love with that Jebediah what's his name, are you?"

"Webster," Felicity supplied, shaking her head. "I don't think I ever was."

"Good." He kissed the end of her nose. "That's good." His lips dropped lower, melding with her in a deep soul-searching kiss. When it was over, his lower body was hard and aching, pressed against hers. He rested his forehead on hers. "I have to go. There are a few things I have to do before we sail."

"You will be careful, won't you?"

"Red, you can count on it." He kissed her once more, and then he was gone. Devon was halfway to the cotton exchange before he realized she hadn't really answered him about staying. But certainly she meant to. Didn't she?

Thank goodness Mrs. Blackstone decided to visit the hospital and took her daughter with her. The older woman seemed to sense Felicity's state of mind over Devon's departure and didn't insist she accompany them. As soon as the door closed behind the two women, Felicity gathered the children in the parlor. Ezra had already been instructed to pack their few belongings.

"I don't know if we should take Mast'a Cock," Felicity said, eyeing the bird staring at her through the slats in the crate. She faced Ezra in time to see the boy's bottom lip quiver. "Oh, I suppose it's all right." She held up her hand. "If you promise to keep him caged up. At least until we reach Nassau."

Hoping she wasn't making a mistake, about the rooster, about stowing away on the *Intrepid*, Felicity and the children left the Blackstone home.

Seventeen

The night was perfect.

Black as pitch without even a break in the smothering clouds to allow a smattering of moonlight to outline a spar or the towering cylinder of a smokestack. Even the mist rising off the swamps seemed guided by Providence as the wispy fingers slid around the *Intrepid's* hull, enveloping the green painted iron in a moisture laden coat of camouflage.

Devon Blackstone stood by the wheel on the cotton packed deck and stared toward the East. They were out there. Waiting. Sidepaddlers and steamers, the blockaders. He took a deep breath, letting the scent of puff mud and saltwater fill his lungs; and he waited.

But the usual heady rush of excitement didn't quicken his pulse. He anticipated the voyage. Yet it was journey's end that intrigued him. Journey's end and the waiting arms of a strawberry blond.

Devon scowled into the darkness. What had come over him? He knew better than most to think of permanence and commitment. The times called for neither. Some in the South might think so. But even now, little over a year into the conflict, the once hot-blooded Secessionists had tempered their stand.

And the worst was yet to come.

With each succeeding voyage the blockade grew stronger, the stranglehold on the Confederacy tighter. Politicians' prophesied aid from England or France was forthcoming. Devon shook his head, dislodging hair he'd finger combed off his forehead. His cousin, Stephen Blackstone, doubted the chances of that happening. A member of the House of Lords, Stephen knew the reality of England's dependency on the South's cotton.

The Confederacy's "ace in the hole" was stockpiled on England's wharfs, and the textile mills were quick to use cotton from India.

No, if the southern states were going to win this rebellion, they would have to do it on their own. And they'd have to do it without the advantage of free commerce and plentiful supplies.

Devon clenched the smooth wheel, made slippery by the damp air. It was not a time for commitment or thoughts of forever. Yet. . . .

He'd devised a plan. When he returned, and Devon had to believe he would, he'd find a way to transport those children to Richmond. Perhaps he'd take them all there himself. Then he'd ask Felicity's father for her hand, marry her, and bring her back to Charleston. Her betrothed, Jebediah "what's his name," wasn't a major obstacle as far as Devon was concerned, though he did have a twinge of conscience about the soon to be rejected suitor. But Felicity obviously didn't love him. And though having her live in Charleston was not what Devon would have preferred, she was as safe there as in Richmond.

"Engine's be stoked, Cap'n."

Devon turned toward his chief mate, who'd just entered the wheelhouse. He could barely see him in the darkness.

"Are we ready to take her out, Mr. MacFarland?" It was time Devon stop mooning over the fire of Felicity Wentworth's embrace and concentrate on running the blockade. The cotton, one thousand bales of it, would fetch a good price in Nassau, and the medicines and supplies he brought back to Charleston were sorely needed.

Yet, even with all his faculties attuned to the problem at hand, Devon couldn't shake the uncomfortable feeling of doom that clung to him as surely as the fine particles of moisture laden fog.

"Aye, we are at that, sir." Devon hardly heard the thick-muscled Scot's response until he added, "We'll slip through the Yankee barricade as slick as you please."

Prosaic words. The Scot said them every time. Like a ritual. Devon smiled, though the old man couldn't see him, and reached for the speaking tube.

"Half speed," he called down to the engine room. To his chief mate he repeated his warning about noise. "Tell the crew, Mr. MacFarland. No speaking above a whisper, and that only when necessary." There were times when they slid by under the hull of a blockader, so close they could hear the melancholy tune the watch whistled under his breath.

"And you've the bag of iron castings?" Devon reached for his mate's arm as he turned to leave.

"That I have. There'll be no telltale hiss of steam escaping through the safety valve. It will all go nice and gentle like under the water."

"Good man." Devon smiled as he clenched the Scot's shoulder. He could always count on his chief mate, as well as the pilot, and all the crew for that matter. They were loyal, and not a one of them had ever shown the white feather when danger flared.

Luck was on his side. Luck and experience, the weather, and even their coal. No soft bituminous coal this trip. The firemen were stoking the furnaces with clean burning anthracite. There wouldn't be a dark cloud of smoke to catch the eye of a Yankee look out.

When the pilot, Mr. Davidson, entered the wheelhouse, Devon relinquished the wheel and went out into the mist to keep watch. Every conceivable space was packed with cotton, so that the crew was forced to stand atop the bales to work the ship. Staying close to the wheelhouse, Devon focused out over the water as the salt-spray peppered his face.

The dull throbbing of the engines and the swish of paddles sounded loud in his ears. He only hoped the lapping waves and noise aboard the blockaders would drown out the sound.

Suddenly a dark shape, black and motionless, loomed out of the darkness. A blockader. With economy of motion Devon leaned into the small enclosed wheelhouse. "Two points to starboard," he whispered. He felt the slight shifting of the schooner, and held his breath. "Steady." Detection could come at any moment. But it didn't. They slipped past, quiet as a mouse.

Yet there were also risks to being invisible.

In the next moment Devon spotted a cruiser dead ahead. He barely could mutter, "Stop," in time to avoid a collision.

Devon sucked in his breath and his pulse quickened. He wondered if the Yankees couldn't hear the pounding of his heart over the sound of their own engines.

"That was a close shave, Cap'n," the pilot muttered, and Devon could only nod his head in agreement. The tension was as thick as the fog as he squinted his eyes, straining to see. He gave the order to proceed, and heard the low whisper, as Mr. Davidson relayed the message through the speaking tube to the crew below decks. Those few men topside crouched behind the bales of cotton, as nervous as he.

The *Intrepid* lunged forward, like a thief in the night. And that's when he heard it. A loud shrill crow that made his blood run cold as the North Atlantic.

"What in God's name . . . ?" The sound rattled the pilot so he forgot to whisper.

But it made no difference.

Blinding rockets exploded overhead. Searching the night for any vessel brave or foolish enough to attempt a run through the blockade.

"Full speed ahead!" Devon thundered the order as the first shells ripped through the spars. They'd been detected and could now do nothing but run for their lives.

And all because of a rooster.

Felicity huddled behind the bales of cotton stuffed into the captain's cabin, her eyes closed, her arms wrapped around Sissy and Lucy.

"I'z really sorry, Miz Felicity. I tried to keep Mast'a Cock hushed."

Her lashes lifted, but Felicity could barely see Ezra squatting to her left. "I know you did." She took a deep breath, waiting for the loud rumble of cannon fire to subside. It didn't, so she yelled over the noise. "It was my fault for letting you bring him." When they stowed away on the *Intrepid*, Felicity just didn't have the heart to tell Ezra his pet had to stay behind. Besides, what harm could a cooped up rooster do?

Felicity took a deep breath and let her head fall back against the bulwark. Apparently plenty. Felicity knew enough about blockade running to appreciate the importance of silence—which is why she'd insisted nobody speak until they heard plenty of commotion above deck. That would mean they were past the blockading ships.

She was also well aware it was more than coincidence that the firing started within moments of Mast'a Cock's strident crowing. A loud boom shattered the night, and the vessel jerked to the right. Lucy, who until now was quietly crying, let out a frightened wail. Felicity did her best to comfort the child, but her soft words were barely audible over the din of canonry and sounded hollow.

Felicity was frightened, for herself and the children . . . and for Devon, who she knew was bearing the brunt of the shelling on deck.

In the eerie light of the rockets, Devon could see the men, chests pressed to the wood decking behind the cotton. Part of the starboard paddle box was shattered, and still the shelling was close.

"More speed, Mr. Davidson," Devon yelled over the din. "Tell them to pile on the coal!" Knifing through the water, the *Intrepid* strained against the pressure. And forward visibility was so poor Devon could only pray that they didn't sail straight into another blockader.

But amid grape shot and canister the *Intrepid* was leaving the blockader astern. The *Intrepid* had finally gotten up full steam and was cruising along at over twelve knots.

"She's giving chase!"

Devon whipped around to see Mr. MacFarland standing by his elbow. As yet another rocket brightened the sky, Devon saw that the Scot was right. A cruiser had come out of the darkness and she was in hot pursuit of them, closing fast.

"We've all twelve furnaces going full steam," the pilot said in answer to Devon's unasked question. "There's nothing more to give."

"Unload some of this weight!" Devon gave the order in a booming voice, then rushed forward to begin the task. He strained against the thickly packed cotton bale, his muscles burning as it slid overboard.

By the time he and his crew cleared the deck, dawn pewtered the eastern horizon and the Yankee cruiser was out of range. The blockader tried signaling for assistance by spewing dark smoke into the twilit sky. But there seemed to be no other ship near and as the *Intrepid* continued at full speed, she left her pursuer in her wake.

"God Almighty!" The Scot scratched at his red beard and leaned against the wheelhouse. "They ain't just playin' around no more, and that's for certain."

"No, they aren't." Devon wiped his sleeve across a sweat dampened forehead. "Any casualties?" When the chief mate shook his head, Devon let out a long breath. "I think our pursuer was the *Connecticut.*"

Davidson's low whistle sounded from inside the wheelhouse. "We're lucky to be clear of that cruiser."

"She's a fast one, and no mistake. But no match for the *Intrepid.*"

"I don't know. I had a moment or two of worry."

"You Cap'n? Now that's hard to swallow." The chief mate pulled his cap lower over his eyes. "What was it do you suppose made that unGodly noise in the first place?"

Devon gave no response, only ordered the mate to set the men to clearing away the rubble left by the shelling, then he headed below.

His fists were clenched as he hurried down the ladder. He was angry, almost afraid of what he might do when he found her. From the moment he heard that rooster crow he knew. She defied him. And very nearly got them all blown to hell in the process.

He threw open every door as he strode along the passageway, but he never really thought she'd be in any cabin but his own.

The portal slammed back against the bulwark, startling Felicity as she stood from kneeling beside the bed. Her hand flew to her throat and she gulped. In the pale wash of light filtering through the porthole Captain Blackstone's face was a study in rage.

"I . . . I can explain. You see . . ."

"Don't say anything," he growled, covering the cabin in three strides and grabbing her by the arm. "Not one word."

"You leave Miz Felicity be!" Ezra shot up to challenge the much taller and stronger man.

Devon jerked his head around to see the boy's defiant stance. He held his rooster, who for the

357

time being rested comfortably and quietly in the crook of Ezra's arm. Before Devon could do or say anything, Felicity reached out and touched the boy's shoulder. "It's all right, Ezra. Captain Blackstone has every right to be angry with me."

"You're damn right I do!" He certainly didn't need her sanctioning his emotions. He hauled her back a step, a movement she didn't resist, then his gaze fell on the child lying in his bed. His grip loosened. "Is she all right?"

Felicity took a deep breath and nodded, her eyes coming to rest on Sissy. "She's tired and frightened . . . and weak."

"Which is reason enough not to have pulled this crazy stunt. What in God's name were you thinking?" Devon didn't expect an answer, and received none. Ezra still stared at him, almost daring Devon to make a move against Felicity. And damn, Negro or not, he respected the boy. With a frown Devon turned back to Felicity . . . and realized someone was missing.

Jerking his head around Devon looked for the youngest child. He caught a glimpse of her cracked leather shoe peeking out from behind one of the cotton bales stuffed into his cabin.

Devon's hand dropped from Felicity's arm and without thinking he crouched down before the child. She stared at him with wide dark eyes, two fingers stuck securely in her mouth. Slowly she pulled the glistening digits out and reached up her hands toward him. It seemed only natural to pick her up and pat her back when the child's arms wrapped around his neck.

"I weren't scared none," Lucy whispered into Devon's ear.

"Good." Devon felt a lump in his chest.

"Miz Felcy, she said you wasn't gonna let nothin' happen to us."

"She did, did she?" Over the child's head Devon's eyes met Felicity's and held. At first her dark auburn lashes drifted down, shielding her expression. But then they lifted and she met his stare.

Devon gave the child in his arms a squeeze and set her down on his bunk beside her sleeping sister. "Crawl down under the covers and get some rest." With his head he motioned toward Felicity. "I want to talk to you."

"You ain't gonna hurt her none, is ye?"

Whether he respected the boy or not, Devon wasn't used to being questioned, not by a youth, and not on his own ship. His jaw tightened.

"Ezra, I think we all know Captain Blackstone better than that." Felicity cocked her head, daring Devon to contradict her, even though she wasn't sure what he was capable of in anger. And there was no denying, by the set of his sensual mouth, he was angry.

"Stay here with your sisters," Devon ordered as he made his way across between the cotton bales toward the door. Felicity followed. She swallowed nervously, but she held her head high.

As soon as the door closed behind them Devon grabbed hold of her upper arm and hustled her

359

along the passageway. He wanted privacy, and that was a precious commodity on a blockade runner. Mr. MacFarland's quarters were to the right, and without thought to propriety Devon flung open the door and shoved her inside.

Cotton was packed to the rafters. The Scot might be a patriot, but he was not adverse to making money. Especially if he could buy some cotton in Charleston, carry it in his cabin and sell it for gold in Nassau. The bales blocked the window so when Devon slammed the door, they were cocooned in their own world of semidarkness.

Felicity took a deep breath. "I know what you're going to say, but—"

"Oh, you do, do you?" Which was interesting because *he* didn't know. Part of him wanted to shake some sense into her. She'd risked her life, and the children and his crew for what? Getting these children back to her Mammy. Of course, she'd been doing as much all along, traveling south during wartime . . . alone. Traipsing off behind enemy lines.

He loomed over her, but Felicity found she wasn't afraid. She didn't step back. Her father's wrath, though it rarely focused on her, was easily swayed by a smile. Felicity moistened her lips, but found herself unable to take that tack. He had every right to be angry, but she also wanted him to know why she felt compelled to do what she did. Felicity lifted her hands. "Don't you see? I have to get those children to their mother." Tears burned her eyes but she blinked them back. She wanted his understanding, not his sympathy.

Devon stood for a moment, jaw rock hard, arms crossed, looking down at her. He could feel his muscles tighten as he fought an emotion much stronger than anger.

But in the end it wasn't worth the effort it cost him to resist. Devon grabbed her to him, backing her up until she was pressed between the firmly baled cotton and his hard body. His mouth covered hers, capturing the tiny cry of surprise that escaped her lips. Anger turned to desire, fueled by the power of the narrow escape they'd just had.

He ravaged, spearing his tongue into the honey depths of her mouth, twisting and nipping, growling when she flung her arms around his neck. Her fingers tangled in his hair, clutching for purchase.

"God, when I heard that damn rooster and knew you were aboard . . ." Devon's hungry mouth forged a burning path down the side of her neck.

"It crowed . . . oh . . ." The feel of his bristled chin sent shivers across her flesh. "I tried to keep him calm."

Devon's response to that statement was to effectively quiet her by melding his mouth to hers. His hands bracketed her face, holding her still for the onslaught of his kiss. When his breath was so ragged he was forced to pull away, he stood, staring at her. Her eyes were closed, a crescent of long lush lashes resting on her porcelain-fair skin. Her lips were moist, slightly open, and more sensually inviting than any he ever saw.

Devon's thumbs swept across the fragile bones of her cheeks. She looked up, studying him with the same intensity he used to memorize every line of her face.

And then he could stand the separation no longer. His mouth lowered to hers again. Deeper and deeper he went until he was lost in a vortex of passion. His hand dropped to her breast, molding the warm soft flesh till he could feel the straining peak of her nipple through the silk.

Instinctively, Felicity arched toward him. Aching. Wanting. She could feel him hard and demanding through the layers of skirt and petticoat and groaned when he pressed his muscled thigh between her legs.

Devon's hand skimmed down her corseted ribs and over the feminine swell of hip. Through ruffles and lace he hooked the back of her knee, lifting her leg up, grinding himself into the V between her legs.

Her eyes flew open, and her fingers dug into the muscle and sinew of his shoulders. Devon rocked forward and her breath caught. She was hot and tight, like a coiled spring, and he wanted nothing more than to be buried deep inside her. He thrust, his erection straining painfully against the taut woolen fabric of his pants.

"Devon."

His name was a cry of desperation as her nails bit into his flesh. The tension in her body, in the soft, sexual sound she made, were almost his undoing. She was as near release as he, and they were both fully clothed, pressed into a standing room only cubbyhole of space.

"Oh, God, Red!" Devon slid his palm between their bodies, searching for the moist heat of her womanhood. His first skimming touch was all it took to send her writhing over the edge. Devon's tongue invaded her mouth as his finger did her body. And he relished the shuddered convulsions as she climaxed against his hand.

She couldn't resist him. Couldn't stop herself from calling his name again and again.

"Cap'n Blackstone."

His name came to him once more as Devon fumbled with the fastenings of his pants. He tried his best to ignore the implication of the thick Scottish brogue, but in the end could not. "Damn." The word he mumbled was heartfelt as he jerked his head around.

"Cap'n where you be?" It sounded as if Mr. MacFarland was close.

"I'll . . ." Devon paused and cleared his throat. To his own ears he sounded like a man wrest from the throes of passion. Which was exactly how he felt. "I'll be there in a moment."

Felicity's eyes were open when he looked back. Still leaning against the bale of cotton she stared at him wide-eyed. With a yank Devon righted her skirts.

"Who . . . ?" Felicity forced herself back to earth. Who is that?" she whispered while frantically repinning her hair. Devon's attempts to right his shirt and pants appeared just as frenzied.

"My chief mate. We're in his cabin."

Felicity's jaw dropped. "Then he'll be coming in."

The words were no sooner out of her mouth when the latch lifted, the door opened and she stared into startled brown eyes.

The chief mate, with his fiery red beard, obviously wasn't expecting to find a woman in his cabin. "And now who might you be?"

"Miss Wentworth is with me, Mr. MacFarland."

Felicity's head whipped around. Devon had managed to squeeze between two bales of cotton and was standing by a desk laden with charts. When Felicity glanced back at the large Scotsman she could tell more questions were on the tip of his tongue. But apparently respect for his captain made him swallow them.

"Were you seeking me for any particular reason, Mr. MacFarland?" Devon kept his body turned toward the desk, waiting for the condition of his lower body to normalize.

"Well . . . aye sir." The chief mate gave Felicity one more furtive look, then concentrated on Devon. "I thought you'd be wantin' to know. No one was hurt. Everyone's as right as rain."

"Thank you, Mr. MacFarland. I'm glad to hear that." And damn if that shouldn't have been his main concern. Certainly more important than making love to Felicity Wentworth. But then he hadn't begun with that in mind. He turned to face the Scot. "And the *Intrepid?*"

364

"No real damage. A spar or two shattered. But the men are jury riggin' them."

"Good."

"We did lose a fair bit of cotton."

Devon nodded. "That couldn't be helped." They'd had to dump as much as they could, as fast as they could to lighten their load and enable the steam engines to send them skimming over the waves out of the blockaders reach. But when Devon said it couldn't be helped, he was lying. And the reason it was necessary was standing by the door, yet to give him an answer as to why she stowed away on his ship.

"Well, Cap'n." The Scot fumbled with the carved pipe in his hand. "If that be all, I suppose I'll be gettin' back to me post."

"That's fine, Mr. MacFarland." Devon had to admire the man's restraint for not asking just what in the hell Devon was doing in his cabin with a woman who wasn't even supposed to be aboard. But the Scot kept his own council, only asking if he could fetch a bit of tobacco before going above.

After he left, Devon stared at Felicity while he turned the only chair in the cramped cabin toward her. "Sit," came his succinct command.

Picking her way around the cotton, Felicity obeyed. She waited, and still he said nothing more. But she knew his anger was back, fueled hotter by their brief interlude of passion. She swallowed. "I'll pay for the cotton you lost."

This seemed to surprise him. He leaned back

against the cluttered desk and crossed his arms. "And what if more than just cargo was lost because of your actions? How could you have compensated for *that?*"

Felicity's lips pressed together. He was purposely baiting her. Trying to make her feel worse when she already regretted her decision to hide on his ship. "You heard your chief mate. Cotton was all you lost. I won't be held responsible for something that didn't happen."

Devon's eyes narrowed. "I don't sell the cotton for Confederate script."

"I'll give you gold."

Devon leaned back and shook his head. "Why in the hell didn't you just wait for me to return to Charleston?"

Felicity took a deep breath . . . and said nothing.

"Was it your betrothed? Were you so anxious to return to him?" Devon hated himself for asking.

Her gaze met his. "No. At this point it has little to do with him."

But not nothing. Devon refused to press the issue. "Did you think I wouldn't keep my word? For God's sake, Felicity, was it because of what I said about loving you? Taking you home didn't depend on you feeling the same. I know I shouldn't have said it, but—"

"No." Felicity bit her bottom lip. "I'm glad you told me." She stopped short of professing her love for him. It wasn't the time or place, and she

366

feared he'd doubt her sincerity. Especially after she said what she must.

Felicity stood, and clasping her hands together moved behind the chair. She wanted as much distance between them as possible. Not that she worried about what he might do. Actually, she feared her own actions. She didn't want to use the sensual hold she had over him to her advantage.

"I decided the best way to get the children to their mother was by way of Nassau."

His expression was incredulous. "I don't understand. Your Mammy is—"

"I don't have a Mammy."

"But those children . . . ?"

"Their mother is a woman I met only once." Felicity clutched the wooden chair back. "A runaway slave who was forced to leave them behind."

"What the hell?"

Felicity almost broke her resolve and went to him. Surely the truth would be more palatable if she were closer? If she clutched his hand and stared beseechingly into his eyes? But she didn't move. After all he'd done for her . . . because of all he meant to her . . . he deserved the unadorned truth.

"I came to South Carolina to rescue them from the clutches of the slaveholders."

"I see." Devon's fists clenched. "We have ourselves an Abolitionist here."

"Not so different from you. I know how you feel about slavery."

"We're not discussing me at the moment." Devon

pushed off from the desk, but didn't move toward her. "I still don't understand how you thought going to Nassau would help get you to Richmond."

"New York."

His eyes caught hers and held. Everything he'd thought about her when they first met came rushing back. Things that he recently was too enamored to notice. Or to want to notice. His jaw tightened. "I think you should explain yourself."

Felicity held up her hands. "What more do you want me to say?"

That you didn't lie to me. That you didn't use me. But he said neither. Instead, he walked past her toward the door.

"What are you going to do?"

His hand paused as it reached for the latch, but he didn't turn to face her. "I, Miss Wentworth, am going to continue toward Nassau and sell the remaining cotton. With the money I make I will buy medicines and whatever else I can to help the citizens of Charleston." When he whipped his head around Felicity was unprepared for the intensity of his sea-green stare. "You may disembark any time you like."

With that he slammed out of the cabin, leaving Felicity to wish she didn't love him so much. Perhaps then she could offer him less than the truth.

Eighteen

"Sissy's gonna die, Miz Felcy."

Felicity shut her eyes and took a deep breath before turning to face the little girl. By the light of an overhead lantern, Felicity saw her. Lucy sat partially wedged behind a bale of cotton. She'd pushed herself back off the blankets Felicity folded for her. It was night, and until Lucy spoke, Felicity thought her asleep, like her brother . . . like Sissy.

The older girl just minutes ago settled into an exhausted slumber after hours of fitful coughing. Because the child was too weak to sit on her own, Felicity had stayed by her side, lifting her head and shoulders when the dry hacking coughs came.

And trying not to accept what she feared was the inevitable. Sissy was dying. Doctor Bateman in Charleston had told Felicity it was probably just a matter of time, till the little girl succumbed to whatever was causing her pleurisy.

Felicity swallowed and moved toward Lucy, bending down and reaching for her, ignoring the ache in her lower back. Lucy scrambled into her arms, snuggling close. And Felicity blinked back the tears that burned her tired eyes.

Wrenching sobs, muffled against her neck, were nearly Felicity's undoing. She rubbed the small back and rocked her body in rhythm with the swaying ship. "Don't cry sweetheart. I know you're sad."

Lucy pulled her head from the nest of Felicity's shoulder. Her face shone wet in the oscillating light from the lantern. "She's gonna die, ain't she?" she said around hiccups of grief.

"I don't know," Felicity answered, but in truth she feared the child was right.

Lucy's response was to nuzzle against Felicity's body again. Within minutes she was asleep, but as Felicity settled her down on the pile of blankets from off the captain's bed, she mumbled a single word. "Mama."

Felicity scrubbed the tears from her face and took a cleansing breath. She sank to her knees beside Ezra and gave his thin shoulders a shake. The boy jerked awake with a start. "What iz it?"

"Shhh." Felicity touched his cheek. "I need you to watch Sissy for a bit."

"Iz she bad?"

Ezra had stayed by Felicity's side, helping spoon some broth into his sister, until he appeared ready to drop from exhaustion. That was about three hours ago, when Felicity had insisted he rest. After a moment's hesitation he'd grabbed his rooster and plopped onto the floor, not seeming to mind the hard oaken planks. Felicity had covered him with a blanket she found in Devon's sea chest.

But now she needed him awake even when she knew he was still tired. But she had no choice. "Sissy's asleep. Maybe a little better," she said, knowing it was wishful thinking rather than fact guiding her words. "But I need to go talk to Captain Blackstone."

Ezra didn't ask why, and Felicity was glad. He simply stood up and walked to the bed.

"I won't be long," Felicity whispered as she left the cabin. Since her encounter with Devon this morning, when she told him the unvarnished truth, she'd not seen him. She returned to his cabin, which he seemed to have turned over to her and the children. He sent down food and water, and the closest thing the *Intrepid* had to a doctor.

But the ship's carpenter could do nothing additional for the child. So Felicity continued to do what she could and hope she could get Sissy to New York before it was too late.

The passageway was damp and poorly lit, smelling of bilge. Felicity lifted her skirts and made her way along the narrow hall, trying to retrace the path she'd used when stowing away. She climbed the ladder and, once through the hatch, took a welcome breath of fresh sea air that whipped through her hair.

The night was clear, the sky alive with twinkling stars. There were several men on deck, each staring over the railing, out to sea. Felicity made her way to the wheelhouse, hoping to find Devon, but

371

instead, saw Mr. MacFarland, the chief mate she met earlier.

"I need to see Captain Blackstone," she said without preamble, hoping this man hadn't been given orders to keep her away. She knew how angry . . . how disappointed . . . Devon was with her.

By the light in the compass housing he studied her, apparently undecided about what to do. Finally he lifted one beefy hand from the wheel and scratched at his beard. "He be in the ward room."

With the directions he gave her Felicity had little trouble finding the room where the officers gathered. But she had to force herself to rap on the paneled door. There was a moment of silence, then a disgruntled, "What?"

It was clearly the captain's voice and he was just as clearly annoyed with this interruption . . . and he didn't even know it was her!

Felicity swallowed and lifted the latch.

The room was low-ceilinged and dark, with only a smoking oil lamp to fight the shadows cast by the overhead beams. Smelling of aged ale and stale pipe smoke, the ward room was nearly as uninviting as the look the captain shot her way when he glanced up from studying the pewter mug that sat in front of him on the table.

"Well, if it isn't Miss Wentworth, the Abolitionist." His tone was sardonic. "To what do I owe this pleasure?"

Felicity stepped further into the cabin and shut the door. His hair was mussed, the maverick lock

372

hanging across his forehead, and he sported a day's growth of dark whiskers across his square jaw. He was unkempt, but Felicity guessed no more so than she. Still, *she* had good reason for her appearance, and it wasn't because she sat, her hand clamped around a draft of grog.

She lifted her chin and tried to keep the emotion from her voice. "Sissy is worse." Felicity hoped she didn't imagine the concern that darkened his green eyes. But it was quickly gone, replaced by an expression she didn't wish to discern.

"I'm sorry." He took a swig from the mug. "I'll send Mr. Lowery to my cabin."

"There's nothing the ship's surgeon can do."

"Then there's nothing *I* can do."

"You can take her to New York," Felicity said on a rush of air.

His bark of laughter was swift and sharp. "I'm afraid you've been misdirected, Red. This isn't a leg of the Underground Railroad."

Ignoring his sarcasm, Felicity stepped forward till her skirts brushed the edge of the table. "I know what I'm asking of you."

"Oh, that's encouraging. You realize you're suggesting I sail into a nest of Yankees."

"It won't be that bad."

"You have the right of it there." Devon lifted the mug in mock salute. "For I shall go nowhere near your blessed New York." He took another swig. "You'll be able to book passage from Nassau. I'll even give you the money." He studied her from beneath narrowed eyes, wishing he didn't care what happened to her. "I believe that was your original plan, was it not?"

"I don't think Sissy will live long enough for that."

His gaze lowered. He took a deep breath. "As unfortunate as that is, I can't sacrifice my ship and crew for her. I'm sorry."

She believed him, believed he cared more about the children than he cared to admit. But telling him so brought an angered snort. "And that surprises you? I'm familiar with you Abolitionists. I ran into enough of them while I was in the United States Navy to last me a lifetime. You all go around blaming the South for all the ills of the world. You act as if we're heartless Simon Legrees who beat and maim and God knows what else, laughing all the while."

"I know different." Felicity's voice was low but it made him pause. His next words lacked the anger of his earlier tirade.

"There's nothing I can do." Devon turned back to the drink he nursed, in a gesture of dismissal. But he wasn't surprised when she didn't leave . . . only by her proposition.

"You'll be handsomely compensated."

Devon purposely misunderstood her. His lazy gaze raked down across her bosom and lower. When he again accessed her face, she was devoid of color, but her stare hadn't flinched. "What type of *compensation* did you have in mind."

Felicity lifted her chin. "Monetary."

"You forget, I've cotton to sell."

"Not a full load."

His brow arched. "And who must I thank for having to toss valuable cargo overboard?"

Felicity refused to be baited. "My father is wealthy . . . very wealthy."

"Is he the one who filled your carpetbag with gold and sent you south? Or was that Jebediah what's-his-name?"

"Neither of them had anything to do with it . . . at least they didn't know what I was going to do," Felicity added truthfully.

"Well that's something in their favor," he mumbled before lifting the mug to his lips.

"Would you stop that?" Felicity leaned forward, her palms flattened on the scarred tabletop. "I'm not interested in discussing this with a drunkard."

Devon upended the mug, keeping his narrowed gaze on Felicity. Then he slowly lowered the mug and pushed forward in his chair. When they were nose to nose he spoke.

"First, I am not, nor have I ever been drunk, while in charge of this ship." He didn't mention that he'd been sorely tempted to break his own long-standing rule after learning the real reason she came south. But he hadn't. He'd nursed this one drink all evening and he resented the hell out of her insinuation.

"And in the second place, there is nothing further *to* discuss."

"My father will pay you handsomely for my safe return. He can get you the drugs and medical supplies sorely needed in Charleston. Cargo you

375

couldn't hope to buy in Nassau." Felicity's arms quivered from the strain of leaning on them, and she wanted nothing more than to fall forward into his embrace, but she didn't. Instead, when he said nothing she continued. "I can guarantee the safety of you and your men . . . and the *Intrepid.*"

"You can?" His tone was incredulous.

Felicity's lashes lowered. "My father can," she admitted. "He's a very rich man."

"So you said."

"And powerful."

Her gaze met his and Devon sensed that power hadn't always been pleasant for his daughter. She stared at him so guilelessly he almost forgot how many times she'd lied to him before—almost. Devon shook his head and grinned, breaking the contact between them. She looked unkempt and exhausted, with mauve circles beneath her blue eyes, and he still thought her the most beautiful woman he'd ever seen.

"Well, Miss Wentworth," he began, sitting back down and leaning his chair back against the bulwark. "I don't trust Yankees. Not rich and powerful Yankees. Or beautiful, red-haired Yankees. I find them an untruthful lot." She flinched then and he could almost feel sorry for her.

"I had to lie to you."

Devon only crossed his arms, and stared at her.

"What would you have me do? Announce to all of Charleston that I was from New York?"

"And an Abolitionist. Don't forget how you

failed to mention that while you took advantage of my grandmother."

Felicity swallowed. "And you." He looked away when she said that, and Felicity let out her breath. "I wanted to tell you, especially after—"

"How much is it worth to you to get to New York quickly?" Devon had no intention of taking her, but he didn't want to hear about his declaration of love. And he most certainly didn't want her feeling badly out of pity for his poor misplaced infatuation. Besides his question had put her off guard, and he liked seeing her that way.

"Well, I . . . I don't know. How much do you think is fair?"

"For me to risk my life and those of my men?" he questioned with a slight shrug. "Not to mention my ship."

"I told you—"

"Yes, I know," he said, his voice filled with disbelief. "But what if your father doesn't see this your way?"

"He will." She would make certain he did. "And even if he doesn't, I have money of my own." Her maternal grandfather had seen to that. "How much would it cost to replace the *Intrepid?*"

"My cousin and I invested about a hundred thousand dollars in her."

Felicity didn't blink an eye. "My father will pay you that much plus the market value for your cotton . . . in gold."

Devon whistled long and low. "You do know

how to toss money around, Red. But what if I want something other than your father's gold?"

"I . . . I don't know what you mean." That light was back in his eyes and Felicity felt a tightening of her stomach muscles.

"You don't?" His expression clearly stated he thought her lying again.

"I don't think you have any intention of taking us to New York so why don't we stop these foolish negotiations." As Felicity spoke she turned and retreated toward the door. But before she could open it, he was there, his muscular forearm above her head, keeping her from opening the door.

"What's the matter, Red? Giving up so easily? I thought you Abolitionists would do anything for the cause. Hell, you have." He could see her shoulders trembling and wanted to stop. To take her in his arms and promise her he'd do anything for her. But the lies were too recent, and he greatly feared what he just said was true.

"You left your nice safe home for the wilds of the heathen South."

"Stop it!" Felicity rested her head against the door. She didn't dare turn to look at him. His presence overwhelmed her. "You are as much Abolitionist as I. Don't forget I saw your letters of manumission."

"Perhaps I hate the institution. But then I also hate the idea of children working long hours in the sweatshops of the North. And I really hate it when people who don't know what they're talking about try to tell me how to run my life."

378

"I didn't do that."

Devon took a deep breath. "No, you didn't." His arm slid down the rough wood, then his fingers tangled in the unruly curls at her nape.

"Don't," Felicity whispered.

"What if this is what I want in exchange for taking you to New York?" Her hair was so soft, so impossibly filled with wild sparks of light, even in the dimly lit room.

"You don't mean that." His fingers on her neck sent shivers down her spine.

"Don't I?" Bending his head Devon placed his lips on the curve of her shoulder.

"Please." Felicity turned enough to push him away. She was so vulnerable to him.

"Please?" He bared his teeth in a mockery of his usual grin. "Please what? Don't act the demure maiden about to be ravished. We both know a kiss is all the force I need."

"No, I don't . . ." But the rest of her words were lost as his mouth swooped down on hers. His lips were hungry and hard. He demanded, his tongue and teeth forcing her mouth open, filling her completely. She could taste his anger, could feel it in the large hands that speared through her hair, and held her head still for his onslaught.

And she acknowledged his claim. He needed no more than a kiss . . . a touch to liquify her resolve. Yet she tried to fight her body's reaction to him, forcing her palms against the solid strength of his shoulders. She pushed, her arms quivering from desire as he thoroughly explored her mouth.

379

Then with a moan, Felicity surrendered, abandoning any claim she had of resisting him. Her fingers spread, tangling with the soft cotton of his shirt.

He was not gentle; nor did she want him to be.

Not releasing his hold on her lips, Devon turned, backing her up till she was sandwiched between the table and him. With a sweep of his arm the mug went clanking to the deck.

Felicity was so aswamp in the fog of desire that she barely felt the wooden table beneath her back as he lowered her. She arched up when his hand covered her breast. Her skirts were lifted and Felicity could feel the rush of cool air on her fevered skin.

Then his mouth was there, setting her aflame. Felicity writhed beneath the onslaught of his tongue, her fisted hands riding his shoulders, then spreading to clasp his head closer.

When Devon lowered himself over her, Felicity was nearly mindless with passion. His first plunge was deep and sure, filling her completely. Sending her over the brink.

His own release was quick and explosive, leaving him spent . . . and hollow. He owned her passion. Since the first time he'd touched her there'd been no question of that. But passion alone wasn't enough.

Devon nestled into her hair, smelling the sweet fragrance, allowing himself one more moment before pushing up. He levered himself free and stood, quickly pulling down her skirts and rearranging his pants.

Felicity waited for him to say something . . . anything. She wanted to tell him what was in her heart, but the words wouldn't come. She feared he wouldn't believe that she loved him. And she wasn't sure she believed it herself. Not with all that separated them. But his rejection, the cut of his jaw as he stood, his forearm against the rafter, staring into the shadows, left little room for dialogue.

As quickly as she could, Felicity righted herself. Then with one last glance at his straight back and broad shoulders, she fled the room.

"Gawd, what's wrong with ye lass?" Mr. MacFarland reeled as Felicity rushed past him. He'd just lifted his fist to rap on the door to the ward room when she flung it open.

Felicity took one startled look at the grizzled man and ran even faster.

"What did ye do to the girl?" Mr. MacFarland said, entering the cabin and shutting the door behind him.

Devon blew out his breath. "We had a disagreement."

"More than that I'd wager." Mr. MacFarland bent and retrieved the pewter mug. "Appears ye let your anger get a wee bit out of hand."

He let something get out of hand, but it wasn't his anger. Devon turned slowly. "Did you want something, Mr. MacFarland?"

"A bit of grog, aye."

Devon shook his head. "And an explanation perhaps?"

"I am wondering what such a pretty mite of a thing is doing aboard."

"She's stowing away in my cabin."

"Ah." Mr. MacFarland rubbed his beard. "Can't bear to let ye go, I imagine."

"You imagine incorrectly." Devon poured brandy into two mugs, handing one to his chief mate. "She wishes me to take her to New York."

Amber liquid spewed from Andrew's mouth. "New York," he repeated as he backhanded his chin. "Does she know what manner of ship this is?"

"She does." Devon turned the chair and straddled it. "But in reality, we're a merchant vessel with British registry."

"Ye ain't thinkin' of slippin' into New York harbor, are ye?"

"No. Duty calls me to Nassau," he said.

But late the next day he wasn't so certain.

" 'Tis a yellow flag, Cap'n," the lookout yelled down after observing the pennant waving above the harbor at Nassau.

"Quarantine," Devon muttered and clenched the polished rail. In aggravation, he gave the order to turn the vessel leeward.

"What does that mean?" The words slipped through Felicity's lips before she could stop them. She'd come above deck to take a breath of air,

382

while Ezra watched his sister. Lucy was by her side, holding onto Felicity's silk skirt with one hand, sucking two fingers of the other.

Devon turned. It was the first he'd seen her since they'd made love in the wardroom the night before. Though she asked him a question, she wouldn't meet his gaze.

"There appears to be some sort of epidemic in the harbor. Yellow fever or small pox, I imagine."

"What shall we do?" There was no way she could expose the children to that. Sissy was holding her own, but just barely.

"We'll have to seek another port. Either that or risk getting caught in the quarantine. And I don't believe anyone aboard wants to risk confinement for twenty-one days."

"But where—"

"Sail ho," the lookout yelled and immediately Devon's attention was diverted.

"Whereaway?"

"On the port quarter, sir and closing fast. They be sportin' the Federal ensign, both of them."

"Damnit to hell!" Devon covered the distance to the wheelhouse in three strides, Felicity at his heels.

"What are you going to do?"

Devon yelled something in to Mr. MacFarland who was at the wheel then jerked his head around. "Get below," he bellowed to Felicity. "And stay there."

With those orders, he turned back to the wheelhouse, leaving Felicity to stare around her in wonder. It seemed every man on board had suddenly come to life. Some climbed the ratlines to unfurl the fore and aft sails. Others scurried below to help shovel coal in the engine room.

Felicity swept Lucy into her arms and headed toward the hatch. Once there, she waited while a member of the crew scurried up the ladder.

"We're headin' right towards them," she heard someone behind her yell.

"Just pray the Cap'n knows what he's doin'," said the man scrambling up on to the deck.

"Oh, I do," Felicity mumbled as she grabbed up her skirts with one hand and hurried past him.

The blockaders were becoming bolder, no longer content to stalk the seaports and sail the Gulf Stream. Now they lay in wait like so many vultures, just far enough from neutral ports to avoid the wrath of foreign governments. Yet close enough to capture unsuspecting Confederate runners.

But Devon didn't have time to ponder this new strategy to cut off the life-blood of the South. The two Federal cruisers were coming at him nearly head on. And there was little or no room to maneuver the *Intrepid* around them.

"Full speed!" Devon called the order down the speaking tube and clutched the wheel. Sweat trickled down his back, and formed on his forehead. But he kept his eyes focused straight ahead as the *Intrepid* closed in on the two ships.

"You're headin' straight at them, Lad." Mr. MacFarland scratched at his beard as he stated the obvious.

"Get down." Devon yelled at the older man without taking his gaze from the narrow waterway between the two cruisers. He heard his chief mate drop to the wooden deck.

And then came the call from the cruiser on port side. "Stop, or we shall sink you."

"I haven't time to visit today," Devon called back as he reached for the speaking tube. "More power if you please."

The opening salvo from the first blockader's rifled cannon screamed overhead. It was followed by another and another as Devon aimed the *Intrepid* toward the swathe of sea churning between the cruisers.

"Stop, I tell you," came another command from one of the enemy ships.

And then Devon noticed it.

The gap between the two vessels widened as Devon steered straight toward them at full speed. Without a glass he could easily see the startled crew on the enemy vessels as he sailed the *Intrepid* between them.

The Federals had stopped their shelling for fear of sinking each other. There was nothing to hear save the thumping of the engines as Devon took his ship, slick as a greased pig, through the midst of the blockaders.

The *Intrepid* shot from between the two cruisers, heading north. By the time the blockaders could back their engines enough to make the turn, the Confederate blockade runners' lead was too great for them to catch.

It was less than an hour later when Devon descended to his cabin. Even though he'd been given daily reports by the steward who provided the children with food, Devon was surprised by Sissy's appearance. Felicity was right to be concerned for the girl's life. He patted the child's hand as it lay on the woolen blanket and turned to face Felicity who sat by the bed.

"May I speak with you privately?"

Felicity glanced toward Ezra. He sat on the floor near the windows busily drawing pictures to entertain his younger sister. "I don't think that's prudent." It was all too fresh in her memory what happened the last time they were alone together . . . what seemed to happen every time they were alone together.

Devon's jaw clenched. "Very well. I wish to discuss with you again the provisions your father will supply."

Felicity's eyes widened. "Anything you wish . . . except weapons. I don't think he'd give you that."

"It was not my intent to ask."

"But drugs . . . opium and morphine, quinine. I know he can and will give you that if only—"

"I've decided to take the risk." He'd almost said "trust you" but that would have been too great a leap. "We are sailing for New York."

Forgetting the children were in the room, Felicity propelled herself into Devon's arms.

Nineteen

Sailing into the enemy harbor of New York was a hell of a lot easier than running the blockade at Charleston. At least it had been to this point. It was high tide and they were crossing Sandy Hook Bar. In minutes they'd pass Fort Lafayette. Devon only hoped his luck held.

During the days since escaping the Federal cruisers near Nassau, the *Intrepid*'s crew was busy. They scraped the painted name from her iron stern and replaced it with *Sea Hawk*, the name of his pirate ancestor's square-rigged ship. Thanks to his cousin Stephen, Devon carried British registry under that name as well. And it only took a minimum of doctoring to make the extra log seem authentic.

On the surface everything about his ship appeared legitimate. There was nothing illegal about sailing a low-drafted vessel painted a dull gray-green to blend with the sea. Even the cargo of cotton could be explained. Granted, importing southern cotton into a Union port was frowned upon by the Republican purists. But unlike England, which had stockpiled cotton before the war, and were importing the fiber from Egypt and India, northern textile mills needed cotton to keep producing.

It was a poorly kept secret that some of the cotton Devon and his crew risked their life to run out of South Carolina ended up, by rook or crook, benefiting the North. He just hoped what he was doing would end up helping his own people more.

"It seems strange . . . being back here." Felicity came on deck to find Devon. But once she found him, leaning against the rail, his gaze fixed straight ahead toward the inner harbor, she hesitated. And now when he looked over his shoulder to fix her with his sea-green stare, she almost wished she had stayed below. As hard as it was not to see him, or talk to him, the alternative was more frightening. The love she'd seen shining in those eyes was dimmed by disappointment and mistrust.

Felicity swallowed. "I'm very grateful that you brought me back—"

"I didn't do this for you." Devon resumed watching the busy harbor, wondering if she knew he was lying. Her safety and getting the children to their mother did weigh into his decision to try this daring scheme. Of course the medicines and supplies she promised had to be his main concern. But damnit to hell, he had to constantly remind himself of that.

"Providing we manage to fool the port authority," he began, his voice a little less gruff. "You and I will go ashore and—"

"What about the children?"

"They'll remain on board." Devon glanced back at her. He didn't like having to do it this way but he had to consider the safety of his crew. God only knew what would happen to them, to him, if they were caught in enemy territory. Probably the best they could hope for would be to sit out the rest of the war in a Yankee prison camp.

"But what about Sissy—," she began but Devon cut her off.

"The children leave the *Sea Hawk* after the agreements have been made," he said and his tone left no room for argument. "If I could manage this alone, you'd be with them . . . as added insurance."

Felicity lifted her chin. "I gave you my word about the cargo exchange."

Devon's brow arched but there was no accompanying grin. "You'll pardon my bluntness, but your word has not always been reliable."

Felicity felt the color leave her face but she refused to look away. "I've explained why I lied to you. The children—"

"Are exactly why you'd lie to me again."

"No." Felicity looked down at her clenched hands. "I need to get them back to their mother, I've never denied that. Nor that I care very deeply for them." Her lashes lifted and she hoped he could read the truthfulness of what she said. "But I love you, Devon Blackstone." Her breath was ragged. "And I'd never, ever do anything to hurt you."

Devon couldn't stop staring into the depths of her blue eyes. His heart pounded inside his chest and he had to ball his fists to keep from reaching for her, from pulling her into his arms.

"Hey, Cap'n, here comes that there pilot to steer us to the wharf."

Devon's head jerked around. He saw the small boat gliding up beside the *Sea Hawk* and realized the first test of his credentials was at hand. He motioned toward the sailor who'd told him about the pilot. "Escort Miss Wentworth below."

"But. . . ." Felicity clung to his sleeve. She'd bared her soul and couldn't stand to leave without a word from him . . . any word.

"Get below, Felicity." His eyes were like green ice. "You have your wish. There's no need for any more charade. Save your words of love for your betrothed."

The expression of pain that crossed her beautiful face tore at his heart. But as she turned away from him, Devon knew there was no help for it. Even if he could believe her.

The port authority accompanying the pilot was a head shorter than Devon, a fact he seemed to compensate for by sticking out his narrow chest. His ears were large, his muttonchop whiskers thick, and his pale blue eyes suspicious.

"You say, Captain Blackstone, that your cargo

was picked up in Liverpool?" Peter Ross slammed the log book shut with a bang that startled the big boned pilot sitting beside him.

They were in Devon's cabin. He'd had all the cotton removed, and what couldn't be squeezed into the hold thrown overboard. It wouldn't do to suggest he was too anxious to sell all the cotton he could. Devon also had moved Felicity and the children to his chief mate's cabin which was why he looked up in surprise when she came through the door.

Felicity smiled, first at Devon, then at the two men seated across his desk from him. It was obvious by the looks she received in return that the two strangers appreciated all the trouble she'd gone to with her toilette . . . and that the captain did not.

"I'm so sorry to interrupt," she cooed, though the tone, once second nature, didn't come easily anymore. "I didn't realize you had visitors." She moved forward, and rested her hand on Devon's sleeve, possessively. He was apparently too stunned by her entrance to pull away as he had on deck. "Well, aren't you going to introduce me to your charming guests?"

He didn't know what she was doing. And that scared the hell out of him. But Devon had no choice other than comply with her request. As he introduced the two to her, he felt like smashing his fist into Peter Ross's big nose. The man could barely keep from salivating as his eyes roamed over Felicity. Devon had to admit she looked good, but then he always thought she did. Even when she didn't twist her red-gold hair up, and flutter her large, thick-lashed eyes.

"Oh, I can't tell you how happy Devon and I are to be safe and snug in New York harbor," she said, her bright smile focused on Peter Ross. "Now that you are here, we know everything will be all right, don't we dear?"

"Actually *dear*" Devon put his arm around Felicity's shoulders, forcing her to straighten and stop giving the small time government official a tempting view of her bosom. "We were just discussing our trip, and I'm sure you'd find it boring, so if you'd just—"

"Nonsense." Felicity turned, managing to free herself gracefully from the arm that tried to maneuver her toward the door. "You know how I find everything about you fascinating . . . as does my father." Felicity shifted her gaze toward the two other men. "Are you acquainted perchance with my father, Frederick Wentworth?"

Peter Ross blinked. "Frederick Wentworth is your father?"

"Why yes. Do you know him?" Felicity was certain her father and this man couldn't possibly be acquainted but she was hoping her father's reputation was known. She wasn't disappointed.

"I know of, Mr. Wentworth, of course. He's . . . well, he's a very powerful man."

Felicity demurred, enchantingly. "To me he's just Papa. But oh," she said with enthusiasm, "Devon and I are so anxious to see him again. I was vacationing in England when he sent my fiancé to fetch me. Papa knows Captain Blackstone would protect me with his life." She smiled up sweetly at Devon. "And now Papa has you two to thank also." Felicity leaned across the desk and clasped each of their hands as they lay on the polished wood. "He will be so grateful. When do you suppose we can go ashore?"

"There is a question about the cargo . . . ?"

"Really?" Felicity's eyes widened as she turned toward Devon. "Isn't cotton what Papa wished for you to bring him?"

"Yes, it is." Devon figured the less he said, the better.

"Well, there." Felicity shrugged her adorably bared shoulders.

"But this cotton probably came from the South and before I allow—"

"Oh my." Felicity's hand fluttered to her chest. It was obvious this minor bureaucrat was a stickler. "You can't possibly think Frederick Wentworth would do *anything* that wasn't completely above reproach. Sir, he's a patriot . . . just like you. Why before I left for England I recall Secretary of State, Seward, sitting at our table saying just that same thing. Do you remember that, Devon dear?"

If the situation weren't so perilous, Devon might have thrown back his head and laughed. As it was he merely nodded. "I do believe he said words to that effect."

"Well, I certainly didn't mean to imply . . . I

mean your father's patriotism is a well documented fact. He's very much admired, by everyone, including myself." Peter Ross turned to the pilot. "Haven't I always said how much we all respect Mr. Wentworth?"

"Uh, yeah . . . yeah. That's the truth of it."

"How sweet. I shall be certain to tell my father of your helpfulness . . . that is, as soon as I see him, I shall."

Peter Ross pushed out his chair and stood. "We should waste no more time. Captain, we will wait upon you in the wheelhouse." After asking their leave, which Felicity was only too glad to give them, the two men left the cabin.

Devon angled his hip against the desk and crossed his arms. "What was that all about?"

"I should think it was obvious. Mr. MacFarland told me you were concerned about the port authorities. I thought I might help."

"By parading yourself in front of them, flirting and lying."

"Me? Lying?" Felicity's hands flew to her hips. "And just what were you doing? I dare say little of your story included the fact that you're the captain of a blockade runner from Charleston with a load of contraband cotton in your hold. Besides." Felicity lifted her chin. "My father will be the first to tell you that flirting is what I do best. You, of course, may disagree, and cast your vote for my ability to lie."

The last word was barely out of her mouth before he pushed off from the desk and with three giant strides closed the distance between them. He hauled her into his arms, and crushed his lips to hers. Before she could do more than cling to him, he let her go.

He left her standing in his cabin wondering what that kiss had meant, and how she was ever going to live without him.

Fifth Avenue was as busy as she remembered. Was it only a matter of weeks since she sold several pieces of jewelry and headed south? Her life had changed so much in that short time.

She stopped just past the corner of Twenty-third and looked up at the imposing four story mansion. "This is it," she said to the tall, handsome man by her side.

He gave a low whistle. "You live good, Red."

Laughing, Felicity led the way up the wide brownstone stairs. He hadn't called her Red since the night she told him who she really was, and she hadn't realized till now how much she missed the colorful nickname.

Her own home seemed so foreign to her that Felicity almost knocked on the elaborately carved door. When she opened it and walked into the huge hallway, a maid came running toward her.

"I'm sorry, Miss, but you'll—" The girl broke off and stared at Felicity from beneath her starched white cap. "Miss Wentworth? 'Tis that yourself? My goodness we never expected. . . . I mean 'tis wonderful to have you home, Miss."

"Thank you." Felicity glanced around, hoping that something would strike a chord of homecoming with her. "Where is my father?"

"Oh, of course, Miss, you'd be wanting to see Mr. Wentworth. He's in the library." The apple cheeked young woman turned, after a surreptitious glance at Devon and led the way up the broad oak stairs. She paused beside the room, third door to the right down the long carpeted hallway.

"You don't need to announce us," Felicity said, excusing the girl.

"Yes, Miss. I'll tell the housekeeper you're home. I'm sure she'll be wanting to tidy your room."

Felicity waited until the maid scurried off around the corner, then she turned to face Devon. "Do you wish to wait here?"

"No," was all he said before turning the heavy brass knob, and ushering Felicity inside.

The room was as dark and dreary as she'd always remembered. The maroon brocade curtains with heavy fringe were drawn against the afternoon light. Several gas lights, with ornate round globes served as substitutes. Her father sat on a velvet settee near the carved marble fireplace. And he wasn't alone.

Though she wished she could back out of the room, Felicity forced herself to move across the Brussels rug. "Hello, father."

At first Frederick Wentworth merely twisted in his seat, then he pushed to standing. "My God,

Felicity." He continued to stand, the heavily carved furniture between them.

It was Jebediah Webster who had the presence of mind to rush forward, though even he stopped short of touching her. "Where have you been? You've had your father so worried."

"I left a note. Didn't you receive it?"

"Yes, but really . . . It was only something about finding Esther's children, hardly enough to—"

"I did it." Felicity looked from one to the other, waiting to see some kernel of admiration for what she'd accomplished in their expressions. "I found her children, and brought them north. They're in New York." Felicity relayed this information without the sense of euphoria she thought she'd have. *She* was pleased with her accomplishment, and she couldn't wait to see the children and Esther reunited. But Felicity no longer cared how Jebediah and her father viewed her self-sacrifice . . . except how it concerned Devon and his men's safety.

"Young lady," her father said, finally regaining his speech. "You have much to answer for. However at the moment Jebediah and I are discussing the possibility that Congress might pass a confiscation act that contains an emancipation clause. Please go to your room and I'll talk to you later."

Ignoring Devon's muttered, "This is Jebediah?" Felicity faced her father. "I shan't run off to my room till you have a moment to spare for me." Felicity paused and took a deep breath. "And what I have to answer for is caring enough to find Esther's children. Now one of her daughters, Sissy, is very ill, so could you please tell me where I can find her?"

Her father's square face turned scarlet, and the veins at his temples throbbed. "Listen here, young lady." He advanced on her but his movement was cut short when Devon stepped in front of Felicity.

"I hate to break up this display of fatherly love, but I think we need to discuss a few other issues."

Frederick Wentworth took one step back and studied Devon through narrowed gray eyes. He was shorter than Jebediah, with a barrel chest that he puffed out beneath his dark frock coat. "Who are *you?*"

Devon bowed slightly, sure this was the first time Felicity's father even realized he was in the room. "Captain Devon Blackstone, at your service."

"Captain Blackstone brought the children and me to New York, Father."

"I see." Frederick shifted his husky body away from Devon. "Now young lady—"

"There's a might more to it than 'I see'," Devon interrupted, regaining the older man's attention. "There's a matter of payment." As much as Devon felt like shaking Felicity's father by his lapels for his callous attitude toward his daughter, he couldn't. He had to remember the precarious situation he, his crew, and the *Intrepid* were in. A situation he had led them into.

"I'll see your good deed is rewarded, young man, however—"

"Captain Blackstone and I made an agreement,

398

Father. One that I intend to see upheld. The captain brought us here at great personal risk." Felicity stepped forward and reaching out, touched her father for the first time since she left home. "He saved my life."

Frederick's gaze dropped to where Felicity's hand rested on the fine dark wool of his sleeve. "Of course, we shall see Captain Blackstone handsomely compensated for his trouble."

"I have approximately eight hundred bales of cotton I wish to exchange for drugs and medical supplies." Devon squared his shoulders and waited.

Jebediah's eyes popped open. "But that sounds as if . . ." He sputtered, seemingly unable to accept what his prominent ears told him.

"That's right." Devon couldn't help grinning. "My cargo originates in the South. And I won't lie to you, that's my destination for the goods you'll supply."

"But . . . but that's impossible. We're at war and besides, it's morally wrong to help sustain a government that fights to retain the worst atrocity known to man. Slavery is immoral and everything that's evil. Why it's—"

"Devon freed his slaves. And his treatment of the Negroes that I've seen, is above reproach. Why the very fact that Ezra, Sissy and Lucy are here today is partly because of him." Felicity's impassioned speech left her chest heaving and she tried to calm the raging emotions that swelled within her.

But Jebediah appeared unimpressed. "How can

you defend him? A man who by your own admission kept slaves. He is the lowest form of life, the—"

"You don't know how it is. You never even traveled in the South. . . . Well, did you?" she demanded.

"No. But that doesn't mean—"

"But it does." Felicity sucked in her breath. "Don't you see—"

"I see that you have changed, Miss Wentworth." Jebediah lifted his head and stared at her down the long expanse of his narrow nose.

"On that we can agree, Mr. Webster. I have changed. And I think for the better."

"Anyone who would willingly consort with a slaveowner . . ." Jebediah's haughty gaze seared across Devon. "Simply because he is handsome of face, is damning themselves to eternal hell." He launched forward, hand raised, only to be blocked by Devon's muscled forearm.

With his other hand Devon grabbed a handful of starched white shirt front. Devon hauled him up, till only the tips of Jebediah's leather shoe toes touched the carpet. "Now, where I come from." His fingers tightened. "We don't insult ladies. And we sure as hell don't strike them. And furthermore, Felicity Wentworth has more goodness in her than you could ever hope to have."

The shove Devon gave him sent Jebediah reeling, arms windmilling and feet searching for purchase. He grabbed for the round marble topped table and was able to right himself without falling on the floor.

"That's enough!" Frederick Wentworth's firm voice stopped Jebediah in his tracks as he fumbled toward Devon, his long, narrow face red, and his cravat askew. "I'll have no more of this in my house." He turned to Devon. "You have my word that whatever agreement you reached with my daughter will be honored."

"But, Mr. Wentworth," Jebediah sputtered. "You cannot mean to—"

"You heard what I said." Frederick Wentworth's words effectively silenced Jebediah. He retreated like a kicked puppy, but his eyes, so often brilliant with impassioned fire, burned cold as he stared at Devon.

"As for you." Felicity's father faced Devon. "My assistant is in the library. Make him a list of supplies you require, and I'll have them transported to your ship as soon as your cargo is unloaded."

Devon nodded. His fist still ached to smash into Jebediah's face, but he realized it would do no good. For some reason Felicity had agreed to marry the man, and at this point in time there wasn't a damn thing he could do about it. He flexed his fingers and walked toward the door.

"As for you, young lady—"

"In a moment, Father." Felicity gathered her skirts and rushed after Devon. She called to him as he descended the stairs. He stopped and turned, waiting for her as she hurried down to him. But when she stood two steps above him, nearly eye to eye, she didn't know what to say.

Don't leave me. That is what she longed to beg of him. But it was such a foolish request. He couldn't possibly stay in New York. Every moment he was here, his life was in danger.

But oh, she didn't think she could stand to let him go. She stared into his green eyes, trying without words to tell him how she felt. "I . . . I . . ." Her breath came out in a rush. "Thank you . . . for everything."

He grinned then, somewhat sadly, but still showing his sexy dimples, and his expression tore at her heart. "All in all, it was a pleasure."

Felicity lowered her lashes, unable to suppress the smile that lit her face. "You truly are a gentleman to say that after all I've put you through."

His finger caught under her chin, lifting her gaze to again meet his. "I meant what I said."

Felicity took another step closer and swallowed. "I love you." It was more plea than declaration.

Devon couldn't take his eyes from hers. His breath was shallow. "I love you too," he said as she took the final step into his arms.

There on the wide oak staircase, carpeted in deepest red, they held each other . . . for the last time.

Felicity clung to his back, trying to memorize the feel of his muscles, the smell of his body. She didn't want to cry, to ruin this moment by shedding tears that could change nothing. But they came anyway, flowing down her cheeks to wet the soft cotton of his shirt front.

"Don't . . . sweetheart. . . ." Devon shifted her so he could look down into her lovely face. His thumbs wiped at tears that shone like prisms of crystal, that rendered him speechless, and broke his heart. If there had been anything he could do he would . . . slay dragons, climb mountains. But he couldn't change the course of the war. Could neither stay nor subject her to the life threatening dangers of returning to Charleston.

He tasted her tears, knew she tasted his, as their lips met. And then, when he could no longer stand the sea of temptation that engulfed him, Devon tore himself away and hurried down the stairs.

Felicity's gown floated out on a balloon of air as she sank onto the riser. Unable to control her grief any longer she lowered her head and sobbed aloud.

"You're looking much better, Felicity." Frederick sipped creamed soup from his spoon and eyed his daughter over a wide expanse of mahogany table. "I'm glad you decided to join me for supper."

It hadn't been so much a decision on her part as a command from her father. If she did indeed look better it had nothing to do with her frame of mind and everything to do with the clothing her lady's maid had poked and prodded her into. Her gown was emerald green silk taffeta, draped low over her shoulders and breasts, and molded tightly around her cinched waist. Addie had washed her hair, brushing it till the curls shone, then piled them appealingly at the nape of her neck.

Except for the mauve crescents that shadowed her eyes she was beautiful, a picture perfect example of the way she used to strive to appear.

And she cared none at all.

"Is there any word when Esther will arrive?" Felicity dabbed the linen napkin to her mouth, then folded it beside the ornate soup bowl. At her insistence her father had sent a coach to retrieve Ezra, Sissy and Lucy from the *Sea Hawk*. Apparently Devon had not resisted the release of his quasi-hostages. He sent the children to Felicity without reserve.

"Jebediah is upstairs. The woman will be along directly." Frederick settled back in the upholstered chair as the servants cleared the bowl in front of him, replacing it with a plate heaped high with pheasant and creamed vegetables. When they were alone again in the cavernous room, he spoke. "I can't imagine what possessed you to run away as you did." He sipped his wine. "Jebediah did relate to me the conversation you had about marriage. You should know he is now quite willing to wed you, and I think the sooner this is accomplished the better."

Felicity's eyes met her father's, wondering what sort of inducement he offered the abolitionist minister to sway him toward her. Whatever, it was all for naught. "I'm not interested in marrying Jebediah," she stated calmly.

"Because of that southerner." His voice rang with contempt.

Felicity refused to look away. "I won't deny my feelings for Captain Blackstone. However, the reason it is impossible for me to even consider marriage to Jebediah is not because of him. It is because of me."

Gaslight reflected off the silver serving dishes as they stared at each other over the long length of polished wood. Finally Frederick tossed his napkin aside. "I just don't understand you."

A discreet knock at the door saved Felicity from responding. "You asked to be informed sir when the Negress, Esther, arrived," the servant, who was dressed grander than most of Charleston's citizens, said.

"She's here." Felicity sprang from her chair and ignoring her father's admonishment hurried into the hallway.

Esther looked very much as she had the one other time she'd seen her. Frizzled black hair salted with white was pulled back from her broad face. She glanced up as Felicity rushed toward her, her almond shaped eyes questioning. "Iz it true what I heard? Did you bring my babies to me?"

"Yes." Felicity grabbed her hands, folding them in her own. "They're upstairs resting. At least I think they are. Lucy is hard to keep pinned down." Felicity smiled and the woman responded in kind. Then there was an awkward moment of silence.

Felicity swallowed. "Before we go up there's something you should know."

"Sissy?" The woman's voice quivered.

"I'm afraid she's very ill." Dr. Brown, who'd been the Wentworth family physician for as long as Felicity could remember, had confirmed the medical opinion she'd received in Charleston. Sissy suffered from pleurisy and wasn't expected to live much longer.

Uncertainty gave way to fear, shadowing Esther's expression. Then suddenly she squared her shoulders and lifted her rounded chin. "I wants to see them."

Continuing to hold her hand, Felicity led the way up the wide stairway. At the top they turned to the left and made their way past the gas lights to the room at the end of the hall. When Felicity opened it, she heard a squeal and Lucy came skipping toward her.

"Miz Felcy! Miz Felcy. Did you come to—" The child stopped bobbing and stood stock still, staring at her mother.

"Lucy." Esther spread her arms, and with only a moment's hesitation the little girl ran into them. Ezra glanced up from the picture he was drawing. Leaving his rooster in the corner, the boy crossed to his mother and was welcomed into the harbor of her embrace.

The three held each other, rocking slightly till a weak voice sounded from the bed. Slowly, Esther extricated herself from her children's arms. "Sissy's sick," Lucy informed her as she moved slowly toward her daughter's bedside.

Esther knelt, placing one work-roughened palm on the child's forehead, the other she used to cover her daughter's hands. "Sissy, Iz so glad we's together at last."

"Mama."

For the second time today tears streamed unabashedly down Felicity's cheeks. She backed toward the door, unwilling to interfere with the tableau of family love before her. The doorknob turned easily and she slipped quietly into the hall. Once there, Felicity leaned against the closed door.

She'd already discussed with her father what was to become of Esther and her family. For all her father's high ideals he seemed unwilling to commit monetarily to the woman. But Felicity had her own money. Thanks to her mother's father she had lots of it. And seeing Esther and her children settled was only one use she planned for it.

Felicity wiped her eyes and started down the hallway. While it was on her mind she would speak with Jebediah. There was no reason for him to worry about her accepting his coerced proposal. She would never marry him.

If she couldn't have Devon Blackstone, she would never marry anyone.

As she approached her father's library, she noticed the door was ajar. Then she heard voices; her father's and Jebediah's. Felicity sighed. She would have to wait to have her talk with the minister.

Felicity turned, ready to go to her room when she heard a name that made her pause. Blackstone. Jebediah was ranting on about her father setting aside his principles to deal with a southern slave owner.

"Do you have any idea where those supplies you're loading on his ship will end up? In the hands of devil slaveholders, that's where. They'll use what you send them to prolong the war. To keep the black man under their thumb that much longer."

Felicity stepped toward the doorway, meaning to enter and set Jebediah straight about the people of the South. But before she could speak her father took issue with Jebediah's charges.

"Would you stop going on so. Nothing of mine is going to aid the South. I made some inquiries about our Captain Blackstone. He's a notorious blockade runner, well known by the Navy. And, I may add, his capture is most desired by them."

"But you told Miss Wentworth—"

"What Felicity doesn't know won't hurt her. She's obviously come under the spell of this Blackstone and it's up to me . . . us, to sever his hold on her once and for all. His ship is currently being loaded, and he plans to sail with the morning tide. However, by dawn, he and his men will be in irons on their way to a Federal prison camp."

Felicity waited just long enough to hear her father's plan before she gathered up her skirts and ran out of the house.

Twenty

By the time Felicity reached the docks, she was breathless . . . and missing two ear bobs. In her haste to reach Devon in time she hailed a passing hansom cab not realizing she had no money. Rather than waste time arguing she'd yanked her mother's emeralds from her ears and tossed them at the driver.

Felicity dodged the stevedores who by the light of burning brands, loaded cargo on the *Intrepid.* Near the gangplank she spotted Mr. MacFarland, leaning against a stack of barrels, his pipe clenched between his teeth.

"Well now lass, I'm surprised to be seein' ye here. He glanced about. "Are ye by yourself? I ain't sure it's—"

"Where's Devon?"

"Why he's on deck, I think, but—" Mr. MacFarland stood scratching his beard as Felicity flew past him, forcing people out of her way as she rushed up the gangplank.

The deck was as crowded as the dock, and for

a moment Felicity could just stand, looking around, her skirts swirling about her ankles. Then she saw him, near the hatch, standing in a line of crew members. He was shirtless, lifting crates and passing each one toward the hatch.

"Devon!" Felicity charged forward, calling his name till his head shot up.

With a nod toward the man beside him, Devon left the row and met Felicity as she rushed toward him. He yanked her close, disregarding the interest of the workers on deck. She was breathing hard. He could feel the rise and fall of her breasts against his chest.

His hands cupped her shoulders, separating their bodies and searching her face as she stared up at him. "What's wrong? Are you all right?" Loose strands of hair curled against her cheeks. Her gown was rumpled, but he could see no sign that she was hurt.

"Not me! You!" Felicity fought to keep herself calm enough to explain. "It's a trap. I'm so sorry." She caught her lower lip to keep it from quivering. From the moment she heard her father's plan she had only one thought—to warn Devon before it was too late. Now, standing loosely in his arms the enormity of her father's betrayal came crashing down on her.

"Oh, Devon, he never meant to let you go. All he said about rewarding you for bringing the children and me to New York was a lie."

"Slow down." Devon's palm curved around the back of her head, nestling her to his shoulder.

"I can't!" Felicity pulled away from his arms. "You have to leave. He's sending men to capture you. They're going to put you and your crew in a military prison." Felicity felt him stiffen. His eyes searched hers.

"How do you know this?"

"I heard them talking, Jebediah and my father. Jebediah didn't like Father helping you and the southern cause. Father told him not to worry. He said you'd never leave on the morning tide, because you'd be captured before that. Oh Devon, I'm so sorry. This is my fault."

"No, it isn't." Devon cradled her in his arms again. His palm rubbed down her back as he stared over her head at the activity on the deck and wharf. The *Intrepid* had unloaded its cargo of contraband cotton, but her hold was only partially full. Even with everyone working to full capacity it would be hours yet until he would have left the pier.

"When?" Devon lifted her away. "What time are they coming after us?"

"I don't know. Before dawn is all he said. Oh Devon, I think you better hurry." In the red tinted light thrown off by torches, Felicity saw him nod.

"Stay here. I'll be right back." Devon moved away and went about quietly warning his crew of their stepped up departure.

"But Cap'n, we ain't just gonna let all this stuff rot here on the dock, is we?"

"Better that than us rotting in a Yankee prison."

Devon clasped the sailor on the shoulder. "We'll make up for it next trip."

By the time Devon returned to Felicity, the *Intrepid*'s crew was busy stoking the engines and stowing as much cargo as they could below deck.

"Take me with you." Felicity rushed toward Devon as he approached. He enfolded her in his arms.

"I can't, Red." Devon took a deep breath. "I can't guarantee we'll get out of the harbor in one piece, and I love you too much to risk your life like that."

"Kidnap me then. The pirate did it. So did your ancestor who fought in the Revolution. Perhaps they won't fire on you with me aboard." Felicity's eyes searched his, imploring him to agree.

But though his expression showed he wanted to change reality, he slowly shook his head. "Even if they knew you were with us, there's no guarantee they wouldn't use the guns at Fort Lafayette. Think, sweetheart, what it was like in Charleston." His large, work-roughened palms bracketed her face. "And it will get worse." He kept her from shaking her head with gentle pressure from his hands. "I won't willingly subject you to that."

All around them was noise and hustle as the crew brought the steam-powered schooner to life. And Felicity felt her own life crumbling around her.

"I can't live without you."

"Don't say that." His heart aching, Devon yanked her to him, gathering her close in the temporary shelter of his arms. "You're strong. I know what you can do when you set your mind to it." Devon lifted her chin and kissed her quickly. "This war won't last forever. When it's over I'll come for you. His eyes shone with intensity. "Nothing . . . nothing will stop me."

Felicity sat huddled inside the coach Devon hired to take her home. She asked the driver to stop before they left the docks. She wouldn't risk Devon's life by delaying his departure, but she couldn't leave without being certain he sailed from the harbor safely.

So she sat . . . and waited.

"Ain't ya ready to be leavin' now, Miss?" the driver said after climbing down from the box and knocking on the door. He shrugged and mumbled something about the rich after she shook her head.

Near dawn, when the pearly sky began silhouetting the eerie forest of rigging along the East River docks, Felicity heard the booming thunder of cannon fire in the distance. But she couldn't tell who was firing or from where. Finally, dejected and sad, she directed the driver to take her to the Fifth Avenue mansion.

Eveline Blackstone sat in the garden. The chill of autumn was in the air and she wore a knitted shawl around her shoulders. In the quiet afternoon solitude her parchment thin eyelids fluttered shut and her chin dropped onto her high-necked bodice. She jerked awake and grabbing her cane pushed up from the wrought iron seat.

It was then she noticed the black-garbed woman standing at the gate. Eveline raised her arthritic-knuckled hand and waved her inside. "I was wondering when you'd arrive."

Felicity drew back the heavy veil of her traveling outfit. "You knew I was coming?"

The older woman shrugged, lifting her shoulders slightly before motioning for Felicity to sit on the bench. Eveline settled back in the chair. "I hoped," she responded succinctly.

"But how did you—"

"I watched Devon when he came back . . . talked to him. He didn't say much, but I could tell he was hurting."

"Is he here now?" Felicity leaned forward on her seat, only to take a deep breath and glance away when Eveline shook her head.

"He managed to bring some medical supplies into Charleston. But he only stayed long enough to reload with cotton and sail out."

Felicity looked up. She swallowed, then wet her lips. "What did he say?"

"About you?" The older woman folded her hands. "Very little. But don't appear so dejected. I raised the boy since his parents died when he was three. And I know him. Enough to realize when he's in love."

Felicity met her eyes, still bright despite the tears. "I love him too."

"Of course you do." Eveline brushed away a pesky bee. "I never doubted it for a moment. Not even when it took you months to get back here."

"I had affairs to put in order before I could leave." She hesitated, then decided Devon's grandmother deserved her total honesty. "I'm from New York."

The slight lifting of the older woman's shoulders seemed to indicate she considered that unimportant. "I took those children there . . . to their mother."

"How is Sissy?"

Tears burned Felicity's eyes. "She died." Standing, Felicity walked to the magnolia and traced one of its broad leaves. "She lived to see her mother." Felicity turned to face Eveline. "I settled them in a small house with a bit of a yard for Mast'a Cock. She blinked. "Esther . . . that's the children's mother, is a wonderful seamstress, and she was able to do sewing for some of New York's finest ladies."

"With your sponsorship, I imagine."

"I did suggest her to several of my acquaintances. But she's the one who convinced them they should stay with her." Felicity's smile was sad. "My friends take their gowns very seriously."

"And Ezra?" Eveline stacked her hands on the head of the cane.

"He's doing very well," Felicity said with pride. "He has a job at the docks. And he's learning to read." Felicity straightened her shoulders and resumed her seat. "Lucy is also fine . . . as precocious as ever. I hated to leave them." Felicity looked down at her folded hands.

Eveline waited a moment, then grabbed hold of her cane and used it to push herself to her feet. "Well," she said when Felicity glanced up. "We must get busy." Without a backward glance, she started across the brick path, through the box-woods, to the house.

Felicity watched her go, wondering if this could be the same woman she'd come across not thirty minutes before. The woman who could barely keep from nodding off to sleep. Now Eveline looked spry, her step, despite the awkward gate caused by her hip, was lively.

Suddenly realizing what Mrs. Blackstone had said, Felicity jumped to her feet. "Get busy with what?" she asked, as she followed her into the house. "What are we going to do?"

There were times during the following month that Felicity wished she never asked that question. This morning was one of them. She stretched beneath the counterpane and watched through her bedroom window. Dawn slowly paled the sky beyond the live oak, and Felicity wished she could stay abed. She was tired, and the now familiar twinges of nausea teased at her stomach.

Throwing her arm across her eyes Felicity took a deep breath and wondered if this morning, like the previous two, she would have to dive for the chamber pot as soon as she sat up.

She inched toward the edge of the mattress, and eased herself up. So far, so good. Perhaps she might make it this morning without being sick. She hoped so. It was becoming increasingly diffi-cult to explain the delay in her toilette to Eveline Blackstone.

The woman was a whirlwind of activity, often making Felicity wonder how she managed at her age. But the work they did at the hospital and the orphanage was important. And though Felicity might at times wish for a chance to sit in the shade and catch her breath, she felt more fulfilled than she ever had. Even amid the war and constant rumors of attack on the city, she was content.

Except for one thing. Devon.

She missed him terribly. Longed for him to slip by the blockade into Charleston. But she also feared for his life. Felicity shook her head, then flipped the thick braid of red-gold hair behind her shoulder.

It was good she had the children at the orphan-age to keep her busy, or she would surely go mad with worry. Deciding she could stave off the nausea this morning, Felicity reached for her wrapper. But her arms were barely in the flowing green gown when she heard a racket below.

There was pounding at the door, and Felicity wondered if somehow the Yankees managed to sneak into the town last night. But as she ran out into the hall, she knew different.

"That ya, Masta' Devon? You sure knows how to take ten years off a body's life."

"My humblest apologies Ruth. Ah, there is my dear grandmother. Looking as lovely as ever."

Felicity didn't hear what Eveline responded to that comment, though she was certain it was caustic. All Felicity could concentrate on was the sound of Devon's voice, so deep and strong, as she padded, barefooted, toward the stairs.

After she descended three steps, she stopped, watching as he leaned forward and kissed his grandmother's forehead. If she made a noise, Felicity didn't realize it. However, just as he pressed his lips to the wrinkled brow, his gaze shot up and locked with Felicity's.

He straightened slowly, never taking his eyes from her. Felicity swallowed, unable to discern what he was thinking behind the unreadable expression on his handsome, sun-bronzed face.

His hands cupped the older woman's shoulders and he gently set her aside.

"Now Devon, you watch what you say and do. That girl's been a God-send to me. Do you hear me, boy?"

"I hear you, Grams." But Devon didn't even bother to glance around as he took the wide stairs two at a time. When he was eye level with Felicity, he swooped her into his arms and carried her the rest of the way upstairs.

Inside his room, he kicked the door shut and set her on the rug. Missing the warmth of his arms, Felicity leaned forward, ready to receive the magic of his kiss. None was forthcoming. Finally she opened her eyes. His square jaw was thrust out and his arms were folded across his wide chest.

"What in the hell are you doing here?" Despite the censure in his words, Felicity thought she noticed a spark of passion burning in his eyes before he narrowed his gaze and looked away. She held onto that vision as he spoke. "Damnit, Red, I leave you safe and sound in New York . . . not because I want to, mind you, but because it's what's best for you. And here you are. God, how did you get here? By train again? Or boat? Please don't tell me you rode a blockade runner in? What about the danger? Didn't you have enough of that before? And what about that fiancé of yours? Isn't he wondering where the hell you are?"

When he finished his barrage of questions . . . which Felicity stood quietly through . . . Devon was by the window. He looked at her over his shoulder when she cleared her throat.

"What do you wish me to answer first?" Since he only glared in response, Felicity decided to tackle the answers at her own pace. "Very well. I came here by train . . . as I did before. I wouldn't trust a blockade runner unless you were captaining it."

His jaw clenched. "I'm not asking for flattery."

"Nor am I giving any. I simply stated why I didn't try to reach Charleston by boat. What else . . . ? Oh yes. My fiancé." Felicity shrugged and her smile was apologetic. "What I do, or do not do, makes no difference to Jebediah. It never did." She took a deep breath. "You see, we never were

419

really engaged. Marrying him was my idea. One of my worst. I only thank God, Jebediah didn't agree to it."

"Wait a minute." Devon turned and extended his hand, palm out. "Are you telling me that you wanted to marry him and he didn't want *you?*" The expression on his face was incredulous.

"Actually, I think I wanted to please my father." Her head tilted to the side. "But, yes, that's how it was."

"The man's a bigger fool than I thought."

"I was hoping you'd feel that way." Felicity took a step toward Devon. "Because, I came south to marry *you.*"

Devon's hands dropped to his side. He rejected the urge to hold them out and block her path as she came toward him. "Didn't I explain why that can't be right now?"

"The war," Felicity said, and took another step.

"Aye, the war."

"And your desire to protect me."

"That's right." Devon forced himself not to back up. The closer she got the harder it was to resist her. And now was the time for reason, not passion, to rule. "What's wrong with wanting you to be safe and protected?"

"Not a thing. But I'm not a hothouse flower. I'm a woman who knows her own mind. And I know that I want to be with you as much as I can. And when you're away, I want to be doing what I can to build our home." She reached up, placing her fingers against his lips when he would have interrupted.

"I know there's a war, and that you feel Charleston is in danger. But I also know that I love you more than life itself. And that somehow we shall see this through . . . together." Her fingers strayed to caress his whisker roughened cheek. "You can't make me leave, Devon. So, if you refuse to marry me, I shall simply have to stay here anyway and be your mistress. Then perhaps when the war is over—"

Felicity didn't have a chance to finish her sentence. Devon yanked her against him.

"God, I missed you so much . . ." His hands tangled with her strawberry blond curls. "If something would have happened to you . . ." His lips touched the pale dusting of freckles on her nose. "Don't ever leave me . . ." His palms bracketed her face. The expression in his sea-green eyes held her spellbound. "I love you . . ." His kiss was gentle. "I'll always love you . . ." His mouth opened, devouring hers.

Felicity melted against him. She was his, body and soul, in this life and beyond. Her arms locked around the strong pillar of his neck and she returned his impassioned kisses in kind.

When Devon's hand slid down the curve of her hip, then hooked beneath her knees, Felicity clung to him. She rained hungry kisses across his face. He lifted her high against his chest and strode to the four poster bed, following her down onto the cool sheets.

His tongue forged into her mouth, finding hers. They clung to each other as the churning sea of temptation swirled them deeper into passion's vortex.

He struggled with the skirt of her nightrail, fumbling in his haste. "Oh God, Red, I want you so much." Devon's lips tore from hers only long enough for the words to come out on a ragged breath.

Felicity couldn't get enough of touching him. Her hands splayed across his back, pulling at his shirt, then thrust lower, frantically shoving his pants lower.

She was hot and incredibly wet beneath his hand. His finger slid inside, in rhythm with his dancing tongue, and Felicity arched off the mattress, renewing her efforts to touch him. Her hands tangled with his, as he aided her quest.

He surged into her hands, thick and full. Felicity caressed, measuring the long length of his flesh, feeling the blood pulse through him.

When he could bear it no more, Devon settled quickly between her spread thighs. His first thrust was deep and strong, filling her completely. She wrapped her legs around his waist, rocking toward him uncontrollably, as each plunge took her higher on the wings of ecstasy.

Devon forgot to breathe. The flaming power of her wiped all but his love from his mind. Deeper and deeper he plunged, till he felt her sweet release. She cried out, a sound captured by his mouth, as the waves rippled through her. His own release was powerful and explosive, putting the memories he'd thought would be his only solace to shame.

When she lay beneath him, replete and silent, save for the soft sound of her breathing, Devon touched the tip of her nose. Her eyes opened, still glazed by passion, and she returned his smile. Languidly, she lifted her hand and traced the indentation on his cheek.

"Does this mean you'll marry me?" she asked, her head tilted to the side.

Devon chuckled and kissed her lightly. "I want nothing as much as to spend my life with you." Doubt shadowed his masculine features. "I can't promise you what the future will bring."

"No one can. What lies ahead is not for us to see, or know . . . or control. But the love we have for each other will survive."

"Always," Devon whispered as his forehead touched hers.

Later, as they lay stretched out, side by side on the bed, Devon began to undress her. Slowly, with deliberate care, he uncovered her soft skin.

"You are so beautiful," he murmured against her breast. "But not just on the outside. In here." He nuzzled the flesh covering her heart. "You are good and strong."

The nightrail slid lower. Down the smooth slope to her waist—over the slight rise of her stomach. Devon paused. With gentle fingers he traced the swell from side to side. He pressed his mouth reverently to her body as realization washed over him. His gaze sought hers, warm and loving.

Felicity threaded her fingers through his hair. "Your grandmother told me a tale of a plant that climbs up the trunks of trees. When there is no rain, the leaves dry up and wither . . . appear dead."

"The resurrection plant."

"Yes, that's it. Times now are like the resurrection plant, dry with the drought upon the land. But when it rains, the vine everyone thought was dead comes alive." Her hand covered his where it rested on her stomach. "This baby is Charleston's rebirth . . . our rebirth." Her fingers linked with his. "No matter what happens, there is always hope with a new generation."

Epilogue

The sepia-toned photograph showing the man and woman on their wedding day was not nearly so grand as the portraits that flanked the room. The portraits of the pirate, Jack Blackstone and his wife Miranda, she'd saved by hiding them in the attic. But as Felicity glanced at the picture of Devon and herself on the table beside her chair she couldn't help smiling.

"Is Baby Thomas tickling you?" Merry asked, looking up into her mother's face from her perch on the stool by Felicity's feet. At four, Merry was an inquisitive little girl, who could name nearly all the animals and most of the plants that grew at Royal Oak.

"No, sweetie." Felicity shifted the infant at her breast, and rested her palm lovingly on her daughter's red curls. "As a matter of fact, I think Thomas is asleep."

"Are you sure? Maybe he's just playing possum?" The little girl's voice rose hopefully.

"I don't think so." Felicity lifted her son, bringing him to her shoulder. She patted his back while he snuggled close to her neck.

Closing her bodice, Felicity rose and led the way from her bedroom to the nursery. Merry followed, her feet scuffing along the threadbare carpet.

"Do I have to take a nap? I'm not the least tired. And I could carry Papa's lunch basket for you."

Felicity settled her two month old son in his cradle, then turned toward Merry, and lifted the child into her arms. The little girl's claim that she wasn't sleepy was refuted as she yawned and cuddled close to her mother. "If you stay up now, you'll be too tired to hear the story Papa will read you tonight. You wouldn't want to miss that, would you?"

"Noooo." Merry drew the word out thoughtfully. "But I think I can do both."

Felicity chuckled. "Not today, Merry." After pulling back the covers, Felicity tucked her daughter into bed. "Have a nice rest, Merry." As the child's eyelids drifted shut, Felicity hurried from the room.

She stopped for a moment in front of the hall mirror to pat her hair into place, then grabbed up the basket she'd packed earlier and left the house. The late summer sun filtered through the live oaks lining the allee as she dashed around the corner.

By the time she reached Royal Oak's wharf she was winded—from her rush, and from the excitement of seeing her husband. It was a thrill to

426

know she could be with him whenever she wished—not like the years the war had separated them. And she never tired of just looking at him.

He stood, knee deep in the river, pounding nails into the dock. In deference to the heat, he'd removed his shirt and she watched as the sweat glistened on his sun-bronzed muscles.

As if he sensed her presence, Devon glanced up. Removing the nails from his mouth he grinned at his wife as she walked out along the dock.

"It looks good," Felicity said when she stood on the wooden planks directly in front of him.

"Thanks." He slid the hammer across the dock. "I was hoping you'd come down. Are the children asleep?"

"They are. Eveline said she'd look in on them. Of course Merry fought it till the end." Felicity settled down on the sun-warmed oak, placing the basket by her side.

"She's like her mother." Devon peeked under the napkin.

Felicity laughed, but argued all the same. "I think she's more like your grandmother than me . . . Who, by the way, says I should make you come up to the house to eat lunch."

"Really?" Devon wrapped his fingers around her ankle. "But does she know what else we do besides eat ham biscuits?"

"No." Felicity felt a blush heat her cheeks. "And you better not tell her either. What are you doing?"

"Taking off your shoes." His dark brow arched.

"Aren't you hot?" He untied the laces, and after removing her shoes, pulled her feet down into the gently lapping water. "Better?"

Felicity nodded, then leaned back as his hands massaged the arch of her foot, then traveled up her calf. Her gaze wandered over the wharf. "Will it be ready in time?"

"It will. In his letter, Stephen said that the ship will be here next week."

"And it will take our rice crop to market," Felicity said with satisfaction.

"And I'll finally begin to repay you for all you sacrificed for me."

Reaching out, Felicity brushed the lock of hair from her husband's forehead. "Don't say that. You've given me more than you can ever imagine."

Devon looked away, and Felicity knew he was thinking of the past, of the final years of the war when he was unable to run the blockade into Charleston, of the Federal victory and the occupation of his beloved home. His eyes met hers. "If it hadn't been for you we never would have been able to regain Royal Oak."

"I invested some money in our future. In our children's future." Felicity shrugged. "You're the one who's worked and rebuilt."

When they returned to Royal Oak after the recantation of Sherman's confiscation order, the plantation was in sorry shape. Overgrown, with the fields gone to seed and the house little more than a hollow shell, Devon and Felicity hired workers and planted rice.

Now they were about to taste the fruits of their labor.

Devon pulled himself from the water and sat on the dock beside his wife. "We can do this, Red." He draped his arm around her shoulders.

She turned into him, loving the feel, the smell of him. Snuggling her face into the crook of his neck she whispered the one word that expressed her faith in their future. "Together."

TO MY READERS

I hope you enjoyed the *Charleston Trilogy, Blackstone Men of the Sea*. Researching and writing about the Blackstones has been a labor of love. First Gentleman Jack Blackstone, the pirate, and his lady, Miranda Chadwick (SEA FIRES—Sept., 1992), then Jared Blackstone and Lady Merideth (SEA OF DESIRE—April, 1993), and finally in the book you just read, the blockade runner, Devon Blackstone and his Yankee bride, Felicity Wentworth. They all came alive to me, as I hope they did for you.

In SEA OF TEMPTATION, as in all my books, I tried to create a true romance between people who love each other and grow as human beings because of that love. I also tried to stay as historically accurate as possible. The Battle of Secessionville happened very much as I depicted—though Devon Blackstone didn't really ride for reinforcements.

The history of blockade runners, those brave men with more than their share of steel nerves and grit, is fascinating. They did their best to sneak through the blockades, aided by cloud shrouded nights and luck. There's even documentation of a rooster's crow calling attention to a ship as it slipped past the Federal squadron . . . the Confederates made good their escape, as did the *Intrepid*.

But is SEA OF TEMPTATION the end of the Blackstones of Charleston? Actually, no. Look for

"Sea of Miracles" in Zebra's 1993 anthology of Christmas stories, A CHRISTMAS CARESS. In "Sea of Miracles" suffragette Margaret Lewis "turns the tables" and kidnaps Devon and Felicity's son, Thomas Blackstone. Thomas is a man who needs a lesson in the Christmas spirit and Margaret is just the woman to teach him. In the process they both learn about the miracle of love.

I'm also excited about MY SAVAGE HEART, which will be released in April of 1994. MY SAVAGE HEART is the Indian love story that has haunted me for years. It takes place during the French and Indian War when Raff MacQuaid, a half-blood Cherokee encounters the beautiful, Lady Caroline Simmons. Unfortunately for the young lovers, Caroline is betrothed to Raff's father. The action is non stop and the passion rages hotter than the Indian uprisings. MY SAVAGE HEART is the first book about the heroic MacQuaid brothers.

I love to hear from readers. For a newsletter and bookmark write to me care of:

Zebra Books
475 Park Ave. South
New York, NY 10016

SASE appreciated

To Happy Endings,
Christine Dorsey